It's just a game, I told myself over and over as I flew toward the jagged edge that zigzagged along the cliff, the soft grasses giving way to loose rocks. I didn't look back, not once, even as the shouts behind me got closer. Suddenly I was six paces away, then five, then four, three, two.

One.

And I leapt.

I flung my body out to the sea, a human stone set loose from a slingshot.

Before gravity took me in its grip and dropped me toward the earth, I saw exactly how far I had to fall. It was as though I'd thrown myself from the ledge of a thirty-story tower, one built on a series of sharp rocks jutting out into the sea like an arrow. The fear, angry and terrible, reared up in me again, threatening to take back control of my mind and my limbs. It wanted to win me over.

But I couldn't let it.

Getting to the Real World depended on my passing this test.

This was just a challenge I needed to clear, one last App working its way through my code that would eventually drain away. That was all this was and nothing more.

Gravity sucked at my feet.

I plummeted toward the sea.

Also by Donna Freitas

The Body Market

UNPLUGGED

Donna Freitas

HARPER TEEN
An Imprint of HarperCollinsPublishers

HarperTeen is an imprint of HarperCollins Publishers.

Unplugged

Copyright © 2016 by Donna Freitas

All rights reserved. Printed in the United States of America.

No part of this book may be used or reproduced in any manner whatsoever without written permission except in the case of brief quotations embodied in critical articles and reviews. For information address HarperCollins Children's Books, a division of HarperCollins Publishers, 195 Broadway, New York, NY 10007.

www.epicreads.com

Library of Congress Control Number: 2015956266

ISBN 978-0-06-211861-5

17 18 19 20 21   CG/LSCC   10 9 8 7 6 5 4 3 2

❖

First paperback edition, 2017

To the Hofstra Honors College, where I sometimes teach Culture & Expression, a course that wakes up my mind and makes it fly. This trilogy grew out of our readings and lectures and conversations one semester. And to Warren Frisina, the dean there, who has always accepted me in all of my academic and writerly weirdness and made me a part of this wonderful community.

I will suppose, then . . . that some malignant dæmon, who is at once exceedingly potent and deceitful, has employed all his artifice to deceive me; I will suppose that the sky, the air, the earth, colors, figures, sounds, and all external things, are nothing better than the illusions of dreams, by means of which this being has laid snares for my credulity; I will consider myself as without hands, eyes, flesh, blood, or any of the senses, and as falsely believing that I am possessed of these . . . just as the captive, who, perchance, was enjoying in his dreams an imaginary liberty, when he begins to suspect that it is but a vision, dreads awakening, and conspires with the agreeable illusions that the deception may be prolonged.

—René Descartes,
"Of the Things of Which We May Doubt,"
Meditations on First Philosophy (1641)

PART ONE

1

Everything comes to a halt

I'LL NEVER FORGET the day the news rang through the App World.

It was early June and I was just another virtual girl, looking forward to unplugging on her seventeenth birthday. I couldn't wait to see my real family again, and decide if maybe, just maybe, the real me was worth hanging on to. School hadn't let out yet for summer and the atmosphere was set at a comfortable seventy degrees. I was at my best friend Inara's house. Her parents, my surrogate family, were there, too. I loved the Sachses' apartment, with its skyline views of the City, its chandeliers, and its plush white furniture where Inara and I would sprawl while uploading our homework.

Wispy clouds floated by and the lights of the nearby buildings began to sparkle. I pressed my palm against the glass of the floor-to-ceiling windows, my eyes on the Empire State Building, then sliding sideways toward the Water Tower. It rose high into the atmosphere, its shimmery blue surface moving like the ocean waves. The Sachses lived in a neighborhood where the architecture was coded with some of the most memorable buildings from the Real World.

Inara joined me at the window and placed her hand next to mine, the lengths of our fingers eerily similar, our skin color identical, the same shade of Caucasian 4.0 as every other citizen of the City. Her eyes were green and mine were blue, her hair a bright shiny blond and mine an inky black, but we shared the same standard settings for height, weight, and general attractiveness for all six-teens—settings intended to highlight the changes that Apps brought to our appearance. We even shared the same birthday. There were slight differences in age among six-teens, just as there were with fifteens and fourteens, and so on and so forth, but adjusting one's age to a standard setting was a normal part of virtual living.

Standard settings helped make the App World a har-monious place. Basic sameness was a right for all citizens. It saved people from enduring the random and often unfair differences that came with being in the real body.

Apps provided all the temporary diversity a person could need.

"I think we should try that Glitter App for Simon's party next weekend," Inara said. "I love the idea of being shimmery from head to toe. Then I would definitely get Simon's attention."

"You don't need to download an App to get his attention," I told her. "You're beautiful as is."

"Right." Inara laughed. "I forgot for a second that you were Miss Au Naturel."

"I am not," I protested. But Inara wasn't far from the truth. I was always wondering what I looked like, and what Inara looked like, too—what we *really* looked like. What kind of body I was in and whether my real face was at all like the virtual one I was staring at now in the glass. The virtual person was infinitely malleable, but when there weren't any Apps intermingling with our code, the virtual self supposedly resembled the real one, especially the bone structure of the face. Nobody knew for sure if this was true until they unplugged. A lot of sixteens worried they'd wake up in their bodies and discover they were ugly.

"Maybe I'll download the Number One Hit App instead," Inara went on, still thinking about how to impress Simon, her crush. "Don't you love that original songs will just come out of your mouth without even having to try?"

"That could be fun," I said, trying to be more support-
ive this time.

"Come on, girls! Dinner is ready," Mrs. Sachs called
from the next room. She was always downloading from
Apps trendy meals by former Real World chefs.

Inara turned to me and rolled her eyes. "You don't
have to yell into the atmosphere, Mom, we can hear you!"
She switched to private chat. *I hope tonight's food is better
than last night's.*

I laughed as these words appeared in my brain. A lot
of people left their minds open to everyone, but Inara was
the only person I allowed to access mine. I took my hand
away from the window. Raised an eyebrow. *What*, I chatted back, *you don't like it when everything on your plate
bursts into vegetable-flavored liquid when it lands on your
tongue?*

I feel ill just thinking about it. Inara touched her fingers to her head. When you live virtually, stomachaches
are experienced in the mind.

I shrugged. *It wasn't that bad.*

*Stop trying to be polite. My mother seriously needs
constructive feedback.*

Yeah, I chatted back. *But you're the daughter, not me.
It's your job to tell her.*

"Skye? Inara?" Mrs. Sachs appeared in the doorway.
"How many times do I have to tell you girls *no private
chatting in this house*! It's rude." Her eyes narrowed.

"Now hurry up. The food is going to get cold." She spun on her spiky heel.

Inara started toward the dining room. "At least that means the food is hot," she called over her shoulder, this time into the atmosphere. Her long hair swayed across her back.

I followed after her and we took our seats.

"How was school today?" Mr. Sachs asked. He sat at the head of the table, his tie loosened and his suit jacket draped over the railing behind him. Mr. Sachs was head of Capital Bank, the largest financial institution in the App World.

Inara studied the quivering brown mass on the plate in front of her, a grimace on her face. "Don't be so boring, Dad."

"It was fine," I told him. "We had a test in App Sorting. I think I did okay."

Mr. Sachs smiled and nodded. "Good, good. App Sorting is an important skill. The market is saturated and it's only going to get worse. Everyone is trying to make their fortune with the next Big App Thing."

Inara poked at the brown square. "Again, Dad, boring."

"Stop playing with your food," Mrs. Sachs said.

"I'm not sure it's really food, Mom."

Mrs. Sachs glared at her daughter. Her ten-carat diamond earrings gleamed on either side of her head. "You shouldn't complain. There are people in this City without enough capital to download the latest in Food Apps," she said, then turned her attention to her own brown quivering mass, looking just as uncertain as Inara.

"Now *there* is a fortune waiting to happen," Mr. Sachs said. "If someone, say, figures out how to make a virtual pizza with the same taste and consistency as real pizza, I'll be able to live here forever a happy man."

"I miss artichokes," Mrs. Sachs said. "And the crunch of a real apple when you bite into it. How the juice of a just-ripe peach makes your fingers all sticky and sweet."

Inara's hands fell to the table with a thump. "Um, can we please stop acting so disgusting at the dinner table?"

Mr. and Mrs. Sachs looked at each other wistfully. They wore sappy smiles on their faces.

"I like hearing about the Real World," I said, feeling a slight pinch of jealousy. Inara was lucky to have both her parents here. My mother and sister never plugged in, and I didn't even know who my father was. But sometimes memories of my real life would flash in my brain. Things like my mother's smile and the sound of my older sister's voice. Sand squishing between my toes on the beach and the words my mother used to whisper to me before bed. *Blue like the ocean and blue like the sky, blue like the sapphire color of your eyes.*

"I'm glad I was a baby when these two weirdos plugged me in," Inara went on. "Saved me the whole Two Worlds Complex and all that."

"We're not weirdos," Mr. Sachs said. "We're your parents."

Inara rolled her eyes. "Exactly."

Inara picked up her fork, but she couldn't seem to bring herself to eat. "Mom, seriously, what exactly are we about to put into our code?"

I bit back a smile—I didn't want to be rude to Mrs. Sachs.

Right then, the signal for the emergency broadcast popped into the dining room. A hologram of Jonathan Holt, the Prime Minister of the App World, appeared. He hovered over the dinner table.

Silverware clattered against plates.

Emergency broadcasts used to be rare, but lately, they were more and more frequent.

The four of us waited in silence for the Prime Minister to speak.

"My fellow citizens," he finally began, "as you know, unrest in the Real World has been growing. There are Keepers who no longer believe in our way of life, who feel that by living virtually we are toying with the very nature of our humanity. There are Keepers unhappy about the high cost required to join us here. But let me reassure you, there are loyal Keepers, too, who are securing the plugs as I speak."

Mrs. Sachs reached across the table to grasp Inara's hand. I waited for her to reach across for mine.

She didn't.

There was a long pause. Jonathan Holt was hesitating.

Mr. Sachs had one hand on his wife's shoulder, and in the other he gripped his napkin in a tight fist. "It's bad enough those Keepers try to conscript our children to unplug for Service." He glanced at Inara, before turning back to the hologram. "One day they're going to go a step further and declare war," he went on. "Our tech specialists need to hurry up with the Cure. Without our bodies to hold us back, the Keepers will have nothing on us."

My jaw fell open. I'd never heard Mr. Sachs talk this way.

"Sam," Mrs. Sachs hissed through clenched teeth. She grabbed her husband by the wrist. "Remember who's here."

Inara and Mr. and Mrs. Sachs were suddenly eyeing me.

My mother and sister were Keepers. They'd volunteered to work on the plugs so they could give me a better, virtual life. All people in the Real World were considered Keepers of some sort, but the ones who worked to keep the bodies were the most important of all.

The hologram sparked and crackled. Jonathan Holt took a breath. "I regret to inform you that the border between worlds has been closed," he announced, his voice hoarse. "To protect the safety of our children, all future Service has been canceled. From this moment going forward, unplugging is prohibited, as is plugging in." The hologram of Jonathan Holt flickered in the light of the chandelier. "This decision was not made lightly. As many of you know, my only son is doing his Service now. This means he is never coming back to our world again. He is lost to me and my wife forever." The Prime Minister cleared his throat. "My family—like so many others—will suffer our shared grief in the coming days."

Inara turned to me. There was a bright panic in her eyes. "Skye?"

I couldn't speak. The words wouldn't come.

Service was *canceled*?

I wouldn't be allowed to unplug—*ever*?

I felt woozy and liquid. My hands were covered in tears, my eyes pouring waterfalls, the sadness overflowing from my brain. When I looked up at the hologram again, something strange happened, something just as shocking as it was confusing.

Jonathan Holt was staring straight at me.

When his eyes met mine they flashed with guilt.

But that was impossible. My imagination playing tricks.

The Prime Minister hung his head low. "That is all for tonight. Thank you for your attention. I leave you in peace and stability on the Apps," he said.

Then the hologram blinked out.

2

Voyeurs

"I REALLY DON'T want to App right now, Inara."

Everything about my virtual self felt heavy. Like my code had been laden with stone. I trailed my fingers along the wrought-iron fence that lined the park outside the Sachses' apartment. I'd needed some fresh atmosphere after the Prime Minister's announcement, and Inara had insisted on coming with me. Really, I wanted to be alone. But I could never say no to Inara.

"Look out," she said.

I ducked just as a skater whizzed by overhead, his board a neon purple and his long hair a bright blue. His virtual skin was covered in tattoos.

People were out and about as though the border

closing didn't matter, as though they hadn't heard Jonathan Holt's announcement, when of course they had—no one can escape a universal broadcast. The City felt like a carnival at this hour, something I'd always loved about this world. But tonight it felt off.

Inara kept walking ahead of me, then turning around to see if I was following. She was anxious. We hadn't Apped in two days. A record for us.

"I know you're dying to App," I told her. "But I can't. Not after everything."

"Come on, Skye. I'm buying."

I was finding it difficult to breathe. "You're always buying."

Inara hopped from one foot to the other. "You could use a little fun. It's the perfect distraction." Her arms were starting to twitch. "Besides, I'm going to get withdrawal symptoms if I don't download soon."

"You already have them," I said.

An icon popped into the atmosphere. Inara immediately reached for it, her code thirsty. A giddy sigh escaped her lips as the download started. A second icon appeared in front of me. Golden wings flapped and waved. It was an Angel App. I ducked under it but it followed me. It buzzed in my ear and I swatted it away. When the icon returned it raced from side to side, blasting through my hair. "Get off me," I yelled, hands swinging. It finally took the hint and gently came to rest above my left shoulder.

At least it had stopped moving.

Inara's download finished and a pair of feathery wings stretched high and wide from her back, shimmering in the evening light. Her skin had a new sheen to it. "Come on, Skye. You love flying. It will get your mind off what happened." She could barely keep her feet on the ground. "Doesn't Apping *always* help us feel better?"

One of the wings of the icon smacked me in the ear. I glared, raising my arm like I was going to hit it. It cowered and fled to a safer distance. "I'm sorry, but I can't. I mean, I just learned I'm never going to see my family again."

Inara grabbed my hand and squeezed it. Her skin had turned ethereal and light, and her fingers floated up toward the heavens, taking mine with them. When her hand was as high as my shoulder she let go. "No, I'm the one who's sorry. I didn't mean to be insensitive."

The icon meant for me vanished.

"I'll walk with you a while longer," she went on. "But Simon chatted me to see if I'd meet him at the top of the Sears Tower to go flying and I *really* want to see him."

My eyes sought the sidewalk. "Go now. It's all right. I don't want you to be late."

"Really?" Inara's voice floated down from above. "You don't mind?"

I looked up at my best friend. Saw how she shined like a silver star in the night sky. Inara was beautiful when she Apped. I felt so dull next to her, in every way. "I'll be fine."

Inara swooped downward and tried to give me a hug. She almost knocked me over with her wings. "Sorry!"

I tried for a laugh, but it sounded like I was choking. "Go meet Simon before you do any lasting damage. Tell him I said hello."

"Okay." Her feet were already a few inches above the ground. She was about to fly off when she turned toward me one last time, hovering there. "I know you're upset, Skye, and I am too." Her eyelashes fluttered and sparkled. "But honestly, I think it's for the best that no one unplugs for Service. When all of this passes, eventually you'll agree. I promise," she finished. Then, quickly, she turned and flew away.

I walked home in a daze. Even the stars couldn't distract me from the thoughts spinning through my mind. Service was *canceled*. Seeing my mother and sister had been *canceled*. Finding out who I was for real had been *canceled*. When I reached Singles Hall, the tall toothpick structure shined with lights in the round windows along its facade. I went inside, my eyes falling across the familiar, brightly colored chairs rising up from the floor like giant bubbles, the great glass dome overhead open to the sky. Normally I found comfort in these things, but all around me was chaos.

Adam Sheridan was making a huge scene in the lounge.

"It isn't fair!" His voice boomed. He must have downloaded an Amplifier App. He seemed bigger, stronger, and taller than normal. Adam was a Single like me, so he was fairly alone in the App World. But I didn't think he had much family left in the Real World to go back to, either. "They can't do this to us! Service is a basic right! They can't prevent the others from plugging back in!"

Some of the other Singles cheered.

But a lot of them were silent.

Adam's skin was turning red. His hands balled into fists, like he was about to hit someone. "Our seventeens must be allowed to cross back! We will not stand for this!"

There were a few weak cheers, and that's when I remembered. Adam had a girlfriend who'd unplugged for Service. Parvda was her name. With the border closed, he'd never see her again. I watched as Adam collapsed into a ball with his head in his hands. Flames shot up from his virtual body and everyone rushed to get out of his way.

It was rare to see so much rage.

I had nearly turned to tears an hour ago, and I wondered how many others would succumb to some similar show. The way our code reacted to intense feeling made us so vulnerable, so naked. I pushed through the circle around Adam, got in front of him, and stuck my hand into the fire, placing it on his back. It burned for a minute but I knew the feeling wouldn't last.

Someone whispered behind me, "Why is she doing that?"

I crouched next to him. "Adam, if you need to talk . . ."

His hands slid from his face. His mouth was an angry red slash. "Leave. Me. Alone."

I got up, stumbling backward. "I was just trying to help. I . . . I didn't mean . . ." I closed my mouth. Adam was glaring at me. "You know what? Whatever." I turned away. The crowd of Singles around Adam had already moved on, distracted by something else.

All over the lounge people were downloading footage from the Cloud. Live holograms of the Holts were projected into the room. There was Lady Holt, the Prime Minister's wife, her face streaked with tears. She walked quickly down one of the boulevards in the Loop, the neighborhood where Inara lived, the collar of her coat pulled high around her neck and face. A crowd of voyeurs trailed after her, whispering and pointing.

"Please." She pulled the collar higher. Her voice cracked. "My son."

Lady Holt could beg for privacy, but there was no hiding for the famous in the App World. People were always making up new aliases so no one could search for them, but celebrities and government officials could never get away with it. Especially not the Holts.

In a separate hologram, Jonathan Holt was sitting at a restaurant by himself, staring into space, maybe waiting for his wife to arrive. Other diners shouted angrily about the safety of our bodies on the plugs.

One man shook his fist. "We should have freed ourselves from the Keepers a long time ago!"

"The Race for the Cure needs to be won!" yelled a woman from halfway across the room.

But another man approached the Prime Minister's table and stuck out his hand. "Good job closing the border."

Jonathan Holt half stood, seeming dazed. He grasped the offered hand.

The man smiled, showing teeth as bright and white as his suit. "We've already got enough poor virtuals looking for handouts. We don't need any more Singles draining the economy." Another man lined up behind him to say more or less the same thing. He wore a suit too, gray like the kind Mr. Sachs put on to go to the bank. Jonathan Holt didn't smile back at the men. He seemed appalled. But then, he still shook those hands.

I looked around at the other Singles. Most of them were silent as they watched people lining up to congratulate the Prime Minister on his decision, but Cecily Gomez was as red as Adam had been before he turned to flames.

"At least we're honest," she yelled at the hologram. "More honest than the rich!"

"They act like we're Lawless," said Jayson Venice

before storming away. The Lawless refused to obey the edicts intended to give our world order and structure. They lived in a part of the City called Loner Town.

"I'm bored," said a male voice to my left.

I turned and saw a large group of Singles surrounding the hologram of a boy, tall and lanky, dressed in the uniform of the Under Eighteens who go to Founders, the school for the children of the most prestigious families in the App World. His dark hair was messy and fell around his face in waves. He leaned against a wall in the courtyard, slouched in his jacket with its golden crest, hands shoved in his pockets.

It was Rain Holt, the son left on the wrong side of the border.

Rain was the obsession of every girl and guy I knew for as long as I could remember, the dream boyfriend, the star celeb, the crown prince of everyone from the twelves all the way up to the nineteens. There were people who would hand over their last bit of capital for the chance to have five minutes alone with him. Inara was always downloading Apps that promised a girl all she needed to know to capture his attention.

Back when she and I were thirteens and Rain was a fourteen, we were voyeuring along with the rest of his millions of fans. He was at this super-exclusive club called Skydive; its claim to fame that it was so high up in the atmosphere it made you feel like you were partying on the moon. To get home you had to download an App that allowed you to jump back to earth. It cost a fortune in capital to get in the door, never mind to get back home again later.

"I can't believe he's out with *her*," Inara had sniffed as we watched.

Rain was on a date with this starlet, Lila, who'd gotten famous by being the first fourteen to open her mind to anyone and everyone—she literally gave people access to every single thing that went through her brain, every observation, every nasty thought she'd ever had about the girls around her. It was because of Lila that Total Access became a trend—that's what people called it when you left your mind transparent. No one else ever managed to get as famous as Lila though. Being first has its rewards in the App World.

Lila and Rain were on the dance floor, not saying much. Just sort of swaying.

Inara was not having it. "All they're doing is posing for voyeurs. She's pathetic."

Rain never cared enough to make the effort to pose, I thought to myself, but didn't mention this.

The two of us sat there on her family's living room couch, waiting for something interesting to happen. Mrs. Sachs had downloaded us these spheres of molten chocolate, and we were popping them into our mouths one after the other. Devil's Drops, they were called. I'd started to tune out, but then there came a sharp intake of breath from Inara.

"He's going to kiss her," she whispered. "I hate that girl. Why does she get to be so lucky?"

The two of us watched as Rain and Lila got closer and closer, until they tilted their heads and their lips met. The lack of gravity was making it hard for them to keep their mouths together, and they kept floating away from each other. Lila actually grabbed Rain's head to stop it from happening. Soon they were making out for all their voyeurs to see.

Inara's sigh was long and heavy. "I wish there was an App to make me stop caring about Rain. Loving him is like, written into my code or something." She reached out to touch the hologram and it disappeared. "I can't watch anymore. It's too upsetting."

I didn't know what to say, so I did the only thing I could think of, which was to put my arm around Inara. She rested her head on my shoulder. Eventually we turned our talk to other things, and ate Devil's Drops until there weren't any more left.

My eyes swept across the lounge. A lot of Singles were downloading footage from Rain's life before he unplugged. Holograms of him were popping up everywhere. Rain walking down the street with a bunch of kids from Founders; Rain at yet another of the hottest clubs in the City; Rain standing there, brushing his hair from his face again and again.

Some of the Singles wept.

Rain was the most searched-for boy in all the Cloud. People would tune in, hoping that maybe, just maybe, he would notice them watching. The thing with being a voyeur was that you could see the person you searched, but they could see you as well. With celebrities, so many people watched at a given time it was nearly impossible for them to pick you out from the crowd. But there were these magical stories of some beautiful famous boy or girl suddenly noticing one of their voyeurs. *Really* seeing them. And just like that, this unknown gets plucked from oblivion, chosen to be special. Lots of Under Eighteens fantasized this would happen to them with Rain.

I suppose now it never could.

"I'm bored," Rain said again as the hologram clip automatically replayed.

I'd seen this particular footage before. It was from nearly a year ago. It had gone viral in minutes because the content was scandalous. This time, I watched alongside everyone else in the lounge.

A crowd of girls surrounded Rain in the school court-yard, their eyes made up to match the abundant, colorful roses climbing trellises and canopies overhead. Their uniform skirts showed off long, thin legs, and they had the supermodel-high cheekbones that only ran through the codes of the richest of the rich. For that kind of perfection, you needed enough capital to buy Appearance Surgery Apps that only had to download once and the changes stayed forever. A group of guys stood off to Rain's side, watching him with envy, yet trying to pretend they weren't. They, too, slouched along the wall.

A girl with long red hair examined her green sparkly nails, looking just as bored as Rain. It was Lacy Mills, daughter of Bryce Mills, CEO of the pornography App industry, a man simultaneously loathed and lauded. "Let's download something super edgy the second school lets out," she said.

Rain didn't even look at her. "No."

The other girls laughed, like he was joking.

Lacy looked up at him. "What do you mean, no?"

"I'm sick of Apps. They're all the same."

A pretty, dark-haired girl reached out and ran a finger down Rain's cheek. "That's not what you said the other night."

The other girls laughed again, though Lacy's eyes flashed with jealousy.

"I'm serious," he said.

The laughter died away.

Rain turned. Stared straight into the paparazzi cam that followed him everywhere. It was supposed to be invisible, its lens as tiny as the point of a pin, but some-how Rain knew exactly where to look. "In fact, I've made a decision and I want the entire App World to know."

The girls hung on his every word.

The boys stopped pretending not to listen.

"I've decided to do my Service," Rain said. "The day I become a seventeen, I'm going to unplug."

"But you can't do that!" the dark-haired girl cried.

"Why would you unplug?" Lacy's long nails sliced green through the atmosphere. "Service is for *Singles*. For people who can't afford to get out of it. For the *poor*."

The group of guys came closer. One of them sneered. "Is there something you're not telling us, Holt? A little hollow sound in Daddy's capital account?"

"Service is supposed to be for everyone," Rain said, unflustered. "For all Under Eighteens who want a taste of the Real World." He looked straight into that lens again. "And I. Want. My. Taste."

The clip buzzed and fizzled, then immediately started from the beginning again.

More Singles gathered to watch the replay.

At the time this first broadcast, nobody could believe the son of the Prime Minister had just announced he would unplug. Lacy Mills was right: only the poor return to the Real World, and when we go, it's because we want to see family or because we lack the capital necessary to sponsor our release. Nearly all the Singles in this room had stories like mine—brothers and sisters, mothers and fathers they hadn't seen since they were three or seven, family that some were too young to even remember. Service affected us the most.

Rain Holt had no such excuse.

Surely he had some hidden agenda with this stunt.

No one ever got an answer that made any sense, though. Jonathan Holt's only comment was that he would miss his son while he was away. I wondered if Rain was punishing his family by making his plan public before they could talk him out of it. He had to know that once the word was out, it would be more scandalous for his father to stop him from unplugging than to allow him to go ahead. If the Prime Minister tried to prevent his son from doing Service because it was dangerous or because it was something only poor Singles did, he would have enraged his more socially conscious supporters.

A flash of anger burned in my middle. "Serves him right," I said to no one in particular.

A nearby Single, Sateen, turned to me. She had long blond hair like Inara, but she was plainer, less glitzy. "What did you say, Skye?"

The hologram of Rain had just reached the part where Lacy Mills was studying her sparkly nails. "Rain unplugged because he was *bored*," I said. "Because he's so rich he had nothing better to do than disappear for a while. He's so arrogant. I'm glad he's getting punished."

Sateen studied me. "You don't mean that. He's still a boy with a family he won't get to see again. He's just like us."

I shook my head. "Rain Holt is *not* like us." Sateen's eyebrows went up. "You heard all those men congratulating Jonathan Holt for closing the borders. They want to keep more people like us from coming here. Unplugging for me was never a joke. Service was the only way I could ever see my mother and sister again."

Sateen put a hand on my arm. "You're upset, Skye. Tonight has been a disappointment and a shock for a lot of us. I understand why you're angry, but don't take it out on someone else's suffering." She was being so rational and reasonable. So kind.

Her words took some of the sting out of my anger, but not all of it. "Rain Holt isn't capable of suffering. He's always so . . . unaffected." I crossed my arms. "I can't bring myself to feel sorry for him, okay? If that makes me a bad person, then so be it."

"You're not a bad person," Sateen said. "But neither was he."

I closed my eyes a moment. Tried to block out the holograms flashing and talking everywhere I turned. "I need this day to be over. I'm going to my room to shutdown for the night."

Sateen gave me a sympathetic smile. "You'll feel better in the morning."

"Right," I said, but I doubted this. How could I feel better when my only opportunity to see my family again had just been rescinded? Before Sateen could move away I stopped her. "I'm sorry for your loss, too."

Her brow furrowed. "My loss?"

"Now you won't get to unplug. You won't see your family either."

Sateen's face brightened. "Actually, I was dreading Service. I'm so relieved about the Prime Minister's announcement. Can you imagine—an entire year without Apps and the virtual comforts of home? I was only doing it because of the obligation, and lucky for me, that obligation is gone, and the guilt along with it!"

I took a step back, off-balance. "Oh. I . . . I . . ."

"More Singles feel this way than you might think," she said when I didn't finish. Then she took off in the other direction.

"I'm bored," said the hologram Rain for the fourth time, or maybe the fifth. I covered my ears even though it was useless. The sound of Rain's voice reverberated through my head.

I needed to get out of here.

I was about to leave the lounge when another hologram caught my attention and I slowed to watch. I couldn't help it.

Rain was gaming with friends, dressed as an archer, moving through a forest of tall thin trees covered in a ghostly white bark, his bow and arrow ready. I knew exactly where he was and what was about to befall him. The game was one of my favorites. A lot of people my age preferred Appearance and Personality Apps, but I liked the ones that would allow me to run fast like a gazelle or swim deep and far in the ocean like a fish. I loved a good Surfing App when I felt like having fun, and I had sharp instincts for danger, and for the right way to go in a maze or on unfamiliar terrain.

In the hologram, Rain dodged a snow-white tiger roaring toward him. The animal turned to dust after Rain effortlessly shot it in the back with an arrow. A big part of me longed to see him fail in a game where someone like me excelled. More beasts awaited him, too. They would come quickly now.

A branch snapped. Then another.

Rain turned toward the sound.

Again, he seemed to stare straight into the tiny camera lens.

Straight at all of us, watching him.

Or maybe not all of us.

My heart quickened.

For the second time that night, I had the uneasy feeling that one of the Holts was looking at me. That of all the millions of voyeurs, Rain Holt was seeing *me*. Logic told me this was as impossible now as it was before, even more so because this hologram was a memory. Rain couldn't pick me out from the crowd because this wasn't happening live.

Yet as I stood there locked in his gaze, it certainly seemed real.

There came the loud crack of another branch.

Rain turned toward it and the feeling evaporated.

3

The last children

THE NEXT MORNING a crowd awaited us outside Singles Hall. The throngs began their assault as soon as I walked through the doors into the sunlight.

"Congratulations!" someone shouted at me.

People roared.

Congratulations?

I looked around, searching for a way through the mob. Inara and I usually met down the block. The only open space was in the center of the street, so that's where I headed. Other Singles followed.

Cecily Gomez was right behind me. "This is insane."

"I don't even know what this is," I said. As Singles we weren't accustomed to being watched. Singles didn't attract voyeurs. "They're cheering for us like we're celebrities."

Jayson Venice caught up to us. "What did we do to deserve this?"

Cecily shrugged. "Stopped sucking down capital now that Service is canceled?"

"Well, whatever it is," he said, "it's kind of fun."

I looked at him. "You think this is fun?"

Jayson shrugged. "My surrogate family got in touch with me for the first time in two years, wanting to know if I was excited about the border closing."

"Mine, too." Cecily huffed. "I was surprised they remembered my name." She eyed me. "At least not all of us have that problem."

"I know I got lucky with the Sachses," I acknowledged, turning away.

I kept searching the crowd for Inara. That's when I began to read the posters people held high in the air.

You are saved! flashed across one of them.

Another said, *Our Under Eighteens are liberated!*

No more buyouts! said yet another.

The crowd was treating the border closing as cause for celebration. An excuse to skip work. A number of citizens had downloaded Apps that turned their hair green or blue so they would stand out. There were men dressed in tuxes and black hats, and more than a few women sparkled with jewels draped across their wrists and necks and had coats of animal fur pulled across their shoulders, the heads of the creatures dangling down their fronts, eyes still blinking. People held long thin flutes that fizzed and popped with golden liquid. They cheered and clinked glasses.

People chanted as we passed. "We are finally free! *You* are free!"

"No more Service!"

"Down with the unplugged!"

"The body is a house of death!"

"The Race for the Cure must be won!"

A man in a glittering suit reached out to grab my hand. "Congratulations," he said giddily. "You're among the last of the Under Eighteens to be plugged in!"

I yanked my hand away and kept moving. Of course, he was right. With the borders closed, no one else would be uploaded to the App World. Within two decades, Under Eighteens would be no more when the youngest of us reached the age of majority. The man spoke as though it was a good thing that the population would be capped.

People tossed confetti and streamers.

Did everyone feel this way?

Anger flashed through my brain. Now that Service was canceled, the wealthy would be even wealthier. They wouldn't have to spend any capital to stop their children from having to unplug.

Well, lucky them.

I hurried along, raking my fingers through my hair,

trying to untangle the tiny flecks of colorful paper cling-
ing to it. My eyes burned but I tried to gain back control
of my emotions. I would not let these people get to me. I
looked around at my fellow Singles, searching the crowd
for a sympathetic nod.

What I saw was startling.

Sateen was a little ways ahead. She was smiling, her
hand in the air, waving at our audience like some sort of
queen.

That's when I began to notice the Apps.

Someone tossed Sateen an icon and she caught it,
grinning at the free download in her hand. She squirreled
it away in her account, only to look up and find another
on its way. Other Singles saw what was happening and
followed her lead. Soon the atmosphere was littered with
so many icons the sky glittered and flashed. Singles were
grabbing at the air, greedy for the kind of App riches
we typically only dreamed about. Soon there were boys
wrestling on the ground, confetti and streamers piling
up on their backs, and girls shrieking at one another over
whose icon was whose. I passed Jayson and Cecily shouting about which one of them would keep the Sports Star
App dangling above their heads.

The crowd looked at us like we were animals. They
threw Apps like they were raw pieces of meat and we
were a pack of hungry dogs. We behaved exactly how
they imagined, too, clawing our way over one another for

whatever we could get our hands on.

My cheeks flamed. I covered my face with my hands to hide these flickers of shame on my virtual skin. I was part of a group to whom people tossed their scraps. Singles rewarded for the mere fact that we would no longer be allowed to unplug and see our Keeper families, symbolic of the end of an era so many people had obviously resented. Amid the frenzy, more App icons rained down. I gave up trying to shake away the streamers and confetti. Twirls of fluorescent purple and green decorated my hair. When my hands slid from my eyes again, I saw Adam. He stood unmoving across the street, a boy statue on the boulevard.

We watched each other through the chaos.

I nodded at him, a strange calm falling across me.

This time he didn't sneer. He nodded back, only slightly, but enough that I saw him do it. Then his attention caught on something else, his eyes narrowing. I searched the crowd for the object of his gaze, but then someone called my name.

"Skye!" Inara's voice cut through the noise all around. "Over here!" *Skye, look to your left*, she chatted in my mind.

I turned and saw her blond hair shining bright in the sun, lighting her up. She waved frantically, beckoning me from the crowd. I glanced back at Adam but he was gone, lost among the other Singles. Inara disappeared around the corner and I went after her, pushing through the distracted onlookers. They were like a forest of trees, each one of them growing taller than the person in front of them with the help of an App to better view the chaos. When I turned down the next street, Inara was waiting there, her father's long black car already running.

"Are you okay?" she asked as I approached.

"Yes. No. I don't know."

She gave me a hug. "This is crazy."

"Let's go to school. The crowds won't be able to get to us there." The downloading of Apps and the presence of voyeurs were prohibited inside the building.

Inara looked at me uncertainly. "Are you sure you don't want a day off?" Her eyes sought the ground. "You know, um, to celebrate?"

My mouth opened in surprise. "How could you even ask that?"

Inara shifted from one foot to the other. "I don't want to lie to you, Skye. Like I said last night, this is probably for the best." She reached for my hand and squeezed it. "Being in the body for a whole year, being trapped in the Real World with the Keepers, it could've . . . it could've *killed* us. The body is fragile and susceptible to disease, and now we don't have to worry about that anymore." Her eyes were pleading. "I know you wanted to see your mother and your sister, but I'm your sister, too. You're the only one I have. You don't have to worry about being separated from your surrogate family anymore. Isn't that worth celebrating?"

I busied myself opening the door of the car. "Sure, of course," I lied, feeling ungrateful as I got inside. Inara joined me in the backseat, but I didn't look at her. Soon we were speeding off to school in silence. Even though I was with my best friend in the entire App World, who thought of herself as my sister, I'd never felt so alone.

Most of my memories of the Real World were hazy or quick, but I remembered the day I plugged in like it was yesterday. My mother and sister brought me to a beautiful old train station in New Port City, the one that wasn't used for trains anymore. At five, I was old enough to understand I was going on an exciting, virtual trip, yet still too young to grasp that it would be years before I'd return.

When it was time to leave, my mother and sister lied to me.

"We'll see you soon, my Skye, my heart, my love, my darling." My mother covered my face in kisses. I had to wipe the red smear of her lipstick from my skin.

I looked up into her wide blue eyes—eyes just like mine. They were glassy. Her tears frightened me. "When will I be back?" I asked. An exact count of days would help me get through the sadness. In my left hand, a soft blue bunny dangled toward the ground, my favorite toy.

It was nearly the same hue as my T-shirt and pants. Blue was my favorite color.

My sister, Jude, put her arm around me. "Stop worrying, Bean. Soon you'll be having so much virtual fun you'll forget all about us."

That was when another woman, the Keeper in charge of children plugging in, came through the door marked *Departures*. I don't remember her face, just that she was tall, impossibly tall, it seemed. So much bigger than me. Her pale, loose garments were bright against her skin.

My mother crouched to my level, two matching streams of water running down her cheeks. "Blue like the ocean and blue like the sky, blue like the sapphire color of your eyes," she sang softly, her voice hoarse. "You'll always be my blue Skye."

The tall Keeper took my hand. "It's time to go."

"No, I won't," I said, my mouth an angry pout.

My sister tried to smile but I could tell she wanted to cry like my mother. "You won't what? You won't go?" she asked.

"No. I won't forget about you," I said. The woman took me into her arms when I wouldn't budge. I looked back at my family one last time. They were waving, tears pouring down their faces. "I won't," I called back.

For a long time, I wrote to them. With the help of one of the School Apps, I composed short letters to the Real World, the best I could manage.

Dear Mom, I love you so much! I miss you and Jude, Love your blue Skye.

Dear Jude, I wish you could read me a story. Love, Bean.

Mom and Jude, when are you coming to live here too? Love Skylar-Bean.

Eventually, the notes I composed grew more worried, more insecure. I didn't bother to sign them—I didn't feel like I needed to.

Did I do something bad to make you send me away?

Mom and Jude, do you not love me anymore?

Have you forgotten me completely?

Each time I finished a new message, Mrs. Sachs would help me post it. At first, back when the letters were sweet, she treated it like a game, checking my spelling and teaching me how to upload communications. Every day I would check my mailbox, and every day I would be disappointed there was nothing from my mother or sister. Months passed. Then years. My insistence that Mrs. Sachs help post my letters wore her down. She became less and less enthusiastic with each new message and her excuses about why I heard nothing back became repetitive and hollow. Then one day, when Inara was busy with homework and I asked yet again for her help, she led me to one of the couches in the living room. The two of us sat down.

"I think you're old enough to know the truth," she said.

I had just become an eight.

"What truth?" There was a tightness in my voice. After three years of hearing nothing from my family, even a little girl gets suspicious.

"About your family, Skye. Their intentions for your future."

I nodded. Everything started to fade as she spoke. Emptied of color and light.

"Your mother and sister aren't coming to get you," Mrs. Sachs said carefully. "They've taken on the important, selfless role of Keeper of Bodies. By doing so, they gave you a better life. But by plugging you in, they gave up all contact. They aren't going to respond to your letters, my dear. They can't. There isn't any point to checking your mailbox for messages. Communication is prohibited. Sending letters to the Real World is only pretend."

Stars clouded my head and made it hard to speak. "But why?"

Mrs. Sachs took my hand. "Imagine if your family was writing you all the time, telling you about life in the Real World, or worse, how they were suffering. The law prohibiting communication between Singles and their families is there to free you, so you can live your virtual life unburdened by them." She shifted a little, the bright flash of her earrings a shock in all the dullness. "Not knowing helps alleviate the stress and despair that comes with feeling so divided."

Even at eight, I knew what Mrs. Sachs meant. It was basic worlds history. Before the first plugs, an early version of the virtual world existed. People carried around handheld devices that allowed them access to it. But the maintenance of two entirely different selves—one real, one virtual—was confusing and exhausting. People became so addicted to looking at their tablets that they stopped going outside and even stopped talking to their real friends and loved ones. The App World saved everyone this division by liberating people from their bodies and allowing them a permanent virtual existence.

But then, what about Singles like me, whose very presence in the App World was the result of dividing a family?

When I didn't respond, Mrs. Sachs sighed. "It's better this way, Skye. It's easier. You'll realize this too, one day."

I could barely breathe. "So I'll never talk to my mother and sister again?"

Mrs. Sachs looked away. She was silent a long time, staring out the window at the tall buildings in the distance. "No. Well. Unless . . ." She stopped.

"Unless what?"

"All children are supposed to unplug for Service. It's meant as a time to experience the Real World, and for Singles to see their families again."

"I want to go. I want to go now." My voice cracked.

"I need to see them." All the questions I wanted to ask my mother and sister swirled in my brain like a bowl of alphabet soup. *Did you abandon me? Do you still love me? Are your lives better without me? Did you really want to give me a better future or was plugging me in just an excuse to make me go away?*

Mrs. Sachs shook her head. "When you're a seventeen you'll be allowed to go."

I held up my fingers and began to count. I was eight and then I would be nine. Ten. Eleven. And so on. "That's so far away."

"Skye . . ." Mrs. Sachs hesitated again. She kept staring at my hand in hers. "Service is dangerous—bodies are dangerous. There are ways to avoid the Service requirement. Inara loves you and it would break our hearts to see her lose your friendship. Mr. Sachs and I are willing to do what it takes so both of you can stay safe in the App World."

"But my mother and sister—" I started.

"Don't worry about that now." Mrs. Sachs got up. "By the time the decision is upon you, I bet you'll have forgotten all about the Real World and everyone in it."

I stood, my virtual legs shaky. "I don't think so."

Mrs. Sachs gave me a hug. "You're so young. A lot can happen in nine years."

This was true. Learning that one day I could see my family again gave me a goal and a purpose. And Mrs.

Sachs was right about something else. Some of the pain I'd felt about not hearing from my family, the fear that they'd forgotten me or had never loved me, was lifted with the news that communication was prohibited. Enough that I felt lighter. More hopeful. While it would be difficult to wait so long to see my family again, I was patient. I could hold out for Service.

When Mrs. Sachs headed back into the kitchen that day, I returned to Inara's room. She was sitting on her bed, downloading her homework. I arranged myself on her violet-covered blanket. "Guess what?"

Inara paused her download to focus on me. "What?"

"When we become seventeens," I said, feeling important, "we're going to unplug."

Inara and I finally arrived at school. Students were celebrating just like the revelers in the street. No one seemed to care about what was happening to those left behind in the Real World. Even Rain was forgotten. Singles were acting like royalty, as though we were the only ones affected by the border closing. As though it was really about us. Everyone was drunk on their new taste of fame.

"I was shocked at first, like everyone else," Sateen was saying to Simon Best, Inara's crush.

Inara stopped to listen.

"Then when it started to sink in," Sateen went on, "I realized this world would be a better place without anyone unplugging or anyone else plugging in." She ran a hand through her hair. It still had a faint shimmer to it, even though the Apps had mostly drained away by now since she was inside the school. "What a relief not to have to unplug!" She looked around, taking in the other students standing in groups, silently chatting one another in their minds or whooping it up loudly in the halls. "Now, it's just us here. We're the last children of the App World."

Simon placed a hand against the wall next to Sateen. "Yeah, it's crazy to think about it. This world is *closed*." He leaned closer, like he might kiss her.

Inara bristled, her skin alive with static. I reached for her, my fingers nearly burned by the sparks that flashed and sizzled.

"We've got enough people to last us, well, forever," Simon added.

"I kind of like the idea," Sateen said. She tilted her chin upward and to the side, ready for Simon to make his move. "Suddenly everything seems so intimate," she breathed.

Inara's mouth was set in a tight, thin line. *Let's get out of here*, she chatted me privately. She walked away so quickly it was practically a run. "I can't bear to watch that girl act like she's so special," she said, out loud this time. Tiny black char marks began to dot her fluffy purple sweater. "Sateen was just a boring Single yesterday and she'll be a boring Single again tomorrow."

I winced. Did Inara think I was just another boring Single, too? "We're headed to assembly, right?" I asked, changing the subject. Reminders about it were pinging all over the hallways. Notices scrolled bright across the wall in all caps, shouting for our attention.

"Yeah. I guess."

We moved through the crowd. "Maybe they'll tell us news of the Real World," I said. "Maybe that's what they want to talk to us about."

Inara shrugged. "I'm sure your mother and sister are fine, Skye."

I shook my head. *I wonder if they're dead* went my mind. I couldn't bear to actually speak those words.

But I didn't have to. My mind was open to chat with Inara, so she heard my thoughts. She spun around quickly, moving in front of me so I was forced to stop. People streamed by us. She put her hands on my shoulders and looked at me hard, her long blond hair lit up by the flashing announcements on the wall behind her. "The government is always being overly cautious. I bet there's nothing wrong in the Real World. Just some rebellious group the Prime Minister freaked out about."

"You don't know that," I said, uncomfortable. Inara's thumbs pushed against my collarbone. "I wish you did, but you don't."

She sighed. "Aren't you even a *little* relieved you're off the hook? I mean, did you really want a whole year away from the Apps? From the constant entertainment of being a voyeur? The Keepers barely even have electricity! They, like, use the sun or something archaic like that."

"Do you really think I care whether I can download a pair of long legs for a few hours or watch Lacy Mills's every move if it means I'll never see my mother and sister again?" I shrugged off Inara's grip. "Without Service, I almost . . . I almost don't feel like I have a future. I'll never know what happened to my family."

Inara's hands returned to her sides. "Skye, you're being melodramatic."

"No, I'm not." My voice filled the hall, sizzling with anger. The words sparked into the atmosphere like fireworks, then burned away. "Melodrama is exaggerated emotion. Do you really think I'm overreacting?" People were starting to stare. The skin on my hands was turning red. "My mother and sister might be dead!"

"Your mother and sister may have forgotten all about you by now," Inara said. Her eyes widened as though even she couldn't believe these words had just come out of her mouth, my greatest fear tossed at me like it was nothing.

"How can you say that?" My voice took flight, the shock so intense that the words appeared in the atmosphere, flying about and bumping into the walls and other students, propelled by all that emotion. People had to duck.

"Shhhh!" Inara hissed. "You're making a scene."

"My family could be in danger and that's what you're worried about?"

Inara smiled at Jackson, an ex of hers passing by, his eyebrows raised. "Lower. Your. Voice. Skylar."

"You're embarrassed by me, aren't you? That of all the Singles, you have to be friends with the one who actually cares about unplugging. Who stupidly cares about the family that gave her up."

"That's not true," Inara said, her voice low and even. "You have no idea what your mother and sister are like after all this time. They might not be the same people you said good-bye to. Your future is *here*. In *this* world. The sooner you accept that, the happier you'll be."

My breaths were rapid-fire. If I wasn't careful, I'd be consumed with rage like Adam was last night, and right in the middle of the school hallway. I conjured up images of ice and snow and felt a chill coursing through my code. My virtual skin became chapped, a web of dry white lines running through it. My stare turned cool on my friend. "You want me to move on as though this isn't a big deal. As though it's cause for celebration."

Inara cocked her head. "Skye." She sounded exasperated. She brushed away a snowflake that had slid down my cheek and onto her wrist. It melted when it hit the floor and disappeared into nothing. "Calm. Down."

But I couldn't. Icicles formed in my hair, pointing into my scalp like tiny sharp knives. "Don't try to pretend you're not mourning your imaginary future with Rain Holt," I said, watching as Inara's mouth opened in shock. People halted midstride, suddenly rapt at the mention of this name. If it wasn't against school rules, someone would be transmitting our disagreement. Under Eighteens loved nothing more than a fight they could upload to the Cloud. "You were always so sure that of all the girls and boys who watched him, Rain would pick *you* out. Everything is always about *you*, Inara."

Her eyes flashed. "Skye, stop," she hissed. "Don't say something you'll regret."

"You know what?" I looked around at the crowd that had gathered. Confetti dotted everyone's clothing. Streamers were laced through their hair. Celebration filled the atmosphere like a balloon expanding and threatening to suffocate me. I shook away the icicles from my limbs and they clattered to the floor, shattering upon impact. "It doesn't matter, Inara. I don't have anything else to lose."

Then I turned on my heel and walked in the other direction.

"Skye!" Inara called after me, but I kept going.

I needed to get out of there. To be somewhere in the City and not stuck in the stale school building. But just as I reached the doors, an unauthorized chat broke into my mind, the words hovering and glowing a bright shiny green in my head.

Meeting, back room, Appless Bar, to discuss unplugging.

Tonight, one a.m. sharp. Come alone. Or you're virtually dead.

What?

My brain spun, dizzy from the invasion. I looked around, searching for the author of the message, but the halls had emptied. I waited a moment longer, but when no one appeared I pushed my way out into the bright light of the day.

4

Top secret

ALL AFTERNOON I wandered the City. People were Celebration Apping everywhere I turned, but I could think of nothing other than the unauthorized chat. Who could have sent it? How did they bypass the firewalls in my mind? How was it possible to unplug with the border closed? Why the threat?

And most of all: Would I go to the meeting?

Inara kept chatting me. At first she sounded angry. *You humiliated me,* she said. *That stuff about Rain was private. How would you like it if I went around telling people you've never had a boyfriend? That you've never kissed anybody outside of a Kissing App?* These mentions set my cheeks aflame and for a few moments my skin began to char like the spots on Inara's sweater. But as the afternoon wore on, Inara's tone changed. *Look, I should have tried to be more understanding about your Real World family. Of course you're worried. I know you've been excited to unplug and see them. I'm sorry Service got canceled. Really. I am.*

Even though I was tempted to respond, for once I ignored her.

Guilt rose in me again and snaked its way through my code. Was I being foolish? Maybe Inara was right, and the border closing was for the best. Even for me.

I rounded the corner and sat down on a bench. Tried to stop my brain from racing. Next to me, a man as big as a giant was towering over the trees of Main Park. A lot of people were walking on air. Kids played soccer in the middle of the street, but everyone was floating three feet above the ground. I watched as a group of Under Eighteens was in front of me one moment and gone the next as they disappeared into a game. A girl not much older than me transformed into a tall, skinny model before crossing the street and heading into an App bar.

I was about to chat Inara, to tell her I was sorry, when a memory flashed—or at least, I *thought* it was a memory. It came in bits and pieces. Lying in a bed. The faraway sound of waves crashing. A face peering at me from above. A curtain of long brown hair. Dark eyes blinking, full of regret. Dark eyes set in a face that I knew, so familiar yet so strange.

"Jude?" I said out loud, as though my sister could hear me. As though she were with me in the App World, right now. She seemed . . . older than in my other memories.

Then her face—and the memory with it—disappeared.

A yearning deep and hungry gaped wide, as though it might swallow me.

I stood up from the bench and headed back to Singles Hall. Tonight, I would go to the meeting. Of course I would. How could I not? I didn't care if I had to go alone. If it got me to the Real World, it was worth the risk.

"Where'd you disappear to today?" a voice asked from behind me.

I turned. "Hi, Sateen." I tried not to stare. "You look different."

Sateen was leaning against the wall across from the entrance to Singles Hall. Or maybe she was using the wall to hold herself up. Unlike this morning, now she was tall and thin, her legs and arms long and lithe, her hips narrow, everything about her stretched and willowy except for her chest, which was bigger and rounder and almost spilling from her top. Her face was bright with makeup, purples and blues and sparkly silvers, her hair styled perfectly, her teeth gleaming white as she smiled. She looked ethereally beautiful—beautiful and aloof and unreal.

"It's the Supermodel App," she said with unmistakable pride, pushing off the wall. Even her walk was different, her hips swaying. On her way toward me she almost toppled over on her six-inch spiked heels. She caught herself before falling, grabbing the back of one of the chairs. "Don't I just look amazing?" she asked, her breaths quickening as she tried to straighten up, only to wobble again.

"Sure." I crossed my arms, taking her in. Apparently, the grace to handle her new height had to be downloaded separately. "But how did you get enough capital for the Supermodel App?"

Sateen laughed, the sound like bells. Her long eyelashes fluttered and flashed. They were so long and thick I could feel a breeze. "How *didn't* you?" She tossed her hair like she had an audience—and maybe she did. Voyeurs were prohibited in our dormitory rooms, but they could access the lounge, and Sateen had become a star among Singles this morning. "I got more free downloads today than I've had in my entire existence."

"But the *Supermodel* App?" In all honesty, I was a little jealous. It's true, I preferred gaming, but sometimes a girl just wants to be beautiful for a few hours.

Sateen's fingers twitched, her manicured nails glittering. Something crossed her face. Sympathy, maybe. "I could share some of my downloads with you." She called up her personal App Store and the icons appeared, orbiting her like she was their sun. She raised her hand, and with one swipe of the air they swirled around her like stars. "Do you want to try on a new face for a while? Or download a celebrity boyfriend for the evening? A bunch of us are going out to celebrate at Crash Club. I was thinking of downloading a cute special someone to kiss myself."

A part of me was touched by Sateen's generosity, but the rest was a little offended—especially by her offer to help me download a new face. "That's nice of you. But I'm staying in tonight," I lied.

She shrugged. "Suit yourself. If you change your mind, I'll be in my room until we leave at midnight. Curfew's been lifted. You should take advantage."

I smiled. Leaving the hall after midnight wouldn't be conspicuous then. Plenty of people would be out and about. "Sure." I watched as Sateen sauntered away as gracefully as she could manage. "Maybe I will," I called after her.

I never did chat Inara.

It was close to midnight when I appeared in the doorway of Sateen's room. She was lying on her bed, eyes wide open but unblinking, long supermodel arms and legs stretched out. Staying still was a way to slow the drain of a download, prolonging an App's life. "Is that offer still open?" I asked her. Crash Club and Appless Bar were in the same direction. I'd decided the best way to get to my destination was to have a full Singles entourage. "I changed my mind about tonight."

Sateen's eyelashes fluttered. Then her knee twitched. Slowly she came alive again and sat up. "That's great, Skye. We'll have fun." She looked me up and down. "Let me at least offer you something for your hair. It's so . . . straight. Maybe a download for your face, too, so it isn't quite so plain?" She studied my eyes, my cheeks, my nose. She took a fistful of my hair into her hand, lifting it and letting it fall back to my head. "It's really limp." Then her eyes traveled lower. "And I'm very happy with my Boob Enhancer. I think you should download one." She laughed. "You could definitely use it."

I laughed along with her, hoping she couldn't hear the false ring. Was I really that boring? "You're sweet," I managed. "I didn't come here for a makeover, though. Just some company on the way to Crash Club." Her lips formed a pout. "You can fix those things about me another time," I added. "I promise."

She extended a thin, delicate hand. "It's a deal."

I took it, then checked the time. It was just after midnight. "Should we get going?"

"I suppose so." Sateen grabbed a sequined clutch, called up a mirror hologram, and studied the second, three-dimensional Sateen that appeared before us. Satisfied, she swept out of the room. Sateen seemed to have a better handle on walking in those heels now.

I trailed after her, trying not to feel as dull and ordinary as I must have looked.

"Come on, people!" Sateen called out to everyone in the lounge. She beckoned with a wave of her hand. At least twenty Singles joined us, most of them transformed by Appearance Apps that made the guys more broad shouldered and the girls thinner and blonder. Though no one looked as good as Sateen. "Isn't this so much fun?" She giggled as we made our way into the night and the City.

I had to take two steps for every one of Sateen's. Her legs were so long it was difficult to keep up. As we hurried down the sidewalk, I took in the scene around me. Other groups of Under Eighteens were reveling in the streets and spilling out along the sidewalks from the bars. Long black cars like Inara's slowly rolled down the boulevard. The Water Tower soon loomed above us, its needle pointing high into the heavens with a colorful blue glow. The urge to chat Inara was as intense as the guilt that wouldn't leave me alone.

But the message had been clear.

Come alone. Or you're virtually dead.

I slowed my pace, falling behind the group. No one noticed me pull back; they were too busy enjoying the feel of so many Apps at once. Then I tossed aside any remaining doubt and slipped away from the group entirely.

Appless Bar was all the way on the other side of Main Park.

The iron gate at the park's entrance creaked loudly as I opened it. Sometimes the effort to make the virtual seem realistic was too well done for my taste. The metal was heavy and cold in my hands and slightly electric. A faint current ran through me until I let go. I looked around to make sure no one had seen me enter. The park was empty at this time of night, everything silhouetted in darkness. The trees were tall shadowy ghosts as I walked, their branches a web of long inky fingers. They reminded me of the Fright Night Apps Inara and I used to download because we liked being scared. We would always end up alone in a haunted wood where we'd have to escape terrible creatures with axes and sharp silver knives.

Empty benches formed a circle around the jungle gym where children played during the day. It was so quiet. Even my steps made no sound in the grass. The City lights glowed reassuringly along the park's perimeter, a reminder that life and other people were still close by.

For some reason, I found myself heading toward the swings. I sat down on one, and the second I closed my eyes a memory flooded my brain. It was different from the one I'd had earlier—longer and more vivid. I was moving through the air, pumping my legs. Swish. Swish. Swish. Everything rhythmic. Laughter rose in my throat as I leaned back, hair flying in the breeze. Then came the voice.

"Do you want to go higher, my love?"

"Higher! Higher," I shouted.

My mother's hands were at my back, giving me a push.

"Be careful, Skylar!"

"Oh, she'll be fine," said another voice, to my left.

As I flew through the air, I saw a girl, about my age now. "Jude!"

"What, Bean?"

"You're my sister."

She laughed. "Of course I am. I hope I don't look like your brother!"

I kept trying to turn around so I could see my mother, but the momentum of the swing kept stopping me.

Skye? Are you awake? chatted Inara into my brain.

"No," I cried out.

The memory faded. I grasped at it again and again with my mind, not quite sure how I'd managed to access it in the first place. It was as though someone had flipped a switch inside me, turning the memory on, then turning it off again.

"What are you doing?" came a new voice.

My eyes flew open. I jumped up from the swing and turned. "Who's there?" I called into the darkness. I searched for the voice's source, but I couldn't see a thing. I turned around again. Still nothing. "Show yourself," I said into the darkness.

Someone stepped out from behind a tree trunk.

A boy. Taller than me, unaffected by any Apps. His curly black hair was clipped close to his head.

"Adam?"

He took a step closer. "What are you doing here, Skylar?"

My heart pounded but I kept my chin up. "I could ask you the same thing."

"I don't need to give you a reason."

"Yeah, well, I don't owe you one either."

We stood there, facing off, neither of us budging.

A strange look crossed Adam's face. "You're going to Appless Bar," he said. It was a statement, not a question.

The message repeated itself in my brain.

Come alone. Or you're virtually dead.

My body tensed. "I don't know what you're talking about."

"You can't lie to me," Adam said. "I know when people aren't being truthful."

"What are you, a psychic?"

"No." His voice was flat.

I reminded myself that it was just Adam. Someone I lived with. But when he took another step closer I took one back.

"You got the same message that I did," he said.

"I told you, I don't—"

"Meeting, back room, Appless Bar, to discuss unplugging," Adam recited. "Tonight, one a.m. sharp. Come alone. Or you're virtually dead."

I opened my mouth. "How did you—" I started, then stopped, midsentence. I came at Adam, arms flying, ready to fight. "You're the one who hacked my brain!"

He caught one of my arms, then the other, my wrists gripped in his hands. "Calm down. I didn't hack your brain," he said. "I was headed to the meeting when I saw you on the swing." Slowly, he let go of me. Waited to see if I'd try to hit him again. "We should go or we're going to be late." Adam started off but when I didn't follow, he turned back. "Come on. We may as well go together."

"Why should I trust you?" I asked.

He shrugged. "Who else do you know who got the message?"

This quieted me. Like it or not, he was right about that part. "It said to come alone," I reminded him.

"Yeah. So? I'm choosing to interpret that as *don't show up with anyone who didn't get this message*." Adam started off again.

Still unsure, I joined him. We walked in silence, side by side. Soon we passed through the gates on the other side of the park, the City blindingly bright after so much darkness. The mood over here was more subdued, the neighborhood not as vibrant. More run-down than on the west side.

The quiet made me uneasy. "It's just a few more blocks," I said.

"I'm sorry I acted like such a jerk last night," Adam said. "I know you were only trying to help."

I turned to him. "Then make up for it by telling me what you know about this message. Why us? How many other people got it? Who sent it?"

He shook his head. "Honestly, I don't know anything more than you do."

We turned the corner, closing in on Appless Bar. Unlike everywhere else, this street was empty. "For some reason, I believe you," I told him.

"You should. I'm not lying."

"Let me ask you something else," I said.

Adam glanced my way. "Go ahead."

We came to a stop before the door of the bar. It didn't exactly look like an inviting establishment. The windows were dark and the outside was dingy, like it hadn't had an architecture update since the first people plugged in. Even the sign was broken down, the name barely lit on the wall and flickering dimly. The second *p* in *App* had gone dark, the download draining away and nobody ever bothering to fix it. The only other thing I knew about this place was that it was coded so no one could App within its walls. Other than schools and workplaces, very few places prohibited Apping.

I took a deep breath, my eyes on Adam. "If whoever called this meeting can really help us unplug—will you do it?"

"Yes," Adam said, his voice full of confidence. "No doubt about it."

"It's because of your girlfriend, right? You have a girl-friend who got left on the other side of the border."

Sadness welled in his eyes. Adam was so different when he wasn't wearing that hard, cold expression. "Her name is Parvda."

I nodded. "I remember."

He hesitated. "What about you? Will you unplug?"

Ever since I received the message, I'd been considering what I would do if this turned out to be a real opportunity. I'd thought about Inara, how she was always claiming we were as real as sisters can ever hope to be, and how leaving her behind would hurt her terribly—it would hurt us both.

"It depends on the circumstances," I told Adam. "But I have a mother and a sister in the Real World and I need to find them. I want to make sure they're okay." I stopped, thinking I'd said all that needed saying, but then realized there was something else. "And I want to find out why my mother thought it was best that I leave the Real World. Whether or not I might still have a place there. And I want to know who I am for real, too," I added.

Adam nodded. "I understand." His expression grew far away. "Being a Single makes it seem like we don't have a place anywhere. Not really."

These words hung between us, their echo full of longing. Adam's honesty made me think he and I were going to be friends.

An alarm went off in my brain reminding me of the approaching hour. "Time to find out who called us here. Are you ready?"

"Yeah. Let's go."

Adam opened the door. Inside, the bar was nearly as dark as the night outside. Adam entered first and I followed. There were a few men scattered at tables, none of them talking, all of them alone. Another man was working, mixing drinks without the help of any Apps, which was a strange sight. He didn't seem surprised to see us standing there, even though we were clearly out of place.

"All the way in the back," he said to us.

Adam and I crossed the room toward another door, this one smaller, crooked, like it led somewhere we shouldn't be allowed to go. Tentatively, I pushed it open. The hinges groaned as it swung wide.

Someone else was already there. Her head snapped in our direction. I knew the girl by sight. She was another Single. She sat at the only table in the room.

"Hi, Sylvia," Adam said as he walked inside, as though

this was just another chance encounter in the lounge at our hall.

I raised my hand in a wave. I'd noticed Sylvia occasionally in the cafeteria and the lounge, but I'd never talked to her. Until now, I didn't have much reason to. It's funny how you can live with someone and not know her at all.

Adam and I stood there awkwardly.

Sylvia spoke, her voice steady. "You guys got the message too?"

Adam opened his mouth to answer, but right then, another person entered the room behind me. His eyes turned icy, frosting over, as he took in the new member of our group.

Sylvia's hands balled into fists.

I turned around to see who it was.

Our newest attendee closed the door with a loud slam, and the rest of us jumped. Her long hair curled down her back, the color of fire. The black dress she wore hugged her virtual body, barely reaching the top of her thighs, accentuating her curves and long thin legs. She crossed her arms and I caught a flash of green sparkly nails.

The smile on Lacy Mills's face was wicked. "Obviously you got my message. How daring that you took me up on it! Perhaps there's hope for us all."

5

Deal with the devil

"WHY ARE WE here?" Adam demanded.

Lacy glared. "Sit down, angry boy, and I'll tell you." The bartender appeared in the doorway with three tall glasses of bubbly brown liquid. For Lacy, there was a thin, delicate flute of something pink and sparkling. "Have a drink." She plucked the champagne from the tray. "This is going to take a while."

When none of us moved, the man set the remaining glasses on the table, then turned around and disappeared into the other room.

Adam walked to one of the empty chairs and pulled it out, the legs screeching against the dusty floor. He eyed his drink, but didn't touch it. Neither did Sylvia. Lacy waited for me to join everyone at the table, but I stayed by the door. I had no reason to trust her, so I wasn't about to go and make myself comfortable.

"Fine, have it your way," Lacy said to me. "You Singles can be *so* overly self-important."

"I didn't come here to be insulted," Adam said.

"Like I said, *so* overly self-important. You take everything *so* seriously."

Lacy was one of the top celebrity Under Eighteens that people loved to hate, but she was turning out to be even nastier in person. I leaned against the wall and crossed my arms. "If you don't get to the point, I'm leaving," I said. Adam nodded in agreement. Sylvia was watching me. "We're *all* leaving.

"I'm not leaving," Sylvia said quietly.

My eyebrows arched. So Sylvia wasn't going to let herself get pushed around.

"Ooh, conflict among Singles." Lacy sounded bored. "How *dramatic*."

I reached for the handle on the door, ready to walk out. Adam got up, knocking some of his drink onto the table.

Lacy put up her free hand, fingers long and delicate. "Fine. Get a grip, everyone. I'll tell you why I called you here."

Slowly, Adam sat down again, taking a long time to adjust his chair. I leaned back, crossing my arms.

Lacy took a dainty sip of her drink, swallowed, and then began to speak. "So. We're at Appless Bar because I needed to make sure you were all, well, *you*. I didn't want anybody showing up as, like, Medusa or a kangaroo or something." She laughed and waited for us to join her. When we didn't, she let out a sigh. "But we're here tonight so we can discuss the current political situation—"

"The political situation?" Adam spat before she could say anything else. "You want to talk to us about politics?"

Lacy batted her eyelashes. "I know, it's hard to believe, isn't it?" She swept a hand across her virtual body. "Totally gorgeous *and* brainy, too." She walked to the vacant chair between Adam and Sylvia at the table and sat down. She crossed her long legs and tapped her nails against her champagne flute. Satisfied we were all listening, she leaned forward. "The three of you are about to get what we all want, which is to unplug and see our"—she paused, seeming to search for the right words—"our *loved* ones in the Real World."

My brow furrowed. Lacy Mills had loved ones in the Real World? I wasn't sure what was more surprising, that she wanted to unplug, or that she and I had something in common. I finally went over to the table and sat down in the only remaining chair. I took a long gulp of the drink that still awaited me. It was bitter.

"In exchange for unplugging, you'll help me get what *I* want. I'm in charge of everyone, of course—the organizer, if you will." She smiled, happy with her status as leader. "What you do on your own time when you're not carrying out orders is your business. You Singles can see your families." She flicked her hand like she was swatting at something distasteful. "Your devoted *girlfriend*. Whatever."

Adam shifted uncomfortably. "I don't take orders from anyone."

Lacy's head snapped toward him. "Maybe *I* should be the one to leave. Then where would you be without my resources? My connections? You think someone else is going to help you unplug?"

Adam got up and started to pace. The floor creaked under his steps. "This isn't a game for me. For any of us."

"Everything is a game," Lacy said. "How do you not know that yet?"

I grabbed the back of Adam's shirt in my fist, and he stopped pacing. I gave him a fierce look. I didn't like Lacy either, but she was right—when it came to unplugging, this would be our only chance. "What exactly do you need us to do?"

Lacy smiled, pleased at my interest. "As you know, dark things are happening among the Keepers—things that could jeopardize the safety and future of every citizen in the App World. There are people on the other side of the border organizing against those Keepers. The three of you are in charge of extracting someone—someone *very* important—from this quagmire and returning him home to his rightful place in Virtual Reality." She took another slow sip of her drink. Lacy was stalling. She obviously loved reminding us that she held all the power.

"But the border is closed," I said.

"Oh! Is it *really*?" Lacy's eyes flashed. "I had no idea! Thank you so much for enlightening little ole ditzy me."

I pressed my lips together. *Okay. Point to Lacy.*

She got up and began to circle the table, steps slow, heels clicking against the floor, dust floating up into the atmosphere. "Obviously, if there are ways around the law forbidding unplugging, there are ways around the law forbidding someone crossing back," she said. "Especially if you're this particular boy."

Sylvia had been quietly studying the glass in front of her. Now her eyes flickered to Lacy. "What boy?"

Lacy's gaze slid across each one of us. "Rain Holt," she finally announced.

I stared at Lacy in disbelief. "Rain Holt?"

Adam looked like he had swallowed something distasteful. "Rain Holt is a useless, rich playboy."

"To you, maybe," Lacy said. "But to me—and to this world and the people who matter—he's priceless."

I eyed Lacy, my brain spinning. "You'd risk everything—your life even—to see Rain again?"

She shrugged. "I need a little excitement."

There was a false ring to her words. Something Lacy

wasn't telling us. The glass in my hand was cold, sending shivers through my code. I peeled my fingers away. "How do you imagine we'll find him? Bodies don't work like virtual selves. Bodies get tired."

"And bodies get damaged," Adam pointed out.

"As for the potential dangers," Lacy began, "why do you think I've invited you three along? Just consider your-selves"—Lucy pursed her lips theatrically—"my advance team if things get dangerous. If I could go alone, I would, but as we've already established, I'm not *dumb*." Lacy rolled her eyes. "And don't worry yourselves too hard. The Real World isn't *that* big. It's pretty much New Port City where all the plugs are and then, well, a bunch of land and abandoned towns." Lacy tapped a finger against her champagne flute. "Besides, I have it on good authority that finding Rain isn't going to be the hard part. The dif-ficulty will be in convincing him to come back."

Something in Sylvia simmered, like a pot on the verge of boiling over. "Why would he need convincing?" She locked eyes with me, then Adam. "Maybe this really is a game to you. Maybe you're just sending us all to our deaths."

Lacy placed her hand on the table in front of Sylvia. Peered into her face. "Well, that's a chance everyone is going to have to take now, isn't it?"

Sylvia said nothing. Just watched Lacy darkly.

"Have a drink, you could use one." Lacy pushed

Sylvia's glass toward her, but Sylvia didn't touch it.

"What's in this for you?" I asked.

Lacy turned to me. "Let's just say that Rain and I have a history," she said. "Besides, think of the scandal when everyone finds out I've rescued the Prime Minister's beloved son! When I've whisked him home to the App World, safe and sound!"

"Whisked *us* home," I corrected.

"Of *course* that's what I meant," Lacy said.

"And this mission, what does it involve?" I asked. "What will we be expected to *do* when we get to the Real World?"

"Patience, Skylar, darling. All will be revealed in time."

I shook my head. I didn't like this.

Lacy sighed. "I know. It's hard not having every teensy detail." Her eyes grew narrow. "But that's part of the deal. You can take it or leave it, and if you leave it, you'll never get to unplug."

I studied Lacy. There was something about her tone that made me wonder if even she knew what we were getting ourselves into, or if she was just as in the dark.

"Why the three of us?" Sylvia asked before I could get to this same question.

Lacy's haughty expression faltered a moment. Uncertainty passed over her face. "I'm not the one who made that decision," she admitted. Then her haughty expression returned, more confident than ever. "But in my *humble* opinion, you three have the most compelling reasons to unplug. Singles who care way more than any others about Service. All lacking in resources. All desperate. All stubborn. All uncharacteristically ambivalent about Apps and virtual living. All unable to let your ties to the Real World go," Lacy went on, ticking off her reasons.

I suddenly found it hard to breathe. "How could you know any of this about us?"

Lacy shrugged. "It's not that difficult to search people's thoughts."

My hand went to my head, as though I could protect it, as though Lacy was digging through my mind right now and I could get her out. "Searching people's thoughts—that's illegal," I cried. "Mind privacy is one of our inalienable rights! Hacking someone's brain . . . It's the lowest of the low!"

Lacy drank the last sip from her glass, unruffled. "You can think those idealistic little things all you want, but it won't make them true. Privacy disappears if you have the right connections." She set the empty flute on the table. "Lucky for me, I do."

Adam grabbed his drink for the first time, and he drained it all in one gulp. "So, when we're not carrying out this 'mission,' we can do whatever we want, right? That's the deal."

"Yes. You can live it up in the Real World all you like. And it goes without saying, but these plans are secret. If

I find out you've told anyone, you're virtually dead. With enough capital, I could *erase* you."

You are evil, went my mind.

Lacy's head snapped in my direction. "No, Skylar," she said. "Just smart." Her expression was fierce, daring me to challenge her.

I glared. "Get out of my head."

"Not until I know that I can trust you—all of you," she added, eyeing Sylvia, then Adam. "Which basically means never, so get used to the fact that your mind is no longer your own. Well, at least until we get to the Real World. Even I don't have a way to create technology where there simply is none."

Sylvia ran her finger in circles along the top of her glass. It made an eerie, mournful sound. "What's the plan, exactly? When would we leave?"

"The plan is simple. The three of you will arrive at a to-be-determined location in Loner Town at the hour I give you," she said. "And you'll each come alone. Traveling in a group will raise too much suspicion."

My mouth fell open. "You want us to just walk into Loner Town, by ourselves?"

"Yes," Lacy said simply. "Our contact for unplugging is there."

"Loner Town is dangerous," Adam said. "We'll go together. And you'll tell us exactly where, now."

"No," Lacy barked. "I'm calling the shots and I will

tell you when I decide it's time. I can't have you Singles blabbing to all the others." Her eyes zeroed in on mine. "Especially *some* people who are *so* devoted to their little best friends! The less you know, the more likely it is you'll keep your mouths shut."

"But—" Adam tried.

Sylvia cut Adam off with an exasperated glare. "Let her finish."

My eyes widened. I was suddenly glad Sylvia was here. It would be good to have someone else around who would help rein Adam in. And maybe Lacy, too.

Lacy uncrossed her legs and recrossed them. Her green nails sparkled as she moved. "As for when we get to the Real World, there are people awaiting our arrival, to help us transition back to the real body. Be prepared— apparently it can take days, even weeks, for the body to support normal functions again like walking and talking. Even seeing."

I nodded. This I already knew. The Preparing for Your Service App that sixteens download explained all of this. It was daunting to think of being that vulnerable, but it didn't scare me. I'd already planned on unplugging, so I'd accepted the risks long ago.

"Though"—Lacy's tone dipped conspiratorially—"there are all sorts of rumors about how being plugged in is changing our brain chemistry. Altering our relationships to our bodies."

"What kinds of rumors?" Adam pressed.

"Of course," Lacy went on, ignoring Adam, "who cares about brains?" She ran a hand along the length of her virtual self. "I can't wait to see Rain's face when he gets a look at the body I'm in. I bet it's gorgeous!"

Adam cleared his throat.

Sylvia rolled her eyes.

But I couldn't help thinking that this was another thing Lacy and I had in common—excitement about seeing our real bodies.

Lacy smacked the table and the three of us jumped. "Now! I'll be in touch again soon with a GPS download for our meeting location. Then we'll be on our way!" She dusted off her hands, like this was all so easy, like everything was decided already.

"I haven't agreed to this yet," I said to her. "To any of it. Including unplugging."

Lacy came over and sat down in the chair next to mine. She scooted closer. "Oh, come on, Skylar! We all know the three of you are going to do this. You're dying to unplug and now you have the means. Besides, think of how pleased the Prime Minister will be upon our return! We're rescuing his *son*."

Adam scowled. "I don't care about pleasing Jonathan Holt. And I'm not coming back unless my girlfriend is coming with me."

"Oh, how noble." Lacy laughed. "You say that now,

but my guess is that when it comes time to get out of that place, you'll be first in line, with or without your girl-friend."

"Can she come with me or not?" he asked.

Lacy rolled her eyes. "Sure." She rapped her knuckles on the table, the line of bracelets along her arm clinking. "Are you all on board, or what?"

Adam nodded, a quick, curt bob of his head. Sylvia closed her eyes, everything about her still. When she opened them again, she nodded, too.

Then everyone turned in my direction.

"I don't know." I glared at Lacy. "I don't trust you. And I couldn't care less where Rain Holt lives the rest of his days."

Lacy studied me. Leaned closer so we were eye to eye. Her perfume was sweet, yet with a bitter scent under-neath. "There are no maybes in this, Skylar. Only yes or no. Do you want to unplug or not?" she pressed. "I don't have all night."

I hated that the government took Service away from us, and I hated that doing this would require me to trust in Lacy Mills on top of everything else, that her plan meant I'd have to prioritize Rain Holt over my own family.

But at least there would be the chance for *some* time with my family.

Some time was better than none.

Far better than never seeing them again.

I took a deep breath. "Yes," I said finally. "My answer is yes."

Lacy clapped her hands. "Oh goody! You Singles will be just like the Three Musketeers, but less valiant and definitely not as good-looking." She readied herself to go. "Make sure you don't say a word to anyone. We leave on Friday! I'll be in touch again soon with the details."

I closed my eyes.

Friday?

Friday was in three days.

When I opened them again, Lacy was gone.

6

Fickle

IT ONLY TOOK one day for the City to go back to normal.

By the next morning, everyone was bored with the Prime Minister's announcement. The Singles were no longer an object of fascination, our celebrity moment past. People forgot about us entirely. For me, this was a relief. Having the world's eyes on Singles wouldn't help any of us—not Adam nor Sylvia nor me—to unplug in secrecy. I was grateful to be a nobody again.

But the wreckage of our abandonment was swift and brutal for everyone else. On my way out of the building for school, the evidence of this was everywhere. The lounge was littered with Singles in various stages of shutdown. People's skin was painted different hues of blue, a sure sign their codes had been overloaded with Apps in an extremely short period of time, after which the downloads had been slashed. The blue color was symbolic, to remind a person that a life without Apps was like suffocating, like real lungs without the air to breathe, and the hangover a reminder that we were all still attached to very real, vulnerable brains that could make us feel pain. I was about to leave the building when I noticed Sateen. Her skin was the color of the ocean. So blue it was almost black.

I went to her. "Sateen? Can you hear me?"

She was draped across a bright yellow couch, lips parted and cracked. Her eyes opened slightly. Even they were clouded with blue. "Hi, Skye." Her voice was hoarse. "You took off on your own last night. Probably a good idea."

"It won't feel like this forever," I told her.

"Won't it?"

I shook my head. "App Hangovers scroll through your code pretty quickly."

"I wasn't talking about the App Hangover," she whispered.

I leaned closer so I could hear her better. "Then what?"

"I'm a nobody, Skye. We're all nobodies again. And we always will be."

"Don't say that."

"Why not? It's true." She blinked slowly, as though it

hurt. "It was almost cruel to have so much attention for a day, only to have it taken away the next morning." Her breathing was labored. She glanced left, looking at something I couldn't see. "The only voyeurs I have left are the ones excited to see my swift and spectacular fall. I even made this list on Reel Time—Top Five Briefest Flashes of Fame Among Under Eighteens."

I wasn't sure what to say. "I'm sorry."

She tried to laugh, but it came out a cough. "At least I'm famous for something."

"Can I help you to your room?" I offered.

"Don't worry," she said, her voice nearly gone. "I'll be okay."

I hesitated. "All right. I'm going to school, but I'll check in on you later," I added.

Her eyes were already closed.

I looked around to see if Adam or Sylvia were nearby. We'd parted ways before leaving Appless Bar so as not to seem suspicious. Three Singles who never hang out seen leaving one of the seedier locales in the City together might raise a few eyebrows. I lingered another moment, as though my presence could conjure theirs. When it didn't I gave up and left for school.

Inara was pacing the corner outside Singles Hall. "You've been ignoring me, Skye," she said the second I was through the door. "Why?" There was hurt in her voice.

"I'm sorry," I said quietly. "I needed time to think."

She crossed her arms. "About what?"

"A lot of things." The urge to tell her everything, about the message, meeting Lacy Mills, that somehow I'd just committed to unplugging illegally, was like an electric current through my code. But Lacy had already picked through our brains once, so it was highly likely she was monitoring my mind right now.

"I'm still upset about the Prime Minister's announcement," I said, which wasn't a lie. It just wasn't the whole truth. "I can't get it out of my mind."

Inara's eyes softened. "I'm your best friend. Please don't ignore me. I wanted to say I'm sorry for the way I acted yesterday. For the things I said."

"Oh." I studied the sidewalk, poking my toe into a small pothole in the atmosphere, watching how it disappeared and reappeared as I moved it. "Thanks for saying that." Suddenly, the thought of leaving Inara without saying good-bye was beyond words. I threw my arms around her in a great hug.

When I let go, she looked at me strangely. "What was *that* for?"

"Just . . . I'm grateful to have such a good friend. A virtual sister."

She laughed. "You don't have to get all mushy. I'm not going anywhere on you. Like, *ever*."

"I know," I said.

Then *but I am,* I thought to myself, feeling terrible about lying.

"We should head to school," Inara said. "No throngs of voyeurs today, but we'll still be late if we don't get moving."

We started to walk. I needed to act normal, as though this was a day like any other, so I turned to Inara's favorite subject. "What's the gossip this morning?"

She immediately grinned. "You mean you don't know? Have you been in, like, shutdown or something?"

I shook my head. "Tell me."

Inara's eyes were bright. "Funeral."

"What?" I asked. "I don't understand. No one ever dies here."

"I thought it was weird too, at first," Inara said. "But then it started to make more sense. The government is holding a massive, state-sponsored funeral for Under Eighteens who got trapped in the Real World. Isn't that, like, the craziest thing you've ever heard?"

"But those seventeens aren't actually dead," I said. But then it occurred to me: maybe they were, and this was how we were finding out. Maybe I'd unplug on Friday and discover a really unpleasant surprise. My eyes widened. "Or are they?"

"They're dead to us." Inara talked with her hands when she was excited, and they waved through the atmosphere now. "To the App World, I mean. They can't come back, so it's kind of like they're dead." Then she shook her head. "I don't think they're *actually* dead. Rain Holt is going to be the star of the show. They're coding giant holograms of all the lost seventeens."

"It isn't a show, Inara," I said quietly. "It's to mark peoples' deaths."

"Come on, Skye. It will be exciting!"

I looked at her in horror. "You're not actually planning on watching it?"

"*We* are, as in you and me, and yes. We're not just going to watch. Daddy got us on the guest list. It's going to be *the* social event of the year. Ten in the morning tomorrow. There's a City-wide holiday."

I stopped. We were almost at school, but I didn't want to go inside. I didn't want another scene, like yesterday. "Inara, this isn't some juicy celebrity hologram with, like, Soda Channing acting like an idiot amped up on downloads and telling her celebrity friends off. This is about families who've lost children." I thought of Adam's girlfriend, Parvda. "People whose boyfriends and girlfriends got trapped in the Real World forever. Funerals are for grieving. Funerals mark tragedy."

Inara listened patiently. "Are you done?"

I stood there in stony silence. We were standing in front of the steps of someone's tall narrow house. I sat down on one of the stairs and put my head in my hands.

Inara joined me. She placed her palm on my back. "I

know it's not a joke. I just want you to feel better. I thought getting dressed up would help. That part was stupid, I guess. But I kind of thought you might like to go to the funeral. You know, that it would allow you to mark what you see as the tragedy of not unplugging to see your family, so then you can move on. And maybe it really will help, Skye." Her voice was pleading. "Please go with me."

I looked up. Turned to those familiar green eyes. A mixture of feelings surged through me. Frustration that Inara could be so superficial sometimes. Gratitude that she always meant well. Guilt that I was lying to her by omitting what I was about to do. And yes, a tiny bit of curiosity about the funeral. I wanted to see the holograms of those left behind. I wanted to see Parvda and, if I were to be honest, I wanted to see Rain.

So I did the only thing I knew how to do with Inara.

I agreed.

"Okay. I'll go."

It was Inara who pulled me into a hug this time.

The two of us walked through the front doors of school arm in arm. The hallways were buzzing with gossip about the funeral. We didn't stop to talk to anyone. Instead, we headed to our first class. Today it was The Body: Its Problems & Perils, a topic that took on new meaning now that the border was closed.

"What are you going as?" Jenna Farrow asked Inara the second we sat down at our download pods. Classrooms were set up like social lounges, everyone facing one another in a circle, with our teacher rotating in the middle. Jenna could never keep a thought to herself, and word bubbles were always popping up from her head and distracting people. She hated keeping anything private.

Inara glanced over at her. "To what?"

"The funeral, obviously."

Inara opened her mouth to respond, but Jenna got there first.

"I'm totally downloading the latest in Widow Apps!"

"Ah, why would you do that?" Inara asked.

She rolled her eyes, like we should already know. "So I can go as Rain's widow. I'm going to wear a grand ball gown, but in black, with a peekaboo veil so people can see my face."

Inara gave me a look, eyebrows raised.

I couldn't hold back my scorn. "You're going as Rain's widow?"

Jenna nodded. "I certainly feel like his widow. I've been watching his holograms on Reel Time ever since I turned twelve. Poor Rain, stuck forever in his *body.*" She shriveled her nose in disgust. "How totally tragic." A bright smile returned to her face. "It's like that famous Real World movie star from, like, a century ago, who died young."

"James Dean?" Inara suggested.

"Exactly," Jenna sighed.

My hands twitched in my lap. Inara was shaking her

head at me. The words *Don't get involved* appeared in my brain. *Jenna's not worth it.* But I was tired of people not caring, people like Jenna who lived as though there wasn't anything else in our world other than an easy life of downloading App after App for her own personal entertainment. *Here we go again*, Inara sighed into my mind.

"Jenna, some people actually care that families are being ripped apart by the border closing—Rain's family, for example," I said. "A funeral isn't a party."

Jenna looked at me pityingly. "But it kind of is, Skye. It's not like funerals happen often and, like, everyone who's anyone is going. Stop taking things so seriously."

Inara got up from her pod. "You know what? I feel a brain stall coming on." She grabbed my hand and yanked me up too. "Walk me into the fresh atmosphere, Skye."

"But—"

"I need you." She dragged me along behind her. When we were outside the room she spun around. "You're not doing yourself any favors by lashing out. Jenna is just being Jenna."

I studied my hands. They were already turning red with anger, and purple with shame. "It's not just Jenna. Everyone is talking like that." I thought of Sateen and the rest of the Singles in the lounge this morning, broken and forgotten. "Sometimes I hate this world."

"Skye," Inara said, more softly this time. "This world is all you have."

Her words stole my breath. They weren't true, but she didn't know that. That they could be true was awful. More and more I was realizing that the App World didn't belong to me like it did to other people—like it did to Inara. And maybe it never had. Maybe it never would.

"You have to let go," she went on. "There's nothing else you can do."

"I know," I said out loud. "You're right. I will," I lied.

Mrs. Worthington, our teacher, had already begun the day's lesson by the time we returned to class. She was perched on a glass desk that turned with the circular podium at the room's center. Her legs dangled, sharp stiletto heels clicking against the side as she spoke. "Before Marcus Holt invented the plugs," she began, pausing to glare at Inara and me as we slid back into our pods before she continued on, "people used real legs to move through the world. This required muscle and tendon strength. But body parts easily stretched and were torn out of shape, causing great pain. Bones were notoriously breakable, especially as a person aged. A simple fall could crush one."

I sat forward, paying attention with more interest than ever. Knowledge about the human body was considered essential because of the Service requirement, but also because a large branch of technological research was devoted to discovering ways to overcome our reliance on the body. Leading App World researchers dedicated themselves to the defeat of death and to the goal of virtual eternity—the Race for the Cure. This class was supposed to encourage us to take up the science of bodily transcendence as a future career. I'd always been annoyed we had to take it, and Mrs. Worthington was my least favorite teacher.

"You never knew who might be capable of making the discovery of the millennium," she was always telling us. "It might be someone sitting in this very room. It might even be one of you Singles!"

Mrs. Worthington called up a hologram.

A three-dimensional image of a human leg appeared, showing the inside. Pink muscle wrapped itself against long thin bone and blue veins shot through everything. The leg began to move, like it was walking along the ground. The foot stumbled on a rock, the knee crashing to the pavement. Muscle separated from bone. Bone chipped. Blood spurted.

Watching this reminded me that the security we enjoyed in our virtual bodies was misleading. I fell all the time when I was gaming, but there was never any lasting damage.

Was the body really that fragile?

Mrs. Worthington replayed the hologram. "See how broken a body can get from just a little fall?" She clapped her hands together. She seemed delighted by the gore.

It made me queasy to look, but I refused to turn away. I needed to know all I could about the body, even if I didn't like its implications.

"Sometimes the damage to the body is so severe," Mrs. Worthington went on, "it doesn't recover and a person can never walk again! Or use their hands. Or even speak a coherent thought. You get the idea."

One pod over from mine, next to Inara, Simon Best sneered. "This is disgusting. I don't want to look at it anymore. It's not like anybody needs to worry about this stuff now that Service is canceled."

Hannah Workman, a classmate who always sat up very straight in her pod, was nodding. She was one of the school's best students and I was surprised to see her agreeing with Simon. "It's true. There really isn't any point to this class anymore."

"Sure there is," Mrs. Worthington said. "What about the Race for the Cure? Even if you can't see the physical human body, each one of you, this very minute, is attached to one. Don't you want to know what could go wrong with it? Don't you want to be informed of its defects and severe limitations? Of the physical and emotional pain it still causes us even as we live virtually?"

"Not really," Simon sighed.

Inara chatted me. *Blah, blah, blah. Mrs. Worthington loves to ramble.*

Shhhh, I chatted back.

Inara pursed her lips.

I stared intently at Mrs. Worthington, waiting for her to go on.

"But isn't it a miracle how living virtually saves us from nearly all of the body's horrors?" she asked. Mrs. Worthington went on to talk about the way skin withers and dies from exposure to the sun and how the sheer presence of the body among real nature and other people makes it prone to disease; how humans pass viruses from one to another by the mere touch of a hand and sometimes just by breathing the air.

Death was around every corner, in other words.

The best we could do was stay plugged in, she explained, our bodies isolated from others.

"What a relief the border closed, hmmm?" Mrs. Worthington said, just before class ended. "What a lucky group of sixteens you turned out to be! You've all been liberated from experiencing those bodily perils and problems firsthand and for free! Even you Singles!"

The rest of the day, her words echoed in my head. I kept thinking about my mother and sister, who'd never had a choice but to live in the real body, risking disease and death every day. I hoped they were living in their bodies still, all in one piece. If they could do it, then why should it be any different for me?

For any of us, really?

7

Research

IT WAS NEARLY midnight, the hour of shutdown. The physical brain needed a break, especially in younger, still-developing, plugged-in bodies. By the time you became a sixteen, you grew to resent this rule. Inara couldn't wait until we could be up twenty-four seven like every other Over Eighteen in the City.

I couldn't stop fidgeting, so I sent Adam and Sylvia a chat. *Let's talk. My room, ASAP.*

Sylvia was the first one to arrive.

"Thanks for coming," I said.

She nodded hello, but didn't speak. I couldn't decide whether she was unfriendly or shy. Adam was right behind her. He stood awkwardly in the doorway.

"We should discuss what's going on," I said. "Don't you think?"

Sylvia's expression was blank.

Adam's hand went to the back of his neck, as though it was hurting him. "Yeah, we should probably . . . um. . . the . . . the . . ." Adam trailed off, unable to find the right words.

Sylvia began to blink rapidly, like there was something in her eyes she wanted to get out. Like they were hurting her.

Virtual tears began to roll down both of their faces.

"Are you guys all right?" I asked, looking from one to the other.

Just then, a faint static started up in my brain. It got louder and louder, my mind growing colder until it felt as though the insides of my head were made of ice. All the air seemed to be sucked out of me. I put my hands to my cheeks and they came away wet.

I was weeping, too.

That was when the download started.

It hit the three of us like a piano dropped from above. We fell to the floor—there was no resisting the force of it. I spread my fingers wide, crouching, leaning into my palms, but I couldn't even hold myself up that far. Soon my cheek was pressed against the hard blue wood. I forced my eyes open and found myself looking into Sylvia's silver ones. They were full of terror.

Information started to appear in my brain, images of a darkened house, broken windows, an ominous tree, its long spidery branches like fingers, a three-dimensional map with an arrow pointing to a single location, its edges sharp and gleaming like the blade of a knife.

Then, a voice. High and piercing. My hands went to my ears, my eyes, my face. The sound seemed to reverberate nowhere and everywhere at once.

"Friday night! Be there at eleven p.m.! We unplug at midnight!"

Lacy Mills.

Each of her words was a scream. I fought against them, pushing the noise away with my mind.

It was as if Lacy knew we'd come together for a meeting without her. And maybe she did. Maybe this was her way of reminding us that she was in control, that she could punish us whenever she felt like it.

At least while we were still in the App World.

"You think this is painful now?" she shouted. *"Wait until we unplug! You've never known pain until you see what it's like to leave this world and wake up in the real body! Consider this a taste of what's to come!"* There was a slight pause. *"Tell anyone and you're virtually dead,"* she finished.

Then the noise, the static, the debilitating cold disappeared.

The three of us were left curled into balls on the

floor of my room. I tried to steady my breathing, began to stretch my legs and sit up. The atmosphere seemed to ooze and I couldn't see clearly.

Adam groaned.

Sylvia didn't move.

I was the first one to stand. Then Sylvia got up and slumped against the wall. Next was Adam, who swayed in the middle of the room like a breeze was buffeting him.

I waited until their eyes seemed to focus. "I can't believe Lacy just broke through my chat walls like that."

Adam ran a hand across his brow. "I can."

Sylvia's face was still shiny with tears, so shiny her virtual skin seemed to be made of plastic. "I've never experienced a remote download. I've heard of their existence, but, I mean, they're illegal. You can't force an App into someone's code."

I braced my hand on top of a table to keep myself upright. I was so tired I worried my brain might shut down. "Lacy's obviously showing us how powerful she is. Showing off those *resources* she was talking about last night."

Adam gripped the doorframe hard, like he might want to rip a chunk out of it. He studied me. "You recovered awfully quick."

"Not really," I said, and shrugged it off.

Sylvia wiped the tears from her cheek. "Do you think

she was telling the truth about the pain of unplugging? Or was she just trying to scare us?"

I'd wondered the same thing. Was this really a glimpse of the mental pain and suffering we should expect? The three of us looked at one another, contemplating this. Adam stopped swaying. Sylvia started to straighten up, able to stand on her own again.

"I don't know," I said. "But Lacy did say she loved to play games. Maybe she's playing one right now."

Adam's cheeks flashed with anger. "I already hate that girl."

I put a finger to my lips in warning. "Careful. She's probably in our heads right now. We don't want her to go back on our deal."

"She won't," Adam said simply. "She wants to rescue Rain."

"Regardless of Lacy," I began, "the three of us need to stick together. When we get to the Real World we'll be all we have. Yet here we are, about to break the law, and none of us knows much about anyone else." I paused, thinking about how to rectify this. "We all must have good reasons to unplug, right? I think we should start by talking about our priorities." I looked at Sylvia and her eyes shifted away. Then I turned to Adam, who was staring back with confidence. "My reason for unplugging is to see my family," I offered. "I have a mother and a sister in the Real World. And Adam's reason is his girlfriend.

And maybe family, too?" I asked him.

"No. I don't have any family," he said, and left it at that.

Sylvia was still avoiding our eyes.

"What's your reason?" I asked her.

"It's kind of private," she said in a small voice.

"We need to be honest with one another," Adam said. "We need to be able to trust one another."

She turned to him. "My reason is the same as yours."

His eyebrows went up. "You have a boyfriend who got left in the Real World?"

She shook her head. "Not a boyfriend," she said. "A girlfriend."

"Who?" Adam asked.

She looked at the floor.

I tried to remember if I'd ever seen Sylvia with someone else during the last couple of years, but I barely remembered seeing her at all. "You know what, Sylvia? It's okay. Thanks for telling us that much." I called up the time. It was nearly curfew. I breathed in deeply, my mind becoming crystal clear. "As for Loner Town on Friday, I'll go first," I offered. "I'll leave at nine thirty. How about you leave at ten, Adam? And you leave at ten thirty, Sylvia?"

Adam and Sylvia looked at each other.

"Sure," Sylvia said.

She didn't sound at all sure though.

Adam shifted from one foot to the other, unable to

stay still. "Sounds like we have a plan." He nodded in my direction. "And it's true, we need to work together." He laughed a little to himself. "Lacy did call us the Three Musketeers."

I joined in Adam's laughter. So did Sylvia. I think it was the first time all three of us were smiling. It was the first moment I felt some hope, too, that everything might be okay. That we all could stick together, and rely on one another. "Yes, she did," I said to Adam. "The Three Musketeers, but less valiant and definitely not as good-looking."

Adam shrugged. "Who knows what we really look like? We won't find out until we unplug and see our bodies."

"True," Sylvia said.

Adam got a strange look on his face—I think it might have been a grin. Slowly, he extended his hand into the center of the circle we made. "All for one," he started.

The smile on my face grew as I realized where he was going. The thought *Adam and I are going to be friends* flashed across my brain. I reached out my hand and joined it with his. Sylvia was next.

"And one for all," we said, laughing.

We stayed like that for a while, looking at one another. Then the bells for curfew started to chime in our minds and flash along the walls. Adam was turning to go. So was Sylvia.

"Will I see you both at the funeral tomorrow?" I asked before they could walk out the door.

Adam snapped back to attention. "You're going?" He sounded incredulous. His voice had an edge.

All that goodwill from just a moment before—I could already see it slipping away. "What about Parvda?" I asked. "Isn't the funeral for her, too?"

He shook his head in disgust. "It is, but I don't have access to that kind of capital. The funeral is for App World families and Parvda was a Single," he said. "It's all a big sham anyway. Just a pageant for rich people to show off." He narrowed his eyes. "I can't believe you're going."

"Adam, I should've known. I'm sorry, I—"

"Save your excuses for someone who cares. See you Friday," he said, and stormed off, leaving me and Sylvia.

"You're not going to the funeral, either," I stated. My tone was flat. I felt deflated.

She shook her head. A tear escaped her eye and ran down her cheek.

"If you tell me your girlfriend's name, I'll look for her hologram."

"That's okay," she said. "But thanks anyway. Good night, Skye," she added in her quiet voice, before leaving the room, her footsteps silent. Like no one was there at all.

I suddenly felt so alone. I went to my narrow bed and sat. I pulled my knees to my chest and rested my chin there, looking around at the tiny room where I'd lived ever since I'd appeared in this world. Everything was a different shade of blue. The chair in the corner and the color of the walls. Even the floor was coded to resemble the sea. *Blue like the ocean and blue like the sky.* Ever since I was small, I'd always wanted blue around me, blue everything, blue everywhere.

Unlike the view from Inara's house onto the skyscrapers of the City, my view was of a courtyard walled in by darkness. The dream of earning enough capital to afford a place where I could see the stars and the clouds used to be so important to me. But those dreams felt far away at the moment.

And so irrelevant.

The bargain we made with Lacy was my worry now.

She might be able to go poking around in our heads whenever she wanted, but she was famous, which meant she had no privacy at all. I wanted a better handle on her. What made her tick? What did she care about most in this world? I needed to find her weaknesses, those vulnerabilities I might be able to exploit one day for sheer survival. Maybe it made me a bad person to think this way, to contemplate how I might bribe or threaten Lacy to get what I needed done. Or maybe it just made me smart.

I raised my hand to call up my App Store.

Icons immediately swirled around me. Apps were designed to make you feel like you were the center of their universe, to make you burn with desire. The pricier ones flashed images of me doing all sorts of things—dancing on a stage, accepting an award in front of an audience of millions, walking a catwalk. One showed me kissing a gorgeous boy and another, kissing a beautiful girl. The gaming ones were always the most tempting. I found it hard to resist a landscape where I could swim across a wide, raging river or one that tested my skills at avoiding predators like a two-headed dragon or a field of vicious tigers.

Thoughts of tigers reminded me of that hologram with Rain.

And I remembered my purpose.

"Lacy Mills," I said out loud.

The icons shifted, replaced by a seemingly endless number to do with Lacy, so many they filled every inch of space around me, all of them boasting footage from her life. Lacy as a baby, crawling across a floor of gold in the Millses' mansion. Lacy as a toddler, frolicking in the grand kiddie pool in her room. One of the more prominent icons was of Lacy as a child, maybe a girl of six or seven. The image that played over and over was of Lacy trying to get the attention of her parents, calling to them, with them acting as though she wasn't there. The way the icon repeated itself, trying to tempt me to download it, was like watching Lacy get abandoned by her family again and again. I almost couldn't look away, even as it pained me to see it.

I shifted uncomfortably.

Once again, the thought that maybe Lacy and I had more in common than I'd originally believed passed through me.

I shook this away. Now wasn't the time to analyze Lacy's relationship with her family. I had to figure out which of the thousands of hours of footage would be useful, otherwise I'd be here for years watching Lacy without getting anywhere. Besides, when Lacy was the center of gossip, the App sponsors wanted you to look at her, and footage was free, but when she wasn't, you had to pay. This meant I would have to be choosy.

I tapped my chin, trying to remember some of the rules our teachers talked about for how to get what you need from the Apps. Hologram footage naturally came up in chronological order, requiring a person to pick the moment in time desired to watch. But if you didn't know the specific time you wanted, you could change how the icons were organized, according to topic or download characteristics.

One subject was more obvious than the others.

"Rain Holt," I said.

Immediately, the footage was reduced by years. At least half the icons blinked out, but so many remained. All the time Lacy and Rain spent together outside of school and in the same vicinity would be included among the icons still swirling around me.

How to get through everything to what I wanted?

"Give me the ten priciest Lacy Mills and Rain Holt moments," I tried next.

Now, almost all of the Apps vanished. No longer did the icons tempt me with images of Lacy dancing at a club or partying in outer space. All I saw was their price.

My jaw fell open.

The cost of watching these ten interactions between Lacy and Rain required more capital than I spent in a month of gaming. I checked the balance in my account and did some calculations. If I started with the priciest downloads and went from there, I could more or less afford . . . three. Buying the right to see a few minutes of Lacy and Rain would drain away all the capital I had left in the world.

But then, what did I need capital for if I was about to unplug?

I reached out and touched the priciest one.

A hologram of Lacy immediately materialized in the room. She wore a short, tight dress that looked like it was made of diamonds. It sparkled like the green on her fingernails. Her hair was pulled back from her face, intricately twisted and braided with shimmery flowers. She looked beautiful.

I sat down on my bed to watch whatever happened next.

"There's something you need to know," Lacy said. She

smiled and posed, jutting out her hip. She knew all her voyeurs were watching. She was playing to them. "It's been on my mind for a long time."

Rain appeared alongside her in the hologram. He leaned against the wall behind him, looking bored, like always. His black T-shirt revealed a sliver of skin at his waist. "Now isn't a good time, Lacy."

The smile stayed put on Lacy's face, but clouds drifted across her eyes. "Now is the perfect time," she said, her voice a little less sure. She took a step closer to Rain, the diamonds on her dress blinking brightly as she moved.

He shifted away. "Lacy," he warned.

She ignored him. She got so close to Rain there was practically no atmosphere left between them. She placed her hands flat against the wall on either side of his head, and leaned even closer, pressing her body against his. Knees, hips, chest.

Rain didn't look bored anymore.

Lacy's lips neared the base of Rain's neck and traveled slowly up to his ear. But when she spoke again, it wasn't in a whisper. "I'm totally and completely in love with you, Rain," she said loudly, ensuring her voyeurs would hear this confession perfectly.

What happened next, Lacy obviously couldn't have predicted, or she would have confessed her feelings where the paparazzi cams couldn't follow, like inside their school.

Rain gripped Lacy's arms—which made her sigh—but then he physically lifted her up and moved her to the side. The look on his face was one of pity, or maybe sympathy. "I'm sorry, Lacy. I just . . . can't," he said, and then walked away, leaving Lacy standing there alone, with only her voyeurs for company.

Lacy's skin drained of its color. The dress still sparkled but her eyes lost their wicked shine. I waited to hear her reaction, to see what she said next, how she recovered from that level of public humiliation, but the hologram buzzed and zapped, got smaller, and disappeared. The remaining nine icons from my search returned, circling my virtual self. One of them neared my left eye, then darted to the right.

I grabbed a pillow the color of the ocean and pulled it to me, hugging it.

So Lacy was in love with Rain. She'd planned a big public unveiling of her feelings and he'd rejected her in front of all her fans. And now she planned on rescuing him and returning him to the App World.

Why?

Was she still in love with him and believed if she offered him a way home he would be grateful and love her back? Or did she hate him so much she wanted to force him home, against his will? She did say Rain would require some convincing. I wondered what could keep him so tied to the Real World.

The second priciest App lunged at me.

I ducked as it zoomed to my left, then reached out and touched it, waiting for Lacy to appear again, curious what new information I'd learn about this girl who'd become so important to my future. And I would need to study Rain a bit closer this time. He was more of a mystery. Much harder to read.

Eventually I fell into shutdown while the holograms still played around me.

I dreamed of Rain, but not Lacy.

Not Lacy at all.

I didn't know why.

8

Masquerade

THE MORNING OF the funeral arrived.

Something nudged at my cheek. When I opened my eyes an App was hovering in front of my face. With consciousness came a saved chat from Inara.

For you. Something nice to wear. Download it. Please? xoxo

I studied the icon. It started out as a pale blue gift box tied up with a looping white bow. As it became aware of my waking state it began to transform. The bow untied and the box fell away. Ribbons twirled around the image of a V-neck dress, clingy and short, that kept shifting color. The style kept changing as I watched. Strapless, column, ball gown with bustle, tie-dyed, sequined, satin, chiffon, seawater, starlight, and silk. The icon turned in a circle so I could admire each new gown. I had no way of knowing what sort of dress would appear on my virtual self until I downloaded it, but one thing I knew for sure was that it was pricey. The kind of App only the Sachses could afford.

Skye?

Hey, I chatted Inara back. *Good morning. I got your present.*

I know you're upset about the funeral and people like Jenna make you angry but this isn't about being like Jenna, okay?

The icon shifted again to reveal a long, beaded gown, the kind girls wore in Miss App World pageants. I sighed. *You know I don't wear dresses. Like ever.*

It's just one day, Inara chatted. *Besides, this was my mother's idea. She gave me one too.*

Mrs. Sachs, who was always so kind to me. I might not have been her biological daughter, but she tried her best to do what she could for me. *Fine. I'll download it. I better not end up in some widow outfit.*

Ew, no! My mother would never let us attend a serious event as widows.

Okay. See you in a few.

The icon showed a pink princess dress with a wide bell of a skirt and puffy sleeves. I waited until it began to shift into something else, just in case the timing of the download might affect what the dress would look like. I hoped the App would choose what would work best for my virtual self.

I reached out and touched it.

The download initiated. I closed my eyes as the App seeped into my code. A slow chill began to work its way through me, starting with the finger I used to touch the icon, then spreading to my forearm and my elbow and up to my shoulder, across my collarbone to my other arm and onward down my torso to my feet.

So the dress would be long.

My body tingled with what felt like tiny flecks of ice.

Unlike last night, this time, the cold was pleasant.

The bonding process began and the chill dissipated. As the download knit itself into my code, my virtual self started to heat up, like the dress was being welded to me. I'd always enjoyed this part. There was something wonderful about all that warmth. It made me feel safe. At least while it lasted.

Finally, it dealt with my hair. There was tugging and smoothing.

This part of an Appearance App I'd always loathed.

Abruptly, the download stopped.

I opened my eyes and called up my self-image.

The mirror hologram showed a version of me that looked uncomfortable. But this Skye didn't look horrible. The gown Mrs. Sachs chose was steel-blue silk. It was long and plain, with just a slight tuck to define my waist. The top was strapless, a straight line across my chest. My hair was pulled away from my face into a high knot at the back of my head. Simple blue shoes peeked out from under the hem. I lifted my foot to better see them. They were flat.

For some reason this detail made me want to cry.

A sad smile appeared on the hologram Skye's face.

Mrs. Sachs knew me well.

Are you ready? Inara chatted. *We're almost to your corner.*

Be there in a minute.

I took one last look before swiping my hand across the mirror hologram. The other Skye disappeared.

On my way out of the building, I ran into Adam. He wore the standard-issue black pants and black T-shirt of Singles on a day off from school. His eyes traveled from my bare shoulders to my feet. Then he scowled. "You're going to the funeral like *that*?"

I crossed my arms over my chest. I didn't like the way Adam was staring. "The dress was a gift from the people who invited me."

"A funeral isn't a party, Skye," he said, using the very same words I'd spoken to Jenna.

Shame burned across my skin. "I know, Adam," I said, already turning to go. "I never said it was."

Inara absently twirled her long necklace of pearls around her finger as the Sachses and I neared the clearing in the park. She'd downloaded a tank dress of light green taffeta that reached her feet. It resembled mine enough that it reminded me of those times when we were small and would download the Twinning App every chance we got. I linked my arm through hers as she gaped at the elaborate building looming ahead of us.

"It's beautiful," she said.

Mrs. Sachs joined us, staring up at the massive church, coded especially for the occasion. "I heard it was designed to be a composite of famous places of worship in the Real World."

Gothic towers pointed toward the sunny sky. Arches jutted out from the stone walls like giant spider's legs. Gargoyles glared at imaginary enemies, their mouths wide, tongues lolling. A great round window of colored glass sparkled high above the doors. Statues of various members of the government stared out from either side of the entrance, the one of Marcus Holt, the inventor of the first plug, taller than all the others. Eleanor Holt, his wife, and the Original Architect of the City, stood next to him, carved in stone. Rain's grandparents. Eleanor and Marcus Holt were already elderly when they'd plugged in, their bodies old and infirm and unsustainable. They only managed to live here during the first few years of the App World's existence. The last important funeral in this City was theirs.

How strange that the next one would also involve a Holt.

Inara leaned against me. "What are you thinking?"

I adjusted the top of my dress. There was a reason I never wore clothes like this. "The cathedral is pretty. Maybe a bit overdone."

The other guests milled around us. They talked and gestured excitedly. There were women in elaborate gowns that belled out to three times their wearers' width or had long trains of silky fabric dotted with tiny roses and peonies that trailed after them as they walked. Hair cascaded in waves down backs or was piled high on top of ladies' heads, tendrils artfully hanging around their faces. Men wore black suits, some so shiny they looked to be made of vinyl. And these were just the conservatively dressed funeral goers. A woman walked by wearing a gown that seemed made of the ocean itself, with silvery fish swimming across it in hues of orange and green and blue. Another looked like a great peacock had loaned her its feathers. More than a few women and men had downloaded Apps that turned them into models on top of the outrageous costumes they'd chosen to wear.

Inara's eyes followed a woman in head-to-toe black lace, a black bridal veil framing her face and falling all the way to her feet. She held a large snow globe with a statue of Rain at its center in her outstretched hands.

"And I thought Jenna was going to look like a fool," I said.

"I did too," Inara said quietly. Then her attention was

caught by Simon Best, who'd just arrived with his parents. "I'll be back in a minute."

"Sure." Mr. and Mrs. Sachs were nearby talking to some friends, but I felt alone in this crowd. I watched as people shrieked and air-kissed. I was about to go up to Inara and Simon when I almost tripped on the hem of my gown. Carefully, I bent down to extract my shoe from the delicate fabric. When I straightened up I was staring into the eyes of Lacy Mills.

Lacy blinked back her surprise. "What are *you* doing here?"

She wore an emerald-green dress, skintight and long. Draped across her arms, her wrists, and her neck were long strings of diamonds, the kind that only come from downloading the Tiffany App. She was so laden with jewels it looked as though she shouldn't be able to hold up the top half of her body.

I felt dull next to so much beauty and glitter. "I'm going to the funeral, same as you." All I could think about was the pain of last night, the way Lacy so carelessly broke into our minds. "Should you even be talking to me?"

The left half of Lacy's mouth curled upward. "Oh, I'll just tell anyone who asks that I'm doing charity work. Bestowing niceties on the less fortunate. Gracing Singles with my presence."

It was difficult to believe someone so famous could be so consistently cruel. "We got your download."

Lacy laughed, like we were having a wonderful time. "Did you enjoy it?" Diamonds swayed as she moved. She wagged a ring-adorned finger. "You Singles shouldn't be getting together without me. I just hate feeling left out."

"This isn't a game."

Lacy eyed me. "People keep saying that."

In my mind, I imagined raising one arm in the air and lashing out at Lacy.

She immediately put a hand to her cheek. "Ooh, I'm so scared!"

I licked my lips. Everything felt dry. "Stay out of my head, Lacy."

Her eyes grew cold. Tiny crystals of frost dotted her cheeks. "Listen up, Skylar. *You* don't get to give *me* orders. And don't flatter yourself. It's not as though your mind is a terribly interesting place. I only go there when I must."

I swallowed, trying to maintain control of my emotions. Out of the corner of my eye, I noticed Inara looking around to see where I was. Her eyes got wide when she realized I was talking to Lacy, and she hurried toward me. "Skye?"

"Um, Inara, this is—"

Lacy stretched out her diamond-laden fingers. "Hello. Lovely to meet you."

A stunned Inara took Lacy's hand.

Lacy pulled it away quickly as though Inara's skin was diseased. "I was just extending my condolences to this sad, lost little Single, doing my patriotic duty and all. Got to go, though! The funeral awaits my celebrity presence."

We watched her totter away on heels too high for anyone to walk in without the help of a special App.

"Do you know who that was?" Inara asked.

"I may not keep up with the Gossip Apps," I said, "but I'm not dead."

"I can't believe Lacy Mills was hanging out with you," Inara said, sounding jealous.

"Trust me, you didn't miss anything," I said. "She's just as awful in person as she is on Reel Time."

Inara studied me. "How did you end up talking to her?"

I watched Lacy swerve through the crowd, air-kissing people as she went. I shrugged. "It was just as Lacy told you," I said, hoping my answer would satisfy Inara and put the topic to rest. A line of long black cars drove up and distracted her.

"That must be the families of the dead," Inara said.

The crowd hushed. They pointed and whispered.

The first limousine came to a stop by the door, the engine purring softly. Out of the back stepped Jonathan Holt, followed by his wife, a long black veil covering her face. The Prime Minister wore a black suit. His virtual skin was off-color. Almost gray. He took Lady Holt's hand and led her to the cathedral's entrance. Their heads were bowed. I hadn't seen the Prime Minister since the night of the announcement. The look in his eyes then—and that of his son's—was burned into my mind.

The doors opened wide.

Before entering, Jonathan Holt stopped. He stared up at the cut-glass windows, then lowered his gaze to the statues of government officials, one of which was in his likeness. His eyes lingered there, as though he wasn't sure what to make of his presence carved in virtual stone. His attention shifted to Marcus and Eleanor, his parents. He walked over to them, studying their faces.

"How moving," said a woman's voice from the crowd. This was followed by giggling and more whispering.

Without acknowledging the other guests, Jonathan Holt returned to his wife, and they disappeared inside. One by one, the rest of the grieving families emerged from the other cars. They were the only people who truly seemed to know the meaning of the occasion, who'd come to this event to pay their respects and say good-bye. The rest of the funeral goers wanted to ogle and whisper and be part of a spectacle, everyone laughing, as though sadness wasn't an emotion they'd known in their lifetimes. When the last family entered, everyone else began to file in after them.

Inara and I got in the slow-moving line. I searched for Mr. and Mrs. Sachs and caught sight of them just before they made it through the doors ahead. It seemed impossible that we would all fit inside this building. A woman wearing a gown made of black calla lilies was in front of us, the perfume of the flowers filling the atmosphere. The woman behind us reached a long, gloved hand between Inara and me, and tapped the other's shoulder.

"What App did you download for that dress?" she asked. "It's lovely. So unique!"

The woman turned, releasing even more of a flowery scent into the air. She smiled at her admirer. "My husband had it created special for today. It's a Juniper Jones original." She plucked a lily from her dress and handed it to the lady behind us. Its stem grazed my cheek. "These are mourning flowers. Isn't that so apropos?"

I resisted the urge to cover my nose. I thought I might choke on the smell.

The woman buried her nose in the flower. "I'm so jealous."

They continued to talk over us.

Inara rolled her eyes. *Let's let this lady up front?* she chatted.

I nodded. As best as we could, we stepped aside so the woman behind us could squeeze by. Which landed us right next to Jenna.

"Hi, guys," she said, all too loudly.

Be nice, Skye, Inara warned in my brain. "Hey, Jenna."

Jenna had dressed as a widow just as she'd promised, the outfit identical to that of the other widow we'd seen, down to the snow globe of Rain. The smooth, round glass was nestled into the crook of her left arm like a basketball.

Inara opened her mouth to say something else, but Jenna, as usual, got there first.

"Don't even mention it." Jenna's lips made a pout. "I already know."

"What do you know?" I asked.

She sighed. "I've seen at least ten Rain widows already. It's humiliating."

"Well," I began as we finally neared the doors, "maybe if you'd—"

"Skye, we need to find my parents," Inara interrupted. She took my arm. Other members of the crowd were already squeezing by us, separating Inara and me from Jenna. "They'll be worried if they don't see us soon. Take care, Jenna," she called over them as she pulled me inside. We made our way up the center aisle, and Inara tilted her head back, sending her eyes upward. "Wow."

The ceiling was high and arched and filled with light. The glass windows let in the sun and refracted it, sending long colorful rays across the cathedral. Each window depicted a scene from an important moment in App World history. The biggest one showed Marcus and Eleanor Holt as the first man and woman who'd appeared virtually. Another depicted a galaxy of Apps that shifted and swirled. But my favorite was the one of Eleanor designing the App that would later download the most famous buildings in the City. The Water Tower rose up behind her in the glass, the first skyscraper she'd coded because of how it reminded her of New Port City.

Inara and I reached the row where Mr. and Mrs. Sachs waited for us. We joined them, and I looked around, searching for anyone else I knew. There were mostly celebrities and wealthy citizens. There was Simon, Jenna, and a few other fifteens and sixteens I knew from school. I located Lacy, too, in the aisle seat of the second row. But I didn't see any other Singles.

This filled me with sadness.

It was cruel that Adam wasn't invited to mourn Parvda, and Sylvia would suffer alone on behalf of her girlfriend. And what about other Singles like me, with family in the Real World? Prime Minister Holt's decree stole away our families and our right to choose. Why didn't this funeral consider our losses too?

Low whispers rippled throughout the audience. Up in front, Jonathan Holt rose from his pew and turned toward the back of the cathedral.

Everyone else followed his lead.

I craned my neck, trying to see.

People's gazes rose toward the ceiling.

Inara gestured above us. "Holograms. Of the dead."

One by one they appeared until there was a long parade high in the air so everyone could see clearly.

"The lost," I corrected. "They're not dead."

The holograms made their way toward the front of

the cathedral, then parted, some to the left, others to the right, hovering in the rafters as they waited for the others to join them. I saw more than a few Singles I recognized, including Parvda. The footage showed her in a simple green sundress with a happy smile on her face. It made me wonder if the footage was taken from a time when she was with Adam. I liked to think this might be true. There were the wealthy App World seventeens, the ones whose parents were patriotic and refused to buy their children out of Service, and those who'd defied their family's wishes and unplugged regardless. As the holograms passed, I wished I knew which one was Sylvia's girlfriend.

Inara reached over and squeezed my hand. A single tear leaked from her eye. "Look. It's Rain."

In the very back, the last hologram began to make its way down the aisle. Rain was so lifelike it was difficult to believe he wasn't actually with us. He appeared to be walking down the street, hands stuffed deep in his pockets, eyes on the ground. I glanced toward the front of the cathedral, trying to gauge Lacy's reaction, but I couldn't tell whether she was looking up at him with love or hate or a mixture of both. Her eyes nearly always seemed to gleam wickedly, as though this were her only expression.

When the hologram of Rain approached our row, I studied him.

Inara sighed heavily. "What a waste. He was so beautiful."

As I took him in, I realized that I was watching to see if he would lock eyes with me again, as he'd done the night of his father's announcement.

Or at least, as I thought he'd done.

A hollowness opened in my chest.

Rain passed me by as though I didn't exist at all.

9

App World 2.0

ONE HOUR INTO the ceremony, after the names of the
lost were read, Jonathan Holt bent down to kiss his wife
on the cheek before making his way up to the stage. He
stood at the pulpit. Everyone waited for him to speak, but
then he held out his hand toward the row of government
officials sitting in the front. Emory Specter, the Defense
Minister, got up from his pew and joined the Prime Minister. The two most powerful men in our world stood
before us, Specter in a bright-red suit, an odd choice for a
funeral.

Murmurs erupted across the cathedral.

The Defense Minister's job revolved around border
maintenance and controlling who was allowed to plug in

and unplug, so he was likely behind Jonathan Holt's decision to cancel Service.

I shifted in my seat. Craned my neck to look at Lacy again.

Was it possible Specter knew we were about to unplug? Was he here to scare us? To scare anyone who had our same plan?

Jonathan Holt gripped the sides of the podium. "Thank you all for coming." His voice boomed through the cavernous space. "Today marks a time of deep grief. My family, like many of yours, has lost a son. Because of this, I requested that someone else in the cabinet speak on my behalf." The Prime Minister sounded like he was having trouble getting his words out. His body arched away from the Defense Minister, as though repulsed. "Emory Specter volunteered to lead us in remembering our loved ones," he finished. Then he went and sat in a chair on stage.

"Distinguished guests, honored citizens of the App World, welcome," Specter began. His hands were clasped in front of him and he rocked on his toes. His gaze traveled from left to right and back as he took in the huge crowd of funeral goers. He raised a hand toward the holograms hovering above us. "This morning we remember our sons and daughters, our brothers and sisters, and our friends who have tragically departed this world. I extend my heartfelt condolences to everyone who has lost someone." A smile played at his lips.

I ran my hands up and down my arms, wishing I had a sweater. Something was off. The Defense Minister was speaking the right words to us, but his demeanor was not one of sadness.

It was more of excitement.

Anticipation.

"But even as we mourn," he went on, "we must also express our tremendous relief that those still with us, our children especially, are virtually safe and sound. And while we regard the real human body as an impediment to leading a fulfilled and happy life, we also depend on that fragile body to maintain the brain, that miraculous organ that connects us to the plugs and allows our virtual selves to exist. I'd like to ask for a moment of silence now, in gratitude to those Keepers working valiantly to protect the plugs, and therefore the brains of all of us, to maintain our safety."

He bowed his head.

Everyone else did the same.

As I stared down at the blue fabric of my dress, the Defense Minister's comments played over in my mind. Even though it made me feel callous, I *was* curious to know why we were all still safe. If I was a Keeper in the Real World who'd lost all possibility of plugging in, I would feel angry and betrayed. I would think the decision to close the border horribly unfair and would want to rebel against it. Strategywise, the most obvious next step would be to attack the plugs and remove the bodies. Every citizen of the App World was dependent on the willingness of the Keepers to maintain us, which was a massive vulnerability. So what possible reason did the Keepers have to comply with Specter? Could they all be like my mother and have a child to protect? Was the answer as simple as this?

Emory Specter raised his head. With his arms outstretched, he went on. "I also stand before you today as a bringer of hope." He glanced at the Prime Minister, who stared stonily ahead. "There could be no better place or time to share the most important news to affect our world since its inception."

The cathedral erupted into chatter.

Inara took my hand and squeezed it tightly. What news could take precedence over the border closing? What could be so important that it should be shared during this funeral?

The Defense Minister raised his hand, calling for silence. He waited until everyone quieted. "For a long time, we've been conducting experiments to discover what will allow citizens of the App World to be free of their bodies once and for all." Specter's gaze traveled across the span of seated guests. He no longer tried to hide his delight. "I am thrilled to announce we have finally succeeded. Within a few months' time, we will be entirely body-free.

Eternal, virtual life has been achieved! The Race for the Cure has been won!"

I almost couldn't breathe. I tugged at the top of my dress, pulling it away from my skin so my chest could better expand.

Some people began to cheer. Others leapt to their feet with applause. Parents and children hugged one another. Chaos broke out across the pews. Only the Holts and the other families in mourning were silent. Inara held on to my hand like she was afraid to let go. She looked at me imploringly. A deep ache began to spread through me, as though someone was scooping out my insides.

The Defense Minister was beaming. "Quiet, please! Quiet, now!" He gestured again for everyone to settle down. "Let me explain how this will happen. In one month's time, the Keepers will begin removing bodies from the plugs. Who will be removed first, you might wonder? When you plugged in, each of you was given a number. Marcus Holt—Apps rest his virtual soul—was number one, and Eleanor Holt, his wife, number two, and so on and so forth. To be fair, the Keepers have been instructed to go in order, beginning with those families who've been here the longest, the pioneers of the App World. Eventually the Keepers will move on to more recently uploaded citizens. We predict it will take about twelve months to give everyone the necessary update. Liberation is set to begin soon!"

I swallowed. Liberation?

Meredith Dowling, one of the founders of the gaming industry and a woman I admired, stood up in one of the front rows. "Minister Specter, as encouraged as I am by your announcement, I can't say I'm thrilled to be a pioneer if that means I am among the first to be separated from my body." There were nods of agreement throughout the cathedral. She stared hard at the Defense Minister. "How do I know it's safe? What if the process doesn't work and I simply . . . disappear from existence? I don't like the idea of funerals becoming a regularity."

She sat back down.

A few people clapped.

The Defense Minister was calm. Maybe he'd anticipated this reaction. "There's nothing to worry about. In the research and experimentation process, some App World citizens were freed from their bodies and they are one hundred percent virtually fine! That's how painless it is. They didn't even know it occurred!" He laughed. "They *still* don't know, actually."

The crowd cheered again, and my stomach clenched. I looked around frantically. Who among us had already lost bodies? Had Inara? Or worse, had *I*? There would be no unplugging if we didn't have bodies to unplug. My eyes landed on Lacy. She was studying her nails, like always, looking unbearably bored.

She obviously wasn't worried.

An ominous wave spread through me. The government would never risk experimenting on someone like Lacy. It would more likely be someone like me. A Single.

Emory Specter smiled from ear to ear, making no effort to conceal his glee. This was becoming less a funeral and more like a political rally by the minute. "I can assure you there is no risk. Many of you have Under Eighteens and young children who've only recently appeared. I want to take this moment to address any worries you might have about their virtual development. As part of the experimentation process, we've removed children at all stages of youth and we can confirm that with our new technology, they will continue to grow virtually as though still plugged in to their real brains." He placed his hands on either side of the podium and leaned forward. "Once the very last body has been removed, the Keepers will destroy the plugs and the App World will officially be self-sustaining. Our population reached optimal levels earlier this year." He laughed good-naturedly. "We no longer have to rely on the Keepers to maintain us. Our way of life will be forever protected. We will be stronger than ever before!"

Men stamped their feet and whistled. Women waved ribbons they'd taken from their hair and tossed flowers into the aisle.

Inara snaked an arm around my shoulders and pulled me close.

I still couldn't wrap my head around any of this. The Defense Minister must have promised the Keepers something, but what incentive could possibly be big enough? And even if we could survive virtually without the plugs and the body, that didn't make it right. It meant the literal and permanent separation of the rich of this world and the poor of the real one. And we were all always supposed to have a choice. People in the Real World could choose a life plugged in and Under Eighteens could choose a life unplugged. We could have a future in only one world or the other, but the decision had always been ours to make.

Until now.

Suddenly the App World felt like a prison.

I looked around at all the wealthy guests in this cathedral, joyfully applauding. Lacy Mills and her family, who profited off the consumption of App pornography. The Harrisons, who profited off the App World citizens' need to be voyeurs. The Jeffries, who grew rich off the desires of people to look like supermodels, and the Monikers, whose wealth depended on people's violent impulses and desire for dominance. The list could go on. It was in their interests that we have no other choice but to live our lives on one download after the other, for all eternity. They stood to profit the most because of our inability to leave.

"Hooray for the Cure," Emory Specter shouted. His smile was so wide I thought it might break his face in half. "The App World 2.0 is almost here!"

People leapt to their feet.

They gave Emory Specter a standing ovation.

The noise was deafening.

Jonathan Holt stared at his colleague. He didn't join in on the cheering. When the Defense Minister stepped down from the podium and returned to his seat, Holt got up and lingered onstage a moment longer, looking out over the crowd. Then his attention went to the hologram of his son floating high above everyone's heads and stayed there for a long time, before sweeping over the other holograms of the lost, reminding the crowd why we had come today.

The cheering finally died out.

"Thank you again for coming to pay your respects," the Prime Minister said evenly. "I wish you all well. I leave you in peace and stability on the Apps," he added, as though there was a bad taste in his mouth. He walked off the stage and straight out of the cathedral. He only paused twice on his way to the doors.

The first was when he waited next to the first pew for Lady Holt to join him.

The second was when he approached the place where I was sitting.

His steps slowed, as though he was tired and gathering his breath. His head turned, only slightly, but enough so that his gaze swept over the crowd. It didn't come to rest until it met with mine. I sat there, frozen, looking into the eyes of Rain Holt's father, still unable to believe they were looking straight back at me. This time, I knew I wasn't imagining it.

Something flickered across Jonathan Holt's face.

Guilt, I thought.

Quickly, he looked away.

Then the Prime Minister and Lady Holt continued up the aisle.

At dinner that night, Mrs. Sachs downloaded a simple meal of something round and white that was supposed to be chicken, with long orange spears on the side. We took our places at the table, and I was reminded of the last time I'd sat down to eat with the Sachses, how the night had ended with Jonathan Holt's announcement about the border closing. For a long time, no one spoke. The only sound was of silverware clinking against plates. The Defense Minister's words weighed heavily. I was curious what Mr. and Mrs. Sachs thought about his announcement, if they were relieved like so many others, or if they were disturbed like I was.

"I'll go download the Dessert App," Inara said when it was clear that none of us could eat any more.

Mrs. Sachs gave her a smile. "Thank you, sweetheart," she said quietly.

Inara got up and stacked the plates of her mother and father on top of her own. She hesitated when she got to mine. "Skye, you barely touched your dinner."

"It's okay. I'm done."

Inara took my plate and disappeared into the kitchen.

I swallowed. "Mrs. Sachs? Mr. Sachs?"

They turned to me.

Mrs. Sachs set her wineglass down. "Yes, Skylar?"

I eyed the doorway. Inara would be back any minute. "I just, um, I wanted to thank you both."

Mr. Sachs dabbed his napkin to his lips, formal as always. "Thank us for what?"

Sadness, like a big, gaping mouth, opened around me. I would miss them. I would miss all of this. The dinners. The time spent here. So much of my life had happened at this house. Most of all, I would miss Inara, my best friend in both worlds. My virtual sister. "I wanted to thank you for everything you've done for me ever since the day I plugged in."

Mrs. Sachs searched my face. "Don't be silly. You're practically a member of this family."

I nodded.

But in truth, the word *practically* dug into me like sharp fingernails. Stung like a splash of cold water. That was the thing: I could only ever *practically* be a member of their family, despite all of Inara's claims that this wasn't true. *Almost* but *not quite* part. Like family but never actually family. An adopted daughter or even a surrogate one, but not the biological equivalent. For that, I had to go to the Real World.

"I just want you both to know that I'm grateful." My voice cracked. "Really and truly grateful. I don't know what I ever would have done without you here. You've taught me order and virtual right from wrong and App etiquette and too many other things to mention. You've given me so much."

The smile fell from Mr. Sachs's face. "Skylar, you're starting to worry me. Is there something you're not telling us? Is something wrong?" He crushed his napkin in his fist. "Are you in trouble?"

"No, no," I said quickly. "Everything's fine." Mrs. Sachs's brow furrowed. Deep lines extended from her eyes. "It really is." Panic fluttered in me. This was a stupid idea. All I'd done was make them suspicious. I needed to backtrack. "I guess, despite the Defense Minister's reassurances, I'm worried that the body removal process might not go well and one of us could disappear at any moment, so I wanted to say those things just in case. Because I mean them. They're all true."

Mrs. Sachs dabbed at her eyes with a tissue. "Skye, you are such a sweetheart. But there's nothing to worry about. No one's going to disappear, just like Emory Specter said. The process is completely safe. We have no reason not to believe him."

"Yes," Mr. Sachs echoed. "We're going to think positive about this! If there was truly a danger, people would have already vanished. But they haven't. There hasn't been a single report of anyone going missing. We're all here and accounted for, safe and sound. Now, while I don't exactly agree with the Defense Minister's choice of venue for his announcement, he wouldn't lie to us about something so important. What reason would he have? The betrayal would be too great and too costly for all of us."

I nodded, like I believed this, too. I wanted to reassure them because they meant me only kindness. Showing them respect felt more important than disagreeing with them about Emory Specter.

Inara returned to the table. "The desserts will finish downloading in just a sec."

"Did you know Skylar was so worried about vanishing?" Mr. Sachs asked her immediately.

Inara raised her eyebrows at me. *Are you really*? she chatted in my brain. "Skye's always worried about everything," Inara said out loud to her parents with a laugh.

I managed a sheepish grin.

Eventually the conversation moved on to other things and we ate our dessert.

But before the night was over, Inara chatted me one last time.

What aren't you telling me, Skye?

10

Tiny betrayals

FRIDAY MORNING ARRIVED. It was my last day in this
world.

A mixture of feelings followed this thought. Sadness.
Nostalgia. Regret.

When I walked into the lounge, Emory Specter's
speech about the Cure was on repeat and Singles huddled
in groups to watch it. I was forced to hear his words about
secret experiments on bodies and the destruction of the
plugs once again. Now fear reared its head inside of me.
Would I have a body to unplug tonight? Would any of us?
If we did unplug, with the plugs soon destroyed, would
we lose our way back?

Even though the body was fragile, prone to disease,

and so many other terrible things, it had always been a consolation to think I was still attached to it, that it was waiting there in case I ever needed it. I wasn't ready to give it up and maybe I wasn't the only one who felt this way. It was wrong for Emory Specter to think he could single-handedly decide to separate all of us from our bodies.

Inara was waiting on the corner by Singles Hall when I walked out the doors. There was a bright-green leaf in her hands that she must have plucked from the tree branch that stretched over the sidewalk. She was smiling down at it. This might be one of the last times I saw that familiar smile. When she looked up, I said something even I didn't expect.

"Let's skip school today."

Inara let the leaf fall gently to the ground. Then she folded her arms across her chest, eyeing me. "But you never skip. Like, ever."

I pulled my hair up into a ponytail. "Exactly why we should do it, right?"

"I don't believe you," Inara said. "I think you're . . . I think you're . . . *joking.*"

"I'm not." I was glad she didn't use the word *lying*, though I knew it had been perched on her lips. "Come on."

A smile tugged at her mouth. "What if I say no?"

"You're not going to, so don't even try. I had you at *let's*," I added with a laugh, but I was less confident than my words. These could be our last hours together and I wanted to do something fun. Something we would both remember. "Please."

"Well, okay, Ms. Cruz. If you're going to beg." Inara joined in on my laughter. "Somebody downloaded a Personality Change App this morning."

I smiled. So we would have our final day of fun. "Speaking of Apps . . ."

Inara rubbed her hands together. She was becoming giddy. "I'm all ears."

I linked my arm through hers and we headed into the park. "Let's definitely not download the All Ears App. Remember that time when Simon did, because he wanted to better eavesdrop on his friend, but the App took forever to wear off?"

"It almost cured my crush on him," Inara said. "Becoming all ears is not attractive, no matter who you are."

"I think that download could cure a crush on anyone." I shivered with disgust. "Hey—remember when we were twelve and you decided you wanted to kiss Jamie Sanders, the son of that famous singer, because you thought he had nice lips?"

"Do you have to bring that up?" Inara said, but she was smiling.

"And when you downloaded his App," I went on, "his lips deflated just before you were about to kiss him because his daily Lip Enhancer wore off and it turned out he barely has lips without it?"

Inara guided us into a part of the park where the trees were always coded for fall. Their leaves shone in hues of bright yellow, orange, and red. It was one of her favorite places in the City. "At least now we know the truth about that not-so-kissable mouth. And while we're discussing our most embarrassing downloadable moments, I'll remind you of the time you tried the Boob Job App and it malfunctioned and got your virtual body size wrong and each of your boobs got as big as a basketball and you couldn't even stand up straight for, like, the entire five hours it lasted."

I grimaced at the memory. "And your mother found me hiding in your closet."

"And she sat us *both* down to talk about age-appropriate downloads. Meanwhile, your boobs were still so big they bulged out from your lap and my mother kept trying not to stare and laugh but she couldn't help it. That was the worst."

Other memories of Inara and me were bubbling up, from the Hide-and-Seek App we downloaded a million times when we were little, to the day we were old enough for Imaginary Boyfriends. I was smiling so wide my cheeks hurt. "Then there was that other time," I started, "when—"

"Skye," Inara interrupted.

I glanced at her. "What?"

"Why are you acting so weird?"

"How am I acting weird?"

She stopped in front of a tree that burned with fiery-red leaves. "Last night with my parents, and today, wanting to skip school, and now, with our greatest hits of Apping."

"That's not what I'm doing."

Inara studied me hard. "Yes," she said. "I think it is."

I looked away. Scraped my foot back and forth along the path, listening to the sound of the gravel. "That's just your imagination playing tricks."

"It isn't, though. I know you better than anyone else in this world, which means I also know when something is up."

I started walking again, keeping my eyes on a tall tree raining down bright-yellow leaves on repeat. "Then you also know I'm going to whoop your virtual butt at Odyssey." I heard Inara's footsteps following after me but I didn't turn around. "I think that's what we should play today. Since we're not going to school," I added.

Inara had almost caught up. "Skye, be serious."

I spun to face Inara, walking backward, sidestepping the pits and dips in the dirt path. Trusting my instincts to keep me upright. "I *am* serious."

Inara threw up her hands. "Fine. I'll humor you since skipping school does make this a special occasion. But this isn't the last time we're having this conversation."

"Okay," I agreed, relieved. Then I realized a problem with my plan. I'd spent everything downloading footage about Lacy Mills. "Um, could you spot me some capital?"

"You don't have any? Odyssey isn't exactly one of the pricier Apps."

"I know, but . . . can you just spot me or not?"

Two red marks appeared on Inara's cheeks. "Sure. Sorry." She knew how much I hated asking for handouts. "I shouldn't have asked."

I felt guilty for holding out on my friend—holding out on so much. "Thanks, Inara." Tears pressed at the back of my eyes. "Really."

"No, it's okay. I shouldn't have doubted you."

Inara's eyes glazed over.

The sound of capital hitting my account alerted my brain. Everything felt woozy and liquid before I pulled myself together. "Inara, that's way too much!" I wiped my eyes, hoping she didn't notice they were wet with tears. She'd put in triple the amount we needed for Odyssey.

When her gaze refocused, she shoved me playfully. "Now if I were you, I'd quit worrying and start downloading. I'm totally going to take advantage of my head start."

"Your head—" I began, but didn't finish.

There was no point.

Inara disappeared from the atmosphere.

She was already in the game.

I took a deep breath. Composed myself. Then I began the Odyssey download. It wasn't long before I vanished into the game, too.

At first, I couldn't see anything.

But the smell all around me was familiar. Salty and fresh, briny and cool. There came the sound of water and the periodic *shhhhh* of waves. I immediately relaxed. The landscape took shape and it was just as I expected. The beach where I stood curved like a long sliver of moon. Inara was already at the other end. We each wore long, billowy linen tunics, our legs bare.

"You cheated," I shouted to her, my voice carried by the breeze.

Inara turned and laughed, walking backward. "Did not! Catch me if you can!"

I started across the sand, my feet sinking among the shifting, sliding grains. They were warm. I didn't rush to catch up. I'd forgotten how much I loved playing Odyssey with my best friend. Of all the games, this one's genius was that you could choose your own adventure. Whoever was leading got to pick the landscape, the terrain, the method of travel, whether the mood was lighthearted and fun or dark and menacing. They even got to pick which other characters would appear to help or challenge players. Everyone loved a villain. There was something so satisfying about fighting off and defeating a person you'd never gotten along with or who'd bullied you as a kid. I wondered who Inara would choose if she stayed in the lead, and I was curious to see where she would take us next.

Up ahead, Inara reached the top of a great sand dune and disappeared on the other side. The sun shone brightly, warming my skin. My tunic flapped against my body and swirled up around my legs in the breeze. I swerved toward the water and waited for it to wash over my feet. My toes curled into the soft, wet sand.

A powerful yearning opened inside me.

I wanted to go to the beach with my family again. My mother and my sister.

And I would. Soon.

"Skye?" Inara's voice traveled over the wind, impatient. "Hurry up!"

I started across the dune in a run, my feet slipping in the unstable sand, and was at the top in no time. I shielded my eyes against the sun's glare. On the other side was another cove. Two tiny sailboats bobbed at the water's edge. Inara was already untying the rope attached to a stake in the sand on one of them. I scanned the water and saw an island not too far out. So that's where we'd be going.

Inara waved when she caught sight of me.

I waved back. "Don't get too comfortable with that lead! You won't have it for long!" I traveled down the rest of the dune with long, leaping strides until I was running along the flat packed sand at the tide's edge.

Inara pushed and shoved until her boat was floating in the shallows. She hopped in. She eyed my own little vessel on the shore. "Good luck with that!"

"Right," I said under my breath. Inara knew I didn't sail. I preferred using my body to do what needed to get done. It cost less capital that way, and the game lasted longer. I reached my boat and stopped. It looked simple enough and it was such a pretty thing, with that tall white sail. But appearances can be deceptive.

Inara was still floating in the shallows, holding back.

"You don't have to baby me," I called out.

She stood, balancing as the boat rocked. "I'm worried I made this too difficult for you."

I laughed. "We may be in your Odyssey world, but don't forget that gaming is my thing." I was untying the rope tethering the boat when I had an idea. The island wasn't that far away. I glanced underneath the tunic she'd given us to wear. There was no bathing suit, but I had on underwear. And it was only the two of us so far.

What, really, did I have to be embarrassed about?

I raised my arms and lifted the dress over my head, tossing it aside.

"What are you—" Inara started, but didn't finish.

I was already running into the waves, the water splashing up around my legs. It was warm, almost tropical. I laughed. There was nothing like going for a swim, nothing better than being here, doing this, on my last day in this world. "Who's worried now?" I shouted.

Quickly, Inara sat back down and put her hand on the tiller. "That's not fair," she cried, guiding the rudder. "We don't have bathing suits because you're not supposed to—"

I dove under and the rest of Inara's words were drowned out by the water. I shot forward, my torso and legs like a spear. Underneath me were fish. Blue and silver and purple and gold. They scattered as I approached. When my momentum slowed I came up for air and started to swim, my arms lifting in arcs above the water, legs kicking. Faster and faster. The next time I lifted my head I glanced right and saw that I'd almost caught up with Inara. Soon I would overtake her. As I propelled myself forward, I wondered what it would be like to swim in the sea of the Real World, a river or a lake, if I would have to start over as though I didn't know how, or if the body would somehow remember this skill, if swimming would be instinctive like it was for me here.

My arms and legs pushed faster.

Ahead, I saw the island. If I reached it first, then the landscape would shift. I wondered what my mind would create for us today. It might be fun to let my unconscious take over so everything that appeared in the game would be a surprise even for me. I'd always liked playing Odyssey this way, discovering what my mind was thinking about that I didn't even realize.

Looking right, I saw that Inara and I were neck and neck.

I dove under again, rippling through the water. I swam as fast as I could, occasionally glancing in front of me to gauge the remaining distance to the island. The bottom of the ocean began to rise. It got closer and closer until I could set my feet down. Inara's sailboat would be harder to get to land. She hadn't accounted for me being able to run once I got to shore.

"Noooo," Inara groaned. "I hate you, Skye," she said, but she was laughing.

I stopped when I was thigh deep in the water. "You don't hate me! I'm your best friend for, like, *ever.*" I watched as Inara climbed out of the boat. I crossed my arms, smirking as I waited for her to catch up, like she'd waited for me earlier.

She dragged and tugged. "You are a mean best friend!"

"What? Like you didn't just do the same thing to me?"

As she struggled with the boat I walked the rest of the way to shore. When I was ankle deep I hesitated. The moment I stepped on dry land everything would shift. The terrain and the objectives my mind conjured were always less . . . tranquil. Maybe it was because I liked running from villains and dangerous animals. When I was gaming I was no longer a Single, dependent on the kindness of others, an outcast in the App World. I had power. Challenges would come my way and I would get through them like I was made for it.

Inara had nearly caught up.

I took my last step onto the sand and closed my eyes.

When I opened them again, the beach, the island, the ocean had disappeared. I looked around. I was in the middle of a city but the streets were deserted. A sharp wind blew leaves along the ground. On my legs were black leggings, and I wore a long-sleeved T-shirt. Thin black shoes clung to my feet. Good for running. Before me, reaching up into the clouds, was the Water Tower.

Of course. It was my favorite.

I craned my neck to see all the way to the top. The facade of the skyscraper seemed to ripple and swell, a trick of the liquid glass used to build it. The whole of it glowed a deep blue.

There was a sizzle and a zap, and then Inara appeared on the corner. "A city, Skye? Really? Couldn't we have stayed on vacation?"

I smiled. "Last one to the top has to eat *all* your mother's dinner downloads for a week." I pulled open the door and went inside, trying not to think about how I didn't have a week left. Not even an entire day.

There was a line of round crystal pods in the lobby, elevators that I knew wouldn't work—they were just for show. This was about climbing. I entered the stairwell and began taking the steps two at a time. They were clear so you could see through to the bottom, as though you were looking through water. Glowing underneath the third staircase were the sharp bright edges of a coral reef. I grabbed the thin glass metal rail and swung myself around to start up to the next floor, the muscles in my legs working and straining. Eventually I heard Inara enter below.

I picked up my pace. Everything about me felt light. My virtual skin hummed with electricity, every bit of my code awake. Then I came to a halt on the next landing.

At my feet lay a bright-blue bag.

I was excited to see what it held, surely a sign of whatever new adventure was in store for us next. I nudged the top open with the toe of my slipper. Inside was a parachute, a rappelling kit, and a pair of wings. So this was how Inara and I would be getting down from the top of the building. Then I noticed something tucked underneath everything else.

The breath left my body.

A gun. There was a gun in the bag.

Why would I ever need such a thing?

When I checked again it seemed to have vanished. I dug around underneath the other things, but it wasn't there. Maybe I'd imagined that cold metal revolver. I hoped I did. I grabbed the parachute. The wings I'd leave for Inara. I started up the stairs again, my mind stuck on the gun. Odyssey was taking a far darker turn than I'd like.

I'd only gotten up three more floors when the lights went out.

Inara screamed. "Skye?" Her voice was faint, it was so far below. "What's happening?"

I tried clearing my mind to reset the game. Conjured up sunlight and peace. Birds chirping and waves lapping against the shore. Emergency lighting buzzed, then flickered on in the stairwell. The glow was weak, but it was better than nothing. "Does that help?" I called down to her.

"I guess," she said weakly. "I want to go back to the beach."

"I know," I mumbled. Odyssey was resisting my wish to override my unconscious. I continued on, not sure what else to do, getting closer and closer to the top of the building. All the freedom I'd felt just moments ago fled. My feet were like lead, each step heavy and loud. I needed the air, the outside, to see the sky and the clouds. If I'd let Inara stay in the lead, we'd probably be doing something silly and fun, like racing to see who could tan the fastest beside a beautiful swimming pool or downing lemonade and apple pie at a Parisian café on a timeout.

I finally reached the top of the staircase. The door to the highest floor swung open and I felt compelled to go through it. I looked around the lobby. Before I had time to process what was happening, there came a crackling in the atmosphere, static prickling across my skin. Then a bright blinding flash. I put my hands up to block it. When the spots faded from my eyes, I took in the sight before me.

A hologram hovered there.

The Prime Minister was standing at its center. His hands were clasped in front of him. He wore a blue suit and his eyes were ringed with purple. His skin was that same gray color I noticed at the funeral.

I blinked at him in shock. Something was wrong with Odyssey. Very wrong. "Why are you here? Did Odyssey conjure you?"

Jonathan Holt glanced behind himself once, then again, as though he expected someone else to appear at any moment. "You must have a lot of questions, Skylar."

A chill raced through my code and I shivered. "You know who I am?"

The Prime Minister's eyes returned to me and stayed there. Something flashed in them briefly. *Guilt*, I thought, for the second time. "There's so much I wish I could explain, but there's no time," he said.

It was difficult to breathe. I covered my eyes with my hands. "I am imagining this," I said out loud. Maybe there was a logical reason why Jonathan Holt showed his face in my game. Maybe it was because his son had been on my mind, because I was about to unplug and find Rain.

Yes. That must be it. Once again, I tried to reset Odyssey. I banished the Prime Minister from my thoughts and I banished thoughts of his son. I waited a beat, then took my hands away from my eyes.

Jonathan Holt was still there, studying me.

The Prime Minister looked behind himself again. "I felt obliged to meet you before you go. It's my duty."

"I don't understand." I stared into his eyes, still unable to believe they were looking straight back at me. My brain kept trying to come up with reasons for his presence. Maybe it was my fear of being found out for unplugging illegally that had brought him here. Maybe I was scared that somehow the government would prevent my return to the Real World, and my subconscious couldn't help but play out this scenario. "This is really happening?"

Jonathan Holt was about to answer when the faint sound of other voices began to come through the hologram. His face grew clouded. "I must go." His gaze lingered on mine. "I'm sorry, Skylar. Truly. Forgive me," he added, and then the hologram vanished.

Sorry? Sorry for what?

My breaths came quickly and I thought I might faint. I headed out onto the roof deck for air. Rather than feeling triumphant about reaching the top, I was exhausted. I waited for the atmosphere to refresh me and for the sunlight to blind me, but instead all I saw were dark clouds, heavy with rain. Thunder rumbled across the sky. Parachute in hand, I stumbled toward the railing and looked down. Lightning flashed, briefly lighting up the City, then leaving everything in darkness again. I'd never been afraid of heights, but the world around me was spinning. Where was Inara? If I let her get ahead, our day would surely turn fun again, like before. I leaned against the low wall. Bent forward to rest my head on the rail. A fat drop of rain landed on my back. Another splashed against my wrist. Thunder rumbled. When it faded, the quiet was eerie. I lifted my head and listened carefully.

There were footsteps behind me.

My instincts told me it wasn't Inara.

My fingers tightened around the rail. The raindrops fell heavier now. I thought about that gun. Wished I'd grabbed it to see if it was real.

Water slid across my skin.

Before I could lose my nerve, I spun around.

Rain Holt was standing there studying me, a confused look on his face. He wore a black jacket and jeans. His hair had its usual shaggy cut and his expression was cold and piercing, like he could see through anything.

"First your father and now you," I said.

Rain's mouth fell open. "You can see me. But how?"

I tried to keep my breathing steady. "You're not really here. My brain is conjuring all of this."

He didn't answer. Just shook his head.

My long hair dripped water onto my shoulders and

arms and I shivered. "Either that or someone is messing with Odyssey."

"Yeah. *You*." Rain's tone was full of awe.

I wrapped my arms around my middle, my clothes soaked through. "This is only happening because I'm about to unplug," I said. "Because I need to find you."

Rain blinked, his eyes all over me, like he still couldn't believe what he was seeing. He lifted a hand to his face. Stared at it. Then he started circling the roof, looking out over the edge. When he stopped circling he turned to me again. "What do you mean you're going to unplug? And did you say something about seeing my father? My father is not—" Rain started, then stopped.

The atmosphere seemed to grow darker. I glanced up at the clouds. They were so close. The water pounding the ground. I shook my head at Rain. "I swear this isn't real."

Lightning struck and lit Rain up. "I swear on my body that it is."

Thunder rumbled, making me jump. "How could you be looking at me, when I'm here and you're in the Real World?" I thought about Emory Specter's words yesterday and something occurred to me. "Do I still have a body? Do you know?"

Rain didn't move. Didn't nod. Didn't answer.

He stepped forward.

I wanted to move away, but he gripped my arm, stopping me. He drew me close. At the last moment, just before his lips were about to touch mine, he shifted away, his breath trailing warmth across my cheek. "You can't unplug," he whispered in my ear. "You'll be sorry if you do."

"Skye?" Another voice wavered across the roof.

I jumped back from Rain.

Inara was standing there, staring like she'd never seen me before. "What is *he* doing here?"

Torrents of rain came down upon us. "I don't know," I choked, each word a sob.

Inara's expression was as gray as the storm clouds above. "Tell me what's going on," she shouted through the din. Came closer. "Tell me . . . or I'm leaving. I'm getting out of Odyssey." Her eyes were cold. "This doesn't feel like a game anymore."

Rain began to fade. I looked at him, needing him to explain what he meant. Then I looked back at my friend. "Inara, don't go. Please."

She crossed her arms. "Then tell me your secret. I know you're keeping one."

"I . . . I can't." Tears rolled down my face. "It's not mine to tell." Inara was shaking her head, her expression full of disappointment. "Please, don't leave!"

But she was already gone.

When I turned around, so was Rain.

I came to from the game and found myself alone in my room in Singles Hall. I looked around, touched the bed, the floor, the walls, to make sure I was really here.

Then I did something I never thought I would do.

I blocked Inara from my mind. Closed her out entirely. She knew me too well. If I didn't, she would figure out my secret and everything would be lost. My ticket to the Real World taken away and everyone else's with it. Lacy Mills's threat of virtual death hung heavy in my mind.

The moment it was done, I felt the cut.

Sensed Inara's sudden, virtual absence.

But the loneliness I felt was all too real.

11

Alone in Loner Town

THE HOUR WE were to meet at the house came up fast.

Too fast.

I had barely any time left in this world and so much on my mind. For the rest of the day I half expected Inara to show up, angry and demanding to know why I'd shut her out, that I explain why Rain had appeared during Odyssey, or even having guessed my secret. I almost wished she would. Maybe she'd convince me not to go.

As I readied to leave Singles Hall for the last time, I was too distracted to do more than whisper good-bye as I walked out the door of my room. The lounge was busy, and things had mostly gone back to normal. Gossip and news holograms flickered around the room. Singles laughed and chatted. But then I noticed Emory Specter's face glowing from one of the walls, his cold eyes staring out at everyone, eyes that I couldn't seem to get out of my head since the funeral. Adam was sitting there, watching the Defense Minister's speech. He glanced at me quickly, and nodded.

Then I walked out of Singles Hall without turning back.

If I let myself see the tall, familiar building, with its warmly lit round windows, I might lose my nerve. I needed forward momentum so I could get through this night without another strange visit from one of the Holts.

So I could finally get to the Real World.

I headed east toward Loner Town.

I'd walked through it once before on a dare and it wasn't something I wanted to do again. Its buildings hadn't had an architecture update since the birth of the App World, and not because the residents couldn't afford one. Most preferred not to leave their rooms and spent every hour gaming or tuned in to the lives of famous people or Under Eighteens trying to claw their way to celebrity status. And these were Loner Town's most normal residents. The worst were the ones who thrived on Black Market Apps that allowed a person to commit virtual crimes. Murders, beatings, terrorist activity, rape, and everything in between. Real World criminals weren't allowed to plug in, but the government soon discovered a person doesn't have to be a true criminal to harbor powerful criminal fantasies. A lot of Loner Town's residents preferred to live these fantasies twenty-four hours a day, sacrificing any social connections, work, and status, secluding themselves in their own corner of the City.

I reached the edge of the park and kept on going, past Appless Bar, still heading east. The farther I walked, the more unfamiliar the City became. Inara and I usually stuck to the crowded avenues in the shopping district, streets lined with App Stores featuring design downloads and restaurants that promised to evoke the intensity of Real World cuisine. I began to see men and women alone, crouched on benches or sitting on the ground. Many of them were catatonic, their clothing in tatters. While sanctioned gaming Apps allowed a person to vanish into another landscape, the Black Market ones often had faulty or substandard codes that left a person sitting in full view of everyone while the brain traveled elsewhere. No one seemed to see me as I passed. I wondered what could be so captivating that these people had checked out of the App World altogether.

The avenues got wider, the buildings shorter and more spread apart. Their color was dimmer, too, more faded. On the next corner I saw a sign and stopped. At one point it must have been bright green, like those on the west side of the City, but now it had darkened to gray with flecks of black where the download had worn out completely. There were thin letters written across it.

You are entering Loner Town.

Underneath the words someone had scrawled, *BEWARE.*

I hesitated.

Then I walked straight past that ominous sign. There would be no chickening out.

The GPS App Lacy had given us automatically turned on in my mind and urged me down a street to my left. It wasn't long before I was deep inside the neighborhood. Loner Town was much bigger than I'd imagined. It spanned dozens of blocks, and it was dark, too. Really dark.

Most of all, though, it was empty.

My hand felt for the wall to my right. I palmed my way down the sidewalk, the crumbling brick as my guide. I thought about downloading a Radiance App but didn't want whoever was out there to see me coming. My mind flickered, nerves racing. Out of nowhere, someone, a man, growled.

"Watch where you're going!" he yelled.

He spoke too late. His legs were stretched across the sidewalk and I tripped, crashing down on his other side, my hands hitting the ground hard, one of them disappearing into a sinkhole in the atmosphere. I'd heard they existed, but I'd never encountered one before now. I winced in pain.

"Sorry," I breathed. I tried picking myself up when I saw a pair of eyes glowing at me in the darkness. There was something in them—rage, or maybe hunger.

"Come here, little girl." He reached out. One of his hands wound through my hair toward my scalp.

My emergency settings kicked into gear and I screamed. With the fear came a great surge of light, my virtual self a fiery glow in the darkness. Sometimes Apps were like a reflex. They were stored in our code, built into the very fabric of our virtual selves, there to protect us if danger was near.

Long claws pulsed from my fingertips.

When Inara was afraid she turned into a bird. I always became a panther.

The man tightened his hold on me the moment I stopped being a girl and became a great black cat with sharp teeth bared and mouth stretched wide.

I hissed, my jaws snapping at him.

"Hey!" His hand retracted.

Then I was speeding away on all fours, smooth and dark as the night around me. I don't know how many blocks I went before the download faded and I was myself again. I stopped at the next corner, panting, my arms and hands reaching everywhere so no one could surprise me from behind. My shirt was ripped at the neck and I did my best to straighten it. My ponytail holder had fallen out. I raked my fingers through my knotted hair, pulling it away from my eyes so I could better look around and get my bearings. The GPS App must have automatically guided me, because it turned out I was exactly where I needed to be. Still breathing hard, I made my way down the final block to the address of the meeting, turning every few steps to check my back. A terrible, acrid smell lingered in the atmosphere, like something was burning. I wrinkled my nose. I took shelter by a tree, the bark dusty and crumbling, like everything else in Loner Town. I peered out from behind it.

Someone was standing in the alcove of the next house.

A man. Tall, wearing a black coat and pants. His hair was a curtain across his cheek, obscuring his face. I wanted a better look at him before I showed myself, but the bark underneath my palms deteriorated to nothing, and then the tree itself began to fade. I yelped and barely caught myself from falling. The man turned. With the movement, his hair fell away from his face, and I saw he wasn't a man after all, but a boy. Not much older than me. His skin glowed pale in the darkness.

"Are you Skylar?" he called out when he saw me there.

"Yes." I straightened up, the tree gone entirely. "Who are you?"

The boy watched me with interest. Then he shrugged. "Lacy's contact."

I took a step closer. "You seem awfully young."

"So?" He sounded defiant.

I walked up to him now, determined not to be afraid. "What are you getting out of this deal? Money?"

The boy was quiet. Then, "Revenge," he said. Like it was simple. He opened the door to the house behind him. "Follow me." He went inside, leaving me alone in the empty dark of the street.

I looked around for the others, wishing Adam would appear, wishing I wasn't the first one here, thinking I probably shouldn't go inside the house alone. But for some reason, when the boy reappeared and said, "I'm not going to hurt you—I promise," I believed it.

And I slipped through the door behind him.

The boy tugged on a string hanging from the ceiling.

A bare bulb above our heads was illuminated.

The inside of the house was almost worse than outside. There was a low couch to my right, the upholstery faded in patches to reveal stuffing and metal springs. The floor had gaping holes, big enough to swallow a person's leg. The pitter-patter of feet, maybe mice, maybe worse, was audible inside the walls. A long thick beam from the ceiling had partially fallen down and blocked the back door.

"Welcome," the boy said. He walked over to the only pieces of furniture that looked usable—an old wooden table and two chairs. He pulled one out for me and sat down in the other. "Have a seat while we wait for everyone else."

I didn't move—I was still taking in the wreckage. I peered down the hall behind the staircase. A thin, dirty mattress was propped against the wall. This didn't seem like a place where a person could unplug. I'd expected sleek chambers and shiny, elaborate machines, not rotting floorboards and the smell of ruin. I joined the boy at the table. Glanced at the door, wondering when Adam would get here, when Sylvia and Lacy would arrive. "Is this your house?" I asked him.

The trace of a smile appeared on the boy's lips. "Maybe."

In his smile I saw something familiar, an expression that reminded me of someone else. I tried to picture him in different surroundings, maybe at school or in the park hanging out with friends on a Saturday afternoon. Aside from the standard features of all boys my age, everything about this one was dark and moody. His hair was black, his eyes were black, his expressions were closed and cautious. His movements were hesitant, like he trusted no one and nothing. But there was something else, too. It was right there, nudging at my brain like an App seeking a download, yet I couldn't quite articulate who, exactly, he reminded me of. "Then why haven't you fixed up the place?"

"I have better uses for capital than redecorating." The boy bent back a long, sharp splinter on the table until it pointed at the ceiling like a dagger. "Why do you care?"

A chill passed through the room and I shivered. "I just . . . I don't like this."

He leaned forward, his dark eyes studying me. He placed a hand over the splinter until it poked the center of his palm. "You're scared."

My heart was pulsating, my code electric with static. "Wouldn't you be, if you were about to unplug?"

The boy closed his hand around the splinter and plucked it from the table, tossing it to the floor. It turned to dust. Then he rose from his chair and walked to the other side of the room. "If I were you, I'd be more worried about what's going to happen when you wake up in the Real World."

I got up and followed him. "I know the deal." I swallowed. "I'm ready for whatever comes."

He leaned against the wall and crossed his arms. "Are you really?"

I tried to soothe the goose bumps along my skin. "Yes," I said, with more certainty than I felt.

The boy flicked dust from his sleeve. "Whatever you say."

I decided to ignore his lack of faith. "What happens if we need to get back here?"

The boy stared at the crumbling wall next to us. It was blurry with age, as though it might turn to dust at any moment, just like the splinter. "I'll come to get you."

"You can just unplug and plug back in when you want?"

"Something like that," he said.

I studied him. This boy was different with each new piece of information I collected. He was unexpectedly young. And now he had ways of moving between worlds as he pleased. "What makes you so special that you—" I began when he turned my way again, and I didn't finish. There was something about the light that hit his face just right. "Wait a minute." I stepped closer. "Look at me."

He shifted. I reached out and brushed the hair from his face. His eyes widened and I saw it again—the resemblance. It was in the shape of his lips and the expression of his dark eyes. The pronounced curve of his cheekbones and the line of his jaw. The way his brow furrowed while he stared at me. There was a hardness about him, a coldness in the way he looked at me. It was there that I saw the stamp of his father, the man whose face I'd been seeing nonstop ever since the funeral.

"I know who you are," I whispered. "You're Emory Specter's son."

He glanced back at the front door, like he suddenly wished the others would arrive. "Everyone in the City knows the Defense Minister plugged in without a family. He has no wife and no children. The perfect circumstances for an all-consuming job like his." His voice wavered, but he didn't confirm or deny the accusation.

"A man can have children and not acknowledge them," I said.

He looked at me hard. "Are you saying I'm illegitimate?"

"No. But in a way," I went on, thinking out what I wanted to say next, "you're a Single like me, aren't you? You're not an orphan, not technically, but you're here alone." I softened my tone. "Sometimes it's worse, isn't it? How even though your family meant well by plugging you in, you still feel like they abandoned you." It pained me to articulate this thought that had long been buried inside me.

He raked a hand through his hair. "Singles aren't abandoned. Your family wanted you to have a better future. My father didn't plug me in. He doesn't even know I'm here."

I took this in. "So you are the Defense Minister's son."

He nodded. For the first time, he seemed vulnerable, like any other boy my age capable of hurt, of sadness. Not so cold. We stood there staring at each other in that decrepit house, with its falling-down ceiling and its walls full of holes. Did this boy scramble for capital just like Singles did, even though he was the son of one of the most powerful men in our world? "You said you were in this for revenge. Revenge against who? Your father?"

He didn't respond. His virtual skin began to darken until it was red. The anger written all over him told me everything I needed to know.

"Listen." My mind was electric with thoughts about what it must be like to be the son of a man like Emory

Specter, a man who so easily used a funeral to further his politics and who was about to enact the most massive change both worlds had ever known—all without giving citizens a say in their fate. "If revenge has anything to do with your father . . ." I hesitated, trying to decide if I truly meant what I was about to say, knowing that I couldn't let the words out unless I was willing to follow through. When I was sure how I felt, I went on. "Then I'm willing to help."

The boy watched me like I was a strange creature, turned mythical by an App before his eyes. "Be careful what you offer. You might not like what it brings you."

"I mean it," I said fiercely.

Slowly, the boy extended his hand. "My name is Trader," he said carefully.

I took it. "It's nice to meet you," I said, just as carefully.

He stared at our clasped hands. Opened his mouth to say something else, when the front door was flung open and Lacy Mills sauntered on through.

12

Border crossings

"WELL, IF IT isn't Little Miss Righteous," Lacy said.

"Hi, Lacy." I wished I could make her walk back out the door so there was enough time to hear what Trader was about to say. A moment later, Adam walked through the door, and not long after, Sylvia. We all nodded hello. Like me, they were dressed in standard-issue casual attire—black long-sleeved shirts and black jeans.

But Lacy had gone all out. She'd obviously downloaded a Manga App. Her hair was a long inky black, as black as Trader's. Her eyelashes were thick and curled up like soft sparkly fans against snow-white skin. Everything about her was exaggerated, either overly big or overly tiny. Her lips, her eyes, and her chest were huge, yet her shoulders, waist, and legs were impossibly narrow. She looked like a cartoon, albeit a gorgeous one. Her dress was an ethereal green, almost entirely sheer, opaque only in the most strategic of places. Its skirt was a series of delicate petals that fell to the middle of her thighs.

Lacy turned to Trader. "Can we get on with this, please?" She sounded bored, but the look in her eyes said otherwise.

Trader gestured for us to follow. He led everyone up the stairs to the second floor of the house. Lacy went first, then Adam and Sylvia. Before I joined them, I looked around once more at the entryway and the living room. This house would be the last thing I saw in this world. How sad. If I had a choice, the last thing I'd want to see was Inara. I followed the sound of voices down the hall. Everyone was gathered in another room where everything looked broken and neglected. A bare bulb dangled from the ceiling, giving off a dim glow. In the center were four ordinary chairs arranged in a tight circle, close enough that whoever sat in them could link arms. The only thing that distinguished them was that they weren't falling apart.

Adam was pacing, as usual. "So? What happens now?"

We all turned to Lacy.

Lacy rolled her eyes. "That's not *my* job."

Trader stepped into the center of the circle. "Once you

unplug, you're going to be disoriented," he warned. "Be ready for that."

"Someone will be there to care for us, right?" Sylvia asked.

Trader nodded. "Each of you has been assigned a Keeper . . . of sorts."

"Who exactly—" Sylvia started.

But he silenced her with a glare. "You'll find out soon enough. More important will be remembering that real bodies are different than virtual ones. You have to be very careful. And not all Real World citizens are friendly— some of them won't want to help you. In fact, they'll want the opposite." Trader's eyes shifted to mine. "You must be prepared to defend yourselves."

Adam and Sylvia erupted into hushed whispers.

"Defend ourselves from what?" I asked.

Before he could say anything, Lacy got between us. Her Apps were already draining away, her eyes growing smaller again, her hair changing back to its standard red color. Lacy glared at Trader. "I'm not paying you to answer lowly Singles' questions. Do your job. It's time for us to go."

Her words quieted us.

"Everyone pick a chair," Trader said. "It doesn't matter which one."

Adam and Sylvia sat down next to each other. Lacy claimed the vacant chair beside Adam. This left only one between Lacy and Sylvia, and I took it.

Adam's right knee bobbed up and down. He was grabbing the back of his neck again. "Now what?"

Trader ignored him. His eyes had grown vacant. When they returned to alertness, he said, "Now this."

App icons appeared in the atmosphere, one in front of each of us. They turned slowly as they hovered.

I should have known. Of course unplugging would involve an App.

Lacy laughed. "Oooh!" She sounded delighted. "One last download before we go!"

They weren't at all typical, though. They didn't shimmer or glitter or even have an enticing image to tempt us. They were dark. Like small lumps of coal. Even though they floated like normal Apps, they seemed heavier, like they would seep into us slowly, instead of racing through our code. Like they might contain poison.

"Where did you get these?" I asked Trader.

"I designed them myself," he said, sounding proud. Then, "It's just about time."

A number—sixty—appeared in the center of the circle.

It immediately began counting down.

Fifty-nine. Fifty-eight.

This was happening fast.

We looked at one another. Adam seemed surprisingly calm, but Sylvia was breathing quickly. Lacy's Apps had drained entirely and she'd returned to her standard virtual self. Without all the downloads to transform her features, she looked remarkably . . . normal. Like she might be any other girl in this City.

Fifty-two.

My virtual heart sped. In a few moments I would no longer exist in this world. I wouldn't live in Singles Hall. I wouldn't wake up and go to school like always. My best friend wouldn't pester me about downloading all of her favorite Apps.

But soon I'd be waking up in the same world as my mother and my sister.

"It's like with any other App," Trader was saying, but I found it impossible to turn away from the black hovering sphere to look at him. I could barely focus on anything else. "It will download into your code. All you have to do is reach out and touch it."

My hand moved out toward the icon, my finger unfurling until it met the surface of the App. A current shivered through me, then that familiar icy feeling began to seep into my code. Instead of enjoying it like I normally did, I felt uneasy, like something was wrong.

Like I—Skylar Cruz—was being erased.

"Be warned," Trader went on. "This App can have strange effects. You may enter the Real World in a dream state, and it may seem endless, but try to stay calm." He came and stood in front of me. "Eventually it will seem like a lucid dream," he said. "And you can take control of it. You should think of it like a game," he added, a whisper in my ear. "You must play like your life depends on it."

Trader's words reverberated through me. The download made my head spin, but my legs, my arms, everything else felt like lead.

"What's wrong with mine?" Sylvia's voice wavered across the room. She sounded fearful. "It's . . . it's like the icon is repelled by me! It isn't working!"

I managed to raise my eyes enough to see Sylvia frantically grasping at her App. It darted away, zipping right, then left. Trader was at her side, trying to fix the glitch.

"Sylvia." I said her name, doing my best to focus. Wanting to help. Her name came out slow and thick.

Trader was shaking his head. He looked down at her. "I'm sorry."

"What's wrong?" I managed, my words distorted.

"She doesn't have a body to unplug," he said. "The App won't connect her to it because her body isn't there."

There came a loud wailing as Sylvia began to weep. "Zeera," she cried, over and over again. Then she got up from her chair and ran from the room.

Adam looked at me through blurry eyes. The App made it impossible to go after her. I was nailed to the chair. But that didn't stop me from filing away the name. *Zeera*.

Thirty. Twenty-nine. Twenty-eight.

The download ran through every bit of me now. I felt its temperature shift from cold to warm, then burning. My gaze went to Lacy's feet—or where her feet should have been.

Little by little, she was disappearing.

The same thing was happening to Adam.

I tried to wiggle my toes but I couldn't.

Even Lacy's eyes held fear. She reached out and grabbed my hand. "Don't let go," she whispered. "Please."

Lacy seemed human, like the little girl I'd seen call to her parents, only to be ignored, so sad to be abandoned. "I won't," I told her. Just as the light began to dim and a strange buzzing sounded in my mind, I added, "You don't have to be afraid. We're in this together."

Her grip on me tightened.

Nineteen.

I could feel someone behind me. Trader crouched to my level. "Be careful, Skye," he whispered.

I was too woozy to respond.

Fourteen.

Right then, an image flashed before me.

Inara.

The atmosphere was flickering in and out.

But I knew that face. I'd always know it. My mind must have conjured up the closest thing I had to safety and security to help ease the transition. My own virtual sister.

"Skylar," she said, but so loudly her voice seemed to fill the room.

Something was wrong. She sounded scared. If my mind conjured Inara to make me feel safe, then why did she seem so frightened?

"Skye," she cried out again.

There it was, the fear. And disbelief. I wanted to respond but words wouldn't form in my mouth. My tongue, my lips were frozen.

"Don't do this!"

Ten.

I tried to lift an arm but I couldn't.

There was a bang and then a thud.

"Let go of me," she yelled.

"You can't be in here," said a different voice now.

Trader.

He'd responded to Inara as though he could see her. Which meant that she wasn't present only in my mind.

Inara was actually here.

"Get out of my way," she said, closer now.

But my brain was already shutting down.

Seven. Six.

The world grew dark, like someone had turned off the lights.

"No, Skye!"

I heard the words, but they were so far away.

Faintly, so faintly I thought I must be dreaming, there

came a pressure on my shoulders. I forced my eyes open.

Inara's bright green ones blinked back at me.

She was right there, but I couldn't reach her.

My arms were gone.

I wanted to say something. I wanted so badly to tell Inara everything, and I knew in that moment I'd made a mistake keeping this secret from her. My true sister, more real to me than the biological one I hoped to find when I unplugged. With all the energy I had left, I opened my mind and chatted her one last time.

I'm sorry, Inara. So sorry.

Three. Two.

It was time.

I began to fall.

All of us did.

But Inara managed to get in a few final words of her own.

"You betrayed me, Skylar," she whispered in my ear.

Then, just like that, I was gone.

INTERLUDE

13

Resurrection

HANDS.

There were hands.

So many of them at my feet, my legs, my middle, my shoulders, my neck, my head. Hands pushing and prodding and shifting me like I was a sack of bones, an inert object, like I was not even human.

I wanted to scream *NOOOOOOO* at the top of my lungs and I wanted to fight them off. Fear built like a sharp knife emerging from within, the point of it lodging in the center of my throat so I couldn't swallow. I wanted to shout my name at them, whoever they were, the owners of these hands, to push away whatever force was holding me under, yell loudly and piercingly, *STOP TOUCHING ME!*

But I couldn't.

The hands slid away, and for a moment, there was peace.

It was then that I realized what this must be.

Trader had spoken of dreams before we unplugged.

This was a dream.

Then, "Careful," I heard. "We don't want anything to break."

And then, after this . . .

There was . . .

Nothing.

I was cold.

So cold.

And dizzy.

Swinging through the air. The breeze, the movement.

Was I on a swing?

There was a noise in my brain, a constant clicking, a chattering in my head, like someone had entered my mind and was chipping away at the code like it was made of granite. But no, the sound was coming from my mouth. At first I didn't understand, then it came to me.

Teeth.

This had happened once before, the chattering, when

I encountered a blizzard in a game and I could barely see, but I'd plowed forward anyway and the App, to make it seem realistic, to make it seem real, sent this noise reverberating through my code because it would happen in a real body that was freezing in the snow.

Was I in the real body? Was this what it was like?

Was I freezing in the snow?

The swinging, suddenly it stopped.

Everything grew so still.

But the fear, the fear grew.

I couldn't move, I couldn't do anything, not even lift a finger or open my eyes to see. Maybe, just maybe I was still in the App World, still disappearing, or in some strange purgatory between worlds.

Yes.

Yes.

I was still between worlds.

The dream world.

With this thought, the fear subsided some, drained slowly, like an App seeping from my code.

But yet . . . there was stone.

I felt stone.

Cold and hard against my back.

I was sure of it.

And ropes—I thought there were ropes—sliding out from underneath me.

And then, then, all of a sudden, again I felt . . .

Nothing.

There came a great crash and a long rumbling sigh, then another, and then again, as though the noise wanted to rock me this way and that, a baby in its arms. The word *ocean* floated across my mind like a tiny vessel heading in toward shore.

Everything was so calm.

I was full. I was nurtured. I was loved.

The Real World was a womb in a great expansive sea. It was the sun high above in the sky, warming the skin and bathing the body with protective light. I could see nothing but I could feel . . . everything. I soaked up the heat, drank in the sweet smell of the air, the breeze that wafted gently against my skin. And my skin, it was so smooth and soft and alive.

I was *alive*.

And then, I felt something new.

A presence. A cool shadow.

"It seems to be waking up."

It?

"That's impossible. It's just the move. The body is confused. The plug is in perfect condition."

"Put an end to its confusion. I can't have interruptions."

That first voice, the voice of a woman, it reached into me like a long curl of black smoke seeking to fill my lungs.

Then hands. Hands again, hands at my shoulders, my arms, my legs, holding me down.

NO! my mind protested again.

I am a girl! A human girl! Not just a body! Not just an it!

These thoughts shouted inside my head.

A jagged pain sheared across my arm.

It's just a dream, cried my brain. *Just a dream.*

But then a great piercing noise filled the air, the world all around.

A scream.

It was coming from my throat.

It sounded so . . .

So real.

I was dreaming again.

In the dream I was lying on a narrow slab of stone. I could feel it against my skin, rough and cold and hard. I tried to open my eyes. Overhead, there was blinding light. Everything filled with glowing spots. Burning orange clouds floated across blackness. Quickly, I closed them again. I heard a murmuring, the murmuring of people gathering in large numbers, talking in low voices, a crowd near me yet set apart. The noise was a great tapestry of words whose threads I could not separate. The last time I'd heard such vast whispering was at the seventeens' funeral, with Inara.

Was I dreaming about the funeral? Would I turn my head and see my virtual sister next to me? The possibility sent a pounding through my chest, a pounding so intense it thumped like it would burst away from my body. Or through it.

It was a heart.

A *heart*.

My real heart?

The heart in the dream was loud. It filled my brain, my mind. My ears. So much throbbing. In between the rhythmic beats, I heard those voices. They were everywhere, all of them strung together and coming at me like a rushing river that tripped and skipped over the pulsing of my heart.

Snatches of speech.

". . . the New Capitalists." *Thump.* "Win . . ." *Thump.* "Freedom . . ." *Thump.* "App World tyranny . . ." *Thump.* "Crisis . . ." *Thump.* "I bid you, come and see . . ."

Wait. No.

These weren't snatches of speech.

They were snatches of *a* speech.

I listened harder, tried to decipher their meaning, any meaning at all, but I couldn't stop that constant noise from pulsating through me and interrupting the words. Maybe if I could manage to see, I would be able to calm down. Yes. I needed to see where I was. That would change everything.

Once again, I let my eyelids slide open.

It took a long time for the spots to fade, for my sight to adjust to the brightness. Too long. I might have been lying there for hours before I was able to focus on the great expanse of blue above me, so big and vast and infinite, but most of all, so so blue. I nearly smiled.

Blue like the sky.

I was looking at the sky.

The real sky.

I was certain of it.

What else could this beautiful roof overhead be?

Now I did smile. Wide and full of joy.

But then I turned my head, turned it ever so slightly toward the murmuring, the whispering that hung around me like a cloud of gnats, and I knew, or, at least, I thought I knew that I'd yet to awaken. There was no way I'd come to from the dreams Trader told us about, because what I saw was impossible.

A thousand pairs of eyes blinked back at me.

Maybe more.

The murmuring shifted until it became a great buzz.

And my smile fell away.

The crowd stared as though they'd never seen a girl before, their faces blank with shock. They were maybe twenty feet away, gathered behind a long curving panel of glass that was anchored to the ground by metal posts. They were dressed in a pale shade of blue, everything about them so still, the glass wall shielding them from the breeze whipping across what looked to be a long, barren peninsula, jutting out into nothingness. I was raised up and apart from them. A sliver of ice pierced me, followed by a fear that was cold and vast and consuming. And then came the shame.

"Don't worry," said a voice from my side of the glass. "The shift in location is a natural shock to her system. The body is merely adjusting."

Were these words for me?

I didn't dare move. I lay there, frozen, afraid to cause another stir. Let them think I didn't understand. Let them believe I was dreaming.

I *was* dreaming—wasn't I?

The crowd, the way they stared, reminded me again of the seventeens' funeral. Could this be my own funeral? Was I a hologram, floating above everyone, as Rain had been just days ago? Was that why I was so high up? Had I died in the process of unplugging?

The crowd's sheer numbers hooked into me next. There were thousands of them, and only one of me. It was as though I'd downloaded some nightmarish version of Odyssey, but driving the momentum of the landscape and the challenges was fear—my fear of the unknown, of unplugging, of being trapped and unable to move. Terror and dread created so much vulnerability, so much weakness.

But then, what else had Trader said before we unplugged?

Think of it like a game.

Play like your life depends on it, he'd said.

I'd learned long ago that I could let a game play me, or I could play it.

A calm spread across me like a healing salve. In a game I could do anything. In a game I could advance. I could get to the next level.

In a game I could *win*.

The prize was getting to the Real World at last.

I lifted my head. Just to see what would happen. If I was going to advance, first I had to figure out the rules.

Looks of astonishment met my eyes. The crowd seemed to see a ghost. I considered their faces differently this time. I sat up now, only a little, to gauge their reaction, a clockwork girl moving in fits and starts. The noise of the crowd shifted along with me, its tenor higher and wider.

"Did you see that? She moved!"

"Is she awake?"

"But she can't be!"

Strength laced itself through my veins, knotting together until it had woven itself into something tough, something durable. Out of the corner of my eye, I saw that a long sliver of slate had come loose on the dais where I lay, the perfect weapon. The crowd's attention briefly turned back toward the voice giving the speech, as though their gaze could will an explanation for the girl who seemed to rise from the dead. I shifted my hand ever so slightly, until my fingers curled around the loose stone's edge, dislodging it.

The audience turned to me again.

Slipping through them would be impossible, and going around the glass to get past them impractical. Their attention was fixed on me like voyeurs' on someone famous. I searched their faces for signs of familiarity, to see if maybe Adam or even Lacy was among them, wondering if all of us were trapped in the same strange and terrible dream, but there was no one else I knew. If I couldn't move through the crowd or around them, I would have to escape by going the other way.

The way of the sea.

I could hear it behind me, the steady crash of it beyond the peninsula. What's more, I could smell it. It called out to me.

But then something else called out to me—someone.

"Skylar!" she screamed over the wind.

I turned toward the voice. A girl with cropped hair that peaked in spikes. The feeling that I should trust her—that I *must*—spread through me.

In games I had allies, and here was one. I was sure of it.

Then others began to emerge.

One, two, then five, then ten, pushing their way

to the edges of the crowd to places where the glass no longer provided a barrier. It was like they were marked with a sign that only I could see, alerting my instinct to trust. Guards emerged too, coming alive like wooden toys. They wore the same pale blue as everyone else, but their clothes were fitted, and on their feet were thick-soled boots. But it was what they wore at their waists that made them seem like guards. Guns. They had guns. The guards began to fan out from the crowd in a wide curving arc. Some of them moved toward the girl, who continued to yell.

"We're here for you," she shouted. "You are not alone! Be brave," she cried when the soldiers seized her.

But the others began to move as well—there were too many allies for the guards to subdue, and the guards seemed as surprised as everyone else by what was happening.

I sat up all the way now, the sharp stone cutting into my palm, assessing the distance between the dais and the ground below. It was covered in golden grass, burned from the sun. The crowd turned frantic, people shoving, fighting, faces pressed against the glass. I was about to jump when my attention caught on a quick movement to my near left.

I turned.

Everything seemed to slow right then.

A woman stood off to the side, alone in front of a

podium looking out at the crowd only a few paces away. She, too, wore the same pale blue.

There was something familiar about her. The woman stared at me in shock, and I wondered if she, too, thought I was a ghost.

"Don't," she mouthed, shaking her head, a mixture of fear and sadness in her eyes. And shame—there was shame in her expression. "Please," she added.

Her voice seemed to reach inside of me. A deep ache yawned and grew until I was nearly consumed with it.

For a moment, I couldn't breathe.

Everything was silent. The crowd held its breath alongside mine.

Then suddenly the game picked up again, time returning to its regular speed, the audience coming to life with shouts and screams. This must be a test, I thought, a test where, at the end, I would get to see my family again. The Real World must be close now. The game was enticing me to move forward.

So forward I would go.

"Run!" someone screamed. It was the short-haired girl's voice again, this time closer. She must have gotten free from the guards.

I braced my body against the stone dais, ready to spring, when one of the guards leapt over the glass wall and two more pushed their way through the angry crowd and around it, headed my way. It was only a second before one of them was on me, throwing himself up toward the place where I was perched. Whether he intended to knock me off or trap me or even kill me, I wasn't sure.

I waited until he had nearly reached me.

Then I plunged the dagger of rock into the guard's chest and moved out of the way. His eyes bulged, a split-second look of shock in them, before he let go a howl so high and horrible it could spur the dead to action. He fell down hard, twisting across the narrow stone.

Then came the blood. So much blood.

Had I ever seen so much blood before in a game?

I couldn't move, fixated on the velvet ooze spreading across fabric and rock and skin—my skin. The girl, the one who'd called out to me to run, was now below me, gesturing frantically for me to join her on the ground. The other guards were nearly on me, murderous looks on their faces, guns in their hands, the metal caught so strangely by the light of the sun. My heart sped. I'd lost my chance to flee.

Then a new voice called out to them.

The voice of the woman behind the podium.

"Don't hurt her!"

The guards froze.

Everyone else did, too.

Now was my chance.

I slipped off the dais to the ground with a heavy thump, and raced toward the edge of the peninsula, the ocean beyond its cliff. There was no time to think *okay* or *yes* or *no*, no time to consider how high or how dangerous, or even ask if I might die. There was only enough time to reach the edge before the guards would overtake me and throw myself into the great expanse of churning blue sea that stretched out toward the horizon.

So that's what I did.

It's just a game, I told myself over and over as I flew toward the jagged edge that zigzagged along the cliff, the soft grasses giving way to loose rocks. I didn't look back, not once, even as the shouts behind me got closer. Suddenly I was six paces away, then five, then four, three, two.

One.

And I leapt.

I flung my body out to the sea, a human stone set loose from a slingshot.

Before gravity took me in its grip and dropped me toward the earth, I saw exactly how far I had to fall. It was as though I'd thrown myself from the ledge of a thirty-story tower, one built on a series of sharp rocks jutting out into the sea like an arrow. The fear, angry and terrible, reared up in me again, threatening to take back control of my mind and my limbs. It wanted to win me over.

But I couldn't let it.

Getting to the Real World depended on my passing this test.

This was just a challenge I needed to clear, one last App working its way through my code that would eventually drain away. That was all this was and nothing more.

Gravity sucked at my feet.

I plummeted toward the sea.

My insides seemed to rise to my middle, my stomach pushing into my lungs, my skin wanting to pull itself up and over my neck and face as though it were a piece of clothing that could be removed. My vision filled with the vast deep blue of the water, of the ocean about to meet my body.

Blue like the ocean, went my memory, my mind.

Blue like me.

I remembered the ways in which I'd felt at home in the sea, as though my legs were meant more for swimming than walking, how I never felt more myself than when I was diving low and fast under the water. My instincts took over just as my body neared the end of its drop and I straightened, toes pointed, arms above my head and hugging my ears, all of my muscles perfectly tight, bracing for impact.

My feet pierced the surface.

The slap was a shock, skin and bone meeting rock.

The rest of me disappeared under the water with a great splash. I kept my muscles tight to manage the blow but the impact knocked my head backward like a punch, even as I continued downward, the ocean gripping my feet and pulling me into its darkness. Water rushed into my nose, a million tiny bubbles blurring my vision. I kept my lips shut tight, holding my breath. If I opened my mouth, this game would be over.

Finally, the downward momentum slowed.

I was able to move my hands, and I pushed them through the water. On my way toward the surface, the sharp edge of a rock slashed across my leg.

The pain was blinding.

Then came the blood.

A cloud of it billowed up around me like red smoke expanding outward until the ocean consumed it. A steady stream poured from a long gash open along my thigh. Mrs. Worthington's voice broke into my brain. *Bodies are so easily shattered.*

My lungs burned with lack of oxygen.

Soon I'd run out.

I looked around underwater, but the ocean was too dark to see anything clearly. A purple fish darted by me and then another, their shiny scales skimming across the back of my hand.

Frantically, I propelled myself upward, knees bending and kicking, leaving behind a long trail of blood. I pushed harder, swimming toward the murky light above, a light that brightened the higher I went, my lungs screaming. The sun shining through the water was my guide, my hope, and I noticed the white bottom of a boat just a little ways off. I darted as fast as I could toward its shape, hoping it was empty.

I broke the surface, gasping.

"There she is! Hurry!"

So it wasn't empty after all.

My eyes stung, my throat burned, my lungs were on fire. My muscles were rubbery and tight all at once. Before I could swim away, the boat was coming toward me, a series of figures hanging off the bow, reaching for me.

"Quickly!" one of them shouted.

Then the boat was upon me. There were arms reaching out, hands, so many hands, grabbing at my arms, my shoulders, my back, dragging me up until I was over the edge, coughing and dizzy, water streaming off me, streaming everywhere, and blood, too. I didn't know how many people were there in the boat, but one of them, a boy, pulled me close, my hair soaking his shirt through.

"How did you do that?" he asked. He sounded incredulous.

I looked up at him. I took in his eyes, his face, his tousled dark hair. I spoke, my voice so hoarse it nearly had no sound.

"I know you," I said.

And then the App, the game, the dream—whatever this was, this purgatory between worlds—it finally drained away.

PART TWO

Ten days later

14

I am born again

EVERYTHING WAS DARK and blurry and my head hurt
like someone was slamming it with download flashes. I
wanted to cry out but my mouth wouldn't make a sound,
like someone had glued my lips together. My throat burned
as though it were on fire and my arms felt like rocks, my
legs aching and throbbing. My nails were knives digging
into tender skin.

My skin.

I was here. I was real.

I'd made it.

My nails cutting into flesh and the pain it produced
was proof of this.

"Stop that. Skylar, don't pinch. You'll make yourself bleed."

What?

My jaw moved side to side and up and down, stretching my tongue. I tried to form words, but it felt as though I was made of rubber, the way everything was twisting this way and that, my throat too hot and sore to produce sound. Why did my throat hurt so much? I lifted my arms, my hands, heavy and solid and clumsy, up and up and out until they hit a wall. But it wasn't a wall in front of me. There was a triangular bump on it and coarse hair tangled together like rope on top and skin, more and more skin, someone else's skin, *not my skin* this time.

A face.

There was a flash of light.

I tried my eyes once more but all they saw were distorted images, squiggly lines and shades of gray.

"I'm glad you're waking up. You've been asleep for a long time. Your body needed to recover."

It was the same voice again, a woman's voice. Smooth and deep and rich.

She came closer. I could hear her breathing. Real ears were so sensitive, like antennae that picked up on everything whether I wanted them to or not. My heart beat quicker now, each pulse accompanying the two syllables that repeated over and over in my brain.

Mo-ther. Mo-ther?

Could it be she was already here? That we were together?

My hands went out to explore the wall that was really a face. I willed all my energy to my eyes, opening them. Little by little, things came into focus, like an infinitesimal number of pixels arranging themselves into a three-dimensional hologram. The light was dim, but I was finally able to make out the other person in the room.

First I saw the color of the woman's skin, which was dark, dark like the earth that has baked in the sun. I tried to fix the blur, tried to make the image of her nose and cheekbones and mouth become sharp, and eventually I got a clearer picture. This woman, with her dark skin and golden-colored eyes, her bone structure, strong and beautiful. She wore a smile on her face.

There was no doubt now. This woman was not my mother.

There was nothing familiar about her. Nothing at all.

"Skylar," she said to me then. "Don't worry, you're safe," she went on. "I am your Keeper." And when I didn't respond—I didn't because I couldn't speak, not yet—she added, "Welcome to the Real World."

15

Lost

I TRIED TO sit up. I couldn't. My brain swam with dizziness and my head throbbed. It wouldn't stop pounding. I focused my eyes on the outline of a chair near the bed. It was too dark to see anything else clearly in this tiny room.

The Keeper put a gentle hand on my shoulder.

Touch in the Real World was heavier, sturdier, but not in a bad way.

"Don't push yourself," she said.

My mind reached into the past, searching for information about my presence in this room, about how I got here, but the search turned up nothing, my memory a vast desert of smooth white sand. I was so tired, too, everything about me aching and sore. Was this what it was like to live in a real body? Pain with every movement? Exhaustion so consuming I could barely open my eyes or form a single comprehensible word?

What was I not remembering?

It was as though my mind had been erased, all except for a series of long, strange dreams.

A crowd, a speech, an ocean, a boat.

The Keeper adjusted the bedspread that covered me. Smoothed it out with her dark-skinned hand, folding over the edge until it made a sharp crease. "What are you thinking, Skylar? I can tell your brain is going. The words are all right there. Try to let them out. Use your mouth. Your tongue. Your breath. It will come. You can do this. You've done it before," she added.

I have?

My mind seemed disconnected from my body and all of its parts. I moved my head up and down and my jaw open and shut, trying to speak, blowing air out of my mouth. "Hvvvvvv." My lips vibrated against each other, my throat dusty with pain.

"You're almost there." The Keeper reached for a small, square towel and wiped my forehead. "In the App World you use your mind to speak, but here you use your mind in conjunction with your body. Let go. Speaking is instinctual."

The suggestion of instincts seemed to flip an invisible

switch. Sounds, syllables began to form in my mouth, my voice rough and hoarse, like I'd scraped the insides of my throat. "Hv. Hv. Hv. *Have.* Have. *How.*"

The Keeper's eyes were wide. "You can do this. What are you trying to tell me? What do you want to know?"

Energy shot through my thighs to my toes, my knees twitching and shaking, every muscle in my body throbbing.

"Do you want to get up? We make sure all the body's muscles are movement ready before Service." The Keeper hesitated. "At least we did until the border closed. Lucky for you, that was very recent."

The word *border* lodged in my brain and opened a geyser of memory. The border had closed. Service was canceled. I'd unplugged illegally. Trader, Lacy, Adam, Sylvia. *Not* Sylvia. Rescuing Rain from the Real World. That was what I'd needed to remember.

Yet.

Something was missing.

Something important.

The reservoir dried up, the geyser petering out.

"Huh, huh, *how,*" I tried again, stuttering along. I tested my lips, my tongue, my vocal cords, until eventually I got the words I wanted so badly out of my mouth and I got them right. "How long have I been dreaming?"

The Keeper's eyebrows arched. She studied me. "I don't

know," she said slowly, carefully, a strange look on her face.

"What aren't you telling me?" I asked, the words falling freely now, the sounds rolling across my tongue and dropping from my lips.

"That's enough for today," was all the Keeper replied. She moved away in the darkness. "You need your rest."

"My mother," I said, the next time the Keeper entered the room. My body still ached as though it were laced through with a permanent App Hangover—and maybe that's all this was—the effects of a lifetime of downloads suddenly stripped away. My mind kept shutting down with sleep, leaving large swaths of time painted black. I couldn't manage to make my legs work so I was left to lie there, waiting for the Keeper to return, testing my memory, poking through all the holes.

The Keeper sat down on the bed, sending creases into the blanket. "You've been through a lot."

"Help me find my family," I said. "Please."

The Keeper looked away. I tried to get her attention, but my limbs were too unsteady. But then I stretched and reached, and this time my fingers grazed the skin of the Keeper's hand and she turned back.

"I'd like to help," she said. "But it's . . . complicated."

I grabbed the Keeper's arm. My fingers curled around it tightly this time. "What's complicated?"

The Keeper hesitated, like she was trying to determine something. Then, "No one can find out that you're here," was all she said, before she got up and left the room.

"Do you know who I am? Who I *really* am? Tell me and I'll give this to you." Trader held an App away so I couldn't reach it. He watched me, his eyes vulnerable even as he tried to bribe me. There was a smile on his face, like he was only playing.

I heard my own laughter. It was so loud in my brain. "Of course. You're Trader." I stretched my arms as high as I could, nearly touching the App, but Trader held it higher. He was shaking his head.

"I know who you are," he said.

I rolled my eyes. "I'm Skylar. Now let me have the App!"

"No." Trader lowered his arm. Leaned toward me. "There is more to you than you realize, just as there is more to me. And I know the *real* you."

I stared at him, confused. "This is the real me," I said.

Out of nowhere, someone else appeared.

Rain Holt.

"I need to understand," Rain said, his mouth so close I could feel his breath. "How did you do it?"

"Don't trust him, Skylar," Trader said.

"What—" I started, but then I heard a third voice.

"Skye?"

Inara.

"You betrayed me," she shouted in my head. "I'll never forgive you. You should have trusted me. You shouldn't have lied."

I woke from the dream, gasping, my own hands clutching my throat.

I felt something at my lips, smooth and rough at once, tiny dents across its surface. The smell was tangy. I opened my eyes.

The Keeper smiled in the dim lighting. "Eat. You need your strength." She held the food to my lips.

My stomach ached with emptiness, a real physical ache that gaped in my center. My lips parted until my tongue, with a mind all its own, brushed along the object's edge. Before I could stop myself I closed my mouth and teeth around it and began to chew.

"Hmmmm."

"Strawberries," the Keeper said.

I gobbled up one, then another, my hand digging greedily into the bowl. I couldn't stop. They were unlike anything I'd ever downloaded. The sweetness, the tart bite of the seeds, the burst of juice when my teeth crushed the flesh—it was so different from what I'd eaten in the App World. A memory flashed as I swallowed another one. Mr. and Mrs. Sachs talking about pizza and peaches. How virtual food couldn't compare to the real thing. And of course, this made me remember Inara.

Her words as I was leaving.

Her words in my dream.

You betrayed me.

The Keeper was about to say something else when a loud knock came from the other room, a rich hollow banging against rough wood. She got up and walked away to answer it, taking the strawberries with her.

I sat up, alert. Listening.

There was another knock, a short, thick thud.

Someone else was here.

My skin tingled and my heart started thumping so hard I thought it must be audible. I leaned forward, my eyes locked on the narrow view I had into the next room, watching as the Keeper pulled open a heavy wooden door. The arc of sunlight revealed was blinding, and I waited for my eyes to adjust.

"You shouldn't have come," I heard the Keeper whisper.

"I had to. You saw what she did! She shouldn't even be here."

The voice was a man's voice, a young man really, or maybe a boy. The sound was familiar. The Keeper and the visitor talked back and forth, too quickly and softly for me to catch all the words.

Gripping the bed for support, I willed myself first to my hands and knees. When I felt steady enough, I put my feet on the floor, the muscles in my legs full of protest.

Bracing myself, I began to straighten up, pushing my body into the wall. Everything about me hurt.

But finally, I was standing.

A wave of dizziness passed over me, the world spinning. It felt as if I was teetering on the ledge of a great tower. Instead of fear or vertigo, there came a thrill, a palpable awareness of the air touching my skin and the rough stucco wall along my back. I swayed, one hand flat on the bed, trying to steady myself. I shifted and, hanging on to whatever I could, moved forward. Curling my fingers around the edge of the doorframe, I pulled myself into the other room.

The boy was speaking. "My father—" he began.

The talking stopped. The Keeper and the visitor froze, watching me.

"Skylar," the Keeper said uneasily. "You're up."

I didn't respond. My attention shifted to the visitor.

He was of medium height, maybe a head taller than me. He wore jeans, the threads fraying at the very bottom, and on his feet were sandals, the kind with the thong between the toes. His T-shirt was black, his hair was dark brown and messy. It fell over his brow in waves and down around his ears and the back of his neck. The color of his skin was much lighter than the Keeper's but definitely not Caucasian 4.0, which made me wonder whether anyone actually had that skin tone in the Real World. His face was caught in the glare of the light, so I couldn't quite make out its features.

Then he shifted slightly.

My heart rose into my throat. "You pulled me into a boat," I said. "You held me in your arms in a dream."

The boy brushed past the Keeper and planted himself in front of me. I reached out to him—I needed to see if he was real—and in doing so let go of the wall behind me.

"We need to talk," he said, reaching back. My fingers grazed his cheek, just as his hand landed on my arm, strong and sure.

"You're Rain Holt," I said. "The *real* Rain Holt." Before he could respond, before I could say anything else, my unsteady body went tumbling to the ground.

16

Suspicious marks

WHEN I CAME to I was in bed, my mind ablaze with surreal thoughts of being watched, being chased, and being rescued from the sea. Of Rain Holt's arms wrapped around me, my head against his chest. A spot on my scalp throbbed. Gently, I touched it with my fingers. A hard bump had formed, the kind of thing that would never happen at home, the virtual self immediately fixable with an App.

But somehow, I felt stronger, too.

I could almost picture my muscles knitting themselves back together, my limbs becoming more nimble and sure. I was getting to know my body. Learning its possibilities and limits, just like I would in a game. My head felt clearer, too.

There was something new at my bedside this morning.

A lamp.

I reached out and turned it on, prepared for the light to blind me, surprised when it didn't. The glow was soft. I pulled the sheet aside so I could get up, and saw the edge of something on my leg. An ugly splotch of purple and blue ran along the bottom of my thigh. I reached out to trace its outline.

It was tender.

Mrs. Worthington would always tell us how even at seventeen when we'd unplug for Service, the skin on our bodies would be like new because during our years on the plugs the bodies had never seen sunlight. Then she'd laugh, and explain how the moment we unplugged, our perfect skin would begin to ruin.

But then, Mrs. Worthington was an idiot.

I drew back the sheet farther. Large round marks on my calves were purple and blue and yellowing at their centers. I took in my arms, thrusting them into the light, only to find that there were plenty more spots.

Bruises, they were called. I remembered them from when I was small.

I had them everywhere.

I swung my legs around to the side of the bed, and the movement tugged the hem of my nightshirt higher. A long, dark seam stretched up the top of my thigh, cutting into the skin, its center a deep, fiery red. I pressed my thumb into it. The pain burned so intensely I gasped.

A memory nudged at me. I couldn't quite make it out.

I shook off the pain and planted my feet on the floor, bracing myself—I expected dizziness, unsteadiness, too—but I was fine. For the second time since waking up, I rose and walked out of the bedroom.

The Keeper was standing in the middle of what looked to be a large living room, folding long, white linen dresses, the kind I was wearing right now. She was piling them onto the end of a sofa that seemed from another era, the 1920s if I had to guess from what I knew from the History Apps in school. The rest of the furniture was the same ornate style. To my right was the door to the outside, the one Rain had come through, and next to it I could see into a large kitchen with a table and chairs. Doors were cut into the center of the living room walls, but they were closed. Crown molding, once elegant but now crumbling, edged along the ceiling. Hanging at the center of the room was a great, decadent crystal chandelier. Its lights were dark, some of the crystals missing from their hooks.

The Keeper looked up from her work. "You're feeling better."

I nodded. "What is this place?"

Her eyes flickered to the chandelier, then to an enormous painting on the wall so covered in grime it was impossible to make out the image on the canvas. "It's one of the old mansions built during the gilded age of New Port City."

Static rushed across my skin. I was born in New Port, a city built on an island by the sea. The sense that after all these years, I was finally home, gave me chills. "Does anyone else live here?"

"No one," she said. "It's abandoned. We're alone."

I sighed. A part of me hoped that once I got my bearings, I would discover that my mother and my sister were right here, waiting for me. That they were close by, somewhere in this city, helped soothe me a little. I walked over to the coffee table in front of the Keeper to look at a tiny bowl the color of the ocean, the only decoration she seemed to have put here herself.

She watched me with narrowed eyes. "Your steps are steady today."

I shrugged. "I guess."

The Keeper shivered. "It's just . . . ," she started. "You know what? Never mind."

I held out my arms in the pool of light left by the lamp. I wanted the Keeper to see them clearly. "Where did I get these bruises?"

She waved her hand through the air casually, like she was tossing something aside. "Probably while you were being unplugged and moved here."

I cocked my head. "Does unplugging involve being

tossed down a flight of stairs?"

"You'll heal soon enough," she said.

I studied the Keeper, who'd gone back to her folding. "I didn't ask if I'd heal." I grabbed the end of the nightshirt in the Keeper's hands so she had to stop. "Rain Holt was here. Why?"

She frowned, but didn't say anything.

I stared at her, waiting for answers. When I got tired of her quiet, I shrugged and headed to the door I'd seen him walk through.

"What are you doing, Skylar?" the Keeper barked from close behind me.

I whirled around to face her. "If you don't want to give me answers, then I'll go find Rain and ask him myself."

She shook her head. "You're not ready to see Rain. You're not ready to go outside either."

I swept a hand across my body. "Why not? Look at me. I'm totally fine!"

The Keeper sighed, long and heavy. Her face seemed to sag. "Skylar. Please."

"Am I a prisoner?" I pressed. "Are you my prison guard?"

"Of course not." She seemed surprised by this question, maybe even a little offended. "I'm here to protect you."

"I don't need protection," I said. "What I need is to see my family. What I need are answers. I want to know what my presence here has to do with the Holts."

The Keeper walked away from me and I followed after her. "Don't be foolish," she said, her voice thick with disapproval. She swiped at the clothing on the edge of the sofa, taking the stack into her arms.

"Why is that foolish?"

She studied me over the pile of folded laundry in her arms. The expression in her eyes softened. "You really don't know," she stated, surprised.

"What don't I know? Tell me," I demanded.

But the Keeper shook her head. Laundry in hand, she disappeared through one of the doors in the wall, leaving me standing there alone, trying to decipher what she could possibly have meant.

I heard a key turn in the lock.

Maybe I was a prisoner after all.

Later that evening, the Keeper made me some tea and asked me questions about life on the Apps. We sat on the couch in the living room, and I told her all that she wanted to know. If I was honest with her, maybe she'd be honest with me in return. I needed to be on her good side if I was going to get access to her keys. The more I talked about my experiences in the App World, the more she seemed unimpressed. "You don't mind the ban on virtual technology here," I finally said.

"No." She took a sip from her cup, eyeing me over the

rim. The hot liquid sent steam curling up into the air. "The existence of the App World is tragic."

I eyed her back. "The only thing that stops people from plugging in is capital."

"No," she said. "Not having enough capital saved us."

I remembered the signs people held after Jonathan Holt announced the borders closing, how so many of them said *You are saved!* Everyone talked about being saved, but from totally different things. "How did the ban save you?" I asked.

"From giving up the body so easily," she said. "Like it means nothing at all."

"Are there a lot of you who feel this way?" I was surprised by her statement. It went against everything I'd learned in school about how all Keepers in the Real World hoped to someday be plugged in. I couldn't help wondering if my mother and my sister might agree.

The Keeper shifted position until she was facing me on the sofa. "It depends on what you mean by a lot. When you plugged in, the population here was already low because of the exodus to the App World. Since then it's diminished drastically. Then a few years ago, an epidemic ripped through the Keepers and another third of our population was wiped out."

I swallowed. I knew that sickness was passed from one person to the next through the body, and how easy it was to die because of this. Living in the App World sheltered us from this sort of danger.

The Keeper dabbed her lips with a napkin. "The last epidemic was over two years ago," she went on. "Everyone is vaccinated now—you were, too, while you were on the plugs. But some Keepers are fearful another epidemic is on the horizon. You know them by the way they wear scarves to cover their faces and protect their noses and mouths from breathing in a virus." She balanced her tea on the arm of the sofa. "Between the epidemic and everyone plugging in, we Keepers had to consolidate territories and jobs. Even if a Keeper doesn't work directly with the plugs and the bodies, they're supporting some task or function that affects maintenance. Little by little, all plugged-in bodies were transported to one central geographic location so we could care for more people with fewer resources. Once the other cities were evacuated, everyone relocated to New Port City."

My throat went dry. Lacy had said something to this effect, but I hadn't known whether to trust her. "New Port is really the only city left?" It was hard to imagine this could happen in a mere decade.

The Keeper nodded. "We had to pool our skills to keep at least one urban area running with electricity and transportation and hospitals. New Port was chosen because of its facilities to accommodate both the plugged-in and unplugged populations, plus it's an efficient place to get around on foot, so we could save energy." She paused to pour more tea. Then she settled the saucer in her hand again. "We're more than Keepers of plugged-in bodies now, Skylar. We're Keepers of humanity's way of life."

I studied her, trying to comprehend all she was saying. "What about the rest of the seventeens on this side of the border? Will they become Keepers, too? And where does Rain Holt fit into all of this?"

The Keeper set her cup back onto the table, so gently it didn't make a sound. "Don't worry about him right now. Worry about yourself."

"But he wants to talk to me," I said, frustrated. "He needs to talk to me. I *heard* him say it. Why don't you just let him?"

The Keeper's hands balled into fists. "When you talk to Rain, I want you to do it on *your* terms, Skylar, not on his," she said. "When *you* are ready, not when he simply decides it's what he wants. He has to learn that the Real World is different from the App World. That everyone isn't at his beck and call." She leaned forward so we were eye to eye. "I risked my life to harbor you here because there are things in both worlds that are unfair. I want so much for you—I want so much for *all* of you—every plugged-in child who will no longer be allowed the freedom of Service, who will soon lose their body once the Cure is enacted. No matter what people tell you about who you are, and what this body means or doesn't—whether it's Rain or someone else, even your family—I want you to discover it for yourself first, because it's *yours*. It will always and forever be *yours*, Skylar. Don't you dare let anybody tell you differently, do you hear me?"

The Keeper's eyes were fierce.

She wanted me to trust her, and I felt myself yearning to. But as we looked at each other now, I also knew that when she said the next time I saw Rain it should be on my terms, what she really meant was on *her* terms, when it suited *her* schedule. When *she* decided I was ready. And her advice was good. I would go to Rain on my own terms.

Just not on hers.

So I nodded slightly. "Yes, I do hear you," I told her, feeling slightly guilty as the words slipped from my lips. Her instincts to keep me safe and hidden were nearly parental, drawn from a well of good intentions, however stifling.

But my instincts pulled me in another direction, and I wouldn't look back.

It's in looking back that we lose the game.

Over the next few days I stretched and bent and worked at my muscles, biding my time, keeping my eye out for the Keeper's keys. The more adept I was at getting around, the more I found that my body was hungry for movement. Each step warranted another. Everything I touched made my hands seek the next thing. It was both exciting and disconcerting to discover how my arms and my legs seemed to have a mind of their own.

I began to feel . . . real.

And in a way that I hadn't in a long, long time.

The Keeper seemed pleased with my progress.

For dinner, she made a big salad with bright-red tomatoes and crunchy green leaves and vegetables. Apps may have made life easier and safer on so many fronts, and even more fun, but nothing compared to real food. Each time I discovered a new texture or flavor I thought of the Sachses. And each time, thoughts of them made me feel sad.

"How much do you know about the Race for the Cure?" I asked her as we ate. "You mentioned it the other day."

The Keeper chewed her food slowly. "Enough."

"Do you know that it's . . . that it's been won?"

She nodded. Then shifted her attention back to the bowl.

I speared a wedge of tomato with my fork. "Liberation is set to begin soon." I'd called up Emory Specter's exact words. They made my stomach queasy.

The Keeper was still staring into her food. "Liberation?"

"Yes," I said. "That's how most App World citizens understand the Cure."

She put down her fork. "The process of removing the bodies will begin soon—that much is true." She snorted. "And I suppose that some App World citizens might regard it as being 'liberated' from their bodies—in a way."

I bit my lip. Focused on the curve of the water glass on the table, the way it caught the light. "What do you mean?"

The Keeper picked up her fork again. Took several more bites of her salad, the crunch of it the only sound in the room. Then she sat back in her chair. "The Keepers have split in two over control of the plugged-in bodies." She clasped her hands and placed them in her lap. "There is a large and powerful group that struck a bargain with Emory Specter, and who've promised to maintain and protect the bodies of citizens in the App World until every last person is unplugged. They call themselves the New Capitalists. The Real World has been dealing with an economic crisis for some time now, and the New Capitalists vowed to solve it, you could say."

My heart was beating faster. We were finally getting somewhere. "This is the first I've heard of any New Capitalists."

The Keeper pushed her bowl away. Like it no longer appealed to her. "Their ideas are rather"—her eyes blinked up at me, then away—"drastic. There's a group of us against them. We've started to organize." She got up to clear her dishes from the table. "Some of the seventeens that got left here have joined with us. Rain Holt is one of them," she added casually over her shoulder.

My eyebrows arched at the mention. I got up and

followed the Keeper to the sink, my bowl in hand. "I thought you didn't like him."

The Keeper dropped her silverware into the metal basin and it hit the bottom with a loud clatter. "Rain Holt is . . . necessary. He has connections that are useful. That we wouldn't have access to otherwise."

I set my bowl on the kitchen counter. The mention of connections reminded me of Lacy. I wondered where she was right now and when I would see her again. "The rich always do."

The Keeper started piling the dishes underneath the faucet and poured liquid soap over them. Then she turned on the hot water. She seemed lost in thought. I watched as soap bubbles spread across the surface of everything. I reached out and laid a hand on a large bubble that had formed over the top of a glass and it popped.

The Keeper scrubbed at the residue on a dish. Then she handed me the plate to dry. Her eyes were ringed with purple. "I know you're eager to see your family, Skylar. But I want to make sure you're ready for whatever happens. The Real World is a complicated place, far more so now than when you plugged in. There are changes that you may find difficult to accept."

I rubbed the dishrag in circles along the smooth white surface, then set the plate carefully on top of the stack of clean ones, wanting her to tell me more. "What are you trying to say?"

The Keeper handed me a glass. When I grasped it, she held on. Her fingers were wet and soapy from the water in the sink. "If I were you," she said, her eyes intense on mine, "I'd be very careful. If your family knew where you were, the outcome would not be good. You'd be in danger. Ask Rain, he'll tell you—" she started, lips parted, about to say something else, but then she closed her mouth, her sentence unfinished.

She let go of the glass.

I felt like I'd been punched. How could my mother and sister be a danger? How could I give up on my plans to see my family? I searched for the right words to respond, but they didn't come. In the silence, the Keeper turned away, dried her hands, and set the towel on the counter. Then she went into the living room. Before she disappeared, something slipped from the cuff of her sweater and settled soundlessly into the thick carpet. I saw the bright glint of silver.

A key.

When I was sure she was gone, I picked it up and tucked it away.

17

Ready or not

ADAM WAS RUNNING.

I could see him far off ahead, his bare feet slapping against the ground, sending clouds of dirt billowing up with each step. Or maybe it was sand. It was white and powdery. He wore jeans and a black T-shirt. I watched him approach a hill covered with tall grass, nearing a bend. Once he rounded it, I wouldn't be able to see him anymore, and I wanted to go to him, to shout his name and get his attention, but I couldn't move or speak. A seagull called out overhead.

Adam stopped suddenly, just before he was about to disappear. He turned back, both hands beckoning me toward him. "Come on, Skye! Hurry!"

His words sped toward me so fast I thought they might knock me over. I tried to reply, but I didn't seem to have a voice, couldn't control my body, my arms and legs held in place, refusing to move.

Adam waited, watching me. He cupped his hands around his mouth. "Don't be scared!" he shouted. "You won't go through this alone!"

Go through what? I wanted to yell. *Have you seen my mother?* I tried to call. *My sister?* Each word echoed in my heart. Then I felt a new presence. Breathing, long and slow and steady. I turned around and jumped back, startled.

The Keeper. She was standing so close, shaking her head. "I'm afraid for you, Skylar," she said. "The Real World is dangerous for a girl with your face."

"What's wrong with my face?" I asked her, this time able to speak.

"Ask your sister."

"Ask her what?"

The Keeper didn't answer. She continued shaking her head, watching me with pity, or maybe sadness. I gripped her shoulders with my hands. Leaned toward her and screamed with all my might. "Tell me what's wrong with my face! Tell me what's happened to Jude!"

My eyes flew open, my breath ragged.

I looked around.

I was in my tiny room, lying sideways across the narrow bed. I'd fallen asleep on top of the sheets.

The word *face* reverberated around me, followed by *Jude*. Maybe I'd yelled out loud in my dream. Sweat covered my skin, soaked my nightclothes and the hair at the back of my neck. I swung my legs around to the floor, the cool wood a relief against the bottoms of my feet. I leaned forward, rubbed my hands across my eyes, my cheek, my mouth, my brow. Everything felt normal, but the dream left me shaking.

I got up and traded my nightshirt for a tank top and leggings. Slipped my feet into the sandals the Keeper had given me to wear around the house. Gathered my hair into a knot to get it out of my face. Then I took the key from the place I'd hidden it under the mattress. The edges were jagged in my hand.

Bad dream or no, it was time to get out of here.

I crept into the living room and went to the door I knew led to the outside. I tried the key in the lock, hoping it would work, but it didn't fit.

I'd have to go out another way.

I went to the only other door where I thought the key might work—the one that opened on to the rest of the mansion. When I reached it, I stopped.

Everything was so silent.

The Keeper had to be asleep.

This time the key slid easily into the lock. I heard the bolt open, and pulled the key out again, tucking it into the band of my leggings. I turned the knob on the door, and it swung wide, the hinges moaning low and mournful. Somewhere in one of the rooms ahead, there had to be a way outside. The Keeper might not think I was ready to go into the Real World, but I knew that I was.

Quietly, I closed the door behind me and headed deeper into the mansion.

For the first few minutes I stumbled around in the darkness. I walked through the first room, then the second, trailing my finger along the backs of dusty chairs and couches covered in old white sheets, my eyes passing across tall gold lamps and delicate china vases. Everything was covered in grime.

Then a breath escaped me into the thick, musty air, and I halted.

I'd come upon a woman.

Dead. Headless.

Dressed for a ball.

I flipped a switch on the wall and a light came on.

The stark white glow of the woman's skin was pale—too pale, even for someone used to the standard Caucasian 4.0 of App World citizens. I went to her lifeless form, touched the smooth round top of the neck.

A mannequin.

The gown she displayed was unfinished. Pins, blackened with age, still held pieces of it together, ribbons streamed down the side, and a long measuring tape was draped across one shoulder. Yards of satin with a structured skirt that belled wide enough for someone to hide underneath it. The color was impossible to discern, the fabric faded until it was nearly gray. I reached out to touch it, but my finger poked right through the delicate material—it was so old it was nearly disintegrating. I snatched my hand back, not wanting to do any more damage. Even though this place was abandoned, it felt wrong to spoil what was here any further. These were the remnants of someone's life. A woman's life.

I turned.

Hanging along the far wall were more ball gowns, some of them big and elaborate like the one on the mannequin, and others elegant slim attire for a dinner or maybe a cocktail party. These were grayed with age, too, and sagging heavily, as though it wouldn't be long before they would give up trying to stay on their hangers.

They must have been beautiful once.

Inara would love this.

This thought crept through my mind, a painful whisper.

I tore my gaze from the dresses. Swallowed around the thick lump that formed in my throat. I was wasting time. The possibility of escape, of gulping real fresh air into my lungs, pressed in on me. There was a door at the other end of the room and I went to it, passing through without looking back, continuing on through the mansion, trying to get my bearings. I moved down a long, narrow hallway and descended a series of three steps where the floor dipped. Like the other rooms, this one was dark. There were no windows and the curtains were shut tight. Great swaths of wallpaper, once grand and colorful, had peeled away near the ceiling, hanging overhead like ragged archways. The floor creaked underfoot, the wood dull and caked with grime when once it had surely shined. At the far end of the hall there was another set of doors, tall and ornate. I wondered if they led somewhere special, into the parts of the mansion where the family who originally owned it used to live and entertain their guests a century ago.

I stopped before a different door that was cut into the wall to my left. For some reason I longed to go through it.

My heart pounded.

It was like my body, my mind—maybe both—knew something I didn't.

I opened it, the hinges creaking through the silence, and flipped another switch on the wall. Everything was bathed in the soft light of a chandelier hanging from the center of the ceiling. Like the other rooms, this one was packed full of furniture covered in cloths to protect it, everything dusty and grayed, but there was one new thing that drew my attention. A tall mirror was propped against the far wall. Its frame, once gilded, was blackened with age, some of the carvings along its edge broken, flowers missing petals, or half a leaf. My mind caught on what the

Keeper had said in the dream about my face.

I went to the mirror and stood before it, the surface smooth and silvery like water, like someone had recently cleaned it.

I stared and stared.

There was a familiarity in the wide mouth I saw there, the small nose, the curve of the jaw. The cheeks had a rosy flush and the lips were full, the skin smooth, the same golden tone people had after they downloaded the Caribbean Vacation App. It was the eyes that told me the truth, however. I zeroed in on their blue color, like the sky in my name. Almond shaped. I would always recognize those eyes. I ran a finger down my cheek and the girl in the mirror did too.

"That's me," I whispered, watching how the words happened on my lips.

I hadn't seen my real face since I plugged in. Until the dream last night I hadn't really wondered what I looked like, whether the appearance of my body would be that much different from the virtual self I was used to at home.

It was.

Similar enough that I recognized myself, but different all the same.

It's strange how the real body can make a person seem . . . changed.

There was nothing wrong with my face. Nothing extraordinary about it either. It was just a face, like any other. I was just a girl, like any other. And the dream was just that: a dream. A strange one, but still a dream.

Quickly, so quickly it passed through me like the faintest of breaths, I wondered how anyone would want to disown the body, be liberated from it. But to be released from the burden of the body was the mark of total transcendence at home. What I used to believe everyone in the Real World aspired to as well.

I turned around and walked back into the hallway. This time I went through the ornate set of doors I'd noticed before, wanting to see where they led.

Soon I was in a ballroom. Whoever used to live here must have once worn those elaborate gowns in here, while people drank and ate and gossiped and fell in love until the wee hours of the morning. The opulence of this place was stunning. Filigreed moldings, once painted gold but now tarnished and falling apart, lined the walls and fixtures. The air smelled vaguely sharp and sweet, like the remnants of spilled perfume. The scent seemed fitting, since I was sure elegant, perfumed ladies once twirled across this floor, leaving trails of jasmine and lilac in their wake as they danced. A great chandelier had crashed in the center of the room, a mountain of glass rising up from the floor. The heap of crystal was taller than me, its round metal top bent inward, five thick broken chains dangling from it helplessly. The ceiling was far away, maybe three stories up. Painted across it were frescoes of angels cavorting with women and men. Hands, feet, the tail of a cloak or the tip of a wing had peeled away.

I thought of Inara again.

If she were here, she'd wish for an App that would let her fly up and examine the scenery above, studying the angels, just as she would have wanted to try on each and every dress I'd seen in the other room. The lump that had earlier formed in my throat seemed to lodge in my center, squeezing against my heart.

I missed her.

But now she hated me.

Other thoughts jostled for attention. My mother, my sister, my reasons for being in the Real World. A pale glow seeped across the floor to my right, spilling from the edges of four tall brocade curtains that cloaked the enormous windows. The sun. It must be rising. To my left, I could see the outline of a series of boarded-up glass doors. Tiny triangles of soft white light spilled through their gaps, sending dusty rays across the room.

The outside.

Finally.

I rushed to the doors like someone was chasing me, pulling and pulling at one of the wide wood panels with my hands, trying to rip it free. A long, sharp splinter broke from the edge, stabbing deep into the side of my finger. I yelped, jumping back. My breaths came in ragged gasps as I stared at the wooden needle piercing that tender flesh, watching as blood bubbled up around it and turned it black.

I closed my eyes and yanked at the splinter.

"*Yuhhhhh,*" I screamed, the pain of it thick and throbbing. I pulled the splinter out and tossed it onto the floor. I went into the next room and grabbed a sheet from one of the chairs. It dragged behind me as I returned to the boarded-up door. Using my teeth, I tore two strips from it, wrapped them around my hands to protect my skin, the blood from my finger dotting the fabric.

No matter what I did, the door wouldn't budge.

I went to retrieve a long iron poker I'd seen a few rooms back, lying next to a stone fireplace that took up an entire wall. The metal was heavy and cold as I carried it. I wedged it between the board and the outside door, pulling on the end. The nails groaned and squealed against the force. Then there came a great crack. All but the very edge of the wood broke away.

The door was comprised of a series of small rectangular glass windows, blackened with layers of dirt. One of the panels at the bottom was broken. I crouched down on my hands and knees, bending my head low.

Air.

It tickled my skin, a million tiny hairs on end all across my arms. I closed my eyes, letting it rush across my cheek, the wind winding gently through my hair. I inhaled, long and deep. The tangy smell of salt, of seaweed, hit hard.

The ocean?

I opened my eyes and took another breath.

Yes. It had to be. I knew that smell, knew it from the Apps and from my dreams, from the time I was small and my mother and sister and I spent our days by the sea. The smell was like its own strange memory, one without words but still powerful. All this time with the Keeper, I'd been next to the ocean, this place I so longed for in my heart that it seemed to sing to me in my dreams. I peered through the opening in the glass, wanting evidence of the sand and the waves, but from this crouched position, it was difficult to see much. There was grass, though. I saw the beginnings of what looked to be a lawn, wild and unkempt and moving in the breeze. It led up to a series of steps and some sort of white marble esplanade that extended all the way to the door. Vines grew across it in places, cracking through its surface. I held my breath and tried to listen, hoping to hear the waves, but there was nothing. Just the *shhhh* of wind across the grass.

I got up, brushing the dirt from my hands and knees. Once I passed through this door I would be in the world. I would be able to search for my family, to find Adam and even Lacy if I needed to, and Rain—I would find him first, so I could make him tell me what the Keeper wouldn't. Everything I wanted awaited me just a few steps away. I closed my eyes. Gripped the knob.

But then I thought about the cuts and bruises I'd gotten

when I unplugged, the intense dream I'd had before waking up here. A crowd. A cliff. A dive. A boat. The long splinter I'd removed from my hand caught my eye, and I thought of the dagger I'd plunged into the heart of that guard. And the blood, all that blood that spilled from his body.

Then Rain. Rain Holt pulling me from the sea.

Pulling me toward him.

I took a deep breath. It had all seemed so real. Too real to be a dream.

I tried the door. There was a crack, and I could hear the wood shift, feel it break free. I pushed my whole body against it with all the force I could manage. It opened, and a pale glow fell across my face. Before I could decide otherwise, I slid my body through the narrow space.

18

The real world outside

AT FIRST I was blinded.

The early-morning sun was a fiery round circle edging up along the horizon. My head swam like someone had spun me around, enormous bright spots dancing across my vision. I blinked and blinked, shocked by the brilliance of real sunlight. After a while, the stinging in my eyes lessened and shapes began to form, outlines of objects like silhouettes against a wall. A tree, tall and gnarled and thick, its branches heavy with green and stretching like long black fingers across the sky, and another with pointy oval leaves that fell like tears all the way to the ground.

I put my hand over my chest, trying to quiet my heart.

Felt the smooth marble underneath my feet, saw the outline of the vines growing across the esplanade and the start of the grass. Heard the *shhhhhhh* of the wind across it. The air was cool against my damp clothing, and it brought that tangy smell of salt from the sea. The ocean was close, but I couldn't see it. My heart pounded harder. The presence of so much reality made it race. The App World sky was beautiful, but knowing it was only virtual, that ultimately it was a projection, diminished the awe I'd had for it.

There came a singing, high and rhythmic. Insistent.

I closed my eyes and listened. Let it fill my ears until it was all I knew. The sound of it seemed to rise, grow bigger, as though it was aware someone had just tuned in. A sense of peace, of hope was carried atop its music as I realized its source.

Crickets.

They sang their last high notes as the night receded completely.

I remembered them from when I was small, how fascinated I was with every little thing that crawled across the earth. My sister had come upon me once, crouched in the grass one early morning like this one, staring at this strange, spindle-legged creature whose song I'd followed until I encountered its ugly brown-black body. She got down next to me, and before I could cry for her to stop, she reached for it—I thought to crush it—but all she did was capture it in her palm so I could get a better look. We watched it, studied its wings, its waving antennae, the way it rubbed its legs together, until it lost patience with us and hopped right from her hand, disappearing back into the grass.

My throat tightened. The crickets seemed to want to remind me of my family, to celebrate the reunion Jude and I would have once I left this place and found her, to tell her and my mother that yes, I was really here. That I'd come for them. I was back, as real as ever, and I'd never forgotten them, just as I'd promised.

The singing stopped abruptly.

The sun inched higher. The Keeper would be up soon. If I was to leave, I'd have to do it now, before she discovered that I was gone and I'd taken her key. I was about to start off when I remembered what the Keeper said about the epidemic that had swept through the Real World, how some Keepers would hide their faces, worried about breathing in some new virus that might overtake the city. I hurried back through the mansion's rooms until I reached the one with the gowns and dresses. I found a pale scarf that would cover my hair and face, and a loose long-sleeved tunic of sorts that reached all the way down to my knees, covering my body. I wrapped the scarf around my head and, just as quickly, went outside again. It wasn't disease, but the strange dreams that haunted me, especially the most recent one, a warning about my face.

It made me think better of simply stepping out into the Real World unprotected.

I walked a few paces, my eyes squinting in the glare of the rising sun, then turned around to take in the house. No, it really was a mansion. It was five stories tall but each level had such high ceilings that it seemed more like ten. Every room had a balcony, with columns reaching between floors, a hundred toothpicks propping up an elaborate house of cards. The French doors and windows were covered with boards, plants and vines overtaking parts of the facade, some of them blooming with tiny white flowers. Solar panels were spaced out across the roof, but only a few were still clean enough to capture the sun and give off any power. Tall, thin windmills reached above the trees. To the left of the mansion were the remnants of a garden, wild and overgrown, great pink and red roses thick and full, their thorns choking away everything else. The marble of the esplanade shone a bright white in the sun. Along the edge of the wide lawn there was a long wrought-iron fence. Beyond it was a sight that made my heart skip.

The ocean.

Dark blue and sparkling in the light. It really was close. I thought of diving in, of swimming in its current and submerging myself in its waters, but it seemed to rear up from below, too far and too dangerous to access from here. The mansion must be built on a cliff. The sky behind everything was bright and clear and blue as a robin's egg.

My blue sky, sang my mother's voice in my head.

The Keeper was wrong about my family, that they could be a danger to me. It was simply impossible.

I would find them and prove this was true.

A gentle breeze rustled the leaves on the trees and rippled across my shirt. I pulled the scarf away from my face for a moment and breathed in, the smell green and sweet, grass and flowers mingling with the dirt.

Summer.

A strange, potent feeling welled inside me. It filled my heart, expanding my lungs and lifting my spirit. There was an ecstasy in the fresh air and real sunlight on my skin, and a peace, too. A pang of sadness drifted through me. I wished Inara were here, experiencing this with me. Longing filled me like water rising to the top of a bottle, longing to see my family again, longing to finally be in a place where I belonged, longing to have my mother and sister assuage my fears that I'd been forgotten or even abandoned. It took up every part of my insides and threatened to spill over.

I started across the lawn. The mansion's immense structure shielded me from whatever lay on its other side. There was a long winding path along the cliff that continued beyond the trees, and I followed it. For some reason, my feet pulled me away from where I sensed the city to be, as though they had a plan of their own, much like how they'd drawn me into the room with the mirror. It was like my body had its own internal GPS. I wandered through grass as high as my knees, the ocean to my left. I passed another boarded-up mansion. It was only one story, but that single story was tall and majestic, with marble columns and great archways sprawling outward on either side, a grand path lined with overgrown bushes winding its way to the entrance. More mansions followed, all of them perched far above the ocean, tempted by the beauty of the water, drawn close by the sight of the sea. Windmills dotted their lawns, slowly turning in the breeze, and solar panels like the ones I'd seen at the Keeper's occasionally caught the glare of the sun as I passed. The path dipped lower. To my right was a wall of jagged stone and to my left, all ocean, the white foam of waves crashing into an ever-shifting outline along the island. The sun was higher in the sky now, bearing down on my bare arms and shoulders. Skin burned, this I knew from Mrs. Worthington's class, but somehow I'd imagined it bubbling over like boiling water, and all I felt right now was the slight sting of heat. There came the sudden crush of gravel behind me and I spun, searching for its source.

But there was nothing.

Only the sight of tiny rocks falling away from the edge of the cliff, loosed by the wind. My hand went to the scarf draped across my mouth and nose, pulling it tighter, my breath hot against the fabric. I looked around, behind me, ahead of me. I didn't see a single soul or other sign of human life. I seemed to be the only person alive and out in all the Real World.

The path was so deserted I half expected an army of zombies to come at me from farther down the cliff, like in that Wandering Dead App I was obsessed with when I was a fourteen. Finally, after rounding another bend, I saw someone. A man was walking far ahead, his attention on the ocean. For a while I followed behind him, wondering if he'd turn around and see me. But he never did—he was too far away—and eventually he disappeared up a path that led away from the ocean toward the trees.

A few minutes later I saw a second person. This time it was a woman, dressed in the same white attire the Keeper usually wore. She was headed toward me, which meant that soon we would be face-to-face. She was out walking her dog.

I put my hand to my mouth and laughed. A real dog! Not one that was downloaded. It was big and tall, maybe tall enough to reach the middle of my thighs, with thick, black, curly fur. His eyes darted everywhere, like he couldn't settle on what was most interesting, and his tongue lolled out of the side of his mouth. More than anything, I wanted to place my hands on his head and touch that fur. I couldn't stop staring at him.

I couldn't even remember one from when I was small. The woman was a few paces away, and I found I couldn't move. She brushed by me on the path without even a glance. The most attention I received was from the big black dog, who pulled toward me on his leash, his nose trying for a sniff.

My lungs let out a big whoosh of air.

I started to laugh again, great and big and uncontrollable. What would the Keeper say if I returned to the house as though it wasn't a big deal that I'd snuck out and said, "I hope you don't mind but I've brought home a new friend," and introduced a big curly-haired dog into our rooms? If it were a girl dog, maybe I would call her *Lacy*. I liked the idea of a loving, slobbery animal with that name.

Thoughts of the Keeper silenced my laughter. I wondered if she was up yet, if she'd realized I was gone. I pressed my hand to my waist, feeling the outline of the key.

I started on my way with more confidence now. The Keeper had been so worried I'd be unsafe out here, but she was wrong. Nobody cared who I was. Nobody even bothered to turn and look at me. I let the scarf slide away from my face and hang across my shoulders. Soon the path bent right and rose until it was level with the top of the cliff again.

Then I stopped, stunned by what I saw.

Far off in the distance were the outlines of New Port City, its buildings rising up beyond a line of trees. The skyline was familiar yet foreign, in the same way that seeing myself in the mirror for the first time had been strange, yet I still recognized myself. Great towers were clustered at the center of the island, as though the ocean had birthed them from below the earth, waves pushing up all that stone and smoothing it across glass. Huge steel and rock structures stretched like needles toward the clouds.

My eyes landed on a skyscraper that was truly familiar.

The Water Tower.

It was dead center, poking up amid the other buildings, the tallest one among them. The sunlight seemed to ripple into bright-blue waves as it hit the side. I was tempted to head straight toward it, across the grass and through the wall of trees until I spilled out into the city.

But my body, my mind, my feet were pulling me elsewhere.

Soon a peninsula took shape up ahead. The narrow strip of land was striking, not only for the way the ocean walled it in, nearly cutting it off from the mainland, but because of the way it jutted into the sea like an arrow let loose from a bow. There was something familiar about it. The wind picked up, whipping across me. I had to hold the scarf in place with my hand. There were no mansions now, no houses either, just wide flat rock that bled into the grass stretching out behind it, a mile of rugged, nearly barren earth that ended with a drop into the sea.

The path dipped again. Up ahead I saw a rough staircase cut into the rock at the edge of the island. My heart rose in my chest until it lodged in my throat. To my left, cutting into the wild, churning ocean below, was a series of enormous sharp rocks that rose from the water. Stepping stones made for giants that ended at the sea. I closed my eyes tight, then opened them once more, as though they might disappear. My breaths were quick and painful as I neared the staircase and started to climb. There was no railing to hold on to, and should I trip or slip, I'd go tumbling into the sea. I barely cared.

I took the last tall step, hoisting myself onto the edge of the cliff.

There it was.

Somehow I'd already known what I was about to encounter, but to see it here made me dizzy, made my stomach churn like the raging water below. I moved forward a few paces so if I fell down it wouldn't be to my death.

In front of me I saw several striking things.

A dais.

A podium.

A wall of glass.

All of it, abandoned. A fight had broken out here. Tufts of grass had been trampled and pulled away. A metal pillar at the end of the wall was lying on the ground, and another was bent at the middle, as though some inhumanly strong person had kicked it. Several long cracks marred the glass. I went to the dais, began wedging my toes into narrow spaces between the rocks, some other force guiding my body, giving it the capacity to climb stone as easily as to walk flat earth. When I reached the top, I lay down, flat on my back, looking up toward the sky, that big blue sky.

I closed my eyes.

Words came to me. Broken and senseless. But I could hear them like someone was speaking them right here, right now.

The New Capitalists.

Win.

Freedom.

App World tyranny.

Crisis.

Come and see.

Come and see . . . what?

Me?

I opened my eyes and turned my head until I was facing that glass wall. A crowd, dressed all in blue, flashed before me.

This was why my body had urged me here, my mind, my feet.

To see this place in person.

To convince me that the dream wasn't a dream at all.

The crowd, the speech, the ocean, the boat. A cliff, an escape, a dive. Nearly drowning. A boy pulling me up from the sea.

Rain Holt pulling me up from the sea.

All those bruises when I'd woken up. That gash in my leg that was becoming a long fine scar along my thigh. None of it was from moving me after I'd unplugged like the Keeper tried to make me believe. It was from when I'd jumped from this dais and leapt off a cliff into the ocean below. Why had I needed to escape? Why had everyone been watching me? Had I been on trial for something I'd done? Was it possible to commit a crime while plugged in?

I sat up on the dais.

Studied it.

There was the place in the rock where I'd loosed the knife. I'd plunged that stone dagger into a guard, a person, a flesh-and-blood body with the capacity to be hurt, to shatter, to be wounded beyond repair. To be struck dead.

I stared at my hands. They were so small. Lines cut across my palms and the tender sides of my fingers, some of them so tiny they were nearly imperceptible, others deep and wide like gullies in my skin. Horror spread through me. In what I'd thought was a game, a dream, had I become a murderer? I swallowed back something acidic. Maybe I *was* a criminal. Maybe that was why the Keeper said I was unsafe, why she came to me in my dream to warn me about my face, because people in the Real World knew it, because I was a wanted girl. Maybe that was why Jonathan Holt appeared to me in Odyssey, because he knew I was a threat to others. Maybe my mother and my sister wouldn't want to see me because they were ashamed of who I was and of what I was capable of doing. Maybe they'd been there that day. Maybe this was what the Keeper meant when she said I should rethink finding my family. Maybe they'd turn me in to the authorities because they'd seen what I was capable of with their own eyes.

I climbed down from the dais and started to run.

I barely remember seeing anything at all as I flew from the peninsula toward the city, barefoot, sandals gripped in my right hand, tunic rippling and rising to the tops of my thighs as my legs pumped, one in front of the other. That stark, rough arrow of land at the point of the island couldn't recede fast enough. The trees that walled the city were ahead of me one moment, then behind me the next. I didn't even notice passing through them, or crossing the first wide empty boulevard that circled the city's outskirts, my body overtaken by something else, maybe instinct, capable of flight when it was required.

Something strange was happening inside of me.

My brain guided my feet, just like Lacy's App had guided my virtual self through Loner Town. But to where? To my mother and sister? It was like that GPS was still working, like somehow it hadn't dissipated once the download was over and had traveled with me as I crossed from one world to the other. Had Lacy tampered with our brains to make this happen? Was it happening with Adam too?

I slowed my pace, panting. Slipped my sandals back onto my feet.

Had someone been experimenting on me?

Could the plugs have . . . changed me? That night at Appless Bar, Lacy had spoken of rumors that being plugged in was altering our brains and our relationships to our bodies.

Could she have been right?

I stopped next to a tiny, narrow house that once must have gleamed a bright shiny green, but now the paint was nearly chipped away. My lungs burned like someone had tossed a lit match inside them, my breaths heaving as I gulped the warm air. I started along the sidewalk, my eyes on the Water Tower, which touched the blue of the sky. I gave my entire body over to whatever was happening in my mind, let my brain guide my feet and my direction. The moment I'd set eyes on that dais a hole had burned through my center, hollowing everything out.

Grass grew up through the cracks in the concrete, the bottoms of my sandals thwacking the pavement. There were potholes in the street the size of craters and I side-stepped them to avoid tripping. Eventually the wooden houses gave way to taller and taller structures. The closer I got to the city center, the more it seemed to wake from the slumber of its outskirts, the windows of the buildings clean and gleaming as opposed to grimy and boarded up, the flowers and greenery pruned and thriving as opposed to wild and overgrown. Solar panels flashed as they drank in the light and windmills rose up everywhere like dandelions in a vast city field. The stormy, briny smell of the ocean permeated the streets, the breeze thick with it. Soon I began to see people. At first it was just a couple here and there like on the cliff. A man way ahead crossing the street. Two women holding hands, heading into a small park thick with trees. But then I turned a corner and suddenly there were people everywhere. Behind me. In front of me. To my left and my right. Not a single one had a face or body altered by an App. There were no supermodels walking down the street or kids caught mid-download as they turned into dragons. People actually looked one another in the eyes as they passed. They paid attention to each other, nodding their heads, some of them saying hello.

My hand automatically reached for the scarf, pulling it up over my hair and across my face.

I searched the crowd for anyone I might recognize, for one of the seventeens who got left on this side of the border, but so far there was nothing. A number of women wore scarves around their heads and pulled up over their faces, the men with wide masks across their noses and mouths. Most everyone I saw wore the same uniform as my Keeper, but there were also women in long, sleeveless dresses smiling up at the sun, and men in short-sleeved T-shirts and loose pants, the exposed parts of their skin a golden tan. Children ran around in shorts and shouted to one another. Everyone, regardless of their attire, wore the same thong sandals, as though these were the only shoes left in this world.

All that talk of division among the Keepers, of war, yet these people seemed happy.

The city was at peace. Idyllic even.

Not a single car rumbled down the street or honked its horn. Everyone was walking. I was taking this in when someone bumped into me so hard I nearly fell down. My heart raced, my pulse signaling danger.

An old man reached out his arm to steady me. He had wild gray hair and a long gray beard. "Excuse me," he said.

I jerked away from him, heart still pounding. "It's okay," I managed, my words muffled by the fabric across my mouth. He cocked his head. Deep lines were etched into his face, around his eyes and across his forehead. I relaxed a little, wishing I hadn't been so rude.

"You seem lost," he said.

I shook my head. "I'm headed to the library," I said, startling myself as these unplanned words leapt from my mouth. Once they were out, I knew they were true. That was where my feet had been taking me. I wondered what I'd find there.

"You're not far." The man turned and pointed. "Four blocks that way, then it will be on your left. You can't miss it. There's a park behind it. Sea serpents guard the front. Not real ones, though. Don't worry." I think he smiled underneath that thick gray beard.

"Thank you," I said.

"Have a good day." He bowed his head a bit and seemed about to move on, but then he placed a hand on my upper arm, his fingers curling around it, and looked at me again, really looked. Peered into my eyes. "Do I know you from somewhere?"

For a second, I froze. Then quickly I said, "No," jerking out of his grip and hurrying away, crossing the street into the shade. I glanced back and saw him standing there, watching me make my way down the block. The heads of others turned as I rushed by. I reached the next corner, my lungs working hard. My body was sweating underneath my clothing and I didn't like the stickiness covering my body. I raced down three more blocks and stopped.

Next to me was a park full of parents and children playing.

"You're it!" shouted a little girl before she ran from the others and hid behind one of the tall leafy trees that lined the perimeter, its branches bending and reaching toward the sky. Keepers sat in pairs on stone benches, some of them with their arms around each other. A couple of girls, maybe not much older than me, were in bathing suits, lying out on towels in the sun. Mrs. Worthington would faint if she saw the risks they took with their skin. A few people with their heads covered scolded them as they walked by.

Beyond the park was the library. It spanned the length of a block, and was much shorter than the buildings around it, but it seemed more immense somehow, and certainly far more beautiful. It was constructed of white marble, and laced along its walls were huge arching windows. The sun gleamed bright against the glass. I made my way to it, up the long block and around the corner toward the front. I saw the two sea serpents guarding it, just like the man had said. The sea dragons roared up over the crests of marble waves, their claws curling out above the water, their backs and the tops of their heads a line of razor-sharp scales. Their teeth were bared. They were at once magical and fearsome, as though to remind everyone that what lay within these walls was the stuff of myth. Immense winding trees grew on either side of the dragons and a wide staircase led up to an entrance marked by columns.

Just like in the crowded park, people sat on the steps out front, eating and enjoying the sun. A few boys played around one of the sea dragons. I could hear the way they roared, trying to mimic the animal's sound. People passed in and out of the library's doors, many of them clutching thick bound volumes of paper in their hands or under their arms.

Books. The old kind.

I'd never seen one before—not a real one. Not even as a child.

By the time I was born, books had become obsolete. With the invention of the plugs, stories and knowledge were downloaded instantly to the brain via the Apps. It hadn't occurred to me that real books might still exist. Maybe with the technology ban in the Real World, the Keepers had no other choice but to resort to the old ways of learning.

I pulled the tunic away from my body and shook it, trying to create a breeze over my sweaty skin. Then I started up the steps one at a time. They were smooth and slippery under my feet. At one point I crouched down to slide my hand along the surface, which felt like hardened liquid under my palm. A huge bug crawled out of one of the cracks in the stairs, all legs and wavy antennae, and my hand retracted.

"It's just a beetle," said a woman sitting to my right, eating her lunch. She laughed. "It won't hurt you."

"I know." But I couldn't stop staring at it. This morning the song of the crickets and now this. We didn't have bugs in the App World. They were considered an unnecessary nuisance and one of the many things we'd overcome by plugging in. I tore my eyes from it, glancing at the woman, nervous she was studying me like the old man had, but she'd gone back to eating her sandwich. I continued the rest of the way up the steps, and took a moment to lean against one of the pillars, suddenly overwhelmed. It was one thing to wander the mansion, and another to walk around all of New Port City.

A murmur rippled across everyone around me.

I looked up, searching for the source of the disturbance.

A group of women and men dressed in blue uniforms and heavy-soled black boots were walking down the street in front of the library, their footsteps loud against the concrete. Guards. I remembered them from the peninsula, the color of their clothing a blue I normally adored.

They were stopping people randomly. Talking to them. Staring at them.

I swallowed hard. It was one of them that I might have killed. I watched now as a male guard halted a woman dressed like me, with a scarf around her head and across her face. She shook her head. She obviously didn't want to do whatever they'd asked. The man in the guard's uniform placed his hand on something at his waist.

A gun.

The murmurs around me grew more pronounced.

The woman reached for the end of her scarf, unraveling it from her face. It fell away, gently floating to the ground. The guard studied her. Got close to her face, then stepped away, the heel of his black boot grinding the scarf into the concrete. Another guard, also with a gun at her hip, came over to consult. They both stared at the woman as though she were an object they might like to buy, or a display item in a museum.

The woman began to cry.

Finally, the guards shook their heads and moved on.

The crowd on the steps seemed to hold their breath until the group of men and women in blue disappeared down the street. Then they let out great sighs of relief. A man went to the crying woman and picked up her scarf from the ground. He brushed it against his pants, trying to clean off the dirt. The woman, still weeping, turned in my direction. It was then that I could better take in her age, her face, her overall appearance. She was younger than I'd imagined. Long black hair, golden skin. She wiped her eyes with her hands. Even from the place I stood I could see that they were a bright, piercing blue.

The blood in my veins turned to ice.

My stomach, my heart, my insides seemed to fall through my body to the ground.

The girl, she looked like me.

19

A rare exhibition

AROUND ME, PEOPLE returned to their lunches and chatted once more with their neighbors. The stream of Keepers heading in and out of the library started up again. My heart began to slow. The resemblance I shared with the girl in the street was probably a coincidence. We had the same features, but aside from that, we looked nothing alike.

I joined the crowd heading inside the building. Got behind a man holding the hand of a small child. He opened the door for his son. Then he looked at me. "Go ahead."

"Thanks." I was nervous, but he turned away quickly and I walked on through.

The library was bustling. People walked about with purpose, traveling up and down the staircase to my left. The sound of paper rustling was everywhere. Long rectangular tables stretched across the room in lines, reading lamps spaced along the surface. Keepers sat before them, books open, noses buried. One of them kept running her finger from left to right, left to right across the page.

The windows edging the top of the building invited the sun through the glass in beautiful, thick rays. The ceiling was so high I could picture birds in flight, zooming across and tucking themselves into the rafters. There were paintings, too, like in the ballroom of the mansion, frescoes with scholars wrapped in colorful robes splashed across the walls. While above me was an open, airy world of beauty and light, down below past the crowded tables was a jumbled maze of towering shelves, metal ladders attached for climbing. Someone teetered atop the highest rung of one of them, reaching for a book. She grabbed it and remained at that same height reading it, as though she did this all the time, as though she knew no fear of falling.

A woman in gray came up to me. Her skin was as dark as my Keeper's, her hair pulled back from her face. She was smiling. "Can I help you find something?"

"I'm just looking," I said from behind my scarf.

"Well, I'm here if you need anything," she said, and

turned to answer someone else who'd come up to her with a question.

I headed toward the maze of shelves, waiting for my internal GPS to kick in. Maybe it had stopped working. I didn't feel pulled in any direction, really. Well, that's not true. I felt pulled in *every* direction. Toward all the books. They covered every surface, overflowing, like someone had tried to store all the texts of the Real World in this one place. They were lined up neatly side by side and shoved haphazardly into wobbling stacks, wedged into every available nook. Some had toppled to the ground in places, creating hills that dotted the walkways. There were even piles on the floor. So many stories and so many words, each one individually set out in lines on pages to be digested one by one.

It seemed so odd. Such a slow way of learning.

Apps sped life up, changing things constantly, updating and altering people and objects so they were no longer recognizable. Icons whizzed by your ears and eyes and bumped up against you, but here everything just waited there, solid and patient, for you to notice it.

I sat down on the floor, the smooth stone underneath me, stretched out my legs, and rested my back against a tightly packed shelf. I plucked the first book from the top of a nearby pile and weighed it in my hands. It was heavy, the cover hard enough that I could knock on it like it was made of wood. Then I remembered it *was* made of wood.

Across the spine, the words *The Subtle Knife* were stamped in gold.

I opened it.

There were so many pages packed together. I couldn't imagine having to read them all, one by one. I ran my hand across the paper. It was creamy and soft, not at all like the sharp edges of an information download hitting the brain. I flipped forward and there they were, more words, hundreds of them strung together in line after line. I pulled the scarf from my face and began to read aloud. "'And Lyra realized with a jolt of sickness what was happening: the man was being attacked by Specters.'" I started at the name. *Specter.* Brought the book closer. Read on as this demon-like creature sucked the soul out of a man until he was lifeless, though not dead. Cut the spark right out of his eyes.

Maybe that was how Emory Specter got his name.

A man who severed us from our bodies until all the spark from our minds had gone out, as though the soul was always a virtual thing that didn't need the body, that could be projected elsewhere and still thrive.

"Excuse me," said a voice from above.

Two feet were planted on the floor next to me. Black, thick-soled boots. The book in my hands fell to the ground with a thump. I looked up. My instincts had been right.

My mind and my body did know how to find things, find people, even when I wasn't trying, even when it was my family I wanted instead.

Rain Holt was standing there, staring down at me.

Nearly all my memories of Rain from the App World were of him hanging out with people like Lacy Mills or Lila Dellman, living his ridiculous, rich-boy life. But I did have one other one—a single experience that was different from the rest. It nagged at me now.

I'd been gaming at the time. I'd downloaded the Mount Everest App, partly because it required so little capital and partly because I loved climbing. Originally, it was supposed to be this wildly popular Adventure App, but it ended up a spectacular failure. Reaching the summit took perseverance and a willingness to be alone with your thoughts. Getting to the top might offer a thrill, but the getting there made people give up. Plus, it was snowy and dark a lot. That's why the App was so cheap.

One time I was picking my way through the snow and ice on the side of the mountain, careful to manage my breathing, when I saw that I wasn't alone.

There was a boy up ahead.

I was surprised to see someone. In an attempt to fix the existential-angst problem of the App, the designers made it so you could scale the mountain with other people.

You'd see whoever else was playing at the same time as you. Even this update wasn't enough to save the game, and I almost never saw anyone else when I was in it.

He was all bundled up, sitting on the very tip of this ice ledge that stuck out from the mountain, his legs dangling over an abyss so vast and deep that if he slipped—even though it was just an App—the drop alone would definitely rattle his code for a good long while. I was afraid to startle him, so I stayed put. I figured I'd wait until he came down from the ledge before heading past. I didn't mind. The sky was a bright, cold blue, and the sun reflected off the snow and ice in such a way that all the nearby mountains were shining. After a while, I began to wonder if the boy was thinking of jumping. Suicide was impossible in the App World, but there were approximations of it, and word got around when people tried. But eventually, the boy got up and moved away from the edge of the ice, and finally, off the ledge altogether.

He stopped when he saw me there.

We nodded at each other as he passed, and that's when I realized two things.

The boy was Rain Holt—there was no doubt about it. I'd recognize him anywhere, even buried under all that gear. To meet up with him in a game like this was startling enough, but it was the second thing that surprised me even more.

His eyes were wet with tears.

Then he went on his way and I went mine.

Rain paled as he took me in, sitting there on the floor. His face flickered with recognition.

My memories of him warred with one another. The Rain I knew best—that all of us knew best—was the playboy prince. But I couldn't shake that other boy I'd seen on the mountain. Technically, it was only one tiny instance against the backdrop of so many other things. Yet there was something that made it significant at this very moment, here in the library. Maybe it explained more about Rain than all the other memories combined. I'd never told Inara about meeting him in the game, partly because I knew she'd roll her eyes and say the opportunity was wasted on me, that she should be so lucky as to meet Rain alone like that. But even telling my best friend seemed wrong. I had no allegiance to Rain, but I could tell when I'd witnessed something private.

Rain's eyes darted everywhere before he crouched down next to me. "What are you doing here?" he hissed in a tone that said it was Rain the Crown Prince in front of me.

I felt a flicker of disappointment. "How about we start with introductions? I'm Skylar Cruz," I said overly politely. "And you're Rain Holt."

There was a stack of books in Rain's arms and he set

them aside. I saw how Rain's eyes were big and green, with brown flecks, like the grass and the earth.

"You shouldn't even be in this world," he said.

I jerked backward, stung. The pads of my fingers pressed hard into the cold floor, as though I could push through it. "I'm here in this world because of you," I told him. "I'm supposed to convince you to go back to the App World," I added, nearly choking on this absurd string of words.

Rain started, seemed repulsed by my mention of home. He turned away, staring down the length of the aisle. "Lacy doesn't get to decide my future."

I blinked at him. "You know about Lacy?"

Rain shifted, his eyes sweeping all around us. "Your Keeper is crazy to let you out," he answered, avoiding my question.

I lifted my chin. "My Keeper doesn't know where I am."

Rain's brow furrowed. His lips parted slightly. He shifted closer, until his face, his mouth, was only inches from mine. He studied me, as though he was looking for something in my face.

Maybe there *was* something wrong with it.

"If your Keeper didn't send you, then how—" Rain started, when someone passed through the aisle. He put a finger to his lips. "Let's go somewhere private," he whispered. Then he held out his hand to help me up off the floor. Stretched his fingers toward me. "It's not safe for us to talk here."

I stared at him. Rain Holt, the *real* Rain Holt, was offering to take my hand. This should be happening to Inara. Someone who could appreciate the gesture.

But it was happening to me.

"Come on," he said, impatient. "And cover your face."

Reluctantly, I pulled the scarf across my nose and mouth and slid my hand into his. Rain's palm was warm with the heat of the day, but something about his skin sent a shiver through me. The touch was over in a second. When I was standing he let go, beckoning me to follow.

"Tell me something first," I began, choosing my next words carefully. "When you said I shouldn't be in this world, what did you mean?"

Rain turned back, his eyes on me. They traveled from my toes over my legs and torso up to my face. Then he cleared his throat. "My father was the one who planted the idea with Lacy to unplug. He knew he could use her. Lacy is . . . lonely. And more complicated than you might imagine."

As we stood there, watching each other, I considered Rain's words about Lacy, how I'd seen glimpses of another Lacy underneath all that meanness, a version of Lacy I might even be able to relate to someday. I nodded at Rain in reply. Wondered how much history he and Lacy really shared.

"The mind is easy to hack when you're the Prime Minister," Rain went on, returning to the subject of his father, his voice hushed. "A lot of things are easy, like communicating with your son between worlds and trying to get him to come home." He dropped this like it should be obvious. "Lacy got in touch with you because that's what my father wanted," he added. "Because he needed you for his plans, too."

I shook my head. That the Prime Minister would need Lacy seemed plausible, but that he would need me seemed outlandish. "You make it sound like I'm supposed to be here."

Rain looked away. He shifted from one foot to the other. "Skylar, my father sent you to this world to die."

I tried to swallow. My throat was full of dust. "Your father wanted me dead?"

Slowly, he turned back. "Not exactly. It was more . . . he knew that unplugging would likely lead to your death." There was apology in his eyes. "That you're still alive is unexpected. I've wondered if my father is relieved or more concerned about the repercussions of it." He drew in a deep breath and continued on. "Me and some of the other seventeens went to the cliff that day to see if we could help, but when we got there, you were already in the process of rescuing yourself." The way Rain stared now, with approval, maybe even admiration, seemed to shine a light on me.

This Rain reminded me of the boy from the mountain.

I suddenly understood what Inara meant when she talked about the power he held over her. I could see it so clearly, how this could happen, how he could do that to a girl. I did my best to shake it off. I didn't like the thought of being under Rain Holt's spell. I had my family to find, and I didn't need to get caught up with the boy whose father apparently wanted to kill me.

But when again Rain said, "Come with me and we'll talk," and extended his hand, this time I didn't hesitate. I reached back and let him take mine into his.

Gently he pulled me forward.

Rain took me to a room with a sign outside that said *Rare Books Collection*. The smell was musty and old. More dusty books were packed floor to ceiling. It felt like we'd traveled back to another time. There was a table at the center of everything.

I pulled out a chair and sat down. Stared at the rough wood. "I saw your father before I unplugged during Odyssey. The same game where I saw you." I raised my eyes to meet Rain's. "It wasn't my imagination. That really happened."

Rain nodded.

"What does your father have against me? I've never done anything to hurt him." I wanted to add, *or hurt anyone*, but that wasn't true anymore, so I swallowed those words back.

Rain leaned against the table. His fingers curled around the edge. There were cuts and scrapes along his skin. "His original intent wasn't to hurt you. But it became clear that if you were allowed to unplug, you'd be in danger. That you probably wouldn't make it through . . . the process." Rain ran a hand down the side of his face. He suddenly seemed tired. "What you did on the cliff surprised everyone."

I closed my eyes a moment. "I wanted it not to be real. I was hoping it was a dream." I slumped in the chair and thought back to that first day. The dais, the audience, the dive into the water. I remembered the feel of Rain's arms pulling me into the boat. My wet hair soaking his shirt through. "I thought I was in a game. I thought I was still between worlds."

Rain's lips were a straight line, his brow furrowed. "Adrenaline is a powerful thing. When it kicks in, it allows the body to do all sorts of things it's supposedly not capable of doing." His eyes held mine. "But it still doesn't add up. You shouldn't have been able to find your way to me today without the Keeper telling you where I am, either."

I got up and went to the wall of shelves behind me. A row of books covered in animal skins—leather, I think it used to be called—stared out at me, and I shivered with disgust. I ran a finger across their spines and it came away black with dust. "I killed someone," I whispered. "Was it adrenaline that helped me stab a guard in the heart?"

Rain stood behind me. "You did what you had to," he said. "If you hadn't stabbed that guard, you might not have survived. We barely got to you in time."

"You keep saying we. Who's we?" I asked. "Are you a New Capitalist?"

"No," he responded forcefully, the single word echoing against the bookshelves. "At first they wanted me on their side." Rain adjusted the neck of his shirt. The heat was stifling. "They showed you to me once, while you were plugged in. Left me there with you so I could consider their plans. That must have been when you were playing Odyssey. I was standing there when you opened your eyes. It was like you knew I was with you." The tired look fell away from Rain's face. "Like you'd woken from the plugs, but without anyone unplugging you first." Rain hesitated. "My father wanted to make an example of you."

I wrapped my arms around my head and groaned in frustration. "That doesn't make any sense. I'm just a Single. Singles don't matter to anyone."

Rain's eyes were sad. "Not here," he said. "And in the Real World you're important to the New Capitalists. To those of us who are against them. People know who you are, Skylar."

I placed both hands flat against the table and leaned into them for support. Looked up at Rain. "Is that why I was up on that cliff with all of those people watching? Is something wrong with me?" I thought about what I'd seen before entering the library, a chill flowing across my skin. "Are there guards looking for me? On my way here, they were marching down the streets, checking people. There was this girl. They made her take off her scarf and she . . . she looked like me." I resisted the urge to wrap my arms around my middle.

Rain's eyes bored into me. "What happened on the cliff was a public event. A celebration thrown by the New Capitalists. All of New Port City was there."

I swallowed. "The whole city?"

He nodded. "Yes. They, ah, they came in shifts." He put out a hand to steady me, as though he expected I might fall. "The New Capitalists struck a deal with Emory Specter. It has to do with the plugged-in bodies. The Race for the Cure." Rain looked at me like I should understand what he meant by now, but I didn't. Not at all. I couldn't speak. "You were chosen as their example," he went on. "They needed a body to display, a body that was symbolic of their deal with the App World. You were up on that dais because the New Capitalists put you on exhibit."

The room seemed to spin. "I was an exhibit?"

"You asked before if there was something wrong with you, but there's nothing wrong, Skylar," he said. "Haven't you looked in the mirror? Seen the real you?"

I nodded. "I did. Today."

"So then you know," Rain said.

I raised my shoulders in a single shrug. "Know what?"

Rain looked at me like the answer should already be obvious. "That you're beautiful," he said simply.

I laughed. "Me?" I thought about what I'd seen in the mirror this morning. The only remarkable thing had been that the girl looking back at me was real. I shook off Rain's comment. "Even if I was, what would beauty have to do with anything?"

"Everything." Rain gripped my arm. He watched me as he spoke. "There are markets for bodies overseas, and the New Capitalists are about to launch the first one of its kind here. The deal with Specter allows them to sell the bodies of the plugged-in to boost the economy. Yours was to be the first." Rain hesitated a moment. Then, "Skylar," he went on, "they were going to auction you to the highest bidder."

20

Negotiations

THE BLOOD SEEMED to drain from my body. It rushed toward the bottoms of my feet. My eyelashes were wet against my cheeks. "I can't breathe," I said. The walls were closing in. I shook off Rain's hand. It felt as though someone had downloaded an illegal Torture App into my mind. The door was right in front of me and in one second I would open it and be through. All I wanted was to get out of this musty room.

But Rain got there first. "If you go out like that, people might recognize you. It's too dangerous."

I stood there, frozen. Now I understood why the Keeper didn't want me outside, why she was so reluctant to allow Rain to see me. She was protecting me from what he might reveal, saving me from people who wanted to sell me for profit. Guilt flowed through me like a download. She must be so worried. I slunk back to my chair.

Rain joined me at the table. "I know this is a lot to take in, but you're not alone. Your Keeper has sworn to protect you." Rain leaned forward. "And there's me, Skylar, and the other seventeens. We'll keep you safe. Hidden."

I sat there a moment, contemplating this. "What if I don't want to stay hidden?"

He frowned. "You heard what I said. Imagine what the New Capitalists would do if they found you."

I looked Rain in the eyes. "I know you have your own agenda, but you need to understand that I have one, too." The wheels were turning in my mind. "The New Capitalists were going to sell me to the highest bidder, which is not only utterly ridiculous, it's criminal." I shook my head in disgust. "What more information could I possibly need to realize I'm against them and everything they stand for?"

Rain opened his mouth, then closed it again. The air rushed from his lungs. He seemed to be debating something. "But it's not that simple," he began. "There are things you don't . . ." He trailed off, uncertain.

I didn't wait for Rain to say what was on his mind. I wanted to get this out before I decided against it. "I'll make you a deal," I told him. "If you help me find my family, if you help get them to safety, far away from the New

Capitalists, then I'll help you with whatever it is you and your friends are planning. Wouldn't it benefit your cause to reveal I was alive and well and fighting on your side?"

Rain took a step backward, leaned against the wall behind him. He shook his head. He seemed stunned by the offer. "But Skylar, that's—"

"Just hear me out," I interrupted. I wouldn't let him say no. He had resources and I wanted access to them. "You tried to rescue me, which means I can trust you. And if you're against the New Capitalists, that means we're already on the same side. Consider the possibilities."

Rain wouldn't look at me. He studied the calluses on his hands, the cuts and the scrapes. "It would be dangerous."

"Up on the cliff, I showed I can take care of myself."

"Yes, you did." Rain started to pace back and forth across the room. It made me think of Adam, made me wish to see him, someone I knew was a friend. I could almost see Rain's thoughts spinning now, the way his eyes burned. "And it's true, we could use you. You could help us." Rain's voice rose in excitement. "Once people hear you're on our side it would give us the advantage. There are Keepers who haven't chosen their allegiance yet and we need them with us." The skin on Rain's face was flushed and his hand waved through the air as he talked. "And the rebellion we're planning involves more than just the Keepers. It involves citizens in the App World and some of the seventeens who got left behind."

I closed my eyes. The possibility of seeing people from home washed over me. That most of them were Singles like me was heartening. "Can I see them? The seventeens?"

Rain was nodding, more to himself. "Yes, you could. And we'd be able to do some tests."

My eyebrows arched. "Some tests?"

"Just trust me," he said. "I'll explain on our way out there. We have a place where everyone is gathered. A secret place."

I got up from my chair. Rain and I watched each other from opposite sides of the musty room as I tried to decide on my answer. "All right," I said finally. "I'm in."

A slow smile spread across Rain's face.

"All right," he said. "Me, too."

I took a step closer.

So did Rain. "I'll come for you at your Keeper's in the early morning, before the sun rises. It will be easier for us to get out of the city that way. Less conspicuous."

I took another step, so Rain and I were face-to-face. "Okay. But let's be clear. I'll join your cause, and in exchange, you'll use your resources to help find my family."

Rain's smile slipped. He hesitated a moment. But then whatever had given him pause fell away and he nodded.

This time, I was the one who reached out my hand. "Deal?"

Rain held my gaze. Clasped my hand in his. "Deal."

The library was still bustling as we moved through it, people coming in and out of the doors, the sun shining through each time someone opened one of them. I turned to say good-bye to Rain, but he was so close behind me we nearly crashed into each other.

He frowned. "I'll walk you back to the Keeper's. She must be worried sick about you. She's going to be angry, too."

I let the scarf slip lower so I could speak. "I got here on my own. I can get back on my own too."

He ran a hand through his hair. "You're stubborn, you know that? If you're not careful, that's going to get you in trouble."

"No, I'm determined to find my family," I corrected. "They're two different things. And it's my determination that's going to help your cause."

He shook his head. Then he shrugged. "Fine. Have it your way."

I studied Rain again, the way his eyes flashed when he spoke to me. This was the Rain Holt I'd seen on the mountaintop, the Rain who would stand up to his father and rescue me, the one who'd rebel against the horrifying plans of the New Capitalists. It was so easy to get caught up in his words and his passion. For a brief moment, I saw what made the Under Eighteens swoon over him at home.

"You're not at all how I imagined you'd be," I said.

Exhaustion flickered across Rain's face, so quickly I almost missed it. Then a lopsided grin appeared to replace it. "I probably don't want to know what you imagined about me from the App World, do I?"

"No, actually." I shook my head, my hand already grabbing the end of the scarf to pull it higher across my face. "You don't."

I managed to get back to the mansion without anyone paying me undue attention. My eyes wanted to close even as I put one foot in front of the other. It was strange how the body could command rest, protesting further use by beginning to shutdown, the mind powerless to its needs. I passed the brightly colored roses, the trees with leaves like teardrops falling toward the ground, and the sea, the smell of it drenching the air. As I neared the door I had slipped out earlier today, I saw the Keeper waiting for me. She was pacing back and forth. I started across the wide marble esplanade.

When she saw me her face lit up with relief, and then darkened with anger. "Where have you been?" she demanded. Her typically neat braids, usually pulled up and away from her face, were frayed and falling everywhere, and her chest rose and fell quickly with great heaving breaths. "I've been so worried! It's dangerous for you in the city. You could have been captured!"

"I'm fine," I told her quietly, caught between regret and guilt. I stopped in front of her, trying to decide what to say next. A bird chirped overhead, the only sound other than the leaves rustling in the breeze. The sun was shining on my face as it dropped low in the sky, making way for evening. "I'm sorry I took your key, but I wish you hadn't felt like you had to lock me in." I looked at her, my eyes wide and honest. "I also wish you had enough faith to tell me the truth about my place in this world."

"You saw Rain," she said. The anger on the Keeper's face began to break apart. "I was protecting you, Skylar." Her voice wavered. "You're only a girl," she added. "I wanted to give you time to adjust to your body, even if it was only a little bit." She regarded me for another moment, her eyes shining like glass. Then she threw her arms around me in a hug. She held me tight, sniffling. "I'm so glad you're okay."

Slowly, I extended my arms around her.

"Come inside," she said after a while, letting me go. "You need your rest." She turned and headed toward the door.

I hung back a moment, not quite ready to shut myself away. I watched the sky turn red and pink as the sun disappeared below the horizon. Not blue like me, not like me at all. For some reason, this thought was a relief.

Hands. There were hands on my skin, my body, pushing me. Shoving me. Hands again. I remembered them from before.

"Don't touch me!" I screamed.

"It's okay, *shhhhhh*, it's okay," came a soothing voice. "It's just me, Skylar. It's only me." The hands slipped away—the Keeper's hands. They'd been on my shoulders, shaking me awake. I opened my eyes. The Keeper turned on the lamp next to the bed, the sudden brightness startling.

"What's wrong?" I asked, squinting, my voice hoarse.

"Nothing's wrong." She sat down on the bed, smoothed the blanket with her palm like always, a gesture of comfort I was growing used to. "You were dreaming. Do you want to talk about it?"

I took a deep breath, the air seeming thicker for some reason. I shook my head. "No. I'm all right. What time is it?" I asked. It felt as though I hadn't slept at all.

"Four thirty in the morning." The Keeper was about to say something else when I saw we had company.

Rain appeared in the doorway of the bedroom. "Good morning." He sounded too awake for this hour. "We should get out of New Port City before the sun rises."

I pulled the sheet up to my neck. "I need to get dressed."

He nodded, and the Keeper ushered him into the other room. She shut the door behind her, but then—ever so slowly and silently—I opened it a crack so I could hear what they were discussing.

"This is happening too quickly," the Keeper was saying. "You're pushing her."

"No," Rain said. "This was Skylar's decision."

"Do you really think that's wise?" the Keeper asked.

"Yes. She can do a lot of good for us."

"Does she know . . . ?"

"Not yet."

The Keeper whispered something else, too low for me to catch.

By the time I finished dressing and emerged from my room, the Keeper and Rain were standing side by side, not looking at each other. I put a hand on the Keeper's arm. "I know you want to protect me, how much you worry, but I'll be fine."

She glanced sideways at Rain. "I'm going to make myself some tea to calm my nerves," she said, and headed off toward the kitchen. When she passed Rain, she added, "I don't like this." I heard the sound of the faucet and rushing water as she filled the teakettle and set it onto the stove to heat.

Rain's eyes went to the scarf dangling in my hand. "You won't need that today."

I set it aside on the couch. Then I stopped in the

kitchen. "We're leaving," I said to the Keeper. Rain had already slipped outside.

She took down a cup and saucer from the cabinet. "Be careful," she said.

"Don't worry. Everything will be fine," I told her. Just before I walked through the door, there came the sharp shriek of the kettle, that awful sound echoing loud and high in my ears like a warning, and I hoped the words I'd spoken to her were true.

21

Field trip

THE WORLD WAS still dark, the only sound our footsteps in the grass as Rain and I stole across the lawn. The moon was a lonely slice of light in the sky. We headed toward the city center, the streets becoming narrower, the buildings rising higher and higher like a stairway reaching for the stars. It seemed as though Rain and I were the only two people in the Real World.

"It's so quiet," I said.

Rain glanced at me, his face in shadows. "It won't be quiet for long. This way." He beckoned me down another street.

Eventually we came to a stop before a staircase that led underground. We walked through a tunnel to an abandoned-looking floor beneath one of the city's buildings. It was so eerily empty it reminded me of Loner Town. The only sound was of water dripping from the ceiling into a puddle. I slowed my pace and shivered. The air was cool amid so much concrete. We turned another corner.

I halted with surprise. "We're taking a car?"

"This place is an old parking garage." Rain walked up to a small black car and knocked on the hood with his fist. It was all right angles and peeling paint. A long cord connected it to a charging station in the wall. "And yes, we are. Where we're going is much too far to walk."

I peered inside the windows. The seats were tan and torn, the stuffing pushing up through the gashes. The car looked like it might fall apart. "Does it still work?"

"Yup," Rain said. He sounded proud. He unplugged it from the charging station. "Real sun and wind is pretty amazing at powering things. Even cars."

"How did you find it? I didn't see any in the city."

He opened the driver's side door. It creaked in protest. "There aren't many left."

I eyed him skeptically. "And you can drive it."

Rain nodded. He took a deep breath and looked at me over the top of the car. "Honestly, I didn't even think to try until I saw what you could do that day on the cliff."

I eyed him back. "What does that"—I knocked on the top of the car with my fist, the metal cold—"have to do with this?"

"Well, there are a number of theories out there about how the plugs are changing our brains. Some of them are pretty doom and gloom, but not all are," he said. "I recently started to test one of them out on myself."

In the silence, the water dripped and plopped from the ceiling into the puddles. I started to put two and two together. "Before I unplugged, Lacy mentioned something about how living virtually might alter brain chemistry, and have an effect on the body. What else do you know?" I asked, genuinely curious.

"Think back to your time in the App World for a minute," Rain hinted. "Think about all the skills you learned, and the kinds of things you do when you're gaming."

I nodded, remembering all the things I used to love to do, especially things like swimming. "Sure, but in the App World, we do everything with our minds."

"Yeah, and that mind is connected to a real brain in a real body."

I shook my head. "You think the skills we learn virtually are transferrable to the Real World?" On one level it sounded impossible, but the more I thought about it, the more it also made sense. It would account for so many things that until now seemed mysterious. On the cliff that day, I'd even imagined I was in a game, and acted accordingly—as though all the skills I'd had when I was playing in the App World were skills I still held and could apply at will. It would account for how I could find my way around New Port City without seeming to know where I was going. I ran my hand along the top of the car, over the rough spots of paint and the smooth metal, seeing it with new eyes. "So you can drive here," I said slowly. "Because you could drive in the App World."

Rain's hand rested on the open door. He nodded. "As it turns out, all those racing games prepared me well. Gaming especially seems to prep your brain so that once you learn to connect your mind to the body's movements, you simply know how to do things here that you thought you could only do in the App World. Or at least, that's the theory," he added.

The possibilities were stunning. And exciting. If this were true, it meant that all that time we spent in the App World had an actual effect on the real body, and how it connected with the brain. It meant that Apping could change us—all of us—and in ways that could be wonderful, or awful, depending on which body, which mind was in control of those skills. "If your theory is right, the implications are huge."

Rain's eyes were alight. "I know. Though I'm not sure if it applies to everyone evenly. The brain is a complicated part of the body."

Then I remembered the guard I'd stabbed. All that blood. "Virtual experience doesn't replace Real World experience, though. The stakes are different here. And so are the consequences," I added. In a game, no one got hurt for real. No one died. I felt my body slump a little with the sheer mental weight of it.

Rain watched me solemnly. "This is true, but don't be too hard on yourself. Now let's go." He got in the car and shut the door.

I shook off thoughts of the guard and slid into the passenger side.

Rain put the key in the ignition and patted the dashboard lovingly. Then he turned it.

The car roared to life.

Rain stepped on the gas and suddenly we were moving. My knuckles were white from gripping the handle on the door. Even though Rain's theory made sense, it was another thing to test it out in a vehicle that could end up killing us. He maneuvered through the underground parking garage until we reached a ramp that led up to the street. We got to the end of it and rounded the corner. The city was still dark as we headed down the boulevard that cut across the island and ended at the cliff. There were no other cars and no one else out so we sped along, block after block, until we reached what looked like a giant gaping arch over the ocean.

A bridge.

"Are we leaving New Port?" I asked.

Rain glanced at me. Bobbed his head once.

It was still pitch-black outside. The only glow was from the car's headlights, two pools of light stretching out ahead and cutting through the darkness as we rose up, up, up over this ribbon of concrete and metal that stretched across the water. Eventually we came to the other side of it and I breathed a sigh of relief.

I turned around and looked behind us.

Through the back window, the skyscrapers of New Port City cut a series of shadows across the darkness. A few lights were on in the buildings, proof that there was still life in the city's midst. Somehow, those tiny sparks were comforting. The sun was just beginning to lift, the warm glow of red burning along the horizon. We raced along the empty road, Rain swerving occasionally to avoid a pothole.

"You really can drive," I said.

"You could, too," he said quietly. "Though you'd have to practice first, somewhere safe, where there isn't anything to crash into."

"Right," I said. "What about piloting an airplane? Or a helicopter?" I went through the list of things I'd learned to do while I was gaming.

"If you could get your hands on one of them, sure," he said. "But I wouldn't want to be on board for the test flights."

The gears of my mind were turning. "So what does this mean for other App World citizens? You mentioned you weren't sure if the way the plugs change our brain chemistry would affect everyone in the same way."

The car leaned hard into a sharp curve in the highway. "That's what I'd like to figure out." Rain shifted the wheel expertly. "In theory, sure, the brain and therefore the body would have the same instincts and skills a person developed while in the App World. But you also have to remember: the real body is vulnerable in ways that the virtual self isn't. So, for example, if a tiger ripped off someone's arm, it would be gone forever."

"Well, that's disappointing," I said. "I liked the idea of those transferrable skills including the one where I can regenerate a limb."

Rain laughed and I joined in. "No kidding," he said.

The sun became a great ball of fire in front of us. Rain put on a pair of sunglasses and handed me a second pair that he pulled from the glove compartment.

I put them on. "How do you think we make all those skills work?" I asked, remembering how when I woke up at the Keeper's, I could barely focus my eyes, how I had trouble speaking, how my legs struggled to hold me up. "Is it always adrenaline that makes them kick in?"

Rain rested his hand on the gearshift. "Adrenaline will do it, sure. But from what I've gathered, you don't always have to be in danger. It's more like, you have to let your body take charge and get your mind out of the way. You have to *not* try so hard, stop thinking about it directly. Just let go into whatever it is you're doing and suddenly"—he snapped his fingers—"your brain and your body start working together and your arms and legs simply know what comes next."

I tried to understand this. "Sort of like the Protection Apps built into our code at home?"

He nodded. "That's a pretty good analogy, actually." He glanced at me. "What do you turn into when you're afraid, Skylar?"

His question surprised me. It was so personal. I took my eyes off the road, staring at my hands clasped in my lap. "A panther. You?"

Rain hesitated. "A tiger."

My mouth opened. "But you were always killing tigers when you were gaming. I saw you do it just before I unplugged. You didn't even flinch. I could never kill a panther, not even if it attacked. It's like, when I look at one, I almost see myself."

"I know." He shrugged. "It was the same for me with tigers."

"But—" I started, then stopped as it dawned on me what he was saying. "Oh." I felt a pang of sympathy for Rain. Thought about him sitting on that ice ledge, his legs dangling over that vast abyss. He really wasn't as carefree—and careless—as everyone thought.

Rain got quiet. I let the subject drop.

The scenery zoomed by outside the window. It wasn't the same as flying on the Apps, or traveling on a train at home—not as fast or quite as free—but it was better in a way. There was something about watching the Real World at this speed, seeing how the sun made its way over the horizon and across the sky, that I didn't want to spoil with any more words. Doing these things in the real body made everything different. More whole. More vivid. More alive.

"Being in this car is pretty great," I admitted after a while.

Rain's eyes were still on the road. "I'm glad you like it."

I started to relax. It was ironic: the farther we got from the city, the closer I felt to finding my family. Joining Rain's cause was taking a giant step toward getting to them by enlisting his help and his resources. Hiding in the Keeper's mansion got me nowhere, and to allow myself to be shut away because a few politicians thought I was pretty enough to sell was ridiculous.

I glanced at Rain and caught him looking at me. His admission that he saw himself in a tiger, yet his impulse was still to kill it, almost made me want to reach out and take his hand. I turned away instead, staring out the passenger side window. After another few miles, Rain pulled off the highway and wound down a narrow lane, walled in by tall, dense, leafy trees. By now, the sun was high. Nothing but green and the road stretching ahead of us. Rain rolled down the window and stuck his left arm outside. The wind struck my face and twisted through my hair. His hand seemed to rise and fall in the air as though it kept rolling over some invisible object.

"Go ahead," Rain said when he realized I was watching him. "Try it."

I rolled down my window and pulled the hair away from my mouth. Then I stuck my arm out, mimicking the movement of Rain's hand.

I started to laugh.

It felt as though my hand was moving over and under bubbles, the air pushing it up and then letting it down again. I decided to stick my head out next. I couldn't help it. The warm wind struck my face and my ponytail flew outside the car, trailing behind me. A feeling of pure joy flooded me. The smell of the air was green and humid, heavy with the scent of summer flowers and grass, and I loved it. I shifted position so only my arm was outside, resting along the bottom of the open window.

Rain smiled. "It's good to see you enjoying yourself."

"I am," I admitted. "But are you ever going to tell me where we're going?"

"Almost there," was all he said.

Soon the landscape changed, becoming more barren, the trees spaced farther apart. Instead of dirt among the plant life there was sand, its grains spilling across the road. The ocean was all around us in New Port City, but the elevation was so high the ocean felt far away, inaccessible. But sand meant it was close. The potholes in the road got worse and worse until the car was bumping over

them nearly constantly. The street widened into a parking lot. Dunes reached up in front of us, sea grass growing
along the hills. "Are we near the beach?"

"Yes," Rain said.

My heart grew wings and I thought it might fly from
my body. "You're taking me to the ocean?"

Rain parked the car and turned off the engine. "In
part."

I threw open the door and got out. I'd always thought
that if I ever saw the beach again it would be with my
family, that I'd be holding the hands of my mother and my
sister as we walked along the sand, like when I was small.
Even though they weren't with me, that didn't quell my
excitement. "How far away are we?"

"Over here." Rain beckoned me up and over the sloping dune.

I took off my shoes.

My feet sank and slid into the shifting grains, and I
remembered my game of Odyssey with Inara. Real sand
and real dunes were different. Each grain was so clear
to my eyes, the heat from the sun burning the bottoms
of my feet. The hurt was strong but not unwelcome. As
we climbed higher, I caught the sound of crashing waves.
"The ocean," I cried, and went faster. "It's right here!"

Soon I reached the top.

Rain was only a few steps behind me.

I blocked the bright glare of the sun with my hand.

A wide beach lay before me. White sand as far as the eye could see to both the left and the right, and after it, deep-blue ocean. A wave crashed into the shore, then another, the surf sizzling as it flowed over the wet sand. I took a deep breath, inhaling the briny smell, the air sharp with salt and seaweed. The breeze was hot with summer.

Far off in the distance I could see the faint outline of skyscrapers.

Rain joined me on the dune's crest. "So what do you think?"

"I think I can't believe I'm at the beach. A real beach!"

"It's beautiful, isn't it?"

I tore my eyes away to look at him. "It's strange to see you care about things," I said. "I'm not trying to hurt your feelings," I added quickly. "I'm just being honest. You always seemed so bored by everything at home."

"I know," was all he said.

Then he kicked off his sandals and headed down toward the water.

I followed him, shedding clothing as I went. It felt so good to have the air on my skin. Without thinking I pulled off the tunic I wore. Underneath I had on the tiny tank top and leggings the Keeper had given me to wear. I loved the feel of the breeze swirling along my stomach.

We stopped at the high tide line. Rain dug his toe into the wet sand. He gestured at the clothing draped across my arm. "I'll hold that for you if you want."

I handed the tunic over. Noticed how Rain averted his eyes. "Thanks."

The sun shone warm on my skin as I stood before the surf.

I smiled—I couldn't help it.

Then I walked into the water, unafraid, and dove under.

22

A body knows

AFTER MY SWIM, Rain and I walked the beach.

There was nothing but sky and ocean and sand. Not another soul in sight. No sign of life, other than the occasional bird flying above or a crab scuttling across our feet. The sun and the heat dried my skin and the wind tangled my hair in knots. I didn't care. I loved how the long black strands were taken up in the breeze and drawn against the wide blue summer sky, as though they had a life of their own. I loved the randomness of the movement, my inability to influence or stop it from happening with an App. I enjoyed the feeling of being unable to control my image, my body, the landscape.

"See that house?" Rain pointed to a gray structure in

the distance that seemed only a tiny speck. It rose up from the place where it was nestled in the dunes. "That's where we're headed."

I'd dried off enough by now and slipped my tunic over my head. "I'm ready. Let's get started."

"Good," he said.

The gray house got bigger as we approached, so big I realized it was another mansion, though very different in style from the one where the Keeper lived. More rustic. My strides got longer. The sand under my feet was packed from waves pounding it incessantly. It made my body itch for movement. I turned to Rain. "Let's test out your theory again."

His eyebrows went up. "What were you thinking?"

"That I would beat you in a race," I said. "I was fast at home."

The left side of his mouth turned up. "You might be a little rusty."

"Let's see about that." I tapped my chin, thinking. "Last one to the gray house—"

"Has to sit in the passenger seat on the way back to New Port City," he supplied.

My jaw dropped. "Seriously? You'd let me drive?"

"Only if you win. Well, and after a little practice in the parking lot."

I laughed. "It's a deal, obviously."

Then I took off into a run.

"I didn't say *go*," Rain protested from behind me.

But I didn't care. I was too busy concentrating on putting one leg in front of the other. At first, my speed was disappointing. I stumbled in the hard sand and swerved left and right. It wasn't long before Rain had overtaken me, and when I looked ahead I saw that he wasn't even trying.

"Don't baby me," I called out to him.

He glanced back, then sped up, the gap between us widening, the house getting closer.

I tried to "let go," as Rain had put it, remembering how when I'd been gaming back home, everything was so automatic. I remembered, too, how fear could propel me, how it had taken over and helped my real body do all sorts of incredible things when I'd woken up on the cliff. Finally, I stopped thinking. Let my legs do what they longed to.

I began to fly.

My strides were long and fast, my feet beating the sand, my tunic whipping against my body. Rain's lead grew smaller. I pumped harder. I was getting closer, but so was our destination. A series of wooden slats set into the sand took shape. They cut the dune in two, leading straight up to the house. Rain swerved toward them and I followed. We sprinted up them, Rain tagging the wall of the house first. He turned to greet me as I arrived, a smirk on his face. I didn't care. All that mattered was what I'd proved to myself on both land and sea: with or without danger, I was fast and I was strong, and with a little more time, I would beat anyone in a race. I couldn't wait to see what else my body could do.

"I guess I'll be driving us back," Rain said between breaths.

I managed to smile, despite the way my lungs were gulping the air. "Next time, you won't have it so easy." My hair was stuck to my neck. I was dripping with sweat. "I could use another swim. We should have raced first, then jumped in the ocean."

Rain nodded toward the house. "You can shower inside."

I looked up. It was three stories tall, the roof flat and covered in solar panels, with windows facing out to the ocean. They shined black in the sun, so I couldn't see through them. Like everywhere else, long, thin windmills rose high like palm trees all around. From the beach, the house's size was deceiving. This close, I could see that it stretched back and back and back—I couldn't even tell how far. Part of it seemed to dip underground, the roof descending until it was covered by sand and sea grass, parts of it peeking up in places throughout the dunes, all the way to the trees by the road. It was designed to blend in to its oceanside location, as opposed to sticking out. Unlike the other mansions I'd seen, it hadn't yet fallen into disrepair. Someone had taken good care of it over the years. "What is this place?"

Rain wiped a hand across his forehead. He beckoned

me to a shady spot under the eaves. "It's called Briarwood. It once belonged to my grandfather."

My eyes widened. I was standing in front of the former house of Marcus Holt, the founder of the App World. How surreal.

"This is where all the seventeens gathered after the border closed," Rain went on. He smiled. "There's a surprise waiting for you inside."

"What kind of surprise?" I asked warily.

"A good one," Rain said. "Promise."

I followed him through a tall metal door cut into the side of the building. We entered a brightly lit hall, the gray slate tiles on the floor cold under my bare feet. I glimpsed the beach through a darkened window, but otherwise we might be anywhere. The air inside was cool, so it was impossible to know that on the other side of these walls was the blistering heat of summer. Recessed lighting lined our way as Rain led me around the corner and down another corridor to a second door. It was made of plain, dark wood. The design was simple—without any embellishments. Rain opened it and went inside. I stood there a moment before I walked in after him.

I found myself standing on a wide balcony that spanned the length of a cavernous ballroom. But, like everything else here, this one was far different from the one I'd seen at the Keeper's mansion. Big, but plain. There were no chandeliers or frescoes.

I joined Rain at the railing.

Then I looked down.

There was a crowd of people spread out across the floor. They stopped what they were doing to watch us. They definitely hadn't been engaged in the dancing for which this space was originally intended.

Some of them stood on thick mats, with padding on their elbows, knees, and fists. One person held a ball in the crook of his arm and another group was gathered inside a series of rings that lined the outside of the room, their chests rising and falling quickly, out of breath. A large area was set up as some kind of obstacle course, with barrels and walls and hurdles, and the entire right wall had been redesigned for climbing.

The ballroom had been transformed into a kind of training gym.

There were as many boys as girls, if I had to guess, with every color of skin imaginable. Almost all the girls had hair as long as mine, but a few had cropped it so short it was difficult to tell their gender.

Then my eyes landed on one boy in particular. He was taller than the rest, almost impossibly so, his skin even darker than my Keeper's. There was something familiar in his face, the way he looked up at me, that revealed his identity.

"Adam?" I called out.

He raised his hand. "Hi, Skylar," he called back.

I looked at Rain.

He shrugged. Then smiled. "Surprise?"

I ran down the center staircase that led to the floor. Adam met me at the bottom. "I can't believe it's really you."

"I feel the same way," he said.

My face only reached the top of his rib cage. "You're a giant."

"Yeah." His voice was deeper. "I was a little surprised about that myself."

I glanced behind him, remembering that everyone else was standing there, watching. A girl approached us. She was tiny, her skin brown, but a different shade from Adam's, her eyes wide and as black as her long wiry hair.

Adam turned to the girl. "Skylar, meet Parvda."

"Hi," she said softly.

"You found her," I whispered.

Adam had love in his eyes as he took Parvda's hand in his, hers so small it seemed to disappear. "When I woke up, Parvda was with me. Not exactly the Keeper I was expecting."

"I'm so happy for you." My voice cracked. "And it's so nice to meet you." I reached out my hand to Parvda and she clasped it.

Tears pressed at the back of my eyes. I was truly happy for them, that they'd found each other again in this world just like Adam had wanted, but I was also jealous. Sylvia had gotten left behind and I hadn't managed to see my family at all. Out of the three of us, only Adam had gotten what he'd wanted. I took a deep breath and willed the tears to stay put. *Soon*, I reminded myself, searching the space until I found Rain again. He was climbing down the stairs to join us, his footsteps ringing out against the wood.

"You were right," I said when Rain reached us. "This was a good surprise." I stood there, thinking, a lump in my throat. "But why did Adam get to wake up here, with Parvda, and I didn't?"

"Adam wasn't on the New Capitalists' radar."

I sighed and looked around. People were whispering and pointing. "So these are the seventeens who have banded together? The ones who got left on this side of the border and didn't choose to join the New Capitalists?"

Rain watched me as he said his next words. "Yes. They witnessed what you did on the cliff. They saw how you fought back. The fact that you *could* fight. It made everyone, myself included"—he blinked—"realize that maybe we aren't so powerless to Real World politics. Maybe not to App World politics either."

I glanced at Adam. He nodded. I watched as one boy ran on a track that circled the gym, and a girl scaled the climbing wall to my right, grabbing at the handholds, occasionally slipping but managing not to fall. "They're testing their skills," I said to Rain. "They're testing this theory about the plugs altering brain chemistry and how this might affect our bodies."

Rain joined me in watching the activity in the gym. "That's the idea," he said. "But we can talk more about it later. There are a few other things I need to show you."

The crowd parted as we moved across the gym, everything coming to a halt once more. All eyes were on us as we walked toward a door at the far end of the room. No, all eyes were on *me*. There were whispers as we passed.

"I can't believe that's really her," said a girl to my left, loud enough to hear.

"She looks different this close up," said another wearing elbow and kneepads, her long blond hair in a ponytail high on her head. "Not as pretty."

The breath left my body, the hurtful remark making me wince. Had everyone really seen me on display? I pulled the tunic closed around my neck, ashamed. Disappointed, too. These were seventeens, sure, but that didn't make them friends. Not yet, at least.

"Yeah," said another girl, sounding defiant. "Well, up close she looks way stronger to me."

This comment turned my head. My eyes went over this newest girl, her clipped brown hair and brown eyes, her skin the same color as mine. Her hands were on her hips. There was something familiar in her expression. "I know you," I said as a memory flashed. "You were on the cliff. You helped me the day I woke up here."

She nodded. "I'm glad you made it. I'm Jessica."

"Nice to meet you. And thank you," I said softly. Then I smiled.

She smiled back. "Nice to officially meet the real you. Welcome," Jessica added.

I headed toward Rain, dazed by all the attention, especially the attention that was unkind. I'd much rather disappear into the crowd than stand out. I followed him out into another hallway, this one dimmer, the walls and floors painted black. The door shut behind us with a soft click.

"It won't always be that way." Rain glanced at me. "They'll get used to seeing you more as just another person involved in our cause."

I shrugged. My confidence seemed to have gone on break. "I guess."

"Try to be patient," Rain said.

I pulled my arms around my body. "But the way everyone stared . . ." I trailed off. "It's just so . . . so hard to get used to."

"Everyone in this city knows about you, Skye, and they all have opinions about you as a result," he said quietly. "It's a lot to take in, but just like they'll get used to seeing you, you'll get used to seeing them. Before, you were the girl the New Capitalists held up as a symbol for their new plan, the girl we were going to try to rescue. Then you were the girl who up and nearly rescued herself.

You surprised everyone. Most everyone in a *good* way. I promise."

Rain stood close. We seemed connected by a strange electric current. It ran across my skin, making the tiny hairs stand on end.

"I think I'd rather go back to being the girl nobody ever noticed."

Rain nodded. "I know what it feels like to have a famous face. I know how difficult it can be, how harsh people can be when they judge you. How it makes you yearn for anonymity." He looked over my shoulder, at some unseen thing in the distance. "One of the things I love most about being in the Real World is that even though the seventeens know who I am, there are only so many people who can watch you at once. Not having thousands of voyeurs has helped me remember—has freed me to be—the person I really am." He sighed. "It's such a relief."

Now I was the one reaching out to Rain, placing my hand on his arm. The touch sent that current from my fingers to my heart. He studied my hand a long while, my fingers curled across his skin. I could see hope enter his eyes hesitantly, and I didn't turn away from it.

23

Behind closed doors

"THERE'S SOMEONE ELSE you should see," Rain said as we continued on through the hall. We stopped in front of another old wooden door. Rain took out a key, unlocked it, and we went inside. A woman, not quite as old as my Keeper but definitely older than us, was sitting on the couch, reading a book. Her hair was long and silky and black, her eyes dark, almond shaped, and set into her face in a way that made them totally unique.

Real World beauty came in so many different shapes and colors.

Rain hung back by the door.

"Hello," I said. "I'm Skylar."

The woman set her book aside. She didn't seem

surprised I was here. "My name is Mae. I was expecting you at some point." Mae looked beyond me at Rain, her eyebrows a question.

"It's all right," he said.

I glanced around the room. It was strangely familiar, set up like a home, the curtains drawn tight over what I assumed were windows, though for all I knew there was a concrete wall behind them. A sofa and two chairs were arranged along the far wall. There were a few shelves with books and a small glass vase, empty of flowers, on a tiny round table. Beyond the living room I could see a kitchen table, a counter, a sink, and a hallway leading down into other rooms.

I'd seen another place set up just like this one.

I'd lived in it.

"Who are you Keeping?" I asked Mae.

She gestured toward the same door that would lead to my room. "Why don't you see for yourself?"

I looked at Rain.

"I'll wait for you out here," he said.

I went to the door and knocked lightly.

Then I listened.

There was no sound, not a word from whoever was inside. I put my hand on the knob and turned it, opening the door a crack. Again I waited to hear something—a cry of protest, a welcome, the rustling of sheets on the bed. But there was nothing. I pushed the door the rest of the way open and stepped inside the dimly lit room. In the bed was a girl. She seemed to be sleeping, eyes closed, her arms resting above the sheet, her shoulders thin and delicate, her skin so pale it was almost translucent. Freckles dotted it, dense in places on her hands and at the base of her neck, but most of all on her face, spread across her cheeks and forehead like spilled ink staining paper.

She stirred.

The movement shifted her long hair into the ray of light coming from the doorway. It was the color of rust.

"Lacy?" I whispered.

Her eyes fluttered open. They immediately narrowed as she looked at me standing there. "Who are you?" she asked. "Where's my Keeper?"

I took a step closer. "You don't recognize me?" I bent forward into the light. "It's Skylar. Skylar Cruz."

Her face changed. Her eyes lost their suspicion, replacing it with surprise. "You're Skylar Cruz?" she whispered. "But you're so . . . so pretty."

I took a step backward. Even though Lacy had given me a compliment, the disbelief in her tone had stung. Hurt edged into my voice. "Do you know where you are?"

Lacy pulled herself to a sitting position. It took a lot of effort and adjusting until she was comfortable, which made me think she hadn't left the bed yet. "The Real World. At my Keeper's house." Each word took a lot of effort. Lacy blinked once, twice. She seemed so disoriented. Then her eyes narrowed again, and I saw the Lacy I knew from the App World in them. The mean girl inside her had returned. "If you're really Skylar, then you should have information for me. Have you made any progress in finding Rain?"

It was like I'd stepped through a time warp, and Lacy was talking about a world I no longer lived in. "You really have no idea, do you?"

"I know plenty," she said haughtily.

But I could hear a flicker of doubt in her voice.

I couldn't decide what came next. It felt unfair that Lacy was so in the dark, that Jonathan Holt had tricked her into unplugging us and unplugging herself too. He'd taken advantage of each one of us, and she seemed just as lost as I felt at different moments. But on the other hand, waking up in the Real World hadn't seemed to cure Lacy of her nastiness. Still, didn't she deserve to know that Rain was just on the other side of the door?

I certainly didn't like it when people kept the truth from me.

"You know what? I'll be right back." I walked out of the room, passing the Keeper, and went straight up to Rain. I grabbed his hand and pulled him into the room with me. "Lacy, I give you the real Rain Holt."

Her mouth parted with surprise. "Rain? Is that really you?" Her eyes blinked, like she couldn't believe what she was seeing.

And I felt so bad for her.

"Hi, Lacy," he said quietly.

Her eyes dropped to our clasped hands, then they traveled back to Rain's face. "I'm here to convince you to go home again." These were her words, but her voice wavered as she said them. "We can leave anytime you want. Your father needs you. *I* need you. Aren't you happy?" she asked, though it came out a whisper.

"Lacy." Rain spoke her name again but this time in warning.

A single tear rolled down her cheek.

I was reminded of that icon of Lacy when she was just a little girl, calling out for her parents, trying to get attention. Having to watch them ignore her again and again, and the way her face fell each time, crushed by this abandonment.

I slid my hand out of Rain's.

Lacy wiped the tear from her face, but it was quickly replaced by another. "You were the only person who ever really saw me, Rain. Who stood by me and not because of my money and fame." She hiccupped, her eyes on him. "I know you didn't love me like I loved you, but I never thought you'd leave me. *Never.*" Lacy leaned forward, reached out her hand to him. It hovered in the empty air, grasping at nothing. "And then you unplugged and didn't even say good-bye. I can't go back there without you. I can't live without you."

I stared at Lacy, shocked by this display of vulnerability

and pain. Despite everything, my heart went out to her. First Lacy's parents had made her feel lost and alone, and now Rain.

Lacy was staring at him, imploringly.

Rain opened his mouth, then closed it.

I went to her and sat down on the edge of the bed, remembering how she'd reached out to me as we were unplugging. I took her grasping hand in mine and lowered it until it came to rest along the crisp white sheet. "You're not alone, Lacy. I'm here. And Adam is right nearby, too. Now that we've found one another, we'll all stick together. We're not going to leave you, I promise."

Lacy looked at me as though she'd forgotten I was there. She retracted her hand. "Don't touch me, Singles trash."

My jaw dropped. "Singles *trash*?"

"That's exactly what you are," Lacy huffed.

"I can't believe I actually just felt sorry for you."

"I don't need anyone to feel sorry for me," she said. "I'm still Lacy Mills and I'll always be Lacy Mills." Her eyes grew small and mean.

And all the sympathy evaporated from mine.

I turned to Rain. "I've seen enough. Let's move on."

Rain cleared his throat. "Okay."

Lacy smacked the bed with her hand, a soft thump. "Rain!"

"Bye, Lacy," I said, disappointed. For a few minutes

I'd felt a kinship with her, realized how much I wanted a friend, longed for another girl in whom I could confide and who would confide in me. I felt stupid for even trying to find this in Lacy. The longer I went without Inara, the more I realized how irreplaceable she was. As we shut the door on Lacy's protests, the quiet that followed, for once, was a welcome relief.

"She obviously cares for you," I said as we walked away from the Keeper's apartment.

Rain shifted uncomfortably. "I know."

The sound of our footsteps was soft against the tiled floor. "I feel like there's a lot more to you and Lacy that you're leaving out," I said. "She *unplugged* for you. She doesn't want to return to the App World unless you go with her."

"Lacy and I go way back," he said. "We have a complicated history."

I stared at him, trying to read his expression. We turned a corner, heading left down a long hallway. "She said she was in love with you. Were you ever in love with her?"

Rain didn't answer. My question hung in the air between us. As the echo of the words drifted away, I realized I wanted the answer to be *no*. Rain's fingers trailed along the wall. "There was a brief time when Lacy and I were together," he admitted.

"Together, together?" I couldn't help asking.

"Is there any other kind?" he deflected.

A silence fell between us, and I contemplated this new information. We reached the end of the corridor. "Where are we going?"

"There's one last place I want to show you," Rain said.

"And then you'll take me back to my Keeper's?"

He tilted his head. "I *could* take you back." He hesitated. "Or you could stay the night. Get to know some of the people here."

Something fluttered inside me. "Won't the Keeper be expecting us?"

Rain shrugged. "I told her we might return tomorrow. If you were open to it."

"I'm open to it."

"Good," he said.

Tension strung itself between us as we continued through the halls. Then Rain gestured toward an imposing metal door at the end of the corridor, unlike all the others I'd seen so far. It reached all the way to the ceiling and it was twice as wide as the others. It had a look of heft to it, like it might lead to a vault. Great round bolts framed its edges. Rain entered a code into a panel on the wall and it sighed open.

"This," he said, "is our weapons room."

I swallowed. "Weapons?"

"Go ahead. Look."

I went inside and found myself in a fortress of sorts. I'd assumed by *weapons* Rain had meant guns and bombs. The word evokes a certain kind of violent object, like the ones I'd seen holstered in the belts of the guards walking the city, or the stone dagger I'd plunged into the heart of the man on the cliff. There were a few guns lined up along the wall and spread across a table in the far corner, but their numbers were small in comparison to what seemed the central weapon of choice that was everywhere I looked.

"I don't understand." I wrapped my arms around my body. It was cold in here. "Video screens?"

Rain's face lit up. "Yes."

There were screens of all sizes, some as big as me and others so tiny they would fit into the palm of my hand. Most of them were barely thicker than a few sheets of paper. They were mounted along the walls and stacked on shelves and packed into boxes sitting on the floor. All of them were dark. Lifeless.

"None of them work?" I asked.

"Not yet," Rain said. "But they will soon. I guess you could say they're our *secret* weapons."

"What are you going to do—hit the New Capitalists over the head and hope they pass out?"

Rain laughed. "Definitely not. That would be a waste of incredible resources." He walked over to one of the boxes and pulled out a screen the size of the cutting board the Keeper used in the kitchen, but paper-thin. Black on one side and silver on the other. He held it out to me.

I could just make out my reflection in the light shining from above. "Does it do anything?" I asked. "Is it a bomb in disguise? Someone picks it up and it explodes?"

"Ah, no," said someone else, a girl who emerged from behind one of the largest screens. "Not that either." There was a tiny silver wand in her hand, maybe a tool of some sort. She was my height, with long thin limbs and dark features, her skin olive in tone, with a strong nose at the center of her face. She emanated strength.

Rain placed the screen back on the table. "This is Zeera, our master of technology. Zeera, this is Skylar."

I took a step back. The name unsettled me. "Do I know you?" I asked, but then I didn't need to wait for her answer. My mind found the memory it sought. "You're Sylvia's girlfriend."

Zeera's eyes immediately glassed over. She wiped her sleeve across them. "I am."

"I'm sorry she's not with us. Sylvia was"—I realized I needed to correct myself—"*is* a wonderfully kind person. At least, from what I knew of her before I left."

Zeera didn't speak. All that strength seemed to soften now, and she became a girl who'd lost the person she loved.

Rain put a hand on her shoulder. "Zeera joined us when she learned Sylvia couldn't ever unplug. She's one of our best weapons scouts," he added.

Zeera straightened, all business again. "The abandoned houses along this beach are a wealth of resources. The people who lived here were rich and sometimes there are up to twenty screens lying around useless on desks and tables."

Rain was nodding. "With the changes in technology and the founding of the App World, the devices of old were considered useless—a pale comparison to plugging in."

Something beeped behind Zeera, and the large screen she'd been working on flickered. She glanced back. "I need to go deal with that," she said. "It was nice to meet you, Skylar. I hope to see you later so we can talk about the people we know in common. Excuse me," she added, and walked away.

I watched her disappear behind the screen. I was glad I was staying overnight so I would have the chance to talk to her again. I picked up the device Rain had placed on the table and looked at it, turned it over in my hands and ran my fingers across the smooth surface. "So if they're not just blunt objects and they don't explode, then what are they for?"

"They're for spying," Rain said simply. "Before the App World existed, the Real World was wired for these devices to connect people to the virtual sphere and to one another. Then the technology ban was instituted and the power was cut. But it's all still there. All we need to do is turn the power back on and *voilà*, we have access to every corner of every street and building in New Port City. We'll be able to see everything. And hear it. And watch it unfolding like with a hologram."

"You're going to become voyeurs," I said, realization dawning.

Rain smiled, but the smile had a bitter quality to it. "Yes. For once, I'll get to be the one watching, not the one being watched."

It didn't seem to matter what world I was in. Here, like in the App World, we wanted to pry into the lives of others, whether they wanted us to or not. But the thought of having to do it through a screen you held in your hand instead of an App downloaded into the brain was difficult to get my mind around. "It doesn't seem fair to watch people when they're unaware and vulnerable. I certainly didn't like finding out that I'd been . . . watched. On exhibit for everyone."

"I understand," Rain said quietly. "But in this world, it's the best weapon we have."

I considered this, and set the spying device back on the table. I suddenly didn't want to be touching it, as though it might turn on and broadcast my face to people I didn't know in a faraway place. Then something else occurred to me. "Can you access the App World with any of these?"

Rain's eyebrows arched. "That's the hope. But at the very least, they'll give us a window to the Real World like never before. And to one another, too."

Rain sounded excited, but I wasn't sure I liked what he described.

He headed toward the vault-like door. As I followed him out of the room, my mind turned over all of this new information. "How did you do it those years in the App World?" I asked him now. "How did you handle the way people always recognized you? How you couldn't go anywhere without them watching you?" The memory of how everyone whispered as I passed them in the gym entered my mind. "I think you must be the expert on this subject. Every second of your life was recorded in the App World. Every turn of your head was discussed and analyzed by your adoring fans."

Rain led us toward the front of Briarwood. "I built walls." He turned a corner and our surroundings shifted. It looked as though we'd entered the wing of a new house. "I lived as though I was made of armor. I put on masks." We passed a darkened glass wall, our footsteps hollow against the wooden floor. "I became a selfish, uncaring asshole who never let anyone in. At the time I thought it was the only way I could keep something back for myself. Then one day I woke up and wasn't sure if there was anything left of me to protect." He eyed me. "When I came to the Real World, bit by bit I discovered that the person I once believed I was still existed. I just needed some time away from all the chaos to rediscover him." Rain stopped before another door, this one made of carved wood, next to a window that looked out onto the ocean. "I'm never letting myself get eaten alive again, not by voyeurs, not by technology," he went on. "If we're not careful, technology starts to use us instead of the reverse."

"What are you trying to tell me?" I asked, struggling to read him.

Rain traced his fingers along the sculpted wood. Then he dropped his hand to his side and looked at me. "There's a gathering on the beach this evening at sunset. You can rest here. There are some clothes for you to change into if you'd like."

"You didn't answer my question."

There was a fierceness to Rain's expression. "Skye, I'm never going back to the App World. Not for all the money and power in the universe. Not for anything," he went on, already turning to walk away. "I'll see you at the party tonight," he called back, and then disappeared down the hall.

24

Revealing

THE ROOM I entered seemed to belong to another era, to someone who must have lived in the original house before it was expanded and turned into a place to prepare for war and revolution. I wondered how long ago Zeera had raided it for weapons and how many she'd found in here. Floor-to-ceiling windows lined one wall and looked out over the ocean. In the middle of them was a glass door. I opened it and saw that there were stairs leading down into the sand, a path cutting through the dunes to the beach. The salty air swept over me and I inhaled it greedily. I couldn't ever get enough of the sea.

I let myself take in the sight of the ocean another moment before stepping back inside the room. At the center of it was a large bed topped with pillows and clean white sheets. A closet was set into one of the other walls, with a tall chest of drawers next to it. I slid the bottom drawer open. It was full of socks. Black, white, green, purple, long, short. For some reason this made me laugh. To have this many pairs of socks seemed extravagant. I went through each of the other drawers. When I came to the fourth drawer, my eyes widened. I pulled out the garment on top and let it dangle from my fingers. Parts of it were a shiny blue, so soft and smooth it was like water spun into fabric, and the rest was lace.

Lingerie.

I peered into the last drawer, the one at the top, and it too was full of dainty, tiny things, but this time they were of a different sort of material, the kind good for swimming. Bathing suits of different colors and patterns. They were nearly all strings. If I dove under a wave in one, I would likely emerge having lost the top or bottom or both.

I felt my cheeks redden. Rain told me I could change if I wanted. Had he known what kind of clothes were in here? Did a part of him hope I would show up on the beach later wearing this tiny bikini? Or that underneath my clothes I would wear lingerie?

No. That's something Lacy would do.

Besides, why would Rain care?

I dug farther down into the drawer.

At the very bottom was a simple black tank bathing

suit. I set it aside on a chair. A yawn pushed my mouth wide and made the muscles in my arms and legs want to stretch. I still couldn't get used to the body's impulse for this. The big white bed called to me, so I crawled on top of it to rest. I wanted relief from the day, to forget about everything, even if only for an hour.

But in my sleep I dreamed of being in a room surrounded by cameras, and that beyond them were people sitting before screens, watching every move I made, assessing my body, my value, my appearance. They could see me, of course, but I couldn't—would never—see them.

When I arrived at the beach later that evening it was already teeming with people. They dotted the sand in groups as the sun went down, chatting and laughing. Some held bottles in their hands and others had small, opaque cups. A number of seventeens were kicking a ball around, running and shouting to one another as they tried to get it past a boy guarding a makeshift goal. A large bonfire burned orange and red, the sound of wood crackling interrupting the crash of the waves.

I wanted to freeze the moment.

I was in the Real World at a beach party, the ocean a few steps away, the horizon on fire with pink, a surreal blue starting to ink its way across the sky. Beyond the ocean the tiny lights of New Port City glinted and winked in the distance. The only thing missing from this moment was sharing it with my sister and mother. I bet they would love this. They used to love the beach as much as I did when I was small.

Soon, I thought. Soon I would find them.

I made my way toward the crowd, surprised to see how many girls were wearing exactly the sort of bathing suit I was too modest to try on. They were so unselfconscious. Even though I'd worn a tank top and jeans over the black bathing suit, everyone turned to stare.

Tentatively, I held up my hand in a wave. Then I smiled.

It was a false smile, at least at first, but then one by one, the people staring at me started to smile back, nodding their heads and returning to their conversations and their games.

I began to relax.

Parvda was heading my way, Adam towering behind her. Her long hair was pulled high into a ponytail, emphasizing her big gorgeous eyes. She, too, was nearly naked and completely unworried about it. I wondered what was passing through Adam's mind as he took in his girlfriend like this, if he preferred her this way as opposed to the virtual Parvda he'd known in the App World. Real bodies were so different, more vulnerable, but also, more sensual and beautiful.

I was suddenly curious if they'd had sex.

Mrs. Worthington had taught us that real sex was

disgusting and caused disease. She would be horrified at the mere idea. The thought of her being horrified put a grin on my face.

"Hi, Skylar," Parvda said. "Glad you could make it."

I was grateful to no longer be standing alone. "Me too, I think."

Adam planted himself next to me. "Hello, o famous one."

A laugh bubbled out of me, a relief after so much tension. "Shut up," I said, and punched him in the arm.

"Ow." He rubbed the place where my fist met muscle.

Parvda joined in our laughter. "Serves you right."

Adam put his arm around me. "I'm enjoying the fame by association, in case you were wondering."

"I wasn't, but thanks for letting me know." It was a little strange interacting with the real Adam after only knowing the virtual one. "Is it me, or is it weird how we all look so similar to our virtual selves, but so different, too?"

Adam grinned. "I think it's just you."

I eyed him. "You are way more relaxed here than you were in the App World." I turned to Parvda. "He was an angry virtual man."

Two spots of red dotted her cheeks. "He's lost without me."

He shrugged. "It's true."

Parvda smiled up at him. "I'm going to get us some

drinks and give you guys a chance to catch up."

Adam's eyes never left Parvda as she walked away. I saw the love in them again, but now I saw the desire, too. As I watched Adam watching Parvda, once more I felt a stab of jealousy that he'd found what he wanted so easily and immediately, and now was so obviously happy. If I had to guess, both worlds could fall into chaos and Adam wouldn't flinch as long as he was with Parvda. But this time I felt something more than jealousy, I felt a desire of my own. If I was to be with someone in this real body, I wanted them to look at me the way Adam looked at Parvda, with love and desire both.

"What's going through your brain, Cruz?" Adam asked, once Parvda disappeared into the crowd.

"Cruz?" I wrinkled my nose. "No one calls me Cruz."

"Well, I'm calling you Cruz."

I laughed. "I was thinking I'm happy you found Parvda. You guys are lucky." Then I remembered who I'd seen in the weapons room and who wasn't so lucky. My mood darkened. "I met Zeera."

Adam's smile disappeared. "Yeah. I know. Poor Sylvia."

Just then the bonfire roared higher, the light of it flashing bright against the windows of the compound. The group of seventeens playing soccer whizzed by us, two girls shouting to each other. Another group splashed through the shallow waves, laughing. "You really woke up here?" I asked. "Staring into the eyes of Parvda?"

Adam nodded. "I'm sorry things have been harder on you," he said.

I wondered if Adam knew that Lacy was right here, inside the house, or if Rain was keeping that information a secret. Then I thought about Rain's father setting me up to unplug and leaving me to die, and another possibility shook me. "Do you think Trader knew what would happen when each of us unplugged? That you'd wake up with your girlfriend, and that I'd wake up . . . how I did?"

Adam grimaced. "I've wondered that myself, but I can't really say one way or the other." He glanced back at the crowd by the bonfire. "All I know is that around here, people listen to Rain and don't ask questions if he doesn't want them to. They accepted my presence like it was normal, like they'd expected my arrival. From what I understand, they took up the task of trying to rescue you because Rain said it was the right thing to do, even if it was dangerous."

I shook my head, mixed emotions warring within. "So it's the same for Rain in the Real World as it was back home. Everyone does whatever he wants."

"Don't be so hard on him, Skylar," Adam said. "He broke off communications with his father because of what happened to you. That's the rumor, at least."

My eyebrows arched. "What other rumors are there?"

"Well," he said, his voice lowered, "I hear different things about Jonathan Holt. Some people think that he's this idealistic leader of the App World, who's working to repair the divide between the Keepers and the citizens at home. And other people think that everything he does is about power, and that the only reason he'd stand up for the Keepers and those seventeens left on this side of the border is because he sees his power slipping away to Emory Specter."

"And what do *you* think, Adam?" I asked.

"I think—" he started, but right then, Parvda returned, a bottle and two cups delicately balanced in her hands. Adam didn't finish. Instead, he smiled and changed the subject. "I think that *you* should take *my* advice, Skylar, and enjoy yourself tonight. One of the great things about this place is that come evening, people like to play. I think it's how everyone stays sane."

I had a million other questions for Adam, and the thought of giving up the chance to ask them immediately was disappointing. "Okay," I told him with a shrug. "I'll go along with it for now."

Parvda handed Adam the bottle. "Beer for you." She turned to me, offering me one of the cups. "And cocktails for us."

Adam raised his bottle. "Shall we make a toast?"

"Definitely," Parvda said.

"To Skylar joining us," Adam said.

I raised my glass first to him, then to Parvda. "To finding the people we love."

Parvda and Adam smiled at each other.

We clinked cups and bottles.

"Be careful with that stuff," Parvda said just as I'd put the drink to my lips for a sip. "It's strong."

"Now you tell me!" I'd already swallowed a big gulp, my eyes bulging, throat burning. If I'd been alone, I might have spit it out. "I'll take a Drunk App any day over this."

"You'll get used to it," Adam said.

"It makes your legs feel woozy," Parvda said.

"My legs?" In the App World, the feeling of being drunk was like fizz in your mind. It blurred the lines of the virtual self in the atmosphere. I took a bigger sip, more prepared for the taste and the burning this time. "What does that even mean?"

Adam snatched the glass from my hand. "Keep drinking that fast and you'll find out."

"Hey! Give that back."

He held it up, looking into my eyes over the rim of the cup, his mouth a grin. "Don't say I didn't warn you." He returned it to me. "It will turn your instincts to mush. Though, now that I think of it, maybe it's just the sort of push you need to loosen up. Like downloading an Antianxiety App." He nodded. "So drink up!"

Parvda punched him in the arm this time. "Stop bullying her."

He looked sheepish. "Why are all the girls hitting me tonight?"

She blinked up at him sweetly. "Maybe because you deserve it?"

"But I'm such a nice guy!"

I saw Rain walking up and over the dune, heading toward the bonfire. "I'll leave you two to work this out alone," I said, and started off in his direction. The rumors Adam told me about were bright in my mind, and I wondered if I would find the right moment to bring them up with Rain. I wanted to know which ones were true, and what Rain thought.

He smiled when he saw me approaching. "You made it."

"Did you think I wouldn't?"

"I don't know," he said. "But I'm glad you're here. Did you get some rest?"

I shrugged, remembering my dream. We fell into step. "A little. That room is beautiful."

"After my grandparents left Briarwood for good for the App World, other families took it over," Rain explained as we walked. "The people who lived in it were some of the wealthiest citizens of the Real World. Then they abandoned it for the App World, too. Everyone here has, ah, co-opted their clothes and rooms."

"Yeah, I can see that," I said.

He glanced toward the group gathered near the fire. "Come with me to grab a beer and I'll introduce you around." He peered into my almost-empty cup as we walked. "Do you want another?"

I thought about Parvda's warning that the cocktail was strong. But then I heard Adam's voice saying it would loosen me up. "Sure," I said, and vowed I'd drink this one more slowly.

A crowd surrounded several large coolers in the sand. Inside them were dozens of dark-brown bottles. Sitting on top of a table were pitchers full of whatever it was I'd been drinking. As night began to cloak the beach in darkness, everyone seemed to become more anonymous, and I felt more anonymous too. Maybe I really would have fun tonight, I thought, as Rain began to pick through the various options.

A tall boy with blond curly hair was next to me. He held up the cup in his hand, then pointed at the pitchers on the table. "Can I get you something?"

I shook my head. "Someone's already taking care of me, but thanks."

The boy didn't go anywhere. Just stood there, looking at me, like he wanted to say something but wasn't sure what. He wore bathing suit shorts, like most of the other boys here. His arms and shoulders were muscular, like most everyone else, too. It was as though the plugs had kept us on a near-constant exercise schedule, toning our arms and legs and bellies, and feeding us nutrients for our hair and skin.

"So," I said, trying to think of what to talk to him

about. "Did we know each other in the App World before you unplugged?"

"No." He smiled sheepishly. "Sorry. It's just strange to see you here so . . . so alive and animated. I'm Rex," he added.

"Skylar," I said.

"Yeah, I know," he said.

I felt awkward. I didn't like being famous, as Adam put it. I was grateful to see Rain heading toward us, a beer in one hand, my drink in the other.

He handed it to me and nodded hello to Rex. Then Rain gestured toward the crowd next to the bonfire. "Let's go meet a few more seventeens."

Rex raised his hand in a wave as we walked away.

Over the next hour I met nearly everyone on the beach. Some I recognized from the App World and others I'd lived with for years in Singles Hall, but we'd never formally crossed paths. As the night wore on and my second drink disappeared, I searched the crowd for Zeera, but didn't see her anywhere.

At one point, Jessica leaned in. "So what do you think of Rain?"

The two of us stared at him across the sand, standing in the middle of a group of girls who were hanging on his every word.

I shrugged. "Rain Holt is Rain Holt," I said, like it didn't faze me. But that wasn't exactly true. Even saying his name made my skin flush red. I took another sip of my drink, hoping to hide this. "What about you?"

"He's not what I expected," she began. She got a wry smile on her face. "Definitely dreamy, you know? Most of the time he seems like a totally different person from the Rain I knew on Reel Time. But then he'll do or say something that absolutely reminds me who he really is."

I laughed. "I know exactly what you mean."

"Yeah?"

I nodded. Soon we were talking and laughing as the evening grew dark, Jessica giving me the rundown on who among the seventeens had kissed so far, and who had crushes on who else but hadn't yet gotten together. It felt good to talk to another girl, one I could imagine becoming my friend eventually. "I know I said this earlier," I said, changing the subject to a more serious topic. "But I'm grateful for your help on the cliff. You risked your life for me." I drained the last sip of my drink. "I hope I can repay the favor someday." As I spoke these words, I realized they were true—that I *wanted* them to be true.

Jessica leaned forward, her long brown hair swinging. "It's okay, Skylar." Two rosy dots appeared on her cheeks. "Singles get one another's backs, right?"

"Yes," I said, and meant it with my whole heart. By the time I made my way to Rain again, the alcohol was buzzing through my veins, making me giddy. Beyond the light of the bonfire, shadows moved toward the ocean, people stripping off clothing and leaving it behind on the sand.

"You were talking to Jessica a long time," Rain said when I reached him.

"I like her a lot," I said, but my attention was still on all the people heading toward the water. "They're going to swim naked?"

Rain laughed. "It's called skinny-dipping. People do it all the time at these parties. There's nothing like being in a real body and jumping in the ocean on a warm evening."

"But does it have to be naked?" Even as I expressed my doubt, I could already imagine the appeal and freedom of it.

Rain shrugged, his eyes flickering in the light of the bonfire. "Sure, why not?"

"You sound like you know from experience," I said.

"I've done it once or twice," he said. "There was at least some truth to the Rain Holt in the App World. I'm still a thrill seeker. I'm surprised you don't want to join them."

The crowd of swimmers kept growing in number. There were shouts and laughter as people splashed and jumped in the waves. "Before I would have probably loved it."

"Before what?" he asked.

"Before I found out I was put on exhibit without my consent or even my knowledge. Before I learned I was an object to be displayed."

"You're not an object," Rain said quietly.

The shouts and laughter got louder. Other people paired off, walking away down the beach, their heads bent close together. "Is nudity required to swim?"

Rain laughed. "I can promise you there are plenty of people wearing bathing suits."

"Good, because I'm going in." I pulled off my tank top and threw it onto the sand. Then I unbuttoned my jeans and slid out of them, leaving them in a pile at my feet. I started toward the water. The cool night air on my skin gave me goose bumps. I turned back to Rain. "Are you coming or what?"

He tugged his shirt over his head and let it fall to the sand.

My eyes slid across his shoulders and chest.

Then I forced myself to look away.

A wave coming in to shore washed over my feet, the cool water making me shiver. I waded up to my knees. Even when I was gaming, I'd never gone swimming in the dark. I knew I should feel afraid, that we were more vulnerable at night without the sun to reveal the dangers in our midst, but for some reason I wasn't. The ocean was gentle, even the sound of the waves soft and hesitant, the tide low and peaceful. The moon above reflected off the surface, swaying and rippling across a slice of water that stretched all the way to the horizon. The ocean swirled around my legs, swelling to the middle of my thighs and subsiding back to my knees. I waded farther and farther out, away from everyone else who was swimming. Soon the water was up to my chest and I was barely able to stay on my toes. The waves wanted to lift me off the ground, so I dove under. The ocean was black around my body, as though I'd submerged myself in a pool of ink.

Then I did something I never did while gaming.

I lay back in the water and relaxed all my muscles, my head just skimming the surface, letting myself float, the waves gently bobbing me up and down, the water lapping against my skin. When I opened my eyes, the night was big and alive and bright with stars. The moon cut a crescent light above. A sense of peace spread from my body to my mind and filled my senses. For the first time I could understand how everything was connected. How *I* was connected. The way the body tied me to the world and reality, to the stars in the sky and the shimmering ocean buoying my back. How I was more than just a brain used to project a virtual image into another world.

I didn't want the feeling to end.

But then I sensed I was being observed. I looked up, pulling my head from the water with a loud splash. Rain was standing a couple of feet away, the ocean rising to his shoulders and falling back to his chest as waves rippled by. The lights of New Port City sparkled far behind him.

I closed the distance between us. "Were you watching me?"

His skin glistened in the moonlight. "I didn't want you to float out to sea."

A gentle wave lifted us off the bottom, then set us down closer together. I laughed. "Sure."

"You're shivering," he said. "We should get out. Tomorrow will be another long day."

I sighed. "You're probably right."

We walked toward the beach in silence. Water from my hair cascaded down my body. I gathered it into my hands and tried to wring it out like I would a towel. The air chilled my skin and now my teeth were chattering. As we headed toward the pile of clothing we'd left behind, sand caked my feet and ankles. I stared down at my tank top and jeans. There was no point in putting them on. They'd only get soaked.

"Here," Rain said, grabbing his shirt and holding it out. "Wear this."

I shook my head. "Thanks, but it'll be drenched the moment it hits my skin."

He shook it. "Take it anyway," he said.

So I did, watching as Rain walked off to say hello to someone nearby. I slipped my arms into it and fastened the buttons up the front one by one. The fabric clung to my body in places, wet all the way through, but it was true—I felt better with it on than not. I extended my arms, studying the way the too-large sleeves belled away from my skin and wrinkled around my wrists at the cuff. There was something intimate about wearing a boy's shirt. About wearing *Rain's* shirt. I didn't remember an App for that at home. *There should be one*, I thought. Then I pushed the thought away and started up the beach toward the dunes.

"Hey, wait up," Rain called just as I'd reached the top.

"I didn't want to bother you," I said.

"Well, I didn't want to miss the chance to say good night."

We descended the other side of the dune toward the house in silence, and in no time we were almost to my room. We stopped at the bottom of the steps that led from the sand up to the door. It was cool on my feet. I knew this was my chance to ask Rain more about his father and his father's plans, but now that I had my opportunity, I didn't want to spoil the moment, or the peaceful end to this evening. "Good night then," I said, but I didn't turn to go.

Neither of us did.

Rain didn't speak. Didn't move. He just stood there looking at me, like he was debating something. I combed my fingers through my tangled, wet hair, unsure whether I should hop up the steps and head inside, or if there was something else I was supposed to do or say. Or that Rain was waiting for me to say. I bet Inara would use this chance to flirt, to win Rain's attention and, at the very least, a kiss. She would never waste the opportunity to capture Rain's heart, even for only a minute. *All boys are an occasion for romance*, Inara always said. But I wasn't Inara. And I reminded myself that I barely knew Rain, and that most of what I did know of him—from the App World, at least—I'd never liked, that no matter how different he seemed here, he still had another side to him.

"Aren't you cold?" I finally asked, breaking the silence.

"No," he said.

I waited for him to go on, but he didn't. I started up the steps. "Okay, well—"

"Don't go." Rain put a hand on my arm and stopped me.

My eyebrows arched. I glanced at his fingers. I was shivering, but I wasn't cold. His hand fell away from my arm. Rain stared at his fingers, turning them over, flexing them, as though touching me had changed them. Then his eyes returned to mine. There was something in them that took me a moment to recognize, and as I did, my heart sped.

Want. They were full of want.

Rain touched a finger gently to my chin.

I held my breath. I wasn't sure what would happen next, but I couldn't believe this was happening at all. I closed my eyes.

But when I opened them again, Rain's hand fell away. The moment had passed.

His gaze was steady. "You should probably get some rest."

"I should."

"Good night, Skye," he said.

I watched Rain walk down the path and disappear over the dune, my hand on the place where his fingers had touched my face. My skin was still warm.

25

Glass houses

I WAS IN the room again, the one filled with weapons.

"Who's there?" I called, banging against the door. "What do you want from me?"

There was no answer.

I pushed against the walls, testing every spot I could reach, trying to find a way through. I'd gotten halfway around the room when the screens buzzed. I stopped to watch what would happen next. The static grew louder. I covered my ears with my hands. My head hurt with the noise, like my mind might explode. Just when it became nearly intolerable, the sound stopped and the screens flickered gray. From the biggest one came a blinding flash of light. I rubbed my eyes, waiting for the spots to fade.

That's when I saw the image.

A face.

I went to the screen and placed my hand on it. "Trader? Is that you?"

His dark eyes blinked back at me. "Do you trust me, Skye?" he asked.

The very next second every other screen in the room flashed. This time I was quick enough to cover my eyes. When the light returned to normal, I pulled my fingers away.

"You betrayed me," said a thousand Inaras all at once, her face repeated again and again, as big as my body and as small as the pad of a fingertip.

"I didn't," I pleaded. "Inara, I'm sorry! I didn't mean to—"

The sound of knocking interrupted my cries. I looked around, searching for its source. The knocking grew louder. Meanwhile, the Trader image and the Inaras started speaking over one another in between all that banging.

"Do you trust me, Skye?"

"You betrayed me."

"You betrayed me."

"You betrayed me."

"Do you trust me, Skye?"

I screamed, eyes shut tight. "Please stop!"

And suddenly, it did.

All that was left was the knocking.

I opened my eyes. I was in my room at Briarwood, lying in the great white bed, my legs twisted in the sheets. When I'd gone to sleep the bed was neatly made, my body barely a small hill marring the order, but during the night I'd pulled the sheets free and now they were hanging down onto the floor, along with the pillows I'd pushed away. Sweat covered my skin.

The knocking continued.

"Skylar?" said a girl's voice. "It's me. Zeera."

I sat up, unsteady, still shaken from the dream. It had been so real, as though it actually happened. As though people were still poking around in my brain. I got out of bed and stumbled toward the door, opening it.

Zeera was standing there. "Are you okay?"

"Yeah. I mean, yes. I think so." My hair hung in my face. I tried to rake my fingers through it, but it was knotted. I must look like a disaster. "Sorry. I was having a nightmare."

Zeera glanced beyond me toward the bed, at the pile of sheets and pillows on the floor. She nodded, looking at me like she knew exactly how this felt. "I just wanted to make sure you were up in time for breakfast," she said. "Just walk out the way you came in, take two rights, go down the long hallway, then hang a left."

"Two rights, long hallway, then a left," I repeated.

She nodded. Then she closed the door behind her.

I stripped off the clothes I'd worn to bed and stepped into the shower, letting the cool water flow over my body and soak my tangled hair. Despite the nightmare, I couldn't help marveling at this tiny luxury. When I was small and in the Real World, I'd only taken baths. My first shower was at the Keeper's house and I could've stayed in it all day, this rainstorm that you can control. I dried off quickly and raked a brush through my wet hair, yanking at it when the bristles hit a knot. The Keeper was so much better at this. When she brushed my hair it felt like I'd downloaded one of those Spa Apps Inara's mother liked so much.

Inara.

You betrayed me, went my brain, echoing her voice from the dream.

I stared at my face in the mirror.

Tired eyes stared back.

When—*if*—I ever saw my best friend again, would she look at this face and only see someone who'd deceived her?

I stepped away from my reflection and got dressed. I was out the door before my mind could decide on an answer.

It was easier that way.

Two rights, long hallway, and a left, I told myself as I walked away from my room, trying to fill my thoughts with something other than the dream. Soon my mind turned to Rain, to our last moments on the beach before we'd said good night, and I felt my cheeks flush. My heart fluttered. *You like him*, it informed me. But then my brain kicked in and shoved those feelings away.

Romance should be the last priority on my list.

I stopped midstride and looked around. I was no longer following Zeera's instructions to the cafeteria. Or at least, my body wasn't. I seemed to be going down, down, down underneath the earth, the halls I followed sloping gently into a series of ramps. I took a step forward, then another, allowing that internal GPS, or whatever it was, to kick in again in my brain.

I decided to follow it.

Eventually I came to one final ramp. At the end of it was a great silver door, similar to the one that led to the weapons room. Huge round bolts framed it. I backed against the wall as someone else approached from down another corridor. I heard a door sigh open. I watched as the woman went inside.

Before the door could close, I slipped in behind her.

A soft glow lit the darkness.

The woman was already gone.

I looked around. The room was cavernous. There came a familiar sound, too, a rushing in, then a retreat, a rushing in, then a retreat, the rhythm of the sea ebbing and flowing, bringing with it the briny smell of salt.

The ocean must be close. Once my eyes adjusted to the dim light, I looked up. It wasn't just that the room was cavernous. The room was actually a cave built into the rocks. The stone glistened with wet, the air humid and heavy. I returned my attention to the ground. At first I thought I was seeing things, hallucinating this vision before me, but it wasn't long before I knew it was all too real. This giant cave housed a library of sorts, with row after row of shelves. But stacked on those shelves were not books.

They were coffins.

Coffin after coffin after coffin, floor to ceiling, coffins everywhere I turned, lit up from the inside by a light source I couldn't pinpoint. They were made of a thin, crystal-clear glass.

My heart raced.

"Oh my god," I whispered, a chill sweeping across my skin. I knew right then what I was seeing.

These were the plugs.

Inside each box was a cradle for the body, designed to rest the legs and the arms, with a special spot for the head that connected to the brain, projecting the virtual self into the App World. The idea that I had spent over eleven years of my life housed in one of these glass coffins was nearly incomprehensible. They were both disturbing to behold but also strangely beautiful.

All of them were empty of bodies.

But they seemed . . . ready to house bodies. Ready to house lots of them.

Why hadn't Rain showed me this place yesterday?

What was he planning that he hadn't told me about yet?

The soundtrack of the ocean was steady all around. I walked down another of the rows, at the very end of which was a single coffin set apart from all the others. When I got close enough for a better look, I halted.

I'd been wrong before.

Not all of the boxes were empty.

Inside this coffin was the body of a man. I pressed my hand against the glass where he lay. My jaw fell open.

The man was Jonathan Holt.

I was staring at Rain's father. That's why he was set apart.

The resemblance was obvious. I could see Rain in the curves of the face and the strong jaw. His limbs and muscles were completely relaxed, his breathing gentle and slow, eyes closed. I took in Jonathan Holt, the man who was willing to let me die. He seemed so peaceful. I crouched down and peered closer.

Was Rain afraid of me knowing his father was here?

I took a step back. Then another.

I wanted to turn away. It felt wrong to watch him when he was unaware. A violation of privacy. Was I any better right now than the Keepers who had made my body available for the entire city to see, to inspect, to witness?

But in the midst of these dark thoughts, a hopeful one struck.

I began to run from coffin to coffin, down row after row, peering through the glass, hoping to find that at least one of them held another body—a very particular body. I don't know how many boxes I saw before I gave up.

Inara.

She wasn't here.

My entire body slumped. I knew it was unlikely I'd find her, but still, for a moment I'd hoped. Shoulders hunched, I headed back the way I'd come. I needed to leave, needed to find Rain. Questions piled onto other questions. My stomach churned. It was only when I passed through the thick metal door into the bright corridor that I felt like I could breathe again. I started up the series of ramps that led to the ground floor. My footsteps, soft against the tiled floor, were the only sounds for a while. But as I neared the top of the last ramp, I heard voices coming from around the corner.

A boy and a girl. Whispering. Then laughter—the girl's laughter. Giggling.

I hung back. Thought of what Jessica had told me last night about which seventeens had gotten together with which others. About Adam and Parvda. I didn't want to embarrass anyone by showing up unannounced and catching them making out when they thought they had privacy. The whispering continued, followed by more laughing.

I could be here all day.

Maybe they were so taken with each other they wouldn't notice me go by. I crept forward a little, then a little more. As I got closer, I began to hear snatches of their conversation.

"She doesn't know. Not a thing."

"How—"

"I missed you so much."

"I'm such a good little actress, aren't I?"

"—her sister—"

And then, a name that rooted me to the floor. "Skylar." Followed by the girl's laughter. "She still thinks you're going to help her find her family?"

My skin raced with static. I leaned against the wall to steady myself, and crossed my arms around my middle, hugging it. I couldn't get air into my lungs. If I was still in the App World, I would literally light up with electricity. I could almost hear it crackling in my ears. Quietly, and ever so slowly, I emerged from my hiding place. I already knew who I'd see, but still, I couldn't quite believe what my ears were telling me. I needed proof from my own eyes.

There he was, his back to me.

Rain.

Leaning against the wall. His body framed by the girl's long flowing hair.

Copper colored and bright in the light.

Lacy Mills was up and about as though she'd been walking around for ages. Her hand rested on Rain's arm with the kind of familiarity that only comes from being together in a romantic way.

I swallowed. Lacy and Rain were a couple.

I'm such a good little actress, she'd said.

Yesterday was all an act?

An act to convince me that Lacy was helpless? That she meant nothing to Rain? And that Rain might actually like me, Skylar Cruz?

Lacy's fingertips slid up Rain's arm, her nails glittering green. Rain leaned forward a little, maybe to hear whatever she whispered to him now.

Maybe to kiss her—I couldn't quite tell.

My face burned with a fierceness that set my skin on fire. Shame consumed me. I was so stupid. Stupid enough to think that someone like me, a nobody Single, might catch the eye of Rain Holt. And he'd let me think this too. He knew it all along, knew what he was doing, knew that he was luring me in, knew exactly how to do it. He used me, was still using me to his own end, whatever that was. He was never going to help me, had planned on betraying me from the very first moment. And I'd let him. I'd let him get in the way of searching for my family, the very thing I'd come here to do. The boy on the mountaintop, that version of Rain, evaporated in an instant, replaced by the one

I'd known ever since I'd plugged in. The playboy all the girls loved and swooned over. He had been that Rain this whole time, and I was foolish enough to think he might be more than that. That I might be more than who I'd always been in the App World too.

Well, I'd learned my lesson.

I breathed deep, in and out. Watched them there.

I would never trust Rain again.

They still hadn't seen me.

I needed to get away without them noticing. I couldn't bear it if they did. Lacy had humiliated me with that act yesterday. It was just the kind of thing I'd expect from Lacy. Before I'd met Rain Holt in the Real World, I would have expected the same from him too.

Tears pressed into my eyes.

I'd really believed that here he was different.

Silently, I backed away. I was nearly to the end of the hall where I could turn the corner and be safely out of sight when Lacy shifted, enough so that I could see her face. Yesterday, when she'd been in bed, she'd seemed so different from the sparkling, made-up Lacy I was accustomed to from the App World. But now I saw her with new eyes, saw how her freckles highlighted an unusual sort of beauty, how her face came alive while she talked to Rain, how she mesmerized him. She'd only seemed different yesterday because I'd allowed myself to think that maybe in the Real World being Skylar Cruz meant something significant, that my body was capable of great things, and that on top of this, here, people thought I was beautiful.

Rain Holt had seemed to think I was beautiful.

But now I knew the truth. Now I knew better.

Liar.

Right then, right when I was about to disappear around the corner, Lacy shifted once more.

This time, her eyes settled on my face.

They were triumphant.

She didn't even flinch, seeing me there.

Her smile grew wider and wider until her teeth gleamed from it.

And, knowing I was watching, she leaned forward, leaned toward Rain, into what would surely become a kiss.

I closed my eyes. I couldn't watch.

Finally, I slipped away.

I emerged from the mansion and ran down the beach. Unlike yesterday, when everything seemed magical, today I barely noticed the crash of the waves or the ocean rippling across the sand. My mind kept going over what I'd just seen, these images on repeat. The parking lot and then Rain's car came into sight over the edge of the dune. Regardless of what I'd just witnessed, one thing hadn't changed. The real Skylar Cruz might not be able to capture the heart of Rain Holt, but she—her body, her mind, at least—was capable of many things.

Like hotwiring a car.

Stealing it.

And driving it back to the city.

I ran straight up to Rain's precious car, opened the door, and went to work. Let my body take over my mind, drawing on those skills I'd learned while gaming at home, and setting my hands to work on those wires. Soon the car roared to life, and I was headed back the way we'd come. At first I swerved left and right, unable to keep the wheel steady, but it didn't take long before I gained control and was speeding fast and sure toward the skyline of New Port City and the bridge that connected it to the mainland.

When I arrived at the mansion on the edge of the sea, I turned off the car. I was about to go inside to see the Keeper when I thought better of it. Could I really trust her? Could I ever really trust anyone?

What if I never found my family?

Would I always be alone in this world?

I got out and stared at the wide marble esplanade on the grounds, at the faded glory of that beautiful house. Of the roses growing wild all over. Then I turned my back on it, on the Keeper, too, and headed into the city.

26

A dangerous view

THE SUN DISAPPEARED behind a series of heavy rain
clouds.

The Water Tower loomed before me, cutting away
an impressive swath of sky, catching the gray light and
turning it into a dark, moving liquid. It seemed to shift
and sway. People were coming in and out of it nearly
constantly. I went inside the entrance behind a Keeper
in a flowing green dress. Even the handles on the doors
seemed made of delicate coral. On any other day I would
be awed to experience the real version of this virtual
skyscraper I'd always loved, but now I was numb to the
momentousness of the opportunity. There was too much
on my mind.

That's why I'd come here.

To think. To get my feelings in order.

The lobby walls were an aquarium of fish. Yellow, purple, blue, striped, and spotted, some with teeth sticking up from ugly jaws. They swam in and out of holes in the rocks, disappearing behind swatches of seaweed. Bright orange and pink anemones grew up from the bottom of the tank like fields of flowers. I watched them for a moment, fixated, until a long shadow that had been lurking way back in the shadows darted forward, its rows of tiny triangular teeth bared as it leapt at the glass.

At me.

I didn't move.

It swam away.

I continued through the lobby. A woman glanced at me twice on her way out of the building, her eyes settling on mine. But then she broke the stare and headed off. A shiver of fear passed over me as I realized I didn't have my scarf. I hadn't had it with me all morning, not when I drove back to New Port City either. I let my hair fall forward, forming a curtain on either side of my face.

Should I go back?

No, I decided.

I stepped into the stream of people moving toward a bank of elevators. The silver doors opened and I was pushed inside by the force of the crowd. The doors shut and my heart clenched. I counted fifteen people packed around me. Was this contraption safe? Could it hold all of us? Maybe I should have taken the stairs.

Too late.

The elevator began to rise.

It stopped and one man got off. Then we were moving upward again, the screen at the top counting each floor. *Sixteen. Seventeen. Eighteen.* When the number hit twenty-nine, the door opened and two women left. Floor by floor, I watched the count climb higher, the elevator emptying out as we went. Soon there was only one woman left besides me. We reached the seventy-fifth floor and stopped.

The woman glanced at me. "It doesn't go any farther. You're out of luck if you want to go to the top. The viewing deck is closed for repairs."

"Oh," I said, disappointed. "I didn't know."

She stepped off the elevator, her arm blocking the doors from closing. "Come on, or it's just going to go back down with you in it."

I exited and found myself standing in a nondescript, white-walled space surrounded by other elevators. "Thanks."

She pointed down the hall. "If you head there and turn left, there's a makeshift viewing deck. It's still quite impressive, though you can only see north," she added with a smile. Then her face clouded over. She stared at me a beat too long, before turning around and walking away.

I stood there, unsure what to do. I didn't come here to see the seventy-fifth floor. Out of the corner of my eye, I saw a sign for the stairwell. Maybe I could continue up through there. The door opened with a loud creak, then swung shut behind me with a heavy slam. Heading toward the lower floors wouldn't be a problem, but going up was another story. A wire gate stretched from floor to ceiling, blocking passage toward the seventy-sixth floor. Posted on the side was a sign that said *No Entry Beyond This Point*. The word *DANGER* shouted in red letters above it. A chain looped around the latch, sealed shut by a heavy lock, but the wire didn't reach across the entire opening. There was a triangle of space just below the ceiling of the next staircase and above the handrail. This was only a small obstacle, to be overcome by hopping up on the lower railing and pulling myself over the higher one. The only difficulty, of course, was that I was in a real body, and at home I'd always been in an indestructible virtual one, enhanced by gaming perks. I could feel my arms twitching at my sides, my muscles and limbs anxious to get going.

I decided to listen to my body.

I kicked off my sandals and hopped up onto the lower rail, my feet balanced along the rung like it was a tightrope, reaching for the higher one where the triangle of space would just allow me to slither through. Muscles straining, I climbed as far as I could, but eventually had to pull myself up and over the rest of the way. After a few seconds of struggling, my waist was even with the bar and soon I was through the opening to the other side.

The floor was thick with dust. Above me there was darkness, but I'd gone to the top of the virtual version of this place so many times I knew it as well as I now knew the contours of my own real body. I started up, plunging myself into the shadows, my left hand feeling for the wall and my right sliding up along the rail. When I reached the top-floor viewing deck, I was winded, but not as much as I would've thought. For a split second my gut clenched in warning, my brain conjuring the last time I'd climbed this building in the App World, how Jonathan Holt had appeared to me in a hologram. There was the gun, the storm, Inara's despair. And Rain, waiting for me at the top.

I shook off the unease.

The moment I stepped through the door, relief swept over me.

The sun shined bright through an opening in the clouds, streaming through the dust on the windows of the top-floor lobby. I pushed my way outside to the viewing deck, and relished the breeze so high up on this sweltering day. Everything was just as I remembered it from the App World, except that here debris littered the ground everywhere I turned. A few broken planters, broken glass, and the remains of what must have been benches. The biggest difference, though, was that the deck was fenced in on all sides by tall iron posts that curved inward. At home, the Water Tower had been a popular launching site for flying and rappelling and parachuting toward the ground, but this one seemed designed to prevent fragile human bodies from throwing themselves to their deaths. I did a lap, careful not to trip on any rubble or cut myself on the broken glass sticking up from the ground. My left hand brushed across the iron posts, hot from the sun.

The view was spectacular, and to have this place all to myself, incredible.

I peered through two of the posts on the south side of the deck. The city was an island surrounded by ocean. There was a series of bridges, and the lonely tops of skyscrapers farther south. On the north side I could see all the way to the peninsula that had been my welcome to the Real World. Down below people were tiny specks on the ground as they went about their business. I'd come here to think about all I'd learned since unplugging, but now, my mind resisted. The impulse to climb to the other side of the fence in front of me, reaching upward toward the sun, was powerful. I even found myself wedging my foot high between the iron posts before I caught myself and stopped. My mind was flooded with thoughts of Rain and the moment I thought we were about to kiss. All over again, my body responded in a way that my mind was powerless to resist.

The body, the real one, had urges and desires all its own.

It made me feel out of control.

But then, what would desire be if we could control it? Something else. Not desire at all.

I willed myself away from the fence and took another lap around the viewing deck. It was strange to think that the last time I'd been here I was a virtual self playing Odyssey. It felt like a hundred years ago. I looked out over the west side of the tower, locating the mansion where I lived with the Keeper. It was so small from this high up.

Then I turned east.

A metal chair was pressed against one of the walls of the viewing deck. It wasn't broken or damaged. It seemed brand-new. What's more, there were discarded apple cores, stems of grapes, and the withered tops of strawberries strewn in a pile next to it. A large green hat with a wide brim was placed neatly on the seat.

The top of this building might be sealed off to visitors, but I wasn't the only person who'd enjoyed the view from the deck. Someone had been coming here. A lot. Most of the apple cores were shriveled and brown, nearly burnt from the sun's harsh heat, but a couple of them were fresher than the others. They'd been left behind more recently, maybe even as recently as yesterday.

I heard the sound of a door opening.

Then footsteps.

And I froze.

They came to a stop behind me, the only sound the sharp intake of breath amid the low whistle of the breeze. The occupant of the chair was back.

My hands balled into fists as I turned around. I put a hand to my chest. "Inara?"

I was looking into the eyes of my best friend in both worlds, eyes I knew almost as well as my own. She was tinier than I was accustomed to, everything about her more delicate, almost childlike. But her blond hair was the same—no, it was far more beautiful now that it was real. It was long and wavy and curled down around her shoulders to her waist. Inara's mouth gaped wide, like she might be seeing a ghost.

I tried to swallow, but I couldn't.

She blinked once, then again. Like she couldn't believe what she was seeing. She held a tiny device with a button on it. I watched as she pushed it. "I knew I'd find you here eventually," she whispered. Before I could respond, she threw her arms around me in a hug. A key dangled in her hand, cutting into my back.

A key to the locked gate?

But how? Why?

I pulled away. "It's really you," I said. There was a moment's hesitation, then joy flooded me. Inara and I would have a second chance! *I* would have a second chance, at least, to make things up to her for leaving. "I've missed you so much."

"This was always your favorite place in the City," she said, but she wasn't smiling now. After our embrace, the joy of our reunion seemed absent for her. "I knew you couldn't resist the real thing for long."

My own smile faltered. "You know me better than anyone."

Inara's eyes were glassy. A tear slipped down her cheek. "Then why didn't I guess you were about to unplug? I thought of you as my sister, Skylar. And then you abandoned me like I didn't matter at all."

"I would never do that, Inara," I said, but even to me the words were hollow.

"But you did," she said. "You chose your *other* sister over me. I thought you saw me as your real sister. You never did though."

"That's not true." I swallowed. "It was never a competition."

She laughed, her face streaked with tears. "Wasn't it, though? Isn't it still?"

I looked at her strangely. Something was off. I could hear it in her voice. Inara had a tell when she was lying.

She laughed a certain way, with a higher pitch. It wavered too much, like she was nervous. And her eyes kept darting everywhere. "How did you get here? Who helped you unplug?"

"You really have no idea what you've done, do you?" she said, sounding choked. "To me, my family, my parents, who treated you like their own daughter. I was forced here, Skylar—at least that's what my parents believe. But honestly, a part of me wanted to come. Even though you lied to me, left me without saying good-bye, you're still my sister. The *only* sister I've ever had. And then another part of me wanted to get you back, but now that I'm here . . ." A sob choked her throat.

"What aren't you telling me, Inara?" I asked.

"It will be easier on everyone if you go willingly," Inara said between sobs.

My heart sank like a heavy stone. "Go where?"

There came the sound of footsteps—many footsteps—on the roof. A line of guards emerged through the door behind Inara, guns cocked.

They were pointed at me.

"Inara," I whispered, my heart pounding with fear. "What did you do?"

"I'm sorry," she whispered, her eyes on the ground. When she looked up again, her gaze shifted to something behind me.

I turned to look.

At first, I saw only more Keeper guards, their guns pointed at my head.

But then Trader stepped out from behind one of them. Of everyone I'd seen first in the App World and now here, Trader looked the most similar to his virtual self. Nearly identical, down to the inky black of his hair and eyes. My brain worked overtime trying to understand what was happening, making me dizzy. My heart was breaking inside my body. I grabbed one of the iron posts surrounding the viewing deck to steady myself.

"You told me to trust you," I said to him.

His eyes were pained. "This isn't what you think, Skylar."

"You did this to Inara, didn't you," I said.

Trader grimaced. Then he walked by me to stand next to her. She looked into his eyes for a moment and something passed between them. "He got caught up in your wake, too, Skylar," she said sadly. "Just like me."

The guards closed in on me from all sides.

One of them clamped onto my shoulder. I struggled and fought, kicking and punching, but it was no use. There were too many of them. One of my kicks finally connected, but not with one of the guards—with Inara. She dropped to the ground with a surprised yelp, landing on a piece of broken glass. There came a loud sob, and when she pulled herself back to her feet, blood streamed from her arm, a long cut like a sliver of moon just below her elbow. Trader went to help her, to console her, but she moved out from under his reaching arm. Pushed through the Keeper guards so she could whisper one last thing before they took me away.

"You betrayed me and now I betrayed you," she said, but she was weeping. "I thought it would be more satisfying to finally say that. But it's not. It's not at all," she added, looking into my eyes.

Hers were full of pain.

27

The perfect prison

I WAS RUNNING.

Running through the unlit streets of Loner Town. Footsteps came after me fast. I turned back but couldn't make out a thing, not even a shadow. Panic rose into my throat and I could feel my nails turn to claws. Suddenly I was flying across the sidewalk on all fours, my feline eyes cutting through the darkness. I spied an alcove and leapt into it, transforming back to my virtual self the second my heart began to slow.

I peered beyond the wall shielding me.

Trader was standing there. "Skylar, let me explain," he said. "Remember that I'm out for revenge against my father. But sometimes revenge is complicated." He took my hand.

I watched him do it, unable to move. My brain reached for a memory. But of what? I was forgetting something—something important. My limbs felt locked. Like someone else was controlling them. Suddenly Trader faded away, and Loner Town with him.

There came a blinding light.

I tried to scream—I thought I had—but my voice was so far away. My eyes wouldn't open. Their lids felt heavy, weighted down, like someone was holding them shut. I raised my hands to my face but someone else—someone I couldn't see—grabbed them and pulled them away. Just then, I managed to open one eye, only a crack. There was that glaring light again, but there was movement, too, a figure flashing across my vision, and the glimpse of a face—brief, but it was there. I worked at my lips, my mouth fuzzy and dry, trying to make them form the word I wanted to say. It came out a mumble, a single syllable muffled by the rubbery state of my face, but still, I spoke it.

"Mom?"

Someone was clawing at my face.

No, at my eyes.

One eyelid was pulled up.

I saw only bright colors.

My head was pounding.

I tried to open my mouth. It felt wired shut.

"She'll keep for another while," said a man's voice.

"Are you sure?" someone asked, this time a woman.

Something pinged in my brain.

Familiarity.

Do I know you? went my mind.

But the words—like before, they wouldn't come.

"Put her back under," said the woman.

Who are you? I screamed inside my head.

There were hands again, pressing at my face.

A sharp pain in my arm.

Then . . .

Nothing.

"Rain, stop!"

I was laughing.

He was laughing too. His eyes were bright with happiness. "Do you really want me to?" he asked. His hands were on my shoulders.

"No," I whispered. "No, I don't."

I looked around. We were surrounded by water. Bobbing up and down in the waves. Floating over the swells as they rolled into shore. I looked toward the beach and saw the compound peeking up from the dunes. Relief reached every part of me like a potent drug.

"I'm so glad I'm here," I sighed. "But how did I get here?"

Confusion crossed Rain's face. "You never left."

"What do you mean? I was taken—" I started, then stopped.

Rain was shaking his head. "You've been with me all along."

"That's impossible." The dread crept back. I fought it off, I'd fight it as long as I could. I studied Rain as though he might disappear at any moment. Hesitant, I reached out my hand to him. Pressed it flat against his chest.

I could feel his heartbeat.

It pounded.

Rain stared at my hand like he couldn't believe it was there. When he looked up again, when he looked at me once more with those soulful eyes, for the first time I saw in them all that I'd ever hoped for: the want was there, just like before, but laced through it as delicate and intricate as a snowflake was love.

I could see it. It was as real as the Real World itself.

I pressed the rest of my body to him, I wrapped my arms around his back, his neck, my fingers winding through his hair, and felt his heartbeat speed even faster against my chest. Or maybe that was my heart going so quickly. We were so close it was difficult to tell.

Our mouths nearly touched.

I could feel his breath, warm and sweet.

"I'm going to kiss you, Skylar," he said, and I could feel his lips moving. "I've wanted to do this for so long."

"Me, too," I whispered back.

I closed my eyes and I waited, ready to lose myself in this.

My first real kiss.

But something was wrong. There was a tightening against my wrists and my ankles, a taut pressure, my limbs pulled apart like wishbones.

"I think she's waking up," came that same male voice again.

"Well, put her out," was the cold reply.

"No," I said. "No, no, please!"

This was all a dream.

Only a dream.

A memory of Lacy flashed—of Lacy and Rain. Together.

"No!" I screamed at the top of my lungs.

But nobody heard me.

It was all inside my head.

When I came to I was lying in a bed, tucked under the covers.

I sat up. The thick blanket slid to my waist. I stared at my arms, at the bedspread, at everything around me. Then I took my forefinger and thumb and pinched the skin at my neck hard, digging in my nails as far as they would go.

Pain seared from the spot.

I drew my hand away. There was blood at the end

of my fingertips. I placed them in my mouth, the taste metallic.

I was awake for real this time.

I slipped out of bed.

My clothes were gone, replaced by a short sleeveless slip. The air was cool and I shivered. My cheeks burned at the thought that someone had stripped me of my tunic while I was unconscious. Then I almost laughed at such modesty. For years this body hadn't been mine, locked in one of those glowing glass boxes I'd seen at Briarwood, bathed and fed and exercised by Keepers I could not see, my body theirs to control. To display. Like some toy rag doll. What I hadn't known had allowed me to live blissfully at ease as a virtual self, but my new consciousness about what this bliss entailed now robbed me of that fragile peace. How could I have so easily surrendered control of this body?

Never again. Not if I could help it.

As my eyes adjusted to the darkness, I looked around. This room was the size of some of the ones I'd seen in the mansion. Maybe this *was* a mansion, one of the others I'd seen along the cliff. It was decorated like a palace. The bed had a great canopy that rose up over it, with ornately carved posts at each of the four corners. A crystal chandelier the size of a small car cascaded down from the center of the ceiling. It seemed dangerous, like it was placed there to crush whoever dared stand beneath it. Keeping to the edges of the room, I moved away from the bed. My feet sank deep into the plush carpet. I tried the door, but it was locked. There was a lamp next to a sitting area, the couch and two chairs upholstered in rich brocade, their legs sloping down to curved feet. I reached underneath the shade for the switch. Soon a soft glow fell across everything.

And I realized something.

Every single thing around me—from the wallpaper to the fabric on the furniture to the canopy over the bed and the sheets tucked across it—was decorated in shades of blue. In any other circumstance I would have loved it. It was as though someone had designed this place especially for me, as though on some level they hoped I'd be happy here. The perfect prison. *Blue like the ocean and blue like the sky, blue like the sapphire color of your eyes*, I sang to myself softly.

But why go to such trouble?

Then something else occurred to me.

Inara knew that rhyme and all about my favorite things, Inara, my best friend, who'd just turned me over to the authorities. If she was willing to do that, then why not something so small as giving over a favorite color? Or a bedtime song for a child from a mother?

You betrayed me and now I betrayed you, she'd said.

I took another turn around the room, examining everything. Sunlight peeked out from heavily curtained windows. It was daytime, but of which day? I had no idea how much time had passed while I was unconscious. I drew back the drapes. I'd been right about the mansion. There was no doubt that I was in one. The grounds stretched out far and wide until they reached the cliff with the ocean beyond, the view from here spectacular. But it was the trees that stole my breath, the ones dotting the lawn. The leaves. They were no longer the bright, heavy green of summer. Oranges and yellows and fiery reds swam across my vision, blurring together.

I swallowed.

Fall had begun.

I had been unconscious long enough for one season to give way to another.

I ran to the door, panicked, and tried the handle once more, pulling on it, turning it as hard as I could, but it wouldn't budge.

"Somebody help me!" I screamed. "Is anybody out there?" I listened for a voice, for footsteps, for any sign of life, but there was nothing. I pounded against the door until my hand was raw with pain. "I need to get out of here," I yelled, my voice hoarse.

Still there was no answer.

I pressed my forehead against the wood and waited for my heart and lungs to slow. When I pulled back I saw there was a note tacked up on the door at eye level. My eye level exactly.

Skylar, it began. *Please dress for dinner. You'll find appropriate attire in the closet next to the sitting area. If you're hungry, there are snacks laid out for you in the next room.*

I looked around. The door which I had thought went to the bathroom must lead somewhere else. Maybe from there I could get out. I went to it and threw it open. There was a tiny round table covered with a cloth the color of the sky. At its center was a silver candelabra, tall bright flames spindling up from the nine candles that I'd counted. Around it were plates laden with sweets and fruit.

Nothing tempted me. Not even a little.

There were two more doors, neither of which led out of here. One opened to an opulent bathroom with a tub nearly big enough for swimming set underneath a series of windows. There were mirrors everywhere, my face reflected back to me from every angle. I blinked, studying myself. My cheeks glowed with health and my hair was clean and styled. Someone had been caring for me. They'd even taken the time to wash and curl my hair and apply rose-red lipstick to my mouth before I'd woken up.

I shivered.

Then I went to the other door. It opened the closet mentioned in the note. My jaw dropped when I saw the lone item inside, the dress that awaited me for dinner.

It was like something from a fairy tale.

Something magical and impossible created from an App.

Like everything else, it was blue, sapphire blue, the same color as my eyes. It seemed spun out of air. The top was strapless and the bodice tiny, but the skirt belled and cascaded and bustled with layers of delicate silk.

Please dress for dinner, the note had said.

I slipped it off the hanger. There must be a hundred buttons. One by one, I undid them, until the dress gaped open like an invitation. Then I pulled the thin night slip over my head, casting it aside, and stepped into the dress's center.

What else was I going to do?

I redid the buttons. It fit perfectly, as though I'd been measured for it. When I fastened the last one I went inside the mirrored bathroom, my steps heavy with the weight of so much fabric, and stared at my reflection. It was the kind of dress that girls my age dreamed about. I didn't know gowns like this existed in the Real World.

Inara would have loved it.

Maybe she picked it out, went my mind.

I blinked at myself once more, then turned away.

That's when I noticed the camera—no, the cameras, plural. Tiny round lenses in each corner of the ceiling, the kind I'd seen in the weapons room out at the compound. I swallowed. I was being watched. Every move I made, viewed by some unseen person. Every glance, every gesture. My cheeks burned as I thought of how I'd just undressed. I began to check the other rooms, the closet. They were everywhere. There was even one mounted into the head of the bed, pointed down toward my body while I slept.

Slowly, I made my way to the door to study the note.

Just then, I heard the bolt slide open in the lock.

I stepped back, looking around for anything that might serve as a weapon, but the door was opening before I could find one.

A woman stood at the entrance of the room, older than me, but not as old as my Keeper. Her brown hair was done up elaborately, her face aglow with makeup, and her ears and neck and wrists dripping with diamonds. She was dressed in a gown of light-green taffeta.

"Who are you?" I asked. "Why are you holding me here?"

But she didn't say anything. She just looked at me like she couldn't believe what she was seeing. Then, finally, she spoke.

"You really don't recognize me?" the woman said.

That voice again. The familiar one.

Then I zeroed in on her eyes.

"Jude?"

28

Reunion

"HELLO, BEAN," SHE said with a smile.

But the smile was sad.

"You really are lovely," she sighed. "Just beautiful."

My arms twitched at my sides. I wanted to throw them around Jude's neck. But I held back. "I've missed you, Jude."

She nodded, blinking, her eyes fluttering rapidly. Then she entered the room and shut the door behind her quietly. "Aren't you a vision in that dress!" Her tone was of forced cheer. She adjusted her skirts and looked around a moment, at the bed, the couch, and the chairs, before her eyes landed on me again. "Do you like your room? I designed it just for you. The gown, too. All in your favorite color."

"You mean you haven't forgotten me?" My voice wavered.

Jude hesitated, like there was something stuck on her tongue. "Of course not, Bean. You're my sister."

I didn't wait any longer. I couldn't. I threw my arms around Jude's neck and squeezed her tight. My sister, here, now, in the flesh. I could barely believe it. But then I remembered how I'd been unconscious for weeks, maybe months. That I seemed a prisoner in this palace.

Jude's arms stayed at her sides.

I pulled back. "Are you here to help me? To get me out of here?" I asked. "Inara—where is she? Is she all right?"

Jude stepped away, green taffeta glistening like grass in the morning dew. Turned her head so she didn't have to meet my eyes. "The situation is complicated." She laughed, but it was a choked laugh, like something was stuck in her throat. "This is all my fault. Bean. I'm . . . I'm so sorry," she added in a whisper.

I looked at her. She still wouldn't meet my eyes. "What are you sorry for?"

"For the way things have turned out," she said. "For having to involve your friend."

I took a step back, and nearly stumbled over the arm of a chair. "How have things turned out, exactly?"

My sister didn't respond. She raised her left arm. A velvet pouch dangled from her wrist. She slid it off and drew open the string, peering inside, shaking it. Then she tipped it over and blue sapphire jewels spilled into her hand. She smiled at me, again with sadness. "The perfect finishing touch, don't you think?" She held them out.

I didn't take them.

What game was Jude playing at?

"You want me to do it?" she asked. My sister pulled up my wrist and lifted my hand so she could fasten the sapphire bracelet. The jewels were enormous, the size of gum balls. They made my wrist seem thin and delicate. Breakable. Jude stepped around the bell of the dress, careful not to pierce the edge of the fabric with her heels. When she reached my back, she lifted my hair and clasped the necklace in place. "For a long time I was angry after you plugged in," she began. "I hated Mom for choosing you over me. Things were so hard for us. We were just lowly Keepers. Expendable. Replaceable. We had nothing."

The mention of our mother made my heart leap, but I held my breath and submitted to Jude's attentions, allowing myself to be decorated like some mannequin. She combed her fingers through my hair, running her hand across the waves. A part of me reveled in this gentle affection, even as wariness settled into my muscles, making them tense.

"I cared for you on the plugs, you know," Jude went on. "I fed you and bathed you. They let me volunteer to be your Keeper because you're my family."

"Oh, Jude," I said, all the air escaping my lungs in one long *whoosh*. I turned to face her again, my hair sliding through her fingers until there was nothing in them but air. I stared into her familiar eyes, took in the curve of the hands that had pushed me on a swing when I was young.

Tears rolled down her cheeks. "Bean, try to understand; the lot we Keepers have, the terrible working conditions, the danger of our jobs, the fact that no one in the App World has ever cared what happened to us as long as we supported their virtual lives—over the years it's created a lot of resentment. We're like janitors of bodies, doing all the dirty work behind the scenes."

My heart broke for my sister. "I'm sorry, Jude. That sounds awful."

She nodded.

I took her hands. Looked at her hard. "But what are you trying to tell me? What are we doing here . . . in this . . . this place? All dressed up?"

She slid from my grip. "I'm afraid to tell you," she said, her voice small. "I'm afraid you'll hate me."

I shook my head. "I could never hate you."

"You say that now." Jude went to the window and looked out. Then she took a deep breath and began to talk. "For a long time we Keepers held on to the promise that eventually we would enjoy the privilege of an easy, virtual future. We believed that someday our work and dedication to maintaining the App World would pay off." Jude went to the window and opened the drapes. She stared out into the early glow of the evening. "Then some of us realized the day we hoped for would never come, that we'd never be allowed a virtual life of our own. The government's promise to us had always been a lie." Jude paused a moment, inhaling the fresh air. "So we decided to rebel."

As she spoke, I thought about the rebellion Rain was forming, how my sister considered herself a rebel too.

Everyone was rebelling against something.

"I'm still listening," I told her.

"We knew about the Race for the Cure," she went on. "One day, while I was laboring on the plugs, I had an idea, one that coincided with something everyone in the App World wanted badly, and one that would help solve the economic crisis here." She stepped away from the window and began to pace the room, the skirts of her gown rustling with each step. I watched her move back and forth. "It was because of this idea that I came in contact with Emory Specter." She looked at me imploringly. Long eyelashes fanning wide dark eyes.

My heart seemed to stop then. This was sounding all

too familiar. "You're one of them, Jude. You're a New Capitalist," I said.

She swallowed. Then she straightened suddenly, her back, her shoulders. "Yes." There was a regal quality in her that I'd never noticed before.

I pressed myself against the wall for support. I didn't trust my legs to hold me up. "Tell me that the idea you're talking about isn't the idea to sell the bodies, Jude."

"Just hear me out," she said. "Let me explain."

I covered my face with my hands. I couldn't look at her anymore while I listened.

"Emory Specter listened to all I had to say. He was fascinated by my idea to fix the finances of the Real World, while liberating citizens of the App World from their bodies. And then, well, he quite literally promised me a new future, and one for our mother, and for so many of the other Keepers who had been suffering. After all those years, we would finally be free. And I would be the person leading them in this effort." She glanced away. "It turned out that Emory Specter and I had more in common than I ever could have imagined."

I let my hands slide down my face. Peered at my sister over the tips of my fingers.

"I'm not just a New Capitalist, Skylar," she added, using my real name for the first time since she'd appeared at the door, as though she needed to provide distance between us. "I'm in charge of the movement."

My hands fell to my sides. "You?"

"Don't sound so shocked." Jude lowered her eyes. Studied the floor. Smooth white marble with tiny black diamonds spaced throughout. Cold. "Emory proposed a deal," she said. "All I had to do was make one simple sacrifice, to prove that I could do what it took to be a true leader, a bringer of change. He explained how his own difficult choices had resulted in his rise in the App World." She raised her eyes to mine again. They were dark with guilt, flickering shadows cloaked in the night.

My heart was in knots. My stomach filled with dread, a black fog spreading. The sun was dropping toward evening, the light from the window disappearing. My shadow began to fade from the floor, evidence of my existence ebbing away.

"The deal was this," Jude said. "If I was serious about my idea, I would have to show I was capable of making hard decisions, just as he had." She hesitated, the room falling silent. She seemed even to stop breathing.

The black fog reached my lungs. I buried my hands in folds of blue silk, clutching at the skirt of my dress. I knew, I already knew. Jude didn't have to say it, so I did it for her. "He made you prove yourself by showing you were willing to sell my body. Your own sister." I began to comprehend what this meant, all of its implications, and I was shattered by them. "Mom," I croaked. "She was just going to let you?"

"Oh, Bean," Jude sighed, going back to her nickname for me, her whole demeanor changing to the way it was before. "When the borders closed, you were never supposed to wake up. You weren't supposed to know a thing, not ever. Then that day on the cliff . . . I saw your escape. I had no idea that you could . . . that you . . ." She trailed off. Sighed. "Your body is capable of far more than anyone ever thought. The bodies of all the plugged-in are capable of more than we'd ever dreamed of. The way the plugs have altered your brains . . ." She trailed off. Her voice had grown tight. "After the guards found you up on the Water Tower, we tried to keep you unconscious. And we did for a long while." She laughed softly. "But your body, it just doesn't want to stay under. It's like . . . it's always wanting to shift between states. Between worlds."

A strangled sound emerged from my throat. I could barely process anything she was saying. "You were the one who put me on display? You were really going to let them . . . sell me?"

Jude blinked. She was wringing her hands again, walking a few steps, then stopping, turning around, and walking a few more. "I could have hidden myself from you tonight, could have hidden this whole situation, but I didn't. I couldn't miss the chance to see you again." Jude beckoned me to the sofa that swirled with shades of blue, like a tornado at the center of the sea. Her heels clicked against the stone floor. She sat down and I joined her. The blue of my own dress melted into the couch, but the green taffeta of Jude's seemed to stand up against it in protest. "Unfortunately, the changes in the plugged-in bodies, the skills people have developed through virtual living, have made their bodies even more valuable. Yours especially." Her last two words were barely a whisper. Then the taffeta of Jude's dress seemed to collapse along with her face, crumpling toward the couch, having lost its battle with gravity. "I'd been having second thoughts for a while, but then seeing the way you fought to be conscious, I realized I couldn't go through with it." She sighed. "But I waited too long, Bean. You've become important to the rest of the New Capitalists, to the changes people have been waiting for. They want their symbol. And you are it."

My nails dug into the arm of the sofa. "But you can't sell bodies, Jude, not mine or anyone else's. We're people! You're selling people."

Anger replaced the sadness in Jude's eyes. "These *people* in the App World? They couldn't care less about their bodies. They gave them up for a virtual life without looking back, perfectly happy if we disposed of them like trash. Why shouldn't we take advantage of their stupidity and carelessness? Why shouldn't we capitalize on their updated brains?"

I studied my sister. "Because it's wrong, Jude. No—" *Wrong* was not what I wanted to say. It wasn't strong enough. "It's evil."

Her brow furrowed. "No, it's smart. Besides, their former owners won't have any idea what's happening. They'll live on happily in their little App World playground, none the wiser." Jude got up again and circled the room, talking as she went. "To think that we Keepers would sacrifice our entire lives on behalf of the App World, without the hope of change or of ever joining them! At best we're like the coal miners of old, but at worst, we're no more than slaves." She stopped in front of me, her eyes hard. "We're done being slaves. Selling bodies is our way out of the life we've been subjected to. The Body Market will function as reparations of a sort. Payment for our services after all these years."

Oh my god.

The Body Market?

"Don't look so shocked," Jude said, her eyes on my face. "It's not without precedent. China has been raising bodies to sell for parts for years now. And Russia has been selling live people—something we would never do. But the technology is such that a fully functioning body and brain, emptied of its personality but still full of all those skills, is a precious commodity in the Real World. In Europe and India, they've found ways to extend life nearly indefinitely by downloading someone's brain into another, younger body, and of course there are plenty of people who are looking for parts. There's also reanimation, which is popular in more than one Eastern nation.

This Body Market was inevitable. It's how we're all going to survive."

I wanted to say something, anything that might soften my sister's resolve. I got up and went to her now, placed my hand on her arm. I looked into her eyes pleadingly. "There has to be another solution. Another way to resolve the economic crisis that's led to this . . . this rift between worlds."

She stared at my fingers like they might not be real. The color of our skin was different. Hers was far lighter than mine. "Do you think we didn't already try negotiations? That we didn't search for another way?" She moved away, and my hand was left grasping for air. I wrapped my arms around my body, a chill settling over my bare shoulders and arms. The light from the window had disappeared, and with it, both of our shadows. "The only way to change our future is to think like the rich. Our worlds turn on capital and people's endless capacity to spend it on things they desire. We realized that with all of these bodies, we were sitting on a gold mine. We'd just failed to extract the goods for our own profit—until now."

Jude sounded so convinced. However misguided she was, I could see how she could easily become a leader. Someone to whom other Keepers listened. "Bodies aren't the same as gold," I said. "People don't put them up for sale."

She picked up a tiny blue china cat from the table in

the sitting area, turned it over in her hands, then set it back down. Looked up. "Tell me. When Emory Specter announced the Race for the Cure had been won and that bodies would be removed from the plugs and destroyed, how did people react? Did they weep and mourn? Did they even care?"

I looked away. I could almost hear the cheers and applause from the funeral. It was such a vivid memory. Even though Jude's words chilled me, in the most messed-up way, a Body Market made total sense. "No," I said quietly. "People were . . . excited. Relieved. They cared only insofar as they would be liberated from the body, and soon. The only life for them is a virtual one."

Jude nodded. "To the App World, bodies are a burden, something to be transcended, to be left behind. But here, bodies are this world's most abundant natural resource. Why shouldn't we exploit it? Why destroy something that has such value to us and to the rest of the world?"

"You really believe this is the right thing to do," I said.

"Yes," she stated with conviction. "I wish you hadn't gotten caught in the middle. If only you hadn't un-plugged . . ." She trailed off.

"But I did. And I'm awake." My voice rose in anger. "So now what? What are you trying to convince me of? Am I supposed to be sympathetic and let you sell me?"

All the air went out of her. "No," she whispered.

"No?" I asked, surprised that this was her answer. "Then what?"

She reached for my dress, fingered the fabric, let it go again. "There is to be a masquerade ball tonight in your honor, and to celebrate the opening of the Body Market—that's what these gowns are for. There are buyers from all over the world who've come to see you. The masks are to protect the privacy of a few of our more skittish guests." Jude's breathing was labored. "Everyone is here to preview the merchandise before we plug you back in."

Nausea grew in my middle. Disgust crawled over my skin.

Jude shook her head. "But I can't go through with it. Not now."

Relief quickly replaced the nausea. I stared into my sister's real face. Saw the lines that had grown around her mouth and her forehead. The way her eyes left purple shadows on her skin. "We'll do this together, then. We'll leave, instead of going to the party. We'll escape. That would make a statement, wouldn't it? If the leader of the New Capitalists didn't show up tonight?"

She hesitated. Gripped her taffeta skirts hard, so hard I wondered if her nails would break through the fabric. "It won't stop the Body Market from opening, if that's what you were thinking. Eventually a new leader will rise and take over."

"So what do we do then, Jude?"

She blinked. "I don't know, Bean."

"Let me help."

She shook her head. "There's a cost to starting a revolution, and then abdicating responsibility."

My heart pounded. "What sort of cost?"

She met my eyes. The color drained from her face. "The deal I made with Emory . . . it was your life, or mine."

I shivered. "What do you mean?"

"He said to become a leader means to take a great risk, to put one's life on the line. And that if I backed down, Mom and I would not only lose everything, but that . . . I would be put to death."

"What?" I looked at her, stunned. "He can't do that!"

She laughed bitterly. "Of course he can. He's the most powerful man in both worlds and he can do whatever he wants. Besides, the first thing I learned about becoming a leader is that the second you do, there are already others planning for the day when they will take that power away and become leaders themselves. There are plenty of New Capitalists waiting for me to fail." A faraway look appeared in her eyes. "I can't disappoint Emory."

I took her hand in mine. "We should run. Please, Jude."

"No," she whispered. "If I run, it will only be worse when they find me. And don't forget Mom. What do you think they'd do to her once I'm gone?"

I wiped tears from my eyes. There were things I needed to say to Jude, that I needed her to hear no matter what came next for us. "You said that you were angry for a long time about Mom plugging me in and not you. But I want you to know that all my virtual life I've been grateful to you, Jude. I've thought about the sacrifices you and our mother made to give me a future in the App World. I longed for the day when I could thank you for all that you've given to me, when I could see you both again, know what you'd become, and have the chance to be a part of your lives again, to see what those lives were after all these years and maybe to stay permanently." My voice cracked. "I always wondered if my life should be in the Real World, with my family. But I guess now I have my answer, don't I?"

"Oh, Bean," Jude sighed.

My shoulders slumped, my lungs empty of air, my heart empty of hope. My mind was racing, my brain leaping from one possibility to the other, trying to come up with an alternative to my situation, to our situation, but finding none. I thought about all the hopes I'd had before unplugging, about the reunion I would have with Jude and my mother, about how all that hope had been for nothing; how I'd betrayed my best friend's trust and then gotten her into this mess, too. I thought about the deal I'd made with Rain, only to find that he'd tricked me, too. That he'd made me think he might care for me, and even made me start to fall for him, when the whole time he'd been with Lacy, and in the end, all he'd done was make me feel like a foolish girl with a crush. It was then that I made the decision I knew was the only one I could make.

I looked up at my sister now. "If you were to sell me," I began, slowly, "what exactly would the buyer do with my body?"

She stared into my eyes. "Why, Bean?" she whispered, shocked. "Why would you want to know something like that?"

"Just tell me."

Jude studied me like I was some strange creature she'd never seen before. "We don't really know what she—or he—will do once the body is officially exchanged, the paperwork signed, etc. That's up to the buyer and I suppose it will depend on the country of purchase."

I swallowed. "And you're *sure* I wouldn't know a thing? I'd be plugged back in to the App World and live on virtually like I'd never left?"

She nodded. "Yes. But what are you saying?"

My stomach churned and roiled. I grabbed the nearest edge of the bed, wrapping my hand tight around the carved wood. Then I took a deep breath. Straightened my back and held my head high. "I'll do it. I'll go to the party tonight. I'll do whatever you need me to do." My throat was dry. "You made sacrifices for me your entire life. So did Mom. Now it's my turn."

"You'd do that for me?" Jude sounded shocked.

I nodded, one quick bob of my head. "Yes. For you and

for our mother. I can't let you die or put either one of you in danger. I can't be the reason for your death."

"Bean—"

"Stop, please! Let's just get this over with. Before I change my mind," I added.

Her lips parted, like she still couldn't believe what I'd said. "Thank you," she whispered, leaning toward me, pressing her mouth against my forehead in a single kiss. Then she reached out her hand and I let her fix my skirts and my dress and walk me through the bedroom door into the hall outside. I was numb as we went, hand in hand, to the place where someone would decide my fate.

We didn't speak another word.

What was there left to say?

We wound through a series of rooms not unlike those in the mansion where I'd lived with the Keeper. The difference here was that they were bright and clean, sparkling with life and opulence. Soon we reached a set of grand carved doors on the ground floor. The sound of classical music played on the other side, beautiful and soft and haunting.

Jude turned to me, her expression full of sadness. "You're not alone in this, Bean. I'm going to be right here with you this whole time. Everything is going to be okay."

I nodded. Put a hand on her arm, stopping her before she could open the door to the ballroom. She looked at me. "I have one last request," I said.

"What is it?"

"I want to see Mom before I'm plugged back in."

Jude nodded. "You will. She's right on the other side of this door, waiting for us," she added as the sounds of the symphony trumpeted our arrival.

29

Belle of the ball

WE STOOD AT the top of a grand staircase.

A lush blue carpet stretched the length of it, ending underneath a chandelier even bigger than the one in my room. Like my dress, the ballroom seemed something out of a fairy tale, I'd always believed such magic was possible only on the Apps. There were circular tables draped with cloth in various shades of blue. At the center of each one was a tall silver vase overflowing with brightly colored flowers, yellow, purple, and pink blooms cascading on soft green vines. A thousand candles hung from the ceiling in tiny gilded cages, a constellation of sparkling stars. At the center of everything was a wide space for dancing.

A full orchestra was next to it, the bows of the string instruments moving in perfect unison, the sad mournful song of the violins carrying high over everything else.

It was appropriate.

This would be my final memory of the Real World, both my reunion and my good-bye with my mother.

"Bean?" my sister urged.

I nodded. Took a deep breath.

She laced her fingers through mine. Her grip was so tight I thought she might crush bone. A single spotlight crossed the room and stopped when it reached our perch above the ballroom. The crowd hushed.

Everyone turned to us.

I'd wanted to search the crowd for the familiar face of my mother—or at least, what I remembered of her—and for Inara, too, but that wish was dashed. It was indeed a masquerade ball, nearly all the guests holding glittering masks to their faces, only their eyes blinking through tiny almond-shaped holes for viewing. The men were dressed in tuxedos, some of them in bright colors, red, purple, even pink, while the women wore elaborate gowns that belled wide across the floor, or sleek, sparkling sheaths that exposed more skin than they concealed. They stared and stared, at my face, my body, my hair. They whispered behind cupped hands and pointed to me.

My free arm snaked around my body, hugging my torso. The delicate dress was so airy and light against my skin that I felt naked, and in the bright glare of the spot-light trained on us the top of it was nearly transparent.

I squirmed under their gazes.

Jude, too, now held a mask in her hand. Peacock feathers of green and blue and black, some the very same color as her dress, fanned out above her head, her eyes shielded by pale, molded silk that left only her nose and mouth uncovered. I wondered if the mask made this party easier for her to go through with, to shield what she was really feeling. I was reminded of the funeral in the App World—the one for the Under Eighteens who weren't even dead—yet this time the funeral was mine, even though I wasn't dead either.

The sounds of the symphony rose higher.

My sister turned to me. She beckoned. Stepped forward, her heels absorbed by the thick carpet.

But I didn't follow.

She turned back. "Are you having second thoughts?" she asked. Her voice wavered—she was scared that I was, what would happen if I did.

I walked forward in answer.

My back was straight, my chin up. I refused to show the guests weakness. I was already vulnerable enough and I would give them nothing more. As we descended the stairs, I looked into their masked faces. Many of the women had chosen the brightly colored feathers of elabo-rate birds like my sister, or mythical sprites and fairies, but the men had chosen more vicious beasts. Bears and lions, tigers and horses and snarling hyenas. I even noticed a few minotaurs and dragons peering back at me as we passed.

I was the animal in a zoo of one, trapped and ogled and oohed and aahed at—a zoo of my sister's making. The irony that I was the only one who'd come to this event in human form wasn't lost on me. Ever since Rain had spoken of how I'd been put out on exhibit, I'd thought it horrible to be on display and be completely unaware. But now I realized how wrong I'd been.

It was far worse to be conscious.

Jude squeezed my arm. I saw how she was smiling for the crowd. "You're going to be okay," she said.

Was I?

"You won't remember a thing after you plug back in."

I nearly missed the next step, but caught myself.

Jude smiled at someone to our left, as though everything was fine. Soon we reached the bottom of the staircase where the blue carpet pooled along the floor like spilled water. She smiled and waved at the attendees.

The guests clapped politely.

"What now?" I asked.

"Eating, drinking, dancing," she said. "I'll show you around. Make some introductions."

I shook my head. Refused to look my sister in the eye. "No. I'm doing enough already, Jude. I'm not going to let you walk me around the room to peddle my body."

"What if it involves seeing our mother?" she asked.

My heart expanded with need and most of all with hope. "Where?" I asked. My voice was hoarse.

"Right over"—Jude craned her neck—"there!"

My eyes sought the place my sister had indicated, cutting through the crowd, who'd spread out through the ballroom again, caught up in conversation. People kept glancing my way. I would be watched all night. "I don't see—" I started to say, but then I stopped.

There was a woman straight ahead, one of the few guests without a mask. Unlike the rest, she was dressed in black, the color of mourning. She seemed older than I would have guessed, her dark hair pulled back in a severe bun, her face thin and drawn, eyes tired. But they never left me.

I could see traces of myself reflected in her features, in the blue of her eyes and the golden-brown color of her skin.

My mother.

After all this time.

Her gaze brightened. Her lips parted. She held out both her arms.

An invitation.

In that moment, the ballroom, the sinister purpose of this event and its guests, my sister, everything else ceased to exist. My only thought was of reaching the spot where she stood there looking at me, at the end of a long and dangerous journey across worlds and over a decade of waiting. I went to her. It was all I could do not to run. I stopped just short of her fingertips.

"Mom?" I needed to hear her voice. I needed to be sure this wasn't another terrible trick.

"Hello, my blue Skye." Her words filled the air around me like a protective shield. Then she pulled me close.

"I love you so much," I said into her neck, inhaling the scent of her skin. "I've missed you."

"Your sister thinks I'm on her side, at least enough to obey," she whispered urgently, clutching me tight. "But I'm not. I promise you, I'm not. As much as I wanted to see you again, I hoped that you'd escape before it came to this."

I blinked, eyes wide with shock. "But . . . but . . ." I stammered in her ear.

"Shhhh," went my mother.

"Skylar was very anxious to see you, Mother," Jude interrupted at my back. "She's been very cooperative," she added. Her tone had changed.

Gone was the repentant sister, replaced by a woman who was obviously in charge.

Someone without remorse about my fate.

My mother released me.

I slid reluctantly from her arms, the long black sleeves of her dress soft against my skin. I straightened up and fixed my skirt so I could face Jude. "Can you give us sone time alone?"

Jude smiled. Her eyelashes fluttered innocently. "Of course," she said, and moved away through the crowd.

A tear slid down my cheek as I stared at my mother, my heart caught in my throat. I waited until Jude was on the other side of the ballroom before I spoke again. "She told me it was her life or mine." I watched as my mother shook her head. "That if I didn't come tonight, if I didn't allow myself to be plugged back in so she could have my body to sell, that she'd be killed," I added.

"Your sister has become quite the actress," my mother said fiercely.

My lips parted, and my chest tightened. Could it be true? Had it all been an act? Like Lacy out at Briarwood, but this time worse, because it was my own flesh and blood? I swallowed. My insides were dry. "Mom, how did Jude get like this?"

She leaned close. "If I'd known what would happen because I chose you to plug in, I wouldn't have separated our family. Jude was never the same after you left. She became obsessed with caring for you—and she did so meticulously for years, lovingly, or so I thought at first. She'd talk about the day you'd be together again, and I thought she meant here, in the Real World for Service, but she believed wholeheartedly your reunion would be virtual. That she would plug in and surprise you." She paused. The sounds of the orchestra played eerily around us. "Little by little, as it dawned on her that this would never happen, she became fixated on how unjust it was, that she was stuck in the body forever, that she'd never have the chance to transcend it. Then she decided to make the most of her lot—of our lot—at least that's how your sister likes to think of it. And I believe you know what comes next," my mother added.

I nodded. "The New Capitalists. The Body Market."

"Your sister is punishing me tonight by forcing me to watch what she's doing to you." My mother's eyes burned with anger. "Only Jude could get you to give yourself up to save her from death! That liar. She's shameless! I'm sure she felt this was the best way—maybe the only way—to go through with her plans," she hissed. "Listen, I've been trying to negotiate a way out for you tonight. I know that this is a lot to take in, but you need to be strong—and you are, my darling. You proved that to everyone the moment you unplugged." My mother cocked her head, took a step back, taking me in. Tears slid down her face, too. "You've grown into such a beautiful woman," she said. "I wish we had more time, my love. Then I could explain everything. There's so much you still don't know about our family." Her eyes darted behind me, as though she was just checking out the crowd at a lovely party.

I blinked back tears. "What do you mean? Tell me."

My mother reached out and touched my hair, fixed it

around my shoulders. Looked at me with eyes full of love. "There is a fanatical streak running through your sister's veins. I didn't see it when she was young, but she has a lot of your father in her."

"Our father?" I asked, startled.

Our mother never talked about him, who he was or where he'd come from, how they'd met or how long they were together. He was so absent from our lives I almost forgot I had a father at all.

"There's something else important you should know about tonight—" my mother went on, but stopped abruptly.

Jude returned to us right then, interrupting whatever my mother was about to confess. "Your time is up, dear Mother," Jude sang. Then to me, she said, "And don't you think you should mingle with the guests?"

"Don't you mean buyers?" I asked, turning away.

My mother laid a hand gently on my arm, the touch so simple and slight, yet I wished she could hold on to me forever. "You should eat something, Skylar. And drink something, too." My mother nodded toward the tables at the edge of the ballroom heaped with edible delights. Fruits and cakes, sea creatures still in their shells, looking as though they could wake at any moment, great bowls of salad and fountains of champagne. "You need your strength. The roast beef is particularly delicious. You must try some."

I looked at her strangely.

Jude seemed pleased at our mother's approval of the feast she'd laid out for everyone. "That's a wonderful idea. Perhaps if Skylar gets something in her stomach, she'll be able to relax. She didn't eat a thing that I left in her room. You must be hungry," she added, nudging me toward the tables, pointing the way with her hand.

"Go on," my mother urged. "We'll talk more in a bit. Do this for me, my Skye. Make a mother happy and feed yourself."

It pained me to cut short our conversation, and I wasn't even hungry. But it seemed a small enough thing that my mother was asking, and though I didn't particularly want to do as Jude told me, I blocked that out for now. What my mother wanted from me was so typically parental, telling a child to eat, making sure I took care of myself, that I found myself obeying her, walking through the crowd toward the other side of the ballroom. People gave me a wide berth, as though they preferred to watch me from afar, or maybe my sister had directed them not to come near the merchandise.

Which was fine with me.

I skipped the plates full of cookies and bowls heaped with trifle, the tables laden with whole roasted fish and lobster tails, and went straight for the one where I thought I might find the roast beef, to comply with my mother's wishes, however odd. I stopped in front of it and my stomach clenched. The smell of cooked animal flesh was sickening. I was about to walk away, to excuse myself to my mother and explain that I simply couldn't get anything down, when something caught my eye and drew me back.

My stomach unknotted.

And I smiled—the first genuine one all evening—as I understood what my mother had really wanted for me.

There were knives. They were small, but they were sharp, meant for carving the thick bloody meat laid out across so many shallow china platters. Their handles were covered in blue mother-of-pearl, and along the side was a long sliver for enclosing the blade. They fanned out across the tablecloth, pretty souvenirs for the guests. They glittered as bright as jewels in the candlelight, reflecting bits of chandelier and pieces of the frescoed ceiling.

Daintily, I piled a tiny plate high with roast beef.

Then I picked up a fork and a knife.

When I was sure no one was looking, I carefully folded it and slid the knife into one of the looping folds of my gown, grateful for the elaborate bustles around the wide, structured skirt. I shifted a little, back and forth, satisfied that the knife was safely tucked away. Then I looked across the long table and saw that next to each plate of pork, of venison, of beef, and of lamb was a new set of knives, all of them decorated with blue pearl handles in various hues to match my dress.

How fitting.

I went down the line, adding each different meat to my plate, and swiping one knife after the other until I could claim a full set hidden in my dress. When I reached the end of the table I was practically floating with hope. I even took the crystal glass of champagne I was offered by a waiter holding out a silver tray. When I turned to observe the merriment of the ball, I saw the party happening around me with new eyes.

Now I was armed.

This changed everything.

I could feel it in the way my heart skipped and my spirits lifted, my mind racing with the possibility of escape. My eyes darted around the ballroom, across the guests, searching for every possible exit. I was sure my sister had them guarded, but I'd gotten out of far more difficult circumstances while gaming. All I had to do was trust my instincts and use the circumstances to my advantage just as I would on the Apps. The only difference was that the stakes here were real, and unlike that day on the cliff, this time I was aware of it.

Not a minor detail, but one on which I wouldn't dwell.

Maybe it was the smile on my face that broke the ice with the other guests, because someone approached me from the left. A man in a lion mask. He held out his hand to me for a dance and, as gracefully as I could manage given my revulsion, I took it. He led me to the center of the dance floor, my bare hand held high in his gloved one.

The orchestra quieted.

"You look lovely tonight," he said in a voice that told me he was older.

The conductor tapped his wand and they started up a waltz.

As we swirled around the room, I made it a point never to look in his eyes. I was stiff in his arms, a wooden doll whose joints could bend. My skirts were heavy with the knives tucked into my dress, and I prayed they would stay. When the song ended, before I could lower my hands, someone else took the first man's place and the orchestra started up again. In the blur as we moved I saw my sister watching, nodding her head, pleased. I glimpsed our mother, too, eyes on me, her mouth a straight, worried line. Then a third man, this one in a pink tuxedo and matching pink mask, fringed with feathers, replaced the second. The only thing that kept me going was the thought of those knives. At one point I fantasized about their blades slicing through the skirt of the gown and nailing the foot of my current suitor to the floor. As the third song came to an end, I was about to claim the need for rest. But then I caught a glimpse of my next suitor. He wore all black and seemed younger than the others—I could tell by the slim, muscular shape of his shoulders and the part of his face not covered by a striped mask.

He'd come as a tiger.

He tapped the shoulder of my current partner, who

sighed and moved away. The new stranger took me into his arms and twirled me across the floor just like all the others. Yet unlike any of them, he leaned close, so close his lips brushed my earlobe, and he spoke.

"Skylar," he whispered, and chills raced up my spine. "Try not to react."

But the moment I'd seen the mask, I'd known. It was Rain's arms around me, one hand in my own, the other resting gently on my back, dancing with me. I felt a million things at once—the pain and hurt of his betrayal, rage about how he'd lied, suspicion, fear, even, that Rain had known all along that my sister was the leader of the New Capitalists. Despite all of this, I felt the rush of seeing someone familiar, someone for whom I had feelings, even as I wished I didn't. And hope, I felt hope, too. That maybe I wasn't alone in this after all. "You lied to me," was all I said.

"I'm sorry, Skylar. But what you saw with Lacy, it wasn't what you think."

I laughed bitterly. "It isn't just about Lacy, Rain. You knew about my sister, didn't you? You knew all along and yet you let me believe that if I helped you, you'd help me find my family. Why didn't you tell me?" I hissed. "You told me everything else, but you left out this one essential part."

Rain was quiet as we turned to the music. The orchestra played a slower, more mournful waltz. "I didn't want to break your heart. Not any more than I already had," he said, his voice low. "But we can talk about all of this after we get you out of here."

I kept my head turned from his. I couldn't bear to look at him. "Did you come with a plan for escape? Because I've been devising one myself."

He laughed softly. "I wouldn't expect anything less." He paused, then said, "I'm sorry this happened to you."

"Not as sorry as I am. How long has it been since the last day I saw you? I still don't know."

"A couple of months."

I tried to ignore the way my stomach flipped at this news.

"Enough time to make a plan," he said.

"Did you come alone?" I asked, my eyes searching the crowd for signs of familiarity. It was no use, though. The masks made it impossible to recognize anyone.

"No," Rain said. "Look left along the back wall—the tall guest with the dragon's eyes. He's holding champagne."

On the next turn I located him. "I see him."

"That's Adam. And two guests away from him—the girl with the bright-purple feathers? That's Parvda."

With every twirl in the dance I studied them. Soon I began to see signs of familiarity in the color of their skin and the way they kept glancing in our direction—and then in each other's. "Is there anyone else?"

"Yes. Zeera volunteered to come. And Jessica, too."

I nodded slightly, my head still tilted away. There was something comforting about knowing Jessica was here. The girl who'd been with me for my ordeal on the cliff. "Where are they?"

"They're not in the ballroom, but they're close. And your Keeper. She insisted on being a part of this."

A rush of relief and affection flowed through me, followed by guilt and worry. "She must hate me now. I put her in a terrible position."

Rain shook his head. "She signed up for rebellion just like the rest of us. And getting you out of here tonight will be the real beginning of it. She wanted to be a part of this."

The current song was winding to an end. My heart was pounding—with nerves, with hope, with the nearness of Rain. "We don't have much time. Tell me the plan."

"It's simple. Parvda is going to come up to you and ask for a private interview. Your sister promised this to guests so they could . . . satisfy their curiosity if they needed to, or had any lingering concerns about your, ah, worth."

My stomach twisted. It was difficult not to cringe. But I nodded.

"There's a room set aside for these conversations," Rain went on. "It's not far from the exit. You'll go with her—it will be guarded—but at least it will get you away from the crowd in here. You'll both evade the guards and get out as quickly as you can. We'll be right behind you. It shouldn't be that difficult. We have the benefit of surprise, but if anything goes wrong, Zeera has control of the lights and the video feeds in this place. She can create chaos if we need her to. But hopefully it won't come to that."

"Jude had cameras all over the room where she kept me," I said, remembering those tiny lenses in the corners of the ceiling.

"She has them in here too."

"I'm tired of being watched," I said.

"I know."

The song ended and my newest partner tried to take Rain's place, but I politely declined. "Find me later?" I told him sweetly. "I need to go to the ladies' room."

"I'll walk you in that direction," Rain offered, an apologetic smile to the man I'd rejected. Then he gestured for me to follow.

We walked off the dance floor and into the crowd of guests who were drinking and eating merrily. I hesitated. "Thank you for coming to get me," I said.

"I know that I broke your trust, but try to believe me when I say that there was no way that we wouldn't. We need you on our side."

Maybe it was the fact that Rain had said *we* instead of *I*, *we* as in the rebellion, the group of people against the New Capitalists, but still, I felt like a grenade being lobbed back and forth between two warring factions. I felt like a pawn in the game they were playing—a game for which I hadn't gotten to devise any of the rules, and one I certainly hadn't chosen to play of my own volition.

But I was in it now, like it or not.

"I'll see you when it's time," I said by way of good-bye to Rain, consoled that it wouldn't be for long. At least not if things went smoothly. I was nearly to the ladies' room, but before I entered, I glanced black, locating Adam and Parvda to Rain's left. I didn't want to lose sight of them. It was right then that I nearly bumped into one of the guests.

"Excuse me," she said in a huff. "Oh!" she added in surprise, just as I'd turned to apologize.

"Inara?" Her long blond hair fell in waves all around a sleek emerald-green gown that looked as though it had diamonds sewn into it. She wore a thin, matching green mask that glittered in the lights. It barely disguised her face, and made her seem like a bandit—a beautiful thief. She looked away from me, as though she couldn't bear my presence.

"I thought you'd be long gone by now, back to the App World," I began, but then I noticed the boy standing a short ways off to the side, behind her. Trader. His mask was thin, but plain and black, as though they both wanted to be recognized, if not by the other guests, then, at the very least, by me. He was talking to a tall, distinguished man in a black tuxedo who wore the mask of a warrior. It was painted with camouflage.

Inara raised a glass of champagne to her bright lips and guzzled half of it down. "I'm not allowed to go home until this deal is done, Skylar."

I blinked. "By deal, you mean my sister selling me to one of these guests?"

She took another gulp of champagne. Then put the glass to her lips again and drained the rest. "It is what it is, Skye. Accept it."

"You don't feel at all badly about your part in this?"

Inara set the flute on the tray of a passing waiter. His eyes flickered along the length of her dress before walking away. "Whatever part I have in this is your doing. If you hadn't lied to me, we wouldn't be in this situation. But we are, and now it's almost over and your sister will return us to our old lives."

"Sure," I said, and laughed again, but this time it was bitter. "And everything will go on as though none of this ever happened."

"Your sister promised me that you won't remember a thing," she said passionately. "And that I won't either. This part of our lives will be a big blank."

My eyebrows went up. "Did she also promise that she won't sell your body?"

Inara shrugged. "I don't really care if she does or not."

"You don't mean that," I said. "That's not how you felt

at the funeral. You were just as horrified at the thought of being separated from your body as I was!"

Inara's eyes flashed. "We're not doing this now, Skye. I'm going to enjoy this party, I'm going to fill up on real food while I still have the chance, and then you and I can blissfully go back to our friendship when we're in the App World since neither of us will remember this nightmare. Though, in a way, that's too bad, since I'm not even sure we have a friendship worth salvaging."

The loud *thump, thump, thump* of my heart beating filled my head. I was done begging for Inara's forgiveness. It was true, I'd lied to her, and for that I was sorry, but she didn't even try to understand my side of things, and why I did what I did. "Maybe you're right, Inara. Maybe there's nothing left to save. At least I have the chance to say that now, before my memory is erased." My eyes slid to Trader where he stood off to the side, still talking to the same man as before. "Have fun with your boyfriend," I added, tossing him a glare. Then I grabbed my skirts, careful not to touch the knives, and walked away without looking back. It was just as I was passing Trader that I saw my sister walking toward me—or I thought she was. She stopped short to talk to the warrior guest.

"Emory," I heard Trader say, with a slight trace of disgust, excusing himself.

Emory?

As in Emory *Specter*?

What was he doing here?

Trader brushed by me. "Things aren't as they seem, Skye," he said out of the corner of his mouth.

I barely heard him. I was too absorbed watching my sister. Jude took up the man's hand casually and leaned in to kiss him delicately on the cheek. He smiled in reply, and for a split second I wondered if my sister and this man—this man who might be Emory Specter—were lovers, even though her kiss had been chaste. But then my sister laughed, her face aglow with delight, and she spoke the following words, one single sentence that turned my blood to ice.

"I'm so glad you could be here tonight, Daddy," she said.

30

Scarred for life

THERE WASN'T TIME to react.

Parvda was headed my way.

"I was hoping we could go somewhere for a chat," she said when she reached me. Her voice was cold. "I'd like to test your skills."

I nodded.

Looks were exchanged between Parvda and my sister. Then Parvda gestured with her finger that I should follow. When I didn't, she turned back. Cleared her throat. "I need you to come with me," she said, slightly urgently.

This time I snapped out of it and let Parvda lead me through the crowd of guests, many of them glancing our way, some of them outright staring. Parvda swerved left before we reached the grand staircase where my sister and I had made our entrance, and led me up to a tall door by the bar. At one point my eyes met Adam's. His small smile was reassuring, at least, that this part of their plan was going well.

Parvda opened the door.

Two guards immediately stepped in front of us. They were dressed the same way as the ones who'd taken me from the roof of the Water Tower and who were there on the cliff that day, with their pale-blue uniforms and with black, thick-soled boots on their feet. My eyes flickered to their waists and came to rest on the guns holstered there.

"I have a private appointment," she said to the two large men with an authority in her voice that was surprising, especially for a girl so tiny.

They nodded and escorted us down the hall to another room lit by a chandelier at its center. There was a sofa and two chairs, with a coffee table between them.

"Sit," Parvda ordered, and I did as I was told. She turned to the guards, who were still standing inside the room. "Which part of *private* do you not understand?"

They looked at each other, whispered something, then left, shutting the door behind them.

Parvda and I were alone.

Could escape be this easy?

Parvda turned toward a tiny round lens in the top right corner of the room and began speaking. "I have her.

It's time for us to move."

I assumed—hoped—that Zeera was on the other end of the feed. "Tell them to bring my mother."

But Parvda shook her head at me. "She's staying. We need your sister to think that your mother has no part in this. It's safer for her that way."

"Leaving my mother with my sister is safe?" I clutched the skirt of my dress. "My sister is crazy. Besides, I need to talk to my mother. It's important." *Essential*, I thought. Potentially life changing, and not in a good way. I couldn't leave without asking her if Emory Specter was my father. The possibility that we shared the same genes was horrifying. It was bad enough that I shared any with Jude at this point.

Then another thought made me blanch.

Did this somehow make Trader and me brother and sister?

A voice came through a hidden speaker into the room. "Jessica and everyone else are almost there," it said. I was nearly certain the voice belonged to Zeera.

"Good. Make sure they take care of the guards outside. There's two." Parvda snapped her fingers in front of my face and I jumped. "Skye? Are you with me? You have to stay focused. We're not out of here yet."

There was a knock on the door.

Parvda's eyes clouded. "That was fast." She went to it and put her ear to the wood. Then, slowly, she opened it.

But it wasn't Rain or Adam or Jessica standing there.

It was Jude. Behind her were the guards.

"Skylar, you're being so cooperative," she said as she swept into the room, pleased. She turned to Parvda. "Have you gotten all the information you need? She can't be away from the party for much longer. Our guests have expectations."

Parvda smiled back. "Of course," she said cheerily. "I understand completely."

"Good," Jude said. "I'll walk you back to the party personally."

Parvda put up a finger. "If I could just have one more minute in private."

Jude's eyes frosted over. "You've had plenty of time. I'll walk you back now."

"But—"

"No." My sister's tone was so cold that if we were in the App World there would be icicles hanging in the air.

"Come now." My sister nodded at the guards.

One of them entered the room. The other gestured for us to follow. We had no choice. Soon we were a parade on our way back to the ballroom, one guard in the lead, my sister behind him, then Parvda and me, after which came the second guard. There was no going anywhere else or waiting for the others.

But the others were already on their way.

They rounded the corner just as we did.

Our two groups nearly collided.

Everyone halted, surprised, facing one another. Adam, Jessica, and Rain blinked, their masks gone from their faces.

"Are you lost?" the guard up front asked them.

"You shouldn't be out here without an escort," my sister said, her tone suspicious.

So this wasn't going to be so easy after all.

I looked at Parvda, eyebrows raised. She shook her head.

Jude tapped her chin with her fingers. "Wait a minute," she said, studying Adam's face. "I've seen you before." Adam began backing away. "You're one of the illegal sixteens! Guards! Take him into custody! Take them all!"

Quickly, before the guards could apprehend anyone, Parvda called up to the video feeds. "Zeera, we need you," she cried. "Now!"

"Seize her," Jude barked to one of the guards.

He was nearly on Parvda when the lights went dark. Shouts of surprise erupted from inside the ballroom. They must have gone out inside there too. There came a giant crash, then another, and the shouts turned into screams. All the doors around us flew open and guests streamed through them, many of them running.

"Everyone, let's go! Now!" Rain shouted above the din.

We all started to run, but it was difficult to move in my dress.

"Get them," my sister shrieked. "Don't let her out of here!"

"Hurry," Adam yelled to us as we rounded a corner, headfirst into a river of guests going the other way.

I grabbed as many of the knives as I could out of the folds of my dress as I ran, and one by one I opened them up and belted them in the fabric at my waist. Then I took the last one and cut away as much of the skirt as I could. The material dropped to the ground behind me in a stream of blue silk.

"Where's the exit?" I asked Rain.

"Almost there," he said, his breaths coming quickly. "Just a couple more turns and we'll be at the back entrance. A van will be waiting for us."

I didn't reply, just ran faster.

A fog seemed to descend around us.

I sniffed the air.

Smoke. Something was burning.

I thought of all those magical candles hanging from the ballroom ceiling. I imagined them crashing to the ground and lighting up the gowns of the guests, the table-cloths catching fire, turning my sister's fairy-tale event into a nightmare for everyone.

"There they are!" someone shouted behind us.

We were running down a long hallway. The end seemed impossibly far away.

A shot rang out.

Then another.

"Don't hit the sister," one of the guards warned. "But get all the others!"

Suddenly bullets were everywhere.

Jessica dropped to the ground ahead of me.

And I screamed.

There was a pause in the shooting as the guards reloaded.

I ran to help her, but she was already dead, shot in the head. Her lifeless brown eyes looked up at me.

"Skye, come on!" Rain urged.

"Jessica," I said, unable to turn away from her, unable to let go of her limp body, but then the shooting started again. I got up to run, and I stopped. I blocked Jessica and Rain with my own body, since my sister had ordered that I not be damaged. "We can't just leave her!"

"We have no choice." He grabbed my hand and pulled me away.

I took one last look at Jessica, this girl who I thought would become my first real friend in this world, before leaving her behind. "Stay ahead of me so you don't get hurt," I yelled up at Rain. I saw Adam and Parvda reach the exit.

Adam turned back, hesitant.

"Go on," Rain urged him. "Make sure the van is ready! We're coming!"

They slipped through the doors.

We were nearly there when a group of guards appeared on our right. We would never reach the exit in time. Without thinking I grabbed one of the knives at my waist and threw it. It hit one of the guards, a woman, straight in the heart. The others seemed stunned, watching as she slid to the ground, her eyes going vacant.

I'd killed her.

I'd killed a real live human being for the second time.

But it was the first time I was aware while doing it.

This wasn't a game anymore.

I grabbed another knife and threw it, then another and another until they were all gone, watching as the guards went down one by one. Rain had been right. Our skills from gaming transferred. Even the killing one.

Rain's jaw fell open as he looked at the bodies lying on the ground.

Meanwhile, the others were getting closer behind us.

"Skye, we can make it," Rain said. "Hurry!"

We stepped over the guards. Rain was through the door to safety and I was about to join him when I heard a familiar voice screaming and I came to an abrupt halt.

One of the guards approached.

He had Inara in a headlock. He dragged her along as she whimpered and cried. There was a gun pointed at her head. He stopped before he got to the first dead guard, maybe ten yards away. My sister was right behind him. Her hair had come loose and her dress was ripped. Gone was the allure of calm that had surrounded her and gone was any of the sympathy she'd shown me earlier. Her eyes were filled with hatred. "How dare you ruin this for me! You've already ruined enough, and I won't let you take this too."

The guard shifted Inara into my sister's grasp, and Jude pressed the gun hard into Inara's temple as she screamed in fear.

"Jude, let Inara go," I said. "None of this is her fault."

"I know, isn't it tragic? She and I have so much in common. You've nearly ruined both of us."

"Please," I begged. "She's my best friend."

My sister laughed. "Not from what I hear."

"Skye, help me," Inara pleaded. Her voice was small and frightened.

"Your choice is simple." Jude's eyes were wide, as though proclaiming innocence. "Turn yourself in, or watch your friend die."

My eyes darted between Inara, the gun, and my sister, looking so smug, sure that she'd won. As my hands clutched at what was left of my dress, I discovered something.

A third option.

There was one knife left, one that I'd missed. It was still hidden in the folds of the tattered skirt.

I sighed heavily, dramatically, as though I was acquiescing to my sister's wishes, and in the process my hand closed around the handle. I'd always been good with knives, but there was no room for mistakes here. Inara's life was at risk. Mine, too. And I'd have to be fast.

"Skye, don't do it, don't surrender," I heard Rain say behind me. He must have come back through the door when I didn't emerge.

"I have to," I said, spinning around to face him, taking this opportunity to ready the knife. "Inara needs me."

Rain's eyes flickered to it. Then very slightly, he nodded.

I would aim for Jude's left shoulder.

I didn't have it in me to aim for her heart.

"Hurry up, Skylar," Jude said. "I want this over. Now."

"I'm coming," I said.

Then, as I was turning back, I raised the knife.

And I threw it with all my might.

I watched it leave my hand and fly across the room. It seemed to travel in slow motion. My sister's face went slack with shock as her eyes saw the blade. Her arm loosened and Inara slipped to the ground. Just as the knife was about to reach its target, at the very last second, Jude moved. She crouched in an attempt to protect herself.

But she calculated badly.

Moved left instead of right.

The knife hit its mark.

It plunged straight into the side of Jude's face.

She let out a bloodcurdling scream.

The guards went to her.

Trader appeared behind them. "I've got Inara! I'll take her to safety! Get out while you can," he shouted to me, but his words seemed so far away.

Blood was everywhere.

My sister's face was covered in it.

"We have to go, we have to go, we have to go now," someone was saying urgently behind me. The words were distant and I couldn't make myself react. Jude's scream echoed in my head.

I thought it might echo there forever.

Then Rain stepped between me and the guards who were helping my sister, between me and Trader, who was helping Inara up. They began to run, Trader yanking Inara along behind him. Neither of them looked back. "Skylar. Wake up." Rain grabbed my arm and dragged me from the room, out the door into the cool night air.

Time blurred.

The smell of burning was everywhere.

A van pulled up and I let myself be lifted inside. I felt the vehicle lurch forward. Around me were Adam and Parvda, Zeera and Rain. Not Jessica. Never again Jessica. In my daze, I noticed someone else in the passenger seat, a girl with long copper hair. She turned around and blinked at me in the darkness.

"What's Lacy doing here?" I managed to ask.

"A lot has happened while you were gone," said a

familiar voice, and I saw that the Keeper was at the wheel. She kept glancing at me in the mirror. "I'm glad you're okay."

I nodded. "Yes," I told her, my tone flat. "I'm fine."

But was I? Were any of us?

As if to confirm this, Lacy reached back—I thought for me, at first—but then I realized she was reaching for Rain's hand. A look passed between them as he took it. "You've got her," she said to him. "Just like you said you would. It's going to be okay. Everything will be okay."

He nodded. They let go of each other's hands.

Lacy turned to me. "I know we've never been friends, Skylar, but I was worried about you, too. I didn't mean to betray you."

I didn't respond. I didn't know what to say.

Lacy settled into her seat again, facing front.

No one else spoke.

People had died tonight, and I had killed them.

I'd come to the Real World with so many hopes.

But now I was a murderer.

A war had begun tonight.

And truly, I was in the middle of it.

They woke me when we reached the ocean.

One by one, we stumbled from the van.

I went to the Keeper and, wordlessly, threw my arms around her. "I didn't know if I'd see you again."

Her arms tightened around me. "I was so worried about you."

Tears rolled down my cheeks. "I'm sorry for everything. I'm sorry I didn't listen to you."

We let each other go and started toward the path in the dunes. Rain waited for us at the top.

"It isn't your fault," she said as we walked. "This is much bigger than you, Skye. I'm sorry you're caught in it."

"We all are," I said. "Aren't we?"

She nodded. Then the Keeper took off to join the others.

I met Rain at the top of the dune and saw the long, curving stretch of beach ahead. I thought about Inara and me on our last virtual day together when she'd landed us by the ocean and the sand. I remembered the tiny sailboats and our race to the island. I remembered how exhilarated I was to be swimming. It was only a couple of months ago now, but it seemed like a hundred years. So much had happened since then. So many terrible things. One last time, I turned to look at the faint outline of skyscrapers in the distance, stretching up toward the sun. The city we'd fled.

But it was only for now. We'd be back.

There was so much more to come.

"Skye," Rain said. "We should go."

I nodded. "You go catch up to the others. I'll follow in a minute. I need some time alone."

"Okay," he said, a little reluctantly.

But then he left.

I watched Rain walk away, pick up his pace until it became a jog and he joined the group, fitting himself between Adam and Lacy. I descended the dune and didn't stop until my toes met the ocean. Then I walked deeper and deeper, and when the water had risen all the way up to my waist I dove into the sea.

ACKNOWLEDGMENTS

The idea for this novel goes all the way back to a wonderful Descartes lecture given by Tony Dardis, a professor and colleague from Hofstra University, on Descartes' *Meditations on First Philosophy*, for a funky great books-like course we sometimes team teach (with many other profs) at the Honors College there. I feel indebted to my time teaching at Hofstra for sparking so many of the big questions that have inspired my thinking and the ideas in this novel (and subsequent novels in the trilogy), and to Warren Frisina, the dean of the Honors College, for having me teach in this wonderful program.

I am grateful for the careful attention and editorial feedback (and the perseverance!) of Tara Weikum, my editor at Harper, for whom I feel so much gratitude, not to mention a slight bit of jealousy since a lot of her editing took place in Hawaii. Everyone at Harper who has worked on and supported *Unplugged*, especially Ro Romanello, Elizabeth Ward, Joey Jachowski, Andrea Pappenheimer, and the marketing, sales, and production teams (especially design!), who have made this process so much fun. I am also grateful to Sarah Barley for all her time and editorial feedback on *Unplugged* during the time when she was still at Harper.

And as always, I want to thank my friends and fellow writers for their input, feedback, and moral support as I've worked on this novel, most especially: Rebecca Stead (for our magic lunch, when what was one novel suddenly turned into a trilogy), Marie Rutkoski, Daphne Grab, Eliot Schrefer, Cheryl Klein, and Alvina Ling. My agent, Miriam Altshuler, is the best, best, best and always has been, and this book wouldn't exist (it really, really wouldn't) without her ongoing support and commitment to me as her author and to all the work that I do. Y, por supuesto a Daniel Matus, la persona que vivió este proceso desde el principio, en este lado del Atlántico y en Barcelona, para tu apoyo y amor y un montón de conversaciones mientras bebíamos vino español, siempre estaré agradecido.

Keep reading for a glimpse at

THE BODY MARKET,

the sequel to

UNPLUGGED.

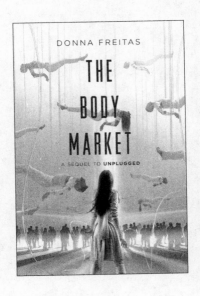

Nature teaches me that my own body is surrounded by many other bodies, some of which I have to seek after, and others to shun. And indeed, as I perceive different sorts of colors, sounds, odors, tastes, heat, hardness, etc., I safely conclude that . . . some are agreeable, and others disagreeable, [and] there can be no doubt that my body, or rather my entire self, in as far as I am composed of body and mind, may be variously affected, both beneficially and hurtfully, by surrounding bodies.

—René Descartes,
"Of the Existence of Material Things and of the Real
Distinction Between the Mind and Body of Man,"
Meditations on First Philosophy (1641)

1

Skylar

sleeping beauties

I ADJUSTED THE scarf around my head.

Only my eyes were visible.

I stepped into the crush of tourists heading inside. A great canopy stretched over us, blocking out the cold winter sun. The floor was polished marble, and it shined so clean and new it was slick as ice. To my right, people emerged from the lobby of the tall, glittering hotel, with its carefully trimmed topiaries lining the entrance.

All around me were voices.

They were speaking in languages I didn't understand. I wished for an App to translate what they were saying and then almost laughed. It seemed like a lifetime ago that Apps were a part of everyday life. An entire world away from the one I was in now. Literally.

I concentrated on the man next to me as we inched forward under the canopy. He held the hand of a woman, maybe his wife. They were nearly the same height, both shorter than me, their hair black as ink, their eyes almond-shaped. I listened to the sounds coming from their mouths, their accents, the tonal cadence of their words. Even with all my gaming and paying attention in Real World History, I couldn't translate the meaning, but with a little effort I could recognize the language.

They were speaking Japanese.

I listened to the others milling around me now, all of us trying to get closer to the main attraction, the reason we'd come. In the span of five minutes I heard a total of seven different languages. First there were the young men speaking in French, and then a large group of people shuffling along whispering to one another in Chinese. There was the tall blond couple talking intimately in Dutch, and another nearly shouting in Spanish. I heard snatches of Italian but I couldn't tell from which direction they'd come, and the same went for the female voice speaking in German. Even more languages swirled in the air around me that I couldn't quite place.

People had dressed for the occasion.

Many of the women had chosen smart skirted suits,

s'pindly heels on their feet and lavish thick coats to protect them from the cold, jewels dropping from their ears. But there were also a few in colorful saris and even more with veils that revealed only their eyes. The men seemed to have coordinated with one another, all of them donning formal black suits and boxy wool coats. The world's wealthiest had spared no expense, traveling from far and wide for this momentous occasion. My flight from the ball and the fire had certainly made a dent in my sister's plans, but in the end it had only delayed the inevitable.

Moving forward was all that mattered.

That's why I was here.

Rain didn't think it should be me, fought me on it. He thought it was too dangerous given my relationship to this place and its founder. But it was because of that relationship that it needed to be me. And then, Rain wasn't high on my list of trusted advisors at the moment. He'd hidden from me the truth about my sister, and he'd openly lied about Lacy.

He didn't get to tell me what to do anymore.

The full extent of the exhibits was a winding labyrinth that covered entire city blocks and extended down, down, down under the earth. The tourists were anxious to get started, excited for the preview they'd been promised. The priciest merchandise had been trotted out to entice and seduce, the rest of it stored away in the underground caverns, waiting and ready. An entire city's worth of goods. We shuffled along together, slowly moving forward in the line. Some people had their heads buried in a map, trying to pinpoint where we were in relation to the various displays.

Finally, we rounded the corner.

At the end of the aisle, someone had constructed a dais made of gleaming white marble. A set of stairs covered in lush red carpet led up to the star attraction. People stood within the space marked out by velvet ropes to get a closer look. I got in the back, and soon dozens more tourists took their places behind me. At least thirty minutes passed as we snaked our way through the maze. By now I could see the ends of the long glass box. It was illuminated from the inside, to highlight the preciousness of its contents.

The two tourists ahead of me—a man and a woman speaking Chinese—talked excitedly as they strode forward. I watched as they circled the box, whispering, pointing things out to each other. They glanced back at me and nodded, just before funneling through the velvet ropes toward the exit.

Then it was my turn.

I stepped up to the box and forced myself to look at what lay before me.

At *who*.

Jude was trying to punish me for my escape.

And she'd done an excellent job.

I pressed my hands against the glass, even though the sign warned me not to. I took in the delicate limbs, the elegant fingers painted a pale pink for the occasion. The way the chest gently rose and fell, shifting the covering that lay across the lower and upper halves of the body. Lips painted red and eyes closed peacefully. Long blond hair that fell across the forehead and down along the shoulder and arms, curled and impeccably styled to show off its lustrous shine. The skin was smooth and unblemished, or nearly so.

A tiny scar curved underneath the elbow.

You had to know it was there to see it.

You had to know it was there to even look.

I stared at the body of Inara, my best friend, on display for all the world to see.

To admire. To envy.

To covet and to buy.

Trader had failed in his attempt to help her escape, and soon Inara would be sold to the highest bidder.

The Body Market was open for business.

READ THEM ALL!

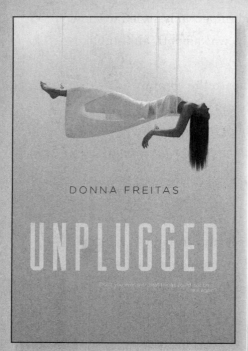

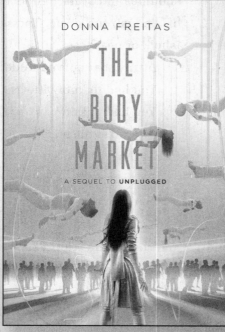